PRASE FOR THE MOON

PRAISE FOR THE MOON

"*The Moon in the Palace* is a colorful and vibrant journey into the grandeur of the Tang Dynasty. Weina Randel weaves a captivating tale about the intrigues of the inner court through the eyes of the woman who would become the most infamous empress in Chinese history, finding a human story of love and hope amid bloodshed and treachery. I couldn't stop reading this exciting debut novel."

—Jeannie Lin, *USA Today* bestselling
author of *The Lotus Palace*

"With fresh, lyrical prose and a true storyteller's flair, in her novel *The Moon in the Palace*, Weina Dai Randel brings seventh-century China to vibrant life. Through the eyes of Mei, a name meaning simply *sister*, given to the middle daughter of the household of her birth, we are submerged into intrigue of the imperial court, where wives and concubines fight for positions of power beside the Emperor, and where men fight to take the Emperor's throne. A story of courage and daring, in *The Moon in the Palace*, a girl without a name takes her destiny into her own hands. A shining jewel of a novel."

Christy English, author of *The Queen's Pawn* and
To Be Queen: A Novel of the Early Life of Eleanor of Aquitaine

"With elegant, modern prose and vivid details, Randel's gorgeous debut novel seductively pulls back the curtain to reveal the heartbreaking world of harem politics in Tang Dynasty China. Exploring the early years of the legendary Empress Wu when she was still a concubine struggling to survive the whims of the man who ruled her, the book's brave and clever heroine finds herself at the center of intrigue and civil war. This is a page-turner that will transport you in time and place. Bravo!"

—Stephanie Dray, author of *Lily of the Nile*

"Randel writes with a fresh, poetic style, bringing to life a time remote from our own, yet filled with the same intrigues, power struggles—and love affairs. For those confined to a claustrophobic existence in the palace, to offend the wrong person was to risk a horrible death. Yet strong women could bend the intrigues to their own benefit—if they dared. This is history, but also a stay-up-all-night read."

—Mingmei Yip, author of *Secret of a Thousand Beauties* and *Peach Blossom Pavilion*

"An astonishing debut! Weina Dei Randal spins a silken web of lethal intrigue, transporting us into the fascinating, seductive world of ancient China, where one rebellious, astute girl embarks on a dangerous quest for power."

—C. W. Gortner, bestselling author of *The Queen's Vow*

"I absolutely loved Weina Dai Randel's *The Moon in the Palace*, which is a truly immersive experience and a rare and beautiful treasure. All I want now is to read the next novel!"

—Elizabeth Chadwick, *New York Times* bestselling author of *The Summer Queen*, *The Winter Crown*, and *The Autumn Throne*

"Mei is a triumph of intelligence and passion, cunning and courage. Randel has provided a strong cast of supporting characters, successfully resisting stereotypes of eunuchs and concubines; in the end, we realize they are all victims of the crucible that is the Imperial Court. Even though I know Mei will prevail to become Empress Wu, I can't wait for the next book and more of Randel's gifted storytelling."

—Janie Chang, author of *Three Souls*

"A must for historical fiction fans, especially those fascinated by China's glorious past."

—*Library Journal* Starred Review

THE

Moon IN THE Palace

DISCARD

WEINA DAI RANDEL

sourcebooks
landmark

For Mark,

whose love gives me a new life

Copyright © 2016 by Weina Dai Randel
Cover and internal design © 2016 by Sourcebooks, Inc.
Cover design by Laura Klynstra
Cover images © Allan Jenkins/Trevillion Images, George Clerk/Getty Images,
tomertu/Shutterstock, ussr/Shutterstock

Sourcebooks and the colophon are registered trademarks of Sourcebooks, Inc.

The characters and events portrayed in this book are fictitious or are used fictitiously.
Apart from well-known historical figures, any similarity to real persons, living or dead,
is purely coincidental and not intended by the author.

Published by Sourcebooks Landmark, an imprint of Sourcebooks, Inc.
P.O. Box 4410, Naperville, Illinois 60567-4410
(630) 961-3900
Fax: (630) 961-2168
www.sourcebooks.com

Library of Congress Cataloging-in-Publication Data

Names: Randel, Weina Dai.
Title: The moon in the palace / Weina Dai Randel.
Description: Naperville, Illinois : Sourcebooks Landmark, [2016]
Identifiers: LCCN 2015009943 (pbk. : alk. paper)
Subjects: LCSH: Wu hou, Empress of China, 624-705—Fiction. |
    China—History—Tang dynasty, 618-907—Fiction. |
    Empresses—China—Fiction. | GSAFD: Historical fiction.
Classification: LCC PS3618.A6423 M66 2016 | DDC 813/.6—dc23 LC
record available at http://lccn.loc.gov/2015009943

Printed and bound in the United States of America.

TANG DYNASTY, AD 631

the Fifth Year of

Emperor Taizong's Reign

of Peaceful Prospect

SUMMER

THE DAY MY FUTURE WAS FORETOLD, I WAS JUST FIVE years old.

I was practicing calligraphy in the garden where Father hosted his gathering with the nobles, scholars, and other important men of the prefecture. It was a brilliant summer afternoon. He was not wearing his governor's hat, and the sunlight sifted through the maze of the oak branches and illuminated his gray hair like a silver crown.

A monk, whom I had never seen before, asked to read my face.

"How extraordinary!" He lowered himself to look into my eyes. "I have never seen a face with such perfection, a design so flawless and filled with inspiration. Look at his temple, the shape of his nose and eyes. This face bears the mission of Heaven."

I wanted to smile. I had fooled him. I was Father's second daughter, and his favorite. He often dressed me in a boy's tunic and treated me as the son he did not have. Mother was reluctant to go along with the game, but I considered it a great honor.

"It is a pity, however, that he is a boy," the monk said as people came to surround us.

"A pity?" Father asked, his voice carrying a rare shade of confusion. "Why is that, Tripitaka?"

I was curious too. How could a girl be more valuable than a boy?

"If the child were a girl, with this face"—the monk, Tripitaka, watched me intently—"she would eclipse the light of the sun and shine brighter than the moon. She would reign over the kingdom that governs many men. She would mother the emperors of the land but also be emperor in her own name. She would dismantle the house of lies but build the temple of the divine. She would dissolve the kingdom of ghosts but found a dynasty of souls. She would be immortal."

"A woman emperor?" Father's mouth was agape. "How could this be possible?"

"It is difficult to explain, Governor, but it is true. There would be no one before her and none after."

"But this child is not of the imperial family."

"It would be her destiny."

"I see," Father said, looking pensive. "How could a woman reign over the kingdom?" Father was asking the monk, but he stared at me, his eyes glistening with a strange light.

"She must endure."

"Endure what?"

"Deaths."

"Whose?"

Tripitaka did not answer; instead, he turned around to look at the reception hall through the moon-shaped garden entrance, where splendid murals and antique sandalwood screens inlaid with pearls and jade covered each wall. Leaning against the wall were shelved precious ceramic bowls and cups, a bone relic of Buddha—Mother's most valued treasure—and a rare collection of four-hundred-year-old poems. In the center of the hall stood the object all Father's guests envied—a life-size horse statue made of pure gold, a gift from Emperor Gaozu, the founder of the Tang Dynasty who owed his kingdom to Father.

Tripitaka faced Father again, gazing at him like a man watching another drowning in a river yet unable to help.

"I shall take my leave now, respected Governor. May fortune forever protect you. It is my privilege to offer you my service." He pressed his hands together and bowed to leave.

What I did next I could never explain. I ran to him and tugged at his stole. I might have only meant to say farewell, but the words that slipped from my mouth were "*Wo men xia ci chong feng.*"

We shall meet again.

Tripitaka's eyes widened in surprise. Then, as though he had just understood something, he nodded, and with a deep bow, he said, "So it shall be."

Any other child my age would have felt confused or at least awkward. Not me. I smiled, withdrew, and took Father's hand.

After that day, I was not to wear a boy's garment again, and Father began to draft letters and sent them to Emperor Taizong, Emperor Gaozu's son, who had inherited the throne and resided in a great palace in Chang'an. When I asked him the purpose of the letters, Father explained there was a custom that every year the ruler of the kingdom chose a number of maidens to serve him. The maidens must come from noble families and be older than thirteen. It was a great honor for the women, because once they were favored by the Emperor and became high-ranking ladies, they would bring their families eternal fame and glory.

Father said he would like me to go to the palace.

He devoted himself to teaching me classical poems, history, calligraphy, and mathematics, and every night, before I went to bed, he would ask me to recite Sun Tzu's *The Art of War*. Oftentimes I went to sleep mumbling, "All warfare is based on deception…"

Days went by, then seasons and years. When I was twelve, one year before Emperor Taizong would summon me, Father took me to our family's grave site. He looked to be in high spirits, his footsteps light and his head held high. He told me old stories of how he, the wealthiest man in Shanxi Prefecture, had funded the war of Emperor Gaozu when he decided to rebel against the Sui Dynasty, how when the Emperor was betrayed and forced to flee, Father opened the gates of our enormous home to accommodate his army, and how, after the war was won, Emperor Gaozu proposed the marriage between Father and Mother, cousin of an empress, daughter of a renowned noble faithful to the empire that had perished.

His long sleeves waving, Father showed me the undulating land that stretched to the edge of the sun—his land, my family's land. "Will you promise to safeguard our family's fortune and honor?" he asked me, his eyes glittering.

Clenching my fists, I nodded solemnly, and he laughed. His voice melted into the warm air and echoed on the tops of the distant cypresses.

The pleasure of pleasing him wrapped around me when I caught a pair of yellow bulbous eyes peering out of the bushes. The forest fell still, and all the chirping and rustling vanished. A shower of leaves, fur, and red drops poured down from the sky, and a scream pierced my ears. Perhaps it came from me, or Father, I was not sure, for everything turned black, and when I came to my senses, I was at the table with Mother and my two sisters, eating rice porridge with shredded pork.

One of our servants rushed into the reception hall, his chest heaving and his face wet with perspiration. There had been an accident, he said. Father had fallen off a cliff and died.

On the day of his funeral, a feeble sun blinked through the opaque morning haze that hovered above the mountain tracks. Slowly, I walked toward his grave. A blister broke on my toe, but I hardly felt it. In front of me, a priest wearing a square mask painted with four eyes hopped and danced, and near him, the bell ringers shook their small bells. The tinkling faded to the distant sky but lingered in my heart. Desperately, I searched my mind to find any clue that might hint at the nature of Father's death, but no matter how hard I tried, I could not remember the details of the day he had died. I knelt, my face numb and my hands cold, as the hearse bearers pushed Father into the earthen chamber, burying him.

I thought my life was over. I did not know it had just begun.

2

WHEN WE RETURNED HOME, A GROUP OF MEN WAITED IN front of my house, their torches roaring in the night like flaming trees, and the black smoke stretching in the sky like the shadowy cobweb of a monstrous spider.

I recognized the magistrate, wearing my father's hat. My heart sank. He had taken Father's position. I knew the law well. No matter how much Father loved me, I was not his son, and thus I could not inherit his governorship. But there had to be another reason the magistrate was there. I stopped Mother and my two sisters, holding them close to me.

"Old woman," the magistrate said to Mother, his hands on his hips, "take your worthless girls with you and get out of here."

I could not stand this man or his utter disrespect of Mother. I stood before him. "Do not speak to my mother like this. If anyone needs to leave, it's you. This is my home."

"Not anymore." He sneered. "It's mine now. Everything belongs to me: the house, the treasure, and all the gold. Now, I order you to get out of my sight." He waved, and his men lunged toward us, pushing us to the road.

"How dare you." I struggled, trying to free myself from the arms that clamped on my shoulders. "You scoundrel!"

A sharp pain stabbed me as the magistrate drove his fist into my stomach. I was stunned. No one had ever struck me before. I dove toward him and kicked with all my might. But another blow fell on my back, and I tumbled to the ground, my vision blurred with pain. For a moment, I could hear only the echoes of loud slaps and my sisters' frightened cries. I shook my head and struggled to rise, because at that moment, I saw that Mother, her hand on her face, fell beside me and gasped. Instinctively, I leaned over and wrapped my arms around her, shielding her as more blows rained down on me.

Finally, all the kicks and commotion died off, and the gates of my home closed behind me. From inside came loud laughter and cheers.

Our servants came to us, all one hundred of them, bearing sacks on their shoulders. They helped me sit up, and then one by one, they bowed, weeping miserably. As they turned around to leave, I watched them, a lump in my throat. I had known them since I was born and called them aunts and uncles, but they had to leave. It was just as the proverb said, "When a tree falls, wretched monkeys have no choice but to scatter."

Pushing back my tears, I turned to my mother and sisters, who sobbed beside me. I held them, trying to comfort them, and I swore I would protect them and take care of them, but I knew there was nothing I could do to take back our home. I could beg the nobles who had served Father to help me, but the greedy magistrate, whose words were law, was their superior, and no one would dare to defy him.

I did not know where we could stay either. All the family members on Mother's side had died in the war, and Father had no relatives in Wenshui. I could ask to stay with neighbors, but we would be like beggars, relying on people's charity. In the end, Mother said we should go to Qing, my half brother, who lived in Chang'an, the city where Emperor Taizong's great palace was located. The eldest son from Father's previous marriage, Qing was a greedy gambler who hated me and the last person from whom I would seek help.

But I decided to listen to Mother. We would go to Chang'an, for once I got there, I would seek every opportunity to see the Emperor and beg him to return our house and belongings to us.

The night grew cold. We huddled together under a tree to keep warm. I was hungry, exhausted, and my body was sore from the beating, but I could not shut my eyes as the night's wind whipped my cold face.

At dawn, Mother sought out a traveling caravan that passed our town and paid them with my jade bangle. Together with my two sisters, I limped to the carriage and climbed in.

My chin knocking against the carriage's window frame, I watched my home fade into the distance. I had drunk Wenshui's water, walked on Wenshui's muddy road, and grown up in Wenshui's air. Now I had to leave.

Father used to say that Chang'an was the most glorious place under Heaven, and many people flocked to the Emperor's city like moths attracted to light. Everyone—merchant, poet, mercenary, and prostitute alike—went there to realize dreams of fortune and decadence. It was also the destination of the Silk Route, where merchants from as far as Persia, Kucha, Kashgar, and Samarkand brought rare perfumes and hard-to-find luxuries for trade.

But when we approached the city wall near the Jinguang Gate, the scenery before me reflected none of Father's description. The gray ramparts, looking like the jagged teeth of a demon, sprawled endlessly in the distance. Around me, many merchants, their faces netted with wrinkles and their lips parched with thirst, faltered on the road in fatigue, and the leaves of persimmon groves near a lake shriveled, looking on the verge of dying.

Once we entered the right gateway, the view of the city surprised me. White stone bridges arched in the shape of half-moons, stands of green willows edged deep ditches, vermillion-colored canoes and indigo-hued dragon boats floated on placid canals, and the enormous walled buildings—the residential wards, Mother told me—stood next to one another like fortresses.

I shielded my eyes to block the bright sunlight reflected from the canal. I did not wish to blink, unwilling to miss anything. The streets were as wide as the sky, and maples, elms, oaks, and junipers were spaced out neatly at the sides. Everything seemed organized and orderly; even the horses stopped nickering, as if awed by a silent code of obedience.

Two streets ran parallel to my left. On the far side, people ambled to exit the city, while the middle lane was unoccupied. Soon, a group of horsemen in hats and boots trotted along that street. At first I thought they were the Emperor's guards, but when they drew closer, I realized they were noblemen. They were better dressed than anyone in my hometown, their hats thick with stripes of fur, their silk sleeves dropping low to their boots. In Wenshui, everyone greeted me on the street, but these people passed us as if we did not exist.

"Where is the palace?" I asked Mother.

"Look over there. See that red wall? That's the palace wall," Mother said, her arms around my sisters. Big Sister was sleeping, but Little Sister, who was born with a weak heart, moaned deliriously. She had fallen sick during the journey.

I stroked her shoulder to soothe her, and when she calmed down, I moved closer to the window. The vermilion gates, studded with bronze balls, were tall and wide, but I was not impressed. They looked similar to our own front gates, but as the carriage moved along, I realized how enormous the palace entrance really was, and it did not have just one, but three entrances—left, middle, and right. The middle one, reserved only for the Emperor and the late Empress—I remembered what Father had told me—was the grandest. It had one arched bridge in the front; two prancing stone kylins, the mythical unicorns; and two watchtowers standing on the top of the wall like pavilions floating in the air.

Father had said that the palace contained 9,999 rooms, an auspicious number to suggest the longevity of the kingdom. Each room was covered with marble, and each pillar was carved with dragons and inlaid with jade and ruby. Day and night, the chambers were filled with the sound of lutes and zithers, and the palace women often sauntered about in rainbow-colored gauze robes adorned with perfumed girdles.

And Emperor Taizong, for whom all the melodies were sung, for whom all the buildings were built...I wondered if he had received Father's petitions. Would he summon me? If he wanted, he could find me easily, since the city kept strict records of who entered the ward and who lived with their kin.

We finally arrived at Qing's house, a small building of packed mud with a thatched roof. The moment he saw us, he asked for Mother's coin pouch and our jewelry. That, I knew, was the only reason he was allowing us to stay.

That night, we shared a bamboo mat in a small room with Qing's two concubines and eight children. I hardly slept. Before dawn, a tattoo of drumbeats rose, the opening signal of the neighboring Western Market. I dressed and left Qing's house quietly. I wanted to see the palace. I would not be able to enter, but perhaps by some luck I would see Emperor Taizong, and with Father's contribution to Emperor Gaozu and the dynasty, surely Emperor Taizong would grant my wish and return our house to us.

Outside Qing's ward, the noise from the market echoed through the thick morning fog like thunder. I paused, shocked to see so many people around me. Vendors chased customers with flaccid quail, rabbits, and pit vipers flapping against their shoulders. Merchants dug their feet into the packed earth and pushed carts laden with bolts of silk. The fortune-tellers paced around, bamboo cards in hands and clouds of coppery dirt at their heels.

I pushed through the crowd and arrived at the Heavenly Street that extended all the way to the palace's front gates. An army of palace guards stood there, checking a throng of ministers holding emblems of a fish: the palace's admission token. Only those bearing the token were permitted to enter the palace. There was no sign of the Emperor.

Disappointed, I turned around and walked back to Qing's house.

Living in Chang'an, I heard rumors about the palace all the time. People said the Emperor would summon fifteen maidens, the Selects, to serve him in the Inner Court that year, and the priority would be given to the high-ranking nobles' daughters. My father, a governor, had been of high rank.

I hoped the Emperor would summon me; it was the only way to meet him. And life in Qing's household was miserable. He was poorer than any of my father's servants. Many days went by without food, and if I was lucky, I ate the burned rice crisp scraped from the bottom of the pot. Big Sister was forced to marry a low merchant in the south so she would not burden us, and Little Sister grew sicker. I made some pickled cabbages and sold them at the market to get her medicine money.

Then one day, my luck changed. Gongs clanged outside Qing's house. A man holding a banner entered the gate. Behind him stood a carriage and a man who looked like a large gourd, with a potbelly, fat torso, and small head.

"All kneel," he ordered as my neighbors, Qing, and Mother gathered before him. Not sure what would happen next, I knelt beside Mother, holding Little Sister in my arms. The gourd man spread out a scroll with gilded edges—the emblem of an edict.

In a singsong cadence, he read, "On the eighth month of the thirteenth year of the Reign of Peaceful Prospect, I, Emperor Taizong, the Emperor of China, the One Above All, the Conqueror of the North and the South, the ruler of all land and the seven seas, hereby do decree that the second daughter of Wu Shihuo, the former Governor of Shanxi Prefecture, the man who provided meritorious services to our kingdom, is to be chosen as one of the fifteen maidens who shall enter the Inner Court. Here, I give my decree."

The crowd gasped, and people surrounded me, shouting their congratulations. I nodded happily, for Father's petitions had been heard, and I would go to the palace, just as he had wished. Yet I could not smile when I looked at Mother and Little Sister. I would need to abandon them; I had not thought of that. And my sister was so sick. Who would take care of them when I was in the palace?

Later, after everyone left, Little Sister dozed off, and I sat on a bench with Mother. She dabbed her eyes.

"These are tears of happiness," she said.

She sounded pleased, but I could still hear pain in her voice.

I did not want to leave her either. In the palace, I would not see her face when I woke in the morning or hear her voice before I went to sleep. I would not be able to wrap my arms around her or listen to her breathe.

"I don't have to go," I said, even though I knew I had no choice. No one dared to defy the Emperor.

She shook her head. "You have to. This is for the best."

My heart heavy, I went behind her and rubbed her shoulders. Her back was hurting her in those days, and I had learned how to ease her pain. I held her shoulders with the strength I was born with, and I kneaded with all the misery and helplessness that bled from my heart. With my thumbs, I circled over her shoulder blades, the top of her shoulders, and then to her back. Under my fingertips, I felt her slack skin and hard bones—solid, resolute, comforting. Like love.

Then I knew. Nothing would ever separate us, be it palace or graveyard.

I eased the pressure and gently tapped her back with my fists. She relaxed and sighed in relief as she always did.

"The Palace Escorts will fetch you in one month. Then you'll start a new life," Mother said.

"A new life." I nodded and looked around the courtyard, where cracked walls enclosed the small space. Before me, a pool of hogwash leaked under a bucket, and near the gate stood a broken spindle and a cooking pit built from mud. That place was not my home, but a reminder of what I had to do for my family—I had to help my mother and sister escape that terrible place, and I had to take care of them. It was possible, since I had been summoned to serve the Emperor. For if I won his favor, I could reclaim my family's home and restore my family's fortune. I could perhaps even fulfill Father's wish for my destiny—to become the most powerful ruler in China.

I went around and knelt before her so I could have a better look at her, at the face that had always looked composed but was recently carved with grief and fear, the face of home, the face that I would die to protect. "Will you take good care of yourself, Mother?"

"I will," she said, her calm eyes seeing through my soul, and gently, she pulled me closer to her. "Mei. You're alone, you have no one to help you, and in your heart, you have too much metal and not enough water. Do you understand what kind of place the court is?"

I knew my words would not soothe her, so I said, "Mother, do you remember that Father used to teach me Sun Tzu? He once explained to me the difference between an ordinary fighter and a good fighter." He had quoted the master's words and told me to memorize them: "'To lift a feather is no sign of great strength; to see the sun and moon is no sign of sharp sight; to hear the noise of thunder is no sign of a quick ear.'"

"Ah." Mother nodded. "So you'll learn to be a good fighter."

"Oh no, Mother." I smiled. "I will be a clever fighter, who not only wins, but also wins with ease."

With that, I hugged her.

AD 639

the Thirteenth Year *of*

Emperor Taizong's Reign

of Peaceful Prospect

AUTUMN

TWO PALACE ESCORTS IN MAROON CAPES CAME TO FETCH me on the fifteenth day of the ninth month. In my full court regalia, a skirt of pink peony paired with white trousers and a green top, I entered a carriage with a blue roof. Near it, Mother dabbed her face. She was alone now. Little Sister had passed away. The horses began to trot, and Mother called out softly, following me. The distance between us grew, and her figure, like a statue on the other side of an opaque silk screen, dwindled and slowly melted away, only her voice, faint but distinct, ringing in my ears.

I leaned back. I would see her again, and when I did, I would make sure she would be safe, happy, and have no fear or worries. I wiped away my tears. Inside, the carriage was dark. The Escort with a patch of purple birthmark covering half of his face, known as the Captain, had closed the window.

The ride seemed to go on forever. We coursed through Qing's ward, where dogs barked and hens clucked. Then we entered the avenue and approached the clamorous outer walls of the Western Market, where people haggled and peddlers called, "Noodles, noodles! One copper a bowl. Fresh, handmade noodles!" Then we arrived at the quiet alleys, where some loud Taoist hymns drifted in the air. I did not know what they meant, nor was I interested. Taoism was the official religion in our kingdom, which the Emperor claimed was founded by his ancestor Lao Tzu. But I had not seen a single Taoist abbey in Wenshui; in the capital, they were everywhere.

The two Escorts' voices came to me through the cracks of the carriage. I listened intently. I wished to know what they were talking about, but I could not hear them clearly above the rumbling of the wheels. I wanted to ask if they had picked up the other fourteen Selects the Emperor had summoned. Or should I say something memorable to them so they would have a good impression of me? I would like them to remember me. It would be useful to have friends in the palace.

My bottom slid on the red cushion as the carriage tilted backward. We were ascending a bridge. I grabbed the window frame to steady myself. The carriage slowed and then raced down. I balanced myself again. More horses trotted outside. It sounded as if we were approaching the boulevard near the Heavenly Street. Soon I would enter the palace's gates. My hands grew sweaty.

Think of Father, I reminded myself. *Think of his dream and how he raised you.* I would not disappoint him, and when I won the Emperor's heart, I would make my father proud, I would restore all the fortune my family had lost, and I would be able to take good care of Mother.

I took a deep breath, and the carriage stopped. We must be at the front gate where the stone animals stood. The Captain announced my arrival. Many footfalls rose at once. A man answered, and the gates clanked open. I leaned forward, ready to disembark.

But the carriage continued to roll, and a wave of voices rose outside the window—men inquiring about one another's health, men shouting at scribes to hurry up, men asking one another's opinions on taxes. I leaned back. So this was the Outer Palace, where the ministers conducted their business. Finally, the carriage arrived at a quiet area, where cries of birds echoed from a distance.

We stopped again.

"Out!" a woman's raspy voice shouted outside.

I balled my skirt in one hand, pushed open the carriage door with the other, and stepped out.

The bright afternoon sunlight blinded me. I blinked, standing in the middle of a pebble path. Facing me were rows of houses with blue roofs and red pillars. The pillars, round and tall, looked majestic, and the roofs were elegant, with tips turning upward at the corners, but when I looked carefully, I could see the surface of some pillars were cracked, exposing dark wood beneath.

It was quiet too. No merry chuckles or sound of zithers in the air. Behind the latticed doors, a shadow slid and peered outside, watching me.

"This way," the raspy voice said again behind me, startling me. The woman was alone. "I shall take you to your room."

The old servant limped past the houses and led me down a narrow trail through elm trees. Her shoulders dipping and rising, she looked like a boat near capsizing, reminding me of Mother's stiff back. I offered the servant a hand, but she only scowled and waved me off.

It was cooler in the shade; a pool of light from the canal shone through the thinning leaves. In the distance, a gray pavilion stood forlornly like a faded parasol. I tried to remember the locations so I could explore in the future, but the path wound around as if to test my memory. Soon, it was hard to tell how far I was from the entrance. We walked by barren flower beds, a greenish pond with withering water lotus, and two zigzagging wooden bridges before reaching a poplar grove. Behind the grove, high walls spread like a gray curtain. I hesitated, suddenly feeling sad. Beyond the wall lay the forest, and beyond the forest was my home and the people I called family.

I composed myself and hurried to follow the servant, who was already a great distance ahead of me. We stopped at a large compound with walls and entered it. Crossing the courtyard, the servant led me to a chamber on the right and pushed open the door. Inside, a group of girls sat on the floor. They looked to be my age, thirteen or fourteen. The colors of their gowns were bright, like the rouge on their faces.

From the way they sat, I could tell they were like Big Sister, who had always behaved like a dainty lady at home. Oftentimes, she had reminded me to cover my mouth when I laughed and instructed me to walk as though bearing a tray of fruit on my head. She had been annoying enough, but I had to deal with fourteen girls like her.

One girl, with eyes shaped like almonds, rose and studied me. Her gaze lingered on my face, my robe, and then paused on my shoes. I curled my toes in embarrassment. Her shoes were made of thick red brocade and embroidered with intricate patterns of yellow flowers, and mine were of plain cloth. But before Father's death, I had worn shoes decorated with gold leaves and jade rings, each costing more than anything the girl wore.

I remembered courtesy. "*Wu an.*" Good afternoon. I bowed.

She only dipped her head, as if she thought she was superior to me.

"If you don't mind me asking, are you a new Select?" I asked, trying to speak pleasantly.

"We are all the new Selects, chosen by the Emperor this year," she said, lifting her chin. "But I arrived here three days ago, before all of you did."

I wanted to ask if she had already met the Emperor, but she walked to another girl near her, cupped her hand near the girl's ear, and whispered, glancing at my shoes. Even though I could not hear her—and I did not need to—I knew what she was saying. My back grew rigid, and my cheeks burned with humiliation.

I turned to study the surroundings. The bedchamber was pitifully small and unadorned. The only furniture was the low table where the other Selects sat. The walls were bare, without a single painting or mural. The famous palace seemed more austere than a servant's quarters in my home.

Two servants brought trays and bowls that contained supper: several bamboo shoots, some soybeans, a chunk of winter gourd, two buns made of corn. No meat. I was disappointed and surprised too. In Wenshui, I had eaten meat and eggs for every meal.

When night fell, the room became so dark that the other girls turned into blots of shadows. They spread out on the floor, sleeping on small bamboo pallets. I looked around. There was one pallet left in the corner, so I took it, spread it out, and lay down.

"Have you ever wondered," said the girl with almond-shaped eyes, who I later learned was the daughter of the Xu family in the capital, "what the Emperor looks like?"

So she had not met the Emperor either. But she seemed to be the one in charge, speaking in such an authoritative tone, and all the other girls fawned over her, calling her Older Sister Xu, although she was neither old nor sisterly.

"They say his skin shines like gold," the Select with a flat nose next to me answered. "He also has the mind of a sage, the strength of a steed, and—"

"The heart of a lion," another added.

Waves of giggles followed.

I did not understand what the joke was, but the tone of their voices confirmed something I had already suspected. I was not the only one who had come with an ambition to win the Emperor's heart.

I slept shallowly and rose before dawn. Watching the others rolling up their pallets, I did the same and put mine away in the corner. The girls sat in front of their bronze mirrors, dabbing red tinctures on their faces, plucking their eyebrows, binding their hair in Cloudy Chignon, a ridiculous style with their hair piled loosely on top of their heads like black clouds. I dressed, wiped my face, and was ready.

"Will we meet the Emperor today?" I asked a girl beside me, trying to start some small talk, but she was too busy to talk to me. With nothing else to do, I simply sat and watched them.

Someone shrieked, pointing at a pimple on her face. The others rushed to her, gasping and groaning as if a tumor had grown on her nose.

The sun rose and poured a pond of golden light through the chamber's open doors. I was getting impatient waiting when an order told us to go to the courtyard, where a woman with hair shaped like a conch and a group of eunuchs stood. The woman would teach us the morning lesson of the Code of Courtly Conduct, she said.

"Conduct, courtesy, and compliance," she said, the tip of the conch hair shaking precariously as she paced in front of us, "share similar sounds but bear one name, the name of virtue. Wear them like your finest gown, carry them like a gold ingot, paint them on your face in the brightest hue, because it is by your courtesy that your goodness is so judged, and, by your compliance, your honor is weighed. Now, repeat after me."

I had never heard of the words before, but I followed her order and repeated them. Then the woman instructed us on the details of the daily court ritual, protocols, etiquette, and taboos. After she was finished, the head of the eunuchs, a man with a bald head, stepped up and said, "If you fail to obey the Code and disrupt the court's peace, you will receive a reprimand, twenty lashes by thick rods, or worse—be sent to the Ice Palace for punishment."

Father had told me about the Ice Palace. It was a euphemism for court prison, the last place a palace lady wanted to go, where the eunuchs stored rods and torture tools. It also, I remembered, had a chamber of reptiles that feasted on the most wicked sinners.

The sun was burning the top of my head by the time the head eunuch finished his speech, and another group of eunuchs came in with baskets that contained threads and needles and piles of handkerchiefs. They all needed to be embroidered in five days, the woman with conch hair said and dismissed us. No one mentioned a word about meeting the Emperor.

"This is it? We'll embroider for five days?" I followed the girls as we returned to our bedchamber, our arms full of handkerchiefs.

For all I knew, embroidery was a craft where women could have an excuse to practice stabbing—not just the fabric, but people as well. I had heard of some embroidery techniques from Big Sister, but I was not interested in it, and Mother had not forced it upon me.

The Xu Girl, the girl with almond-shaped eyes, glanced at me. "Come, Selects, let's take a look at the embroidery technique on the sample handkerchief. Here, I have the sample." She gathered us around her, and I sat across from her in the outer circle. "We will start with the partridge. Let's look at the satin stitches used in the feathers. Isn't this fabulous?"

Nodding, the girls stroked the partridge's tail.

"Look how even these stitches are."

"And the threads are so shiny!"

"Well, we shall start embroidering," the Xu Girl ordered and stuffed the piles of handkerchiefs into our hands.

I stared at the vague bird-shaped pattern on the cloth. In my right hand, I held a needle, but it felt like a slippery eel. Crouching carefully, I wrestled it between my thumb and forefinger, suspending my right arm in midair, and traced the edge of the vague pattern.

Soon my eyes were sore, my neck stiff, and my hands cramped, while my mind was knotted like a skein of yarn. When would I see the Emperor?

And I was hungry. I wanted my midday meal.

"So I heard this from the head eunuch when I arrived a few days ago. He said if you wish to see the Emperor, you need his summons," the Xu Girl said.

I raised my head, surprised. I had assumed that since I was in the palace, I would see him immediately. Perhaps we would all gather in a courtyard, and he would pace before us and ask questions, similar to Father interviewing a group of scribes. But the Xu Girl could be right. The One Above All, the lord of the wind and the sand, the ruler of those flying and those walking, must elude others' eyes.

"Whom will he summon first?" the girl with a pimple asked, glancing at all of us. "There are fifteen of us."

"I suppose he will summon us in the order of age, pedigree, or the rank of our family," the Xu Girl said.

A wave of voices exploded. "Then he would summon you first," one said, pointing at the other.

"No, I think it's you," another added.

They sounded courteous, but a shade of uneasiness lurked in their eyes, telling me that they were not truly friends but rivals.

"If he summons us in the order of rank, shouldn't he see the titled ladies first?" I said, fingering the needle between my thumb and forefinger. Everyone in the kingdom knew the Emperor had many titled ladies serve him.

"You mean the Four Ladies and the Ladies-in-Waiting?" The Xu Girl dismissed me with a wave. "Perhaps he will summon them first, and then he should see us."

"But there are so many." I could tell she disliked my interruption, but she did not seem to know how many titled ladies there were. "If you include all the ladies of nine degrees."

She glanced at me and then looked down at the handkerchief in her hand. "Nine degrees?"

"Yes."

The highest ranking of all titled ladies was the Empress, the chief wife, but she had died the previous year, so the Emperor had his consorts, the second-degree ladies, whom we called the Four Ladies; the third-degree ladies, known as the Ladies-in-Waiting; the fourth-degree ladies, the Beauties; the fifth-degree ladies, the Graces; the sixth-degree ladies, the Talents; the seventh-degree ladies, the Baolins; the eighth-degree ladies, the Yunus; and the ninth-degree ladies, the Cainus.

"Where did you learn that?" the Xu Girl asked me without lifting her head.

"From the Sui Book."

"What book?"

I could tell the Xu Girl, like Big Sister, was not interested in reading, or perhaps she could not read at all. After all, reading was usually reserved for the noble boys. Many women, even the noble ones, did not have the privilege. But Father had given me all types of books: history books, Confucius's *Analects*, poems and rhapsodies, and Sun Tzu's *The Art of War*. I had enjoyed reading them. "The history book about the Sui Dynasty. It says the palace women were ranked in nine degrees, like the ministers in the Outer Palace. Emperor Gaozu adopted the same system when he founded his dynasty."

She waved her hand, frowning. "Fine. Nine degrees of ladies. We know that now. Only a dozen women."

"No, no. Not a dozen. Each rank consists of a different number of women. There are top-ranking ladies: the four Ladies, and six Ladies-in-Waiting. Then the middle-ranking, the fourth-, fifth-, and sixth-degree ladies. Each of those ranks has nine women. And then there are lower-ranking, the seventh-, eighth-, and ninth-degree ladies, and each of those has twenty-seven."

The Selects stared at me, their mouths open in shock, and the Xu Girl pulled the thread abruptly, looking frustrated. "Twenty-seven lower-ranking women? What is the total of the titled ladies then?"

I added the numbers quickly. "One hundred and eighteen."

She was quiet. Someone else dropped her needle.

"Are you sure?" the Xu Girl finally asked. "One hundred and eighteen titled women?"

"Yes," I said. An army of the Emperor's women. My stomach clenched as the true meaning of that number sank in.

If the Emperor shared one night with each titled woman, it would take him more than three months. About seven months if he ordered a second round, and if he was happy with his bedmates, it would probably take at least a year before he summoned one of us.

"Nobody told me that. You certainly know more than any of us," the girl with a pimple said with a sigh.

"Well, I did not want to tell you this." The Xu Girl flipped her handkerchief over and touched the stitches. I could tell she was unhappy because I had gotten attention from the other Selects. "The head eunuch also told me that..." She gathered the others around her and whispered.

I could see the wall she built to isolate me. I frowned, pulling a thread through the fabric. I did not care if she liked me, but I desperately wanted to know what she was saying.

"Really? Three hundred women?" The girl with a pimple gasped.

"What three hundred women?" I asked. Then I understood. The Selects who had come before us.

"They have waited for years. Some have been here for ten years. But they have never received a summons." The Xu Girl glanced at me. She looked triumphant that she had known that.

"They never met the Emperor?" someone asked.

"No, the head eunuch said that their hairs have grown white and their faces are wrinkled. They have never even glimpsed the Emperor's face."

That night, I lay on my pallet, eyes wide-open in the dark. Would I wait in the bedchamber until my hair grew white, like those old Selects? I would not accept that. I could not let my father's wish turn into a dusty cobweb, and besides, I needed to get our house back and give Mother a comfortable life.

If the Emperor would not summon me, I would go find him myself.

I was already inside the palace. I needed only to walk around, locate the Emperor's chamber, and introduce myself. No one could stop me.

I waited until the girls' rhythmic breathing rose. Then I slipped off my pallet, unlatched the oak bar between the two brackets, and pulled. The door squeaked open. A cold draft rushed in, and my eyes watered. A girl shifted on her pallet, and I froze. When I was certain she was still sleeping, I slipped out the door, closed it, and stepped into the corridor.

Before me, the smooth ground of the courtyard, coated with a thin layer of frost, glimmered in the moonlight like a damask tapestry woven with silver threads. In front of the bedchamber, two pillars stood silently like watchful giants, while the tips of the flying eaves soared into a starless sky.

Footsteps paced outside the courtyard. The building was guarded, and it was impossible to escape.

AD 640

the Fourteenth Year *of*

Emperor Taizong's Reign

of Peaceful Prospect

SPRING

MONTHS PASSED. NO SUMMONS CAME FROM THE EMPEROR.
I learned I was living in the Yeting Court, which was located on the west side of the Inner Court. Heavily guarded by female guards twice my size, it was the home for old and new Selects, exiled ladies, slaves, and many unhappy women. At the northern end, when I walked far enough, I could see the towering trees from the Forbidden Park on the other side of the high wall. At the southern end of the court, near the hill, stood the Ice Palace and the gray brick buildings where the eunuchs lived. That area had no gardens or pavilions. It was often quiet, a place even birds seemed afraid to enter.

The titled ladies lived in a compound on the other side of the wall, the real Inner Court. The Emperor, of course, dwelled there with them. The walls were so high between us, even if I stood on tiptoe, even if I climbed the tree next to the wall, I could not see the face of the man who could change my family's future.

I sank into the tedious routine of the court like a rock dropping in the river. I rose before dawn, ate my breakfast, and worked on my embroidery. There were endless pieces of fabric waiting for me: gowns, tunics, shawls, skirts, shoes, sleeves, padded jackets, and trousers. They were all for the titled ladies who lived in the Inner Court, I was told. When I finished one, another was pushed into my hands. Taking a break was not allowed, and if I slowed, I would hear harsh scolding from the eunuchs who supervised us. Over time, my embroidery skill improved greatly, and when the eunuchs compared my work with the other girls', they could not tell the difference.

I seldom joined the girls' conversations, which were mostly about facial creams or how to draw beauty marks, and the Xu Girl began to take an interest in my accent. When I commented on something, she would sniff and imitate me. The others tittered. Born in the capital, they spoke with a typical Chang'an accent, which was rigid and carried a light nasal sound, but I still spoke with a heavier nasal sound, the voice of Wenshui. I was determined to change. Whenever I had a chance, I silently practiced Mandarin. Soon I could speak as well as them, and they had to stop teasing me. But still when I sat in a corner, I felt like a stag among a herd of horses, where my own difference stuck out like antlers.

I missed my family. I worried about Mother every day. What if Qing refused to give her food? What if Qing beat her? Who would protect her? And Father. How tall the grass in front of his grave must have grown. Was he disappointed in me? When I thought of them, when I thought of how much Mother needed me, I could hardly sleep. I grew desperate.

I needed to get summoned.

✦ ✦

One morning, I went to fetch water to wash my face. A woman in the pavilion called to me. "You're new here."

I had noticed her before. Like me, she was always alone, sitting at a low writing table in the pavilion. Although she did not look old, she had white hair that reached her waist. When she bent to the table, she looked as if she had been showered by snow.

"Do they give you any trouble?" She glanced at the Xu Girl, who passed by me with the other Selects.

"What makes you say that?" I walked to the pavilion. Perhaps the woman had noticed my unhappiness or heard the others make some comments about me.

She smiled, tucking a handkerchief in her pocket. "It would be hard to live here for anyone, especially if you have difficult chamber mates."

I put my basin down and sat on the windowsill. "I agree."

"You do know they dislike you because you are more intelligent than they are, don't you?" She was drawing something on the table while a basket of fabric, unembroidered, lay near her feet.

I was rather flattered. "How did you know that?"

"It's my secret. But I see you're more beautiful than they say too."

And she certainly knew the right things to say. "You're very kind," I said. When I was at home, I had not cared about my looks, but after spending all these months with the Selects, I understood a woman's beauty was important. Still, it bored me to spend hours dabbing white cream on my face.

The woman herself was stunningly beautiful. She had willowy eyebrows and a small cherry-red mouth. Loops of white fringed her forehead, while two heaps of hair stood at both sides of her head like the pointy ears of a feline.

"How old are you? Fifteen?" She smoothed a scroll on the table and anchored the corners with the ink stone, ink sticks, and a calligraphy holder painted with white clouds and red peonies.

"Thirteen." Most of the Selects were fourteen—another reason I did not fit in. I had bled for the first time the month before I came to the palace. My body was changing too, and my breasts were sore. But I still had the slender figure of a girl.

"So young," she said. "They call me Jewel."

"I'm Mei."

"Of the Wu family."

"You know my family?" I could not have been more proud.

"I heard the eunuchs talk about you when they were discussing the summons."

"Summons? Have you met the Emperor?"

She shook her head, her gaze fixed on me. Her eyes were like a cat's, inscrutable, observing me quietly but refusing to be observed. I wondered what she was thinking.

"How long have you been here?" I asked.

"Long enough." She picked up a calligraphy brush on the table.

"From what others have said, it sounds like we could be waiting forever. I do not like it, waiting here and wasting time."

"There are some ways that can help you obtain the summons."

"Really? What ways?"

She dipped her brush in the ink stone, her left hand holding back her right sleeve. "If you have a powerful relative in the court." She dabbed it against the stone to remove excess ink and began to draw a few lines on the scroll. Her hand was steady, the strokes smooth and thin. Soon the lines formed a large blossom. I could not criticize her skill. She was a good painter. "A truly powerful one, a first-degree minister, or second-degree, who will have opportunities to exalt your beauty to the Emperor. When he hears it, he'll surely be eager to see you."

"Ah, connections." That was how the world functioned, of course. People with good connections received good opportunities; people with no connections received no opportunities. "What are the other ways?"

She glanced at me. "Bribe the eunuch who's in charge of deciding the Emperor's night companions. He'll whisper in the Emperor's ear about your beauty when he has a chance. When the Emperor gets curious, he'll summon you."

I wanted to groan. I did not possess anything valuable that could be used as a bribe, not a jade pendant or even a silver bangle.

"I did not mean to upset you, my friend." She put down the brush. "Let me tell you something else. Every year on his birthday, the Emperor accepts gifts from his concubines, including us in the Yeting Court. If you give him an unforgettable gift, he may honor you by seeing you."

"Oh, really?" I was excited. "What kind of gift?"

"Something unique."

"It has to be, doesn't it?" There must be thousands of gifts from all the ministers, titled ladies, and all the other ladies. How could one gift stand out and attract his eye? "What have the ladies given him in the past?"

"Gold or expensive toys, jewelry, silk robes, lapis lazuli even. I once offered him a horse."

A horse! One of the most treasured animals in the kingdom. The rebellion against the Sui Dynasty had cost many precious steeds. With peace at hand, horses were cherished and desired by every man. A conqueror like the Emperor certainly understood their value. "And he didn't summon you?"

Jewel shook her head.

"If he is not interested in seeing us"—I frowned—"why does he summon maidens to the palace each year?"

She sighed. "All I can tell you is our Emperor is a collector."

"Collector?"

"A general is no general if he has no soldiers, and what kind of emperor would he be if he cannot have any woman he wishes in the kingdom?"

I would rather not think of myself as something to be collected, like the piece of bone relic Mother cherished. "So he would summon us, any of us, if he is interested in the gift?"

"That's right." She nodded, gazing at a group of women coming down the winding path to fetch water from the canal. "But let me tell you—for seven years, no one from the Yeting Court has impressed him."

The women came closer. I did not recognize them. They were probably the other Selects who had come years before. Their white gowns fluttering in the wind, they glanced at me and frowned.

"Do they know about giving gifts?" I asked.

"They live for the Emperor's birthday and the chance to impress him. We all do. Once the Emperor summons us and honors us with a title, we will move to the real Inner Court and receive monthly allowances, beautiful gowns, and good food. We will not need to do any embroidery or laundry. Perhaps we will even have maids to serve us. Who does not wish for that?"

I had to agree with her. Embroidery was a slave's duty. "What are you going to give him this year?"

She shook her head. "I don't know yet."

I had a feeling she was unwilling to share her idea. I did not blame her. She must have desperately wished to impress the Emperor and move to the real Inner Court.

I watched her finish painting the flower. A black peony. It was strangely appealing. When it was time to leave, I took my basin and thanked her for telling me about the Emperor's birthday.

I came to the pavilion often after that day. Jewel was not like the Selects in my chamber. She was not talkative. She always looked quiet, and many times she fell into a serene repose that reminded me of a figure in a painting. It was only her catlike eyes, deep and unfathomable as a summer's pond, that made me wonder whether, like me, she had experienced a great pain in her life. I did not inquire, as I thought of Confucius's advice: "The friendship between gentlemen is plain as water." I believed it should apply to women as well.

5

SOON THE SELECTS HEARD OF THE BIRTHDAY AS WELL. SO excited, they spent day and night discussing what gifts they would give to the Emperor. The discussion intensified as the date of the Emperor's birthday approached. One night, a Select mentioned consulting her family; the next night, another declared her family would send her gold and silver to present to the Emperor. It seemed there was no limit to what they would give.

Some Selects worked on their embroidery fervently. They fought over the colorful threads and tried to hide their designs as they labored, afraid the others would steal their inspirations. I often awoke in the midnight hours and saw shadows crouching by the hemp oil lamp, the threads flying between their fingers.

Sitting in front of my bronze mirror, I stared at my reflection. This was perhaps my only chance to get noticed, and I had to choose a good present, an unforgettable present.

What should I give to the Emperor?

There were no exotics he had not seen, no finery he had not touched, no prizes he had not won. He could have had anything he wanted, and he would not care what treasure he received or who gave it to him. And if I was right about the court protocol, the only people who would see the presents would be the court recorders, who might neglect or misreport the items, and the Emperor would never know, or care, who gave him what.

Perhaps I should have considered him not as the Emperor, who owned the kingdom's extravagance, but simply a man.

What would a man want?

Many things: big or small, expensive or cheap. But there was nothing I could afford.

I thought of Sun Tzu. What would the master advise me to do if he were me? "All warfare is based on deception," he had said. That did not help. I needed only a suggestion for a gift. Gift giving was not warfare, and his strategies of attacking were not relevant to my need. But wait…did he not say that prior to attack, one must hold out bait to entice the enemy?

Bait…

I had an idea.

A week before the Emperor's birthday, the eunuchs came to collect the gifts. There were handkerchiefs lined with silver threads, belts encrusted with jade, fragrance sachets embroidered with flowers and love ducks, and vests with images of dragons and phoenixes. The Xu Girl had the most precious present—a pair of rhinoceros horns with gold tips. She wrapped them in a piece of red silk she had embroidered and handed her package to the eunuchs with care. I slipped mine into the bottom of the pile.

Then we waited.

"What did you give to the Emperor?" I asked Jewel in the pavilion that afternoon.

She leaned over the table to paint. "Myself."

I stared at her. "You gave him a portrait."

How clever. She was a beautiful lady, and I could imagine how attractively she had painted herself.

She nodded. "What present did you give him?"

"I can't paint, and I do not have anything valuable." But wealth and treasure would not be what the Emperor sought, if he sought anything among us.

"You did give him something, didn't you?"

"Yes." I cleared my throat and recited:

"I have no beginning nor an end,
I have no mother nor a friend.
Seldom do I give you warning or fear,
but when you think of me, you shall shed a tear.

"So fair and just I'm known,
Like the wind and air that you cannot own,
On and on I shall continue,
When your heart hardens to a stone."

Jewel arched her painted eyebrows. "What is that?"

"A riddle."

She paused for a moment. "You gave the Emperor a riddle for his birthday?"

It was a good choice, I saw it in her eyes, for she looked surprised and then almost rueful, as though regretting why she had not thought of it. "Do you think he'll like it?"

"I like it. An ingenious thought. But I have never heard of the verses. Where did you find the riddle?"

"I wrote it."

She was quiet again. "I certainly did not expect a girl of your age would have such an inspiration—a riddle for the Emperor!—and express it so poetically. But I wonder. Are you not worried you would offend him? It is rather bold, isn't it?"

It was risky. The Emperor owned everything and beyond, and what I said in the riddle could certainly be read as a challenge. "I took my chances."

"So what is the answer?"

I told her.

"My sweet friend," she said. "I hope this will earn you a summons."

If she was distressed by the possibility that I would be summoned instead of her, I did not see it on her face.

The Emperor's birthday came, and the celebration started.

There were musician troupes, parades of floats, and festivals on the dragon boats, but none of us in the Yeting Court had the honor of attending. The Emperor did not summon the Xu Girl, Jewel, or me. Jewel was disappointed. "I should have known," she said. "The Emperor is surrounded by beauties. My picture will not attract him."

I shared her distress. It seemed my efforts were no better than drawings in the water.

✦ ✦

Weeks passed. One day, a eunuch led me to the entrance of the Yeting Court, where two ministers—one old, one young—wearing black hats stood. They verified I was the sender of the riddle and then explained the reason for the interview. When they recorded the gifts, they said, some of the court scribes were intrigued by my riddle. They looked through the classics and consulted many books and songs, but they were unable to decipher it. The ministers wanted to know the answer.

"It's time. The answer is time," I said. It was a good sign. The ministers had noticed me. Perhaps the Emperor would notice me too.

"So where did you find the riddle?" the old minister asked.

When I explained I wrote it, he looked shocked. "Where did you get the idea to compose a riddle like that?"

I had to be careful. Anything I said could be my undoing. I replied, "I have the immense honor of serving the Emperor in this palace. Every morning, I rise from bed, checking my appearance in the bronze mirror. I look different from how I was at home. I thought of how wondrous time was and its mighty power to transform what we are and what we see. That is where I got my inspiration."

The two ministers exchanged looks. The old one frowned while the young one's face remained as blank as a swept courtyard. Then they left.

I wrung my hands. Were they going to report me to the Emperor? Had I offended him?

That night, the Selects were chattering about the Emperor again.

"I certainly hope a summons will come to us very soon," one of them said. "He's bound to like our gifts, isn't he? Those gifts are expensive and unique."

The others agreed. Certainly the Emperor would love the vests with the satin stitches, one said. Or rhinoceros horns, another added. Then they leaned over to the Xu Girl and murmured something.

"Yes, what a shame," the Xu Girl said. Her voice was loud enough for everyone to hear. "When you're poor and inept, what else can you give as a gift other than a stupid riddle?"

She was mocking me. She must have heard me explaining the riddle. I let her be. Criticism would not hurt me.

"I have so many peasants at home who act just the same, and they cannot afford to wear a pair of decent shoes," she continued. "Speaking of them, I don't like peasants looking at my shoes. They always think about stealing them. But I daresay it's her mother's fault. She forgot to teach her. But perhaps she is ignorant as well. You know the saying goes, 'Like mother, like daughter'?"

I rose from my pallet and walked to her so she had to look at my face. It was fine if she mocked me, but not my mother. "You may have a thousand pairs of shoes, but it does not make you a thousand times better than the others. If I were you, I would keep my eyes on my shoes and keep my mouth closed."

She growled. "Who needs your advice? You're no better than a peasant's daughter."

Peasants were the lowest social class, and it was the worst insult she could give me. "I would like to tell you my mother is a cousin of an empress and my father was a governor—"

"Peasant!" she spat at me.

I raised my hand to slap her. She had gone too far.

Something smacked my head. I staggered backward and stepped on something soft. A pillow? No. Someone's leg. "I fell, and before I could get up, fists, spits, taunts, and scorn rained down on me.

Someone yanked my hair, another girl pounded on my back, and yet another kicked my arms and legs.

"What's going on there?" someone shouted from outside.

They stopped.

"Coward, that's what you are," the Xu Girl hissed.

I did not have strength to speak. My head was hurting. I lay down on my pallet and curled up. I was angry, yet there was nothing I could do. For the rest of the night, I stared at the swirling lattices of the window. They seemed to whirl and spin out of control.

The morning light shot into my eyes. I rose stiffly, my body sore. In front of me stood the head eunuch, the Xu Girl, and the other Selects. They were smirking.

My heart tightened. I ignored my headache and bowed. "*Zao an.*" Good morning.

The Xu Girl pointed at me. "Here she is. She slapped me!"

I straightened and turned to the eunuch. "You shouldn't listen to her. She is lying."

The eunuch scowled, waving his hand. "The guards heard your voice. The girls here confirmed what happened."

"But they are all lying."

"There's no point in denying it. You, the daughter of the Wu family, attacked your fellow Select and disturbed the court peace. You must be punished. Guards, take her to the Ice Palace."

I felt chilled. The Ice Palace. The last place where a palace lady would want to go. "No...please don't... I can't... I... What about the Emperor? He will not allow it!"

"There is no need to bother the One Above All." He waved at the female guards behind him. "Take her now."

Like vultures, they dove at me. I drew back to the corner of the bedchamber, but their hands came anyway. I threw them off. "Get away from me. I will walk myself."

I hurried out of the bedchamber, passing the girls quickly so they would not have the satisfaction of seeing my tears. It was my own fault. I had underestimated them and let this happen.

"Wait," a voice called out when we turned on the pebble path outside of the compound where I stayed. The air was cold, and the sun spread its golden rays through the thin branches and reflected on the bare garden rock beside me. But I did not feel the warmth. "Where are you going?"

Jewel.

"To the Ice Palace," the eunuch replied.

"What?" Jewel's fan paused in midair. Behind her, some girls who were pounding their laundry with flat wooden clubs at the bank of the canal stood up, craning their necks in my direction. A group of older Selects, who were on the way to fetch water, came around the pavilion to watch me.

"What happened, Mei?" Jewel asked.

"I…" I stared at the treetops in the Forbidden Park, unable to bring myself to recount last night's story. The wind whipped my loosened hair around my face. I gathered it in front of my chest and held it there, but still the wind plucked at the strands and sent them flying. I wished it could blow me away.

"Was there a fight?" Jewel said, glancing at the Selects on my left, who had followed me. "My respected head eunuch, perhaps you may not wish to rush into decisions. She is only thirteen. So young! She does not deserve to be punished in the Ice Palace. Perhaps you may wish to ask more questions?"

"Stay out of this, Jewel. I do not like people questioning my judgment." He looked down his nose at us.

Jewel sighed. "Yes, my respected head eunuch, I shall not question you, lest you throw me into the Ice Palace too. I do wish, and kindly beseech, that you will give this incident some thought and give her another chance." She pulled me beside her, and before I knew what she wished me to do, she bowed. Deeply. Three times. "If there is anything I can do to make you change your mind…" she said.

I was grateful to her. She was the only woman who dared to help me.

"I have made up my mind." The eunuch waved at the guards. "Take this disobedient girl now. Let's go."

They held my arms and pushed me. All Jewel's pleadings were wasted.

"Halt!" An elderly man scurried along the trail toward us. I recognized him—the old minister who had asked me about my riddle. "My lady," he said courteously to me when he approached. "I have been searching for you. The servants told me to find you here. I'm to deliver you a message." He unfurled the scroll, which was colored in imperial yellow. An edict.

"Is this from the Emperor?" Jewel sounded surprised. She tucked her fan into her girdle.

"Yes," he replied.

So the Emperor had heard of the fight. I was doomed. Despair and regret expanded inside my chest.

The minister cleared his throat and began to read. It sounded like something I had heard before, but his words pelted me like heavy raindrops that wet my head but could not penetrate it. When he stopped, gasps rose around me, and Jewel clutched my hand, her eyes as large as lanterns.

"Mei, I cannot believe it!" she cried out.

I stared at the minister. "What…what? Did you…did you say the Emperor summoned me?"

The minister gave me a firm nod. "Yes, Select. After our interview with you, the court ministers had a heated discussion about the riddle. The Emperor happened to pass by and overheard it. He was intrigued. He would like to honor you by meeting you."

It was true. The Emperor had summoned me, but I continued to stare at the minister, not knowing what to say.

"Can you believe it?" Jewel tapped my arm. She looked delighted too, her cherry-red lips widening to a lovely curve. "For seven years, not one of the ladies in the Yeting Court has had the honor to see the One Above All's face. You sent him a riddle, and now he wants to see you."

"I know, I know. I am fortunate." My heart sang. Finally, I

would meet the Emperor! I would tell him what happened to my family, and Mother would have a comfortable life again...

"Yes, indeed you are." Jewel smiled. "Now, I think you should get busy. We shall not waste time."

"Why?"

"You did not hear it?" She showed me the edict.

I followed her forefinger, which traced the lines on the golden paper. "Oh." It was not a simple meeting after all. He had summoned me for tonight. I stopped smiling. Every maiden understood what a night summons meant. "What should I do now, Jewel?"

She spread the fan in her hand, a smile on her face. "First, you're going to the bathhouse."

6

ON THE WAY TO THE BATHHOUSE, MY STEPS WERE LIGHT, and my heart was filled with joy. I thought of what Father had told me. The second son of Emperor Gaozu, Emperor Taizong, whose given name was too sacred for human mouths to speak, was a great conqueror and also a master of war.

The night Emperor Gaozu defeated the Sui army, Emperor Taizong was only twenty years old and a duke commanding a small cavalry. While his father celebrated in the palace, he sought out the Sui ruler's young son and nephew and took the children as prisoners, sending them to the Sui general, who escorted the fleeing ruler to the south by Grand Canal. Taizong proposed that the general should rule the kingdom in the south with the imperial descendants if he killed the defeated ruler. The general agreed and assassinated the Sui ruler while he was drinking on his five-story dragon boat. But when the general delivered the body to the shore, he was greeted by Taizong's army, who held sabers at his neck.

Still a duke, Taizong would later persuade his father to give the throne to him instead of his older brother, the heir, or his younger brother, Emperor Gaozu's favorite son, and claimed himself as the One Above All.

"We are here," Jewel said as we turned right on the pathway before a pear grove. At the end of the path stood a one-story house

I had never seen before. "Remember the court protocol? It is the first and foremost requirement that no dirt or grime shall cling to your body before you step into his bedchamber."

I nodded. "What else should I know?" When the etiquette teacher cited the rules to me after the announcement of the summons, I had been too excited to pay attention.

"That should be all," she said, and paused to let me walk ahead of her. "The bookkeeper and other helpers will wait for you when you arrive. You need only to follow their directions."

I turned to her. "Why did you help me, Jewel? When the head eunuch was taking me away?"

"I don't like the Selects. Besides, what could the eunuch do to me? Come." She pushed open the bathhouse door.

I stepped inside. A wave of hot steam rushed to my face, blurring my vision. Batting the steam away, I saw a wooden tub at the center of the room. It was so large it could have held my whole family. I walked toward it, passing shelves holding bowls of red soap beans, brushes with long handles, stacks of towels, and balls of dried vegetable fiber used for scrubbing. Then I stopped.

A group of men emerged before me. Some carried pails of hot water and poured them into the tub while some scattered flower petals in the water. One walked toward me, his hand extended.

"Where are the women servants?" I asked Jewel. Usually, the female servants performed the intimate task of bathing.

"This is the eunuch in charge of the Emperor's night summons. We call him Eunuch Uncle Ming." Jewel, already disrobed, stepped into the tub. "Is there a problem?"

"No…" I did not realize Jewel would bathe with me. But I should not object. She had been so kind to me. "I just did not know, that's all."

"You will get used to the eunuchs," she said. "And they will take you to the Emperor's bedchamber when the water reaches the line six." She pointed at a water clock on a stool.

"All right." I undressed and joined her in the tub. A eunuch, who appeared to be deaf and mute, came to me with a bowl filled with soap beans, while the others all filed out of the room, except Eunuch Ming.

I hunched my back to let the water cover my chest and inhaled the sweet flower scent, all the while deeply aware of how transparent the water was. Jewel looked relaxed, leaning against the tub with her eyes closed. The water reached just below her breasts, her pink nipples leaping in and out of the petals floating in the water like curious children playing hide-and-seek. A clear stream glided down her pale neck and plunged between her breasts.

I sank farther. I was not as pretty. Her breasts looked supple and perfectly sized while mine were small and unimpressive. She had lush hair under her armpits and below her stomach, blooming gracefully like a collection of ornamental grass in a garden. But mine was sparse and ungainly, shriveling pitifully like a handful of weeds in a desert.

"Are you nervous?" Jewel's voice drifted in the vaporous steam.

"No," I said quickly. "Well, maybe just a little." I arranged my long hair to cover the front of my chest. Pink petals floated toward me, and my hair drifted in the water like black clouds. "I just realized I don't have decent gowns."

Jewel pursed her lips as if to suppress a smile. "Gowns? You don't need any." She pointed at a red mantle hanging on a peg near a bucket I had not noticed before. "Eunuch Ming will wrap you in the thick cover and carry you to the quarters."

I sat up. "Just the mantle, nothing else?" Eunuch Ming was examining something among Jewel's clothes. He picked up a small golden thing, Jewel's bangle, and pocketed it. He was stealing! I gestured to alert Jewel, but she only shrugged.

"I am only trying to tell you this is the routine," she said and stretched out her arms as Eunuch Ming returned and washed her with a ball of dried gourd fiber. "You go there naked and empty and come back naked, but with his seed."

The bedroom affair. It sounded crude coming from Jewel's mouth. "Oh…"

She gazed at me, her eyes sparkling. "It's always difficult the first time."

The deaf eunuch waved a ball of gourd fiber and gestured for me to raise my arms. I obeyed, relieved to be distracted.

"Well, I assume you've heard of this…" Jewel paused as Eunuch Ming whispered something in her ear, and she continued, "bedding. The Emperor requires special instructions."

I watched the two of them. I wondered what the eunuch had told Jewel. "What special instructions?"

She chuckled. "Knowing *The Manual for a Pure Maiden* is not enough, Mei. After all, he's the Emperor, not an ordinary man."

"What manual?" I wanted to bite my tongue. I had heard of it, of course. When a daughter's wedding night approached, her mother usually hid the manual at the bottom of the clothing trunk. It contained various ideas to conceive boys as well as many rules, taboos, and suggestions about the bedroom business. Its importance was similar to scriptures for religious followers who sought guidance and principles. But I had never seen it. Mother had not given it to me.

Jewel swam to me, her eyes boring into me. "You haven't heard of *The Manual*?"

There was something light and flirting in her eyes. I felt my cheeks warm. I hunched my shoulders. "No, I was just asking…"

"Have you seen it?"

The eunuch scrubbed hard on my raw skin, and my nose touched the hot water. "Well…"

Jewel swam back to her side of the tub. "What are you going to do now? You don't know anything."

The challenging tone in her voice made me straighten my back. "I'll do whatever is asked."

Surely I would not be the first woman who did not know any bedding secrets, and if I were, it would not be a disaster either. The Emperor, among all men, should be most familiar with his battle.

Jewel shook her head. "That's not enough, Mei. You need to do more than is asked. This is your first chance, and perhaps only chance, to win his affection. You do not wish to ruin it. If you like, I can teach you the tending, the intimacy, and all."

Teach me?

"Or I have another idea." She leaned outside the tub, squeezing her breasts against the rim. When she straightened, she held a wine cup in her hand. "Drink this. It'll give you a man's valor."

"I don't like wine."

During festivals, my parents had filled my cup with specially prepared plum wine. I had sipped some, but what I really enjoyed was the company of my family.

"Do you want to ruin your first, and probably only, chance?"

She had a point. I grabbed the cup and drank the liquid in three gulps. "Thank you."

I gave the cup back to her and leaned against the tub. The deaf eunuch began to wash my hair with soap beans, his nails scraping my scalp. "Tell me about the Emperor, Jewel. What have you heard about him? What did the eunuchs tell you?"

There was silence. "He could be many things you imagined and hoped, save for one."

"What?" A bonfire of heat erupted in my stomach and rushed to my chest then my head. It was so powerful I shivered. Jewel's drink was much stronger than Mother's homemade plum wine.

"A lover."

There was something in her voice, something subtle that made me sit up. "You have met the Emperor before, haven't you?"

"Hmm?" She turned to me. Her face was wet with vapor.

A lover. Only a woman who had a history with the Emperor would say something like that. "You told me you never met him. But you did. You know him. You know him well."

She blinked, as though I had wronged her, but I knew I was right. She was hiding something from me. "Are you lying to me, Jewel?"

She sighed. "I would never do that. You are a good friend of mine. If you really wish, I shall gladly tell you my story over the warmth of fire and music someday. I fear I shall bore you."

"I shall not be bored." I felt deceived, and the wine simmered in my stomach, burning quietly and persistently.

She drew a line in the water with her finger. The water rippled;

the petals leaped up and down. "I was once the Emperor's favorite. He adored me, giving me a chamber inside the Inner Court and bestowing on me many gifts and servants. He even promoted my father and brothers within the court. But then he exiled me to this place—this doomed Yeting Court—like a slave."

I could hardly believe my ears. "Why? What did you do?"

"I did nothing. Someone hated me and said something about me, I suppose, so he lost his interest in me." She paused. "But that was not all. He took everything, and everyone, from me. All my family members, my father and brothers, all the people who served me or were related to me, gone."

I shivered. That was the most horrific story I had ever heard. "When did that happen?"

"Seven years ago."

She had been exiled to the Yeting Court for seven years. I stared at a petal in the water. My anger dissipated. "That is a long time."

"I was eighteen when he exiled me. Now I am twenty-five. I spent my most precious years here, inside the Yeting Court. No one knows me. No one wants me. I am no longer the same girl I used to be. And the Emperor? His wife is dead, and he likes one woman today and another tomorrow, changing them like cups of wine."

I could not help pitying her. "This must be hard. Do you…" I swallowed the word *hate*. "Do you still wish to see him?"

"You wish to know if I hate him?" She had read my mind anyway. "Of course I did. For a long time. But then I learned it was not him, really. He was deceived. He still favored me, I knew, or he could have ordered me killed. But that was seven years ago." She leaned back. "And all these years, I have tried to see him. Giving him unique gifts. He has never summoned me. He perhaps has forgotten me already." She sighed. "Seven years is a long time."

That was why she sent the Emperor her portrait—to remind him of her.

I wiped sweat off my face. I was growing hot. "When I see him, I will speak for you."

"You will?" She sounded delighted, but then she sighed again.

"I wish I had not been so naive then. Had I known what kind of a man he was, I would not have ended up here." A veil of emotion vibrated in her voice. What was it? Regret? Resentment? Determination? Eunuch Ming coughed, and Jewel lifted her head, smiling at me. "But this is your night. You must prepare yourself. Don't you wish to please him? And become Most Adored?"

"Most Adored?" I had heard of the honorific, an unofficial title referring to a woman who won the Emperor's favor and received as many bestowals and privileges as the high-ranking ladies. In the past, some of those women with that title had been elevated to Ladies, second only to the Empress, and brought eternal glory to their families. Perhaps that was what I had to do—become Most Adored and then request the Emperor to restore my family's fortune.

"Yes, you would need to share his bed more than three times during two moon's cycles, which means he must upset the court bedding schedule—"

"What bedding schedule?" I had never heard of it.

"Oh, I'll tell you more when you're ready. For now, all you need to know is you must keep his interest so he'll summon you again."

I agreed. She was very sensible. It was almost six o'clock, and I should not waste time. "Are we finished?"

"Almost," she said, her eyes on me. She seemed to watch me, expecting something, and Eunuch Ming was staring at me too. His eyes were sharp and unkind. I did not like him. "Are you certain you do not need my help to please the Emperor?"

"Yes." It was so hot. I wiped my face again. I could hardly breathe.

"Then let him rinse you."

The deaf eunuch poured water over my head, and I sighed. It felt good to have cold water on my scalp. But I wished I had not drunk the wine. It was giving me a headache. I leaned back and gazed at the ceiling, where mists surged from the tub and clung there. Lightly and tenaciously. I could see that someday a crack would appear in the wood, and then the moisture would rot the whole ceiling. I blinked. The mists seemed to drift, and slowly, they converged to form a familiar face. Father's.

I reached out, but how strange. I could not raise my hand. I tried again. My hand, stiff, remained under the water.

"This is odd," I said. Hot steam ran across my forehead and flowed into my eyes. I shook my head. The house seemed to whirl around me. The roof wavered, slowly driving toward me like an enormous net.

"Is something wrong?" Jewel's voice sounded far away.

She looked strange too, her limbs twisting like ropes and her head bouncing like a ball. "Jewel?" I struggled. "What's happening..."

"Steady." A pair of slippery arms held me. It was Jewel's voice. "We can't let her drown... Get her out... Put her on the towels here..."

"No...wait...why..." My eyelids grew heavier and heavier. Then I could no longer see or speak.

I awoke to eerie silence. Jewel and Eunuch Ming were not there. It was only the deaf eunuch and me. I sat up, looking for the water clock. It was reaching the line of seven. I should have gone to the Emperor's bedchamber an hour ago.

I leaped to my feet, but I stumbled, my legs weak and my head dazed. I could not understand what had happened to me. But the summons!

"Wake up." I nudged the eunuch, dozing on a step stool. "We're late."

He rubbed his bleary eyes. Then he grabbed a cover from a peg and wrapped me from head to toe. Carrying me above his chest like a bundle of firewood, he headed into the dark night.

"Stop." The guards outside the Yeting Court blocked us. "What is the purpose of your leaving the court?"

"Ah...ah...ah-ah..." the deaf eunuch answered.

"The Emperor's order?" one asked.

They hesitated. Then they whispered among themselves for what seemed like an eternity. Finally, the heavy gates opened. The eunuch continued to walk. More guards and more questions. At last, a voice announced we were to enter the Inner Court.

My heart pounded. Pulling away the folds around my head, I peered out. Nothing, save the starless night, dark as the bottom of an abandoned well.

I wiggled more determinedly. But the wrapping wound tightly around me, and I grew tired, my neck hurting from straining below the eunuch's shoulder. I was going to give up when the eunuch flipped me around as if to ease his arms, and the wrapping loosened.

I pulled down the folds and turned my head.

The Inner Court looked like a deep cavern, with many buildings sitting around like small mountains. The buildings' flying eaves protruded like ragged cliffs while the red rays from glowing lanterns streamed like a river of rubies. The eunuch walked up a platform, stepped down into a courtyard, and then entered a hallway. Then another platform, another courtyard, and another hallway. It seemed he would never stop walking.

Sometimes, I heard murmurs of women from the chambers, their light footsteps, their labored coughs, and their heavy sighs. I wished I could see their faces. Were any of them the Four Ladies, the highest-ranking ladies?

Finally, we arrived at a large courtyard adorned by a single tree. The eunuch put me down. Gesturing at the central chamber, he mumbled something and left me.

This must be the Emperor's quarters.

I stared at the latticed windows, where warm, yellow lights illuminated the opaque window covers. Some soft shuffling came from inside, but no one greeted me. And there were no book-keeper or helpers.

I was alone.

Gripping the cover, I ascended the stone stairs flanked by a pair of stone kylins, the mythical unicorns. When I arrived in front of the chamber, I pushed open the door. There, I hesitated for a moment and stepped across the high threshold.

In front of me stood a bed, the largest and most ornate bed I had ever seen. The headboard and footboard were encrusted with jade and rubies, and red cloth draped across the frame held by four round posts. On top of the posts sat dragons, whose heads raised skyward, each holding a green ball in its mouth. The bed was empty and bare. There were no quilts or pillows, as though no one had ever slept on it.

In the corner, fire sputtered in a tripod brazier and reflected on the scrolls of couplets hanging on the walls. I would have loved to get closer and read them, but it was not the time.

A sweet aroma drifted in the air, perhaps from perfumed candles, the rare type made of beeswax, but I was too nervous to tell what scent it was.

Where was the Emperor?

The mural on my left seemed to tremble. I looked again. It was not a mural, but twelve painted screens with embossed frames. A shadow flew across the screens. My chest tightened. Before I could speak, a breeze swept my nape. Something icy pressed against my neck, and a grim voice said, "Speak! What are you doing here?"

I COULD HARDLY BREATHE. THE BLADE FELT COLD AGAINST my skin. "I...I was summoned."

"An ill-mannered servant!" The man sheathed the sword with a clang and headed to a stool near the oversize bed. He had a large frame: his shoulders were broad and his head was round like a festival lantern. His face was mercifully masked by the darkness.

Emperor Taizong. Who else would speak in such a manner, as if he were discontent with my behavior even though I had done nothing? He did not possess a lion's roar. His voice was grim and somehow raspy. He did not walk like a powerful lord. He shuffled, his shoulder tilting to one side, and he looked like he was having trouble holding his back straight. He also groaned as though his bones ached.

That man was the mighty conqueror everyone talked about? The most formidable man of the kingdom, the one who was above everyone else? He had just celebrated forty years of mortality, I remembered, but he looked old, irritated, and morose, as though he resented the world and held grudges against everyone.

With a loud grunt, he sat down on the stool facing the bed. He did not ask me about the riddle—perhaps he had forgotten it, or perhaps he was no longer interested—nor did he question me about my fight with the other Selects.

I stayed where I was, remembering the code, which dictated I must not do anything until I was told. Certainly I could not sit. The superior sat while the subordinate stood. But what should I do? A drop of water slid from my hair to my earlobe, dropped on to my shoulder, and slithered down to my stomach. I shivered.

A splutter came from the brazier, startling me. I glanced at the Emperor. He did not move.

Was he going to sit there forever?

Suddenly, he stretched out his arms. "Now."

It looked as though he wished me to disrobe him. I tied the corners of the cover sideways at my chest and scurried toward the stool.

Carefully, I held the collar of his robe, pulled back the fabric from his shoulder, slid it down his arms, and took it off. Then I knelt on the floor to reach for the drawstrings of his loose underpants.

I thought of what would come next. My hands trembled.

"What are you waiting for?" He slapped my hand.

I shrank back. Did he wish me to take off my cover? My nerves tightening into a ball, I dug my fingers into the knot and loosened it. The cover slipped from my shoulders and dropped on the floor. Goose bumps spread on my arms, and I stood, unprotected like a plucked hen.

He did not move.

Cold seeped into my skin. I hugged my chest and crossed my legs, but immediately I realized that was a mistake. I dropped my hands to my sides.

"What are you doing?" he said sharply. "Here." He pointed to his back.

I looked behind him. Nothing. Hesitating, I then walked there.

"Never stand at my back," he barked.

I quickly stepped aside. Something poked my leg—the sword, its hilt inlaid with jade and gold. It was strange he would keep a sword in his bedchamber, but perhaps he wished me to give it to him. I stooped to pick it up.

"Never, ever touch my sword." His voice was louder, and the sword slid aside, out of my reach.

I straightened. It was so humiliating. There I was, naked, standing, trying to please him. But he shouted at me as if I were nobody.

"Put these on." A pair of leather gloves dropped at my feet.

I picked them up, not knowing what to do at first. Then I understood. Of course. I must not touch his skin directly.

He wiggled impatiently, his finger pointing at his right shoulder. "Here!"

Suddenly, everything was clear to me. He did not wish me to strip, nor did he desire me to pleasure him. He only needed my fingers to scratch his back.

I tapped the skin beneath his shoulder blades. He let out a loud grunt. "Harder!"

I increased my pressure.

"Harder!"

I scratched with all the strength I could muster. He sighed in relief, and then he lifted his feet. "Foot bath."

I searched for containers. There were two basins filled with water near the brazier. I wanted to cover myself first and then fetch the water, but I was afraid to keep him waiting. So I went to one basin, carried it above my chest, and left it before him at the stool.

He thrust his feet into the water. They made squeaky noises as he rubbed, and then he leaned against the wall, staring at the ceiling. For a moment he seemed to be soaked in a stream of thoughts, and then he closed his eyes. Soon, soft snores rose into the air.

A strand of damp hair fell over my eyes. I tucked it behind my ear. It seemed ironic to me that the Emperor, who conquered the vast land for the kingdom, would sleep on a stool.

I found the cover and tied it around me. I was glad he was asleep so I could study him. He had long, curled whiskers, which shook gently as he breathed. His skin was dark, leathery, and wrinkled, and there were some dark specks around his cheekbones, like smeared flies. He did not have much hair on his head, and a deep scar snaked from his neck to his chest where his underrobe failed to cover. Still, judging from his square face and straight nose, I could tell he had been handsome once, and with his broad shoulders, he must have been a fierce figure on the battlefield, a frightening presence when he commanded an attack.

He was a powerful ruler, the first emperor who had conquered the troublesome Eastern Turks, forcing their neighbors, the Western Turks, to flee to the farthest northern border, and expanded the edge of our kingdom to the snowy mountains near Tarim Basin. He was also known as a cunning strategist. When he faced the undefeated elephant armies of the Champa kingdoms in the south, he had trapped them in pits and shot the elephants with crossbows, causing them to trample their own soldiers in fear.

But he was old now, so withered and unattractive. If I passed him on a street, I would not look at him twice. And to want to please him? Forget about it. But he was the Emperor, whose words could change my family's fate. I must do whatever I could to make him love me.

Suddenly, he gazed at me, his eyes bright like a wolf's eyes sparkling in the darkness.

My knees grew weak. He could order my death for staring at him.

But his eyes rolled and then snapped shut, and as though he had not noticed me, his head lolled to one side and his snores filled up the chamber again.

Perhaps the Emperor was testing me. Or perhaps he was indeed sleeping? For a long time, I stood rigidly, not daring to move. But he did not wake again.

Flames burst in the brazier and danced in the air. The fire cast my shadow on the wall scroll and covered the couplets. Slowly, I walked to a mat near the brazier and sat down, my head resting on my knees.

Something was wrong.

Yes, I had been late for the summons. But where were the servants and the bookkeeper who was supposed to record my night with the Emperor? And why did he treat me like I was a servant?

I looked around, searching every corner of the chamber. The incense sticks had burned halfway down, the fire in the brazier was burning bright, and the cushions on the floor were stacked against the wall. Everything appeared neat, and no one else was around.

The door squeaked. A woman stepped over the threshold.

I could not believe my eyes.

"Mei?" She was shocked to see me too, her hand frozen on the cover she wore, a cover similar to mine.

My hands turned cold.

Jewel had stolen my summons. She had come in my place to meet the Emperor, who had mistaken me for a maidservant. The bookkeeper and servants were absent because the bedroom affair was already over, or perhaps the Emperor had sent them away.

So that was the secret she had shared with Eunuch Ming. She had bribed him to bring her to the Emperor's quarters. No one would know it was not me, since she was wrapped in the cover. But the deaf eunuch, unaware of their scheme, had carried me to the Emperor's chamber.

And she had drugged me.

"What are you doing here? Go to your chamber." Jewel stepped forth and held my shoulders. "I will explain later."

"There's nothing to explain." I shook her hands off. A fire burned inside me. Pretending to be my friend. Bathing with me. Deceiving me. Jewel was worse than the Xu Girl.

"He's here. Don't be foolish." She glanced at the Emperor on his stool.

I did not care. I shoved her with all my might. A loud thump. She crashed onto the foot of the bed, and the screens toppled to the floor. Water splashed. The basin, spinning, flew to my feet.

"What is it?" the Emperor roared, standing up. "What's going on?"

I kept my eyes on Jewel. When she rose, I would slap her and make her suffer. And I did not care that the Emperor was watching.

She did not rise. Instead, she slipped down the bed, her head drooping, her arms sprawling.

"What's this?" The Emperor walked to her. "Rise now."

No response.

I blinked. Did I hurt her? Did she...?

The Emperor shook Jewel's shoulder, but she wobbled like a lifeless doll. Frowning, he pulled her into his arms. Then he pinched her cheek and patted her face. Jewel made no movement.

He stood up and turned to me. "What did you do?" he bellowed. "Who are you?"

"I...I..." Blood rushed to my head, and the room swam before me. Jewel was dead? But I had not meant to harm her. I was angry. That was all. She had deceived me!

There was a groan like that of a small animal, coming from somewhere. Like that of a cat. I recognized the voice.

Jewel's.

"Oh, I'm fine. Don't worry. I was only getting a rest." And there, one hand holding the bedpost and the other touching the back of her head, she rose, smiling, as if nothing had happened.

She had feigned it. She had made me believe she was dead. Never had I felt so angry. "Jewel!" I lunged for her. But somehow I ended up on the floor, and my head knocked against the hard wood. A stabbing pain hammered my head, and I could not hear or see. I was also soaked, my feet were cold, my hair was tangled, and water was everywhere.

"Get out." The Emperor stood before me. "Get out now."

My head spinning, I looked from him to Jewel.

"You should go." Jewel stood next to the Emperor. Gently, she stroked his shoulder, her head leaning toward him, her slender, tapered fingers clinging to him like vines.

I scrambled to my feet.

"Wait. Perhaps you'll mop up the water before you leave?" she said.

All I could do was take the rag from her hand and kneel. I wiped the area near the bed, behind the screens, under the drapery, and around the stool where the Emperor sat. When the rag was soaked with water, I straightened and wrung it above the basin. The bedchamber darkened momentarily before me. My kneecaps were tender, my back ached, my fingers were cold, and my head throbbed.

Jewel whispered to the Emperor while I cleaned. He smiled and nodded. He seemed to enjoy her company, and finally, he leaned against the wall and closed his eyes.

When I straightened again, Jewel came to me. "Now, you may

leave," she said, her catlike eyes as deep as a treacherous abyss. "And thank you for your riddle."

I stumbled out of the chamber, and the door shut behind me.

For a long time, I stood in the corridor outside the bedchamber while a stout girl holding a broom watched me. I pulled the cover tighter and went down the stone stairs.

Beyond the courtyard, the lights had been extinguished. There was nothing but darkness ahead of me.

O

AD 640

the Fourteenth Year *of*

Emperor Taizong's Reign

of Peaceful Prospect

WINTER

W INTER REFUSED TO LEAVE. E VERY DAY AFTER THE midday meal, I walked to the arboretum in the back of my bed-chamber, where high walls divided the court from the forest in the Forbidden Park.

The air was chilly, and it pressed against my face like an icy veil. Above the tall poplars, clusters of gray smoke gathered and stood still like a pond of shadows. The wind came and the smoke drifted, stretching like a stream, and then it bent again, settling in the sky like a misty bridge I could not cross.

I had heard that Jewel had told the Emperor it was her riddle, and she had given my name because she was worried he would not receive her. But when she took my place and met him, he obviously remembered her. He also seemed interested in her again, and she had stayed with him that night.

Jewel had moved to the Inner Court. Rumors said the Emperor enjoyed her company so much that he took her to all the feasts and festivals. Some even said she had been summoned every week. She would soon be Most Adored. It sickened me to hear.

I tucked my hands into my sleeves and walked, my shadow dragging at my feet. I wanted to think everything through and sort out what I had done wrong. I had been too trusting, too eager to make friends. That was my undoing. As long as we all strove to win the Emperor's heart, there would be no friends in the court.

Frost moistened the cloth soles of my shoes and sent a chill through my body. I wrapped my coat tightly around me. It had been over a year since I had left Mother. I remembered my last days with her. She had appeared fragile then, her steps slow, her hair gray, her eyes rimmed with worries.

Did her back still hurt? Mother would reach the age of Knowing Heaven's Mission this year. What if something happened to her and she fell sick? What if she could not wait for me?

I shivered. I must do better. I must see the Emperor again.

I kept walking. I imagined Father watching me, his eyes sparkling with expectation. What would he say to me if he learned of my situation?

"The good fighters of old first put themselves beyond the possibility of defeat, and then waited for an opportunity of defeating the enemy," Sun Tzu had said. Waiting for an opportunity... There was always next year's birthday, was there not? I had no idea what I could do to attract the Emperor's attention, but I had to think of something.

Meanwhile, I had to learn to read people's faces as well as their words. I had to learn to perceive the dagger hidden behind a woman's smile and know how to fend it off. And more importantly, I had to learn to deliver a dagger myself.

Spring finally came. Birds chirped in the Forbidden Park. Rabbits, foxes, and weasels dashed through the bushes, and trees swayed under a clear sky. I went to the arboretum again, pacing between the poplars and the wall. The other Selects gathered around the rocks in the sand garden. They covered their mouths, laughing.

The poplars grew green shoots with thick coats of hair. I snapped off a few, held them, and then let them fall through my fingers. The wispy white fuzz drifted to the ground like a string tugging at my memory, and those images, vivid but puzzling, rolled in my mind like a scroll blown by a gust. There was a pair of yellow, bulbous eyes, the sudden silence of the forest, a shower of leaves and red drops, and a desperate voice.

What did these visions mean? I wished I could understand them, but a thick blanket of fog seemed to shroud my head, and no matter how hard I tried to uncover it, it returned to coat my mind.

But it must have had something to do with Father—it had to— for I remembered clearly that on that same day, Father had died.

"What are you doing, Pheasant? Bring the horse back here. Now!" a man's voice shouted from the Forbidden Park on the other side of the wall. His voice was deep, rich, and thick with a man's valor.

I took a few steps back and raised my head. It was the first time since my arrival that I heard a male voice that was not the Emperor. All the eunuchs sounded like shrill, querulous housewives. Who was the man on the other side of the wall?

"I'm trying," another male voice answered. "But horses are like girls. You can tell them what to do, but they still do whatever they like."

A different voice. Youthful and joyous. Infused with spirit and good humor. The young fellow called Pheasant. He must have been good-looking. He had to be. Anyone who spoke with such liveliness had to be beautiful.

I stood on tiptoe. I wished to see who these two men were, but the high wall was impossible to climb. I took a few steps farther and looked again. Nothing but the flowing treetops. I listened intently. There was the rustling of leaves and a horse's grunting. Then nothing.

Who were those men?

They must have lived or worked in the palace, or they would not have had permission to come to the park. Perhaps they were ministers, scribes, or guards. The first man with the deep voice sounded older; he was in command. The second man, Pheasant, seemed to be his groom.

Could the first man with the deep voice be the Emperor's son?

The Emperor had ten living sons, ranging from twenty years old to less than a year.

I waited a bit longer, listening intently, but no more movement came from the other side. Soon, I left the arboretum as well, but I could not stop thinking of the two men.

✦ ✦

A few days later, I had almost fallen asleep when I heard the other Selects whispering on their pallets.

"I cannot wait," someone said, beginning her nightly chorus with the others. "Only two more months!"

"Me neither," another added. "How exciting! We will see all those people—the counselors, the ministers, the dukes, and the princes."

I pricked up my ears. They were talking about the Adulthood Ceremony of our Taizi, the Crown Prince. To celebrate his coming of age, the Emperor would gather all the important ministers and the imperial family members to attend the ceremony in the Altar House. He had also given permission to his women, including us in the Yeting Court, to watch.

I would go to the ceremony! That meant I would see the Emperor again. I wanted to know the date the ceremony would be held, but the girls went on to discuss what to wear and how to shape their hair.

"Look!" a loud voice called out, and gasps rose.

I pulled down the blanket. The Xu Girl and the others were sitting up, peering outside, where a bolt of stark white light flared and flew across the sky like a burning candle. Surprised, I sat upright.

The girls rushed to the corner of the chamber, trembling. Confused, I ran to the doors, opened them, and looked up. Another bolt of light, like a silver fish, swept across the black sky.

A comet.

My hands turned cold. Comets possessed evil power that could bewitch a human's mind. It was also a sign of Heaven's wrath and spoke of looming calamity to the kingdom.

Father had often said that an emperor founded a dynasty not

by superior military acumen, nor noble lineage, nor the number of decisive battles in which he defeated his foes, but because he was chosen by Heaven. And when Heaven was displeased with the chosen one and his reign, it gave signs, like comets, eclipses, and shooting stars. Disaster and chaos then ensued, the dynasty collapsed, and the emperor's rule ended.

In *The Art of War*, Sun Tzu had called Heaven's intention the Moral Law, which compelled people to comply with their ruler. If one lost it, the reign would end. That was what happened to the Sui Dynasty, the empire before the Tang Dynasty. Emperor Gaozu, who had been a general of the Sui's army, claimed Heaven had revoked its consent to the Sui Emperor and started the rebellion. He was backed by all men he sought to support and then succeeded in overthrowing the Sui Emperor.

I covered my eyes to block the sight of the comet, but in my mind I could see it was like a sword, a mighty blade of fury Heaven used to pierce the heart of the kingdom.

What evil would befall us? A poor harvest? A flood? A drought?

I shut the doors and went back to my pallet.

The chamber was silent. Then someone whispered in the dark, "This is a bad omen."

"Do you think the Emperor will cancel the ceremony?" another asked.

"It seems unlikely," the Xu Girl said. "The date of the ceremony was chosen last year, and it would be difficult to change it."

"So I will still see everyone, then." The girl sighed with relief.

I rolled on my side, tucking my hand under my head. But I was not ready to sleep yet. Because I just realized an opportunity had presented itself.

I knew what I must do.

◆ ◆

On the day of Taizi's ceremony, I left the Yeting Court with the other palace ladies, passed the Inner Court, crossed the Chengtian

Gate, and arrived at the Outer Palace, where the ministers conducted their daily work. When I had first entered the court two years before, I was inside the carriage and did not realize how vast the palace was, but since then, I had gotten an idea of its immensity. When we left the Yeting Court, it was at dawn, but by the time we reached the Altar House, the sun was hanging on the top of the trees, and I was tired, my legs sore from walking.

"This way, this way." The palace's Gold Bird Guards directed us across from the yard in front of the Altar House. Wearing maroon capes and shining breastplates, they looked stern, their eyes scanning here and there. Since the comet, rumors suggesting that the Emperor was unfit to rule had swirled about the palace, and I had heard the news of insurgence from the northern border. It was an important day today, and with all the imperial family members and ministers gathering, the guards had to be extremely vigilant.

We were ordered to stay in a corridor at the end of the yard, perhaps the least favorable place to watch the ceremony. In front of me stood many court ministers, imperial members, Taoist priests, and ladies dressed in different colors of gowns. Jewel might have been among them, but I could not find her. I was still angry, and for many nights I had thought about how to confront her. But to do so would be stupid. There was no point letting her know my anger, since she had the Emperor's ear. In fact, I must play coy when speaking to her, as though nothing had happened between us.

Standing on tiptoes, I searched for the Emperor, who sat on a raised platform in the center of the massive yard before the Altar House.

He wore a bejeweled mortarboard on his head, a splendid golden robe with rectangular sleeves draped to the floor, and two swords at his waist. He looked different from the dark man dozing on his stool all those months ago. If the man I met in his chamber were a naked cat, the one in formal attire resembled a true tiger. He looked larger, more solemn, more distant, and more frightening.

What could I do to attract his attention?

Taizi, the Crown Prince, cloaked in bright yellow ceremonial regalia, walked to each minister and thanked them for their presence. He had a deep voice that seemed to echo in his chest, and his tone was short and precise.

I recognized that voice. He was the man in the Forbidden Park who had shouted for Pheasant. When he talked to the ministers near me, I studied him. He was the tallest, most robust man I had ever seen. His neck was thick, his shoulders wide, and he towered over the other people by a head. Each time he approached a minister, he cracked his knuckles and then bowed. He also seemed to be uncomfortable in his regalia; each time he rose, he pulled at his sleeves and frowned.

I had heard stories about him. The firstborn of the Emperor and the late Empress Wende, he was twenty years old. He had grown up in the military camp when his father and his grandfather were warring against the Sui Dynasty. A mighty wrestler, Taizi had never lost a bout since he was nine years of age, and I would have said he was built more for wrestling than for ruling.

"He would make a fine ruler," a lady in a blue gown near me said.

"Not so loud." An old lady with her hair shaped in Cloudy Chignon elbowed her. "The spies are everywhere."

I fell on my heels and turned to her. Who would object to Taizi's rule? "Whose spies?"

"Oh." The old lady coughed and glanced at me. "I know who you are. You gave the Emperor a riddle. Very clever. You were summoned."

I smiled to let her know I meant no harm. "Yes, and I may never be summoned again. Who are you worried about, if you don't mind me asking?"

"Ah, I should not say this, but have you noticed the Emperor's uncle?" The old lady pointed at an old man holding a cane. Clearly most revered for his age and rank, the Uncle stood among a group of ministers with high hats who bowed constantly as he spoke, his finger stabbing in the air.

"He does not look happy," I said. Father had said the Uncle had gone through many battles with Emperor Gaozu and helped found the dynasty. He would have been the one to inherit the throne if the Emperor had begotten no sons.

"For a good reason," the lady with the blue gown said, pointing at Taizi as he left the ministers to kneel before the guest of honor, a tall man, to receive his three hats—a skintight silk wrapping, a leather cap, and a square black hat embroidered with golden dragons flying through clouds. Each hat carried profound meanings. The wrapping signified his responsibility as a man to himself, the cap to his family, and the black hat to society.

I understood immediately. The Adulthood Ceremony was one of the four most important ceremonies in a man's life. The guest of honor, who would confer the hats on the heir, was supposed to be the most senior member of the imperial family, who I assumed would be the Uncle, but the man who held the wrapping appeared to be in middle age. "Who's the guest of honor?"

"That's the Duke, the late Empress's brother, the Emperor's brother-in-law," the lady in the blue gown said. "He—"

The old lady coughed, and the lady in blue swallowed her words. I did not ask more questions. There was no need. Clearly, the Duke and the Uncle did not get along.

It was getting hot. The morning air turned fetid with the odor of scorched pigskin on the sacrificial tables and musk and camphor from burning incense. Layers of heavy clouds pressed against the roof of the Altar House. It would rain soon.

The ministers lined up before the platform to praise Taizi. First the Uncle, then a hunchbacked man wearing jade pendants, Chancellor Wei Zheng. Following him were more ministers. They bowed constantly, their heads springing up and down like hungry birds pecking at grain.

When they finished, the Duke cleared his throat and shouted from the platform. "Today, we are here to witness one of the most important rituals in life, the Adulthood Ceremony, for my great-nephew, our Taizi, Li Chengqian, the heir of Great China." He held a wrapping above Taizi's head. "I now have the honor to recognize you, the firstborn of the Li family, whose ancestry is of the most supreme in this kingdom, son of the late daughter of the Changsun clan, now a man worthy of trust. You shall prevail on occasions of stress and moments of adversity…"

I wiped the perspiration from my forehead. I was shorter than the women in front of me, and, for a long time, I did nothing but stare at their backs.

Finally, the Duke concluded the ceremony and people began to disperse, the tide pushing me toward the entrance gate. The guards on the other side of the ladies waved, shouting for us to return to the Yeting Court. Someone around me mentioned the feast, and the ministers became animated, rubbing their bleary eyes.

I craned my neck in time to see the Emperor enter the Altar House, accompanied by three Taoist priests with long ponytails. One sprinkled yellow water in the air, as if to prepare for a divination. I glanced at the guards standing near the entrance. If I left, I might never see the Emperor again. I ducked under the arm of a minister robed in purple, went behind a painted pillar, took another turn at a corridor, and scurried in the opposite direction.

At the end of the corridor stood a small door. I pushed it open and quickly shut it behind me. The door led to a small garden. An ancient oak, its trunk as large as a round table, stood to my right. Bundles of hay were stacked on the left. The place appeared to be a temporary stable for imperial members who lived outside the palace.

I decided to hide in the garden and wait for the guards and ministers to leave. Once no one was around, I would go out and see the Emperor.

"Who is it?" a voice called.

I jumped, my heart leaping to my throat. A guard? I must not be caught!

"Are you alone?" A boy poked his head above a stack of hay against the wall.

"Oh." I was relieved. The boy pushed a bundle of hay away from his face and jumped to the ground, his arms casting a graceful curve in the air. "I'm… What are you doing back there?" I asked.

He did not seem to hear me. "Quick." He whistled and patted the haystacks behind him. "Come out now."

From where he had first appeared, a girl in a red gown stood. She climbed down and tidied her creased skirt. Glancing at me, she whispered in the boy's ear. He nodded, and she ran to the door, covering her face with her sleeve, and disappeared through the entrance from where I had come.

The boy coughed. "Well... We were looking for something."

"In the haystack?"

"Yes," he said, a piece of straw dangling from his mouth.

"I see. Could it be a needle?" I said, trying to help him out. He looked my age but was taller than me and dressed in a plain white tunic, the color for a commoner. He had a well-chiseled face, a straight nose, and a square jaw. He was like an image whom a painter had taken great care to paint—and the most attractive boy I had ever seen.

"That was it. A needle." He laughed. "What's your name?"

I hesitated. It was not wise to identify myself, yet I wanted him to know me. The wind blew my hair to my face, ruffling my bangs. I arranged my hair carefully with my fingers, hoping the wind did not mess it up. I had taken care to style my hair in Cloudy Chignon that morning, and I hoped I still looked presentable.

He leaned against the haystacks. "I'm Pheasant, like the bird. That's what my brothers call me."

This was Pheasant? I remembered his comment that girls were like horses. "So you are the heir's groom." He looked confused, and I explained. "I heard you talk to him in the Forbidden Park once."

"The heir? Right... Is he finished with the ceremony? It was boring, wasn't it? Whoever sits through that ceremony should be crowned as a saint, not just an adult."

A fair statement. I laughed, liking him.

He took out the straw in his mouth. "I like the way you laugh."

I stopped. I had forgotten to cover my mouth. Was he criticizing me for showing my teeth? I did not think so, but still I was displeased. "Well, you should be careful. Someone might tell the Emperor what you were doing here, and he will not be happy."

"You won't tell." He stepped closer to me. His eyes were bright, shining the limpid color of newly brewed ale, clear, light, and inviting. "And you are not supposed to be here either, sweet face."

I studied him. He did not look menacing. "All right," I said. "I'll keep your secret if you agree to keep mine."

"That's fair." He nodded and then froze.

I froze too. Faint voices came from the corridor outside the garden. They were heading toward us.

Pheasant raced to the door and opened it a crack. Then he closed it. "It's the Captain of the Gold Bird Guards."

My heart raced faster. If the Captain found me, I would be doomed. He would perhaps punish me, and I would never see the Emperor again.

"You should go," Pheasant said.

"Go where? I don't have time." I looked around for an escape, wishing I had never gone there in the first place.

Pheasant hesitated. "Come. Help me move this." He sprang toward the haystacks in the corner and lifted a square bundle of hay.

"What are you doing?"

"You'll see. Quick. They're coming." He heaved, and behind the bundle a small hole appeared. A hideout.

"You go in," he said. "I've never told anyone else about this place. Saving it for a special moment."

I peered inside. The opening was too small for two people. "What about you?" Was he not afraid of getting caught?

The footsteps grew closer, and a man's voice rumbled. Louder now. It sounded like the Captain who had escorted me to the palace. "Where is the intruder?" he asked.

There was no time to think. I ducked under Pheasant's arm and went inside the opening.

"I'll be fine." He moved to close the haystacks behind me.

Squeak. The door opened.

"Captain!" Pheasant said. "What's wrong? Is your horse hungry?"

"I'm searching for an intruder. Someone reported it to me." The Captain sounded suspicious. "What are you doing here?"

"I came to get some hay for the horses. Who are you looking for?"

There was a pause, and the Captain said, "Guards, take him. Keep him until I get back."

"What did I do wrong? Watch out. Hey! Get your hands off me. I only came to fetch some hay..." Pheasant's voice grew lower, and it soon faded in the corridor.

No one in the garden spoke, but the Captain and some of his men were still there. I could hear someone stomping across the ground, a sword slashing here and there. So nervous, I could hardly breathe.

"Search the haystacks," the Captain ordered, and a chorus of voices answered.

Perspiration poured down my forehead and ran into my eyes. Tightly, I pressed my back to the haystacks. My arm swept something solid, and I heard a rattling sound. There was a secret door beside me. Elated, I pushed it open, and fresh air sailed to my nose.

I peered out. In front of me was a long corridor with latticed windows and a vast courtyard, and at the end stood a house with a blue roof and red beams. The Altar House, where the Adult Ceremony had taken place.

No one was in sight. The ministers must have been feasting in the hall. It was quiet too; only wisps of gray incense smoke spilled from the ceremonial bronze pot.

The Captain shouted something in the garden. I scrambled out of the hideout, stood up, and swept straw off my face. My tunic and my undergarments were soaked with perspiration, but I was relieved. If it had not been for Pheasant, things would have turned out badly for me.

I did not want to take more risks to see the Emperor anymore. I just wanted to get out of the courtyard and return to the Yeting Court as soon as possible. Looking around, I found the entrance in the distance and scurried down the corridor.

I heard a loud crack, as if roof tiles had split under a heavy weight. I paused, looking up. There, between the branches of the oak tree, I caught sight of a large shadow. Was that...a man? I blinked and looked harder. The shadow was gone.

In the sky, clouds gathered, but still no rain.

I was not sure what I had really seen. Frowning, I turned to face the wide Altar House. Its doors were ajar. The Emperor's golden regalia flitted across the gap, and he shouted something. I could not understand what he said, but he sounded angry.

What was going on? I crept closer to the building. I was not allowed to enter it, for the Altar House was sacred and reserved for only men and high-ranking women, but what if the shadow on the roof was a man... I could not help myself. Carefully, I walked down the corridor and went up the stone stairs stained with the yellow water the priest had sprinkled earlier.

I stopped in front of the House and listened. It was quiet inside. I peered into the gap between the doors. It was too dark, and I could not see anything. Hesitant, I held the door frame and pushed. My hand touched something soft. I looked down.

A hand with yellow stains on the fingertips. The priest's hand, clutching the door frame from the other side. I started and glanced up, expecting to see his reproachful face.

But there was no priest.

9

A SEVERED HAND!

I shrank back, an uncontrollable shiver rushing through my body. The priest's hand. Still grasping the door frame.

My teeth chattered. I grabbed the other door for support. It swung away from me, and I fell facedown inside the room.

A peculiar odor—a mixture of mold, acid, musk, and camphor—assaulted my nose. My head swam.

A pair of red eyes gazed at me. The priest. Or rather, what was left of him.

I stared for a moment. Then I screamed.

That was what the comet had brought us. An unthinkable, unspeakable crime. Right in the sacred Altar House. And the Emperor. What had happened to him?

A loud thump rose somewhere. I froze.

"Who's there?" I asked and searched. But a thick gloominess draped before me, and I could not see anything.

A groan came from deep within the House.

My throat tightening, I rose to my feet. "The One Above All?" There was no answer.

I blinked. I wanted to back out, but I could not do it. I had to find out what was going on. My hands shaking, I walked toward the center of the House. The long panels, draping from the ceiling, brushed my shoulder like the cold tail of a snake. But my eyes had adjusted to the dark, and I could see banners, bamboo sticks for divination, incense, and paper money scattered on the ground. Ahead of me, rows of mortuary tablets stood like miniature tombstones, while burning candles appeared like weeping statues.

The cloth covering the altar table fluttered. A man leaned against the table, his bejeweled mortarboard at his feet.

"Oh heavens, oh heavens!" I rushed to the Emperor. Blood gushed from his mouth, and his face looked gray like ashes. "What happened, the One Above All?"

A tremor passed over his lips, and he pressed his hand on his blood-soaked shoulder.

"Leave him," a voice said, and a figure emerged from the dark.

The killer! Still inside the building! I released the Emperor and scrambled backward. "Who...who are you?"

The killer inched closer, dressed in a vest, a skirt, and leggings. He limped a little. I wanted to run but could not find strength to lift my feet. Where were the Emperor's personal guards? Two had followed him when he'd entered the building, but most of them, I understood, had been dismissed by the Emperor prior to the divination, and they were dining in the feasting hall. They would not hear my screams over the rowdy drinking and loud fife music.

The killer raised his sword.

"Guards, guards!" I pulled up my skirt and ran. Panels brushed my face, and I pushed them aside. Behind me, the killer's heavy footsteps followed. I kicked away a crumpled banner on the ground, ducked behind a small table, and passed an incense pot. I skidded on something slippery. Under my feet, a pool of blood spread like a thick, luxurious Persian rug. At its edge, a body...no, two bodies sprawled—the guards!—one with a dagger in his chest and the other with his throat slit.

Metal clinked behind me. The killer was catching up! Gripping my skirt, I raced toward the half-open door, where bright daylight poured through.

A cold breeze grazed my cheek, and my ear stung. I did not slow down. The door was closer. Five paces. Warm liquid trickled down the side of my face. Three paces. I stretched out my arm. I could smell the fragrance of wine and cooked meat in the courtyard. I surged forward, my fingertips touching the solid wood of the door, and gratefully, it squeaked, opening wider.

A large figure appeared in the center of the courtyard—the Captain. He shouted at me, but I could not understand him. The killer! The killer! I wanted to scream, but before I opened my mouth, a hand clamped around my throat and everything went dark.

✦ ✦

The moment, dark and dreamless, swallowed me. I could not breathe, see, or hear. I was going to die, I knew it. But I did not want to. I must not die. Mother was waiting for me. I had not done anything to make my father proud yet... Suddenly, sweet air poured in my throat. I gasped again and again. I could breathe!

But I could not see well. Everything appeared blurred. I rose, wobbling. Somehow I was in the corridor, where bolts of bright daylight blinded me, and shadows of people, screaming, flitted around me.

Some guards carried the Emperor on a stretcher and laid him down. A dozen imperial physicians knelt beside him, while a ring of guards surrounded the physicians.

The body of the assassin was carried out too, and the Captain waved at the people, asking them to step aside.

My ear throbbed. Some blood had stained the shoulder and the front of my robe. But it was only a skin wound. In a day or two, it would heal. Someone bumped into me, and I almost tripped. I kept walking.

I had to stop to lean against a kylin statue. The stone felt warm, but I shivered. Behind the roof of the Altar House, clouds flooded the sky, and the oak tree, its lush leaves drooping, curved over the roof like a giant sickle about to tip over. The storm would arrive soon. I wanted to get out of there. Now.

"Where are you going?" A man in a splendid, embroidered purple robe stepped in front of me.

The Duke.

"I—"

"Who are you? What were you doing in the Altar House?"

"What?" My throat hurt. It was hard to swallow.

"You're a woman, and a Select!" He scanned my green robe. "What were you doing in the sacred Altar House?" His voice was louder.

In a moment, the crowd swarmed around me like a human siege wall—the Emperor's uncle, the Chancellor, other ministers in red, green, purple robes and high hats, Taoist priests, the guards bearing swords and clubs, and Taizi, who cracked his knuckles, as if readying to throw me over the roof.

I dropped to my knees. "Mercy, esteemed Grand Duke. I trespassed."

He paced around me without a word, then his ominous voice rose again. "Who is the killer?"

I shook my head.

He circled me again and then tossed something to the ground. "Do you know what this is?"

"A fish emblem." I heard the hollowness in my voice. Everyone knew what the carved emblem meant—admission to the palace. Anyone who requested to enter the palace, including the ministers, had to present it to the sentries at the watch tower, who verified its authenticity by matching it with a counterpart before granting entrance.

"The Captain found this on the assassin's body," the Duke said.

I wanted to ask how the assassin could have gotten access to the carp, but I could not speak. An ominous feeling clouded my heart.

"Did you steal this and give it to him?" he asked. "Or did someone ask you to give it to him?"

His words sent a jolt down my spine. "What? No!"

"Then why were you in the House?"

"I...I don't know." I should have ignored the shadow on the

79

roof. I should not have gone inside the House. I should not have hidden in the garden at all. If I had just left the yard, nothing would have happened to me.

The Emperor's uncle threw his hand in the air, looking outraged, and the crowd murmured in anger. I curled my hands into fists, refusing to let tears roll. An ant crawled out of a crack in the stone floor. Probing with its tiny antennae, it veered toward my hand but slid and fell on a tuft of grass.

The Duke stomped on the grass. "Why didn't he kill you?"

I felt like the wretched ant under his foot. But I refused to let the Duke stamp me with his hand-stitched leather boots. I faced the Emperor's stretcher. "The One Above All, it was wrong that I entered the House, but I am telling the truth. Believe me. I swear on my father's honor."

The Emperor did not answer. The physicians glared at me as though they believed it was better for the Emperor to save his energy rather than my life.

"Your father?" the Uncle asked. "Who is your father?"

"He was Wu Shihuo, the governor of Shanxi Prefecture," I said.

"So you are the maiden who composed a riddle." He nodded, looking less angry. "I've heard of him too, the wealthy Wu Shihuo from Shanxi Prefecture. He was a man of meritorious service in founding our dynasty."

"That was twenty-five years ago, venerable Uncle." The Duke frowned.

"What are you going to do, Grand Duke?" a minister in a red robe asked.

"Secretary Fang, it is my recommendation that we torture this maiden so she will reveal her conspirators. I am certain there are some," the Duke replied.

"Is that all you can do, Duke?" The Uncle knocked his cane against the ground, each pounding my heart like a hammer. "What would you recommend, Chancellor?"

Chancellor Wei Zheng stood beside me. "Venerable Uncle, it is my understanding that since each carp is issued and recorded in palace journals daily, the Grand Duke might find it helpful to check with the court recorder."

"That's a fine idea." The Uncle nodded.

"We'll interrogate the recorder in no time." The Duke waved. "Meanwhile, this suspect must undergo investigation." He turned to the stretcher. "I'm certain the One Above All would approve of my suggestion."

And the Emperor, to my dismay, still did not answer.

"So it is." The Duke clapped his hands in the air. "As you wish, the One Above All. Guards, take her! Guards!"

The Captain clamped his iron-like hands on my arms, his purple birthmark twitching on his face.

"Do not touch me." I struggled. But he lifted me up and walked across the courtyard as if he were holding a dead hare.

I did not care about anything anymore. I kicked. My feet were in the air. My life hung in the air too. "Don't touch me! I saved the Emperor. Can't you see? I saved the Emperor!"

"Halt," a quiet voice said. The Emperor's.

"Bring her to me," he said.

I floated, like the heavy clouds above the roof, as the Captain carried me to the stretcher. I could not imagine what fate the Emperor would order for me. When the Captain dropped me, I knelt, moisture stinging my eyes.

For a long moment, he only breathed heavily. "So listen, Select, this is what will become of you." He took another labored breath. "I hereby bestow the title of Talent upon you."

His voice was thin, like a thread drifting in a gust of wind, but it struck me like thunder. He had just conferred a title on me. Talent, sixth degree.

"The One Above All?" The Duke stepped closer to the stretcher. "Are you feeling well? All your servants are waiting to serve you."

The Emperor raised a forefinger to stop him. "I recall a woman in the Altar House. She cried for help, Duke. Guards, guards, as you just called."

"Indeed?"

The Emperor nodded.

"So it is, the One Above All." The Duke bowed.

I could hardly move. I was now a Talent, a sixth-degree lady, a titled woman. It changed everything. It meant I would leave the Yeting Court, move to the Inner Court where the Four Ladies and other high-ranking ladies resided. I would also receive an additional silk gown in the spring, a coat in the winter, and relish one serving of meat in my victuals on a monthly basis. But most importantly, I would be closer to the Emperor. I would have opportunities to beg him to help my family.

"I am honored—" I bowed deeply.

My forehead touched the ground three times, and I did not rise when the physicians, guards, and ministers poured forth to surround the Emperor. The feet of the guards shifted, and then they left the courtyard. The ministers and servants trickled out as well. When the courtyard quieted again, I rose.

As I stepped out of the gate, the first drop of rain pelted my face. The storm had arrived. I spread out my arms and welcomed it.

○

AD 641

the Fifteenth Year *of*

Emperor Taizong's Reign

of Peaceful Prospect

SUMMER

LATER, I LEARNED THAT THE IMPERIAL GOLD BIRD Guards, led by the Captain, went to interrogate the court recorder that afternoon. They found nothing, because when they arrived at the Outer Palace, the recorder was already dead. Poisoned. No one knew if he had killed himself in fear or if he had been poisoned by someone else.

An extensive search was conducted to find any possible conspirators in the Outer Palace, and a strict curfew was imposed in the Inner Court. Every night, the guards' footsteps echoed in the corridors, and many rats died, pierced by arrows, mistaken as human invaders scurrying on the ground. All the trees, those century-old elms, oaks, and maples, were chopped down so they would not provide any convenience to evildoers in the future.

The Gold Bird Guards expanded their search to the city. Sketches of the assassin were posted on the gates of the Western Market and the Eastern Market. The Emperor put out a reward for anyone who identified the man. A few days later, a hostel owner near the Northern District, where courtesans and unscrupulous, drunken men gathered for entertainment, reported that a man of similar description had lodged there three months before and that he was accompanied by two foreign-dressed men.

With the help of the hostel owner's clue, the Guards expanded their search and found the two men, who were connected to the son of a chieftain of the Western Turks, the enemy of our kingdom.

The imperial cavalry, followed by many conscripted peasant soldiers, was soon dispatched to the border near the Western Turks' territory. A punitive war started, turning the border towns into rubble, and many garrisons were established and enforced. Forts were built; more paid soldiers were enlisted. The news of the dust of the war and the cries of the dead were told in the palace for months.

✦ ✦

I heard it all from within the safety of the Inner Court's walls. Sometimes I thought it ironic that an evil plot had provided me with an entrance to a life I had dreamed about, but such was the design of life, that one could never foretell.

Inside the Inner Court, the maids looked much more splendid than the Selects did. They wore bright pink robes and long, transparent shawls. Their makeup was colorful, and they wore jade hairpins in their Cloudy Chignons. They glanced at me curiously, whispering among themselves. Obviously they knew I had saved the Emperor's life, but when I nodded at them, they looked away.

When I passed the courtyards, flocks of golden orioles leaped and dove before me; roses, chrysanthemums, asters, and azaleas bloomed by the paths winding through gardens of peonies. In the large, silvery lakes, blue water lilies floated placidly, while frogs croaked and goldfish swam near the red-roofed pavilions. The land rose slightly in the distance and blended into the cloudy horizon; from afar, it seemed as if a garden had grown in the sky.

The beautiful scenery reminded me of the garden at home. The creation of a garden was meant to duplicate the paradise of the after-life, Father had said, and its most important feature was the rocks, which must be placed carefully to resemble the islands of Penglai, the haunts of the Eight Immortals. I had seen many shapes of rocks in Father's one-acre garden, but in the Inner Court, the scale of the garden and the number of unique rocks surprised me. There were rocks with perfectly smooth edges resembling giant eggs, rocks with perforated holes like beehives, rocks with deep hollows as wide as windows, and rocks bearing grotesque angles and shapes that suggested the peaks and valleys of the Tai mountain.

Father would have been happy to see that lovely garden.

I wished to tell him that I still remembered the promise I had made at our family's grave site. I wished to tell him too that I still remembered how he had raised me and what he had wanted for me when he was alive. Born a humble man, Father had started out with selling lumber, built his fortune with his mere hands, and rose to be a powerful man who helped destroy a dynasty and found another. He wanted me, his daughter, his heir, to accomplish more than what he had achieved, to perpetuate his fame, and to reach a height no ordinary men, or women, could possibly dream of.

I would not disappoint him.

I was assigned to a bedchamber in a walled compound at the west side of the court. The eight other Talents were my roommates, and the Graces and Beauties shared the other houses in the compound. The area was far from the Quarters of the Pure Lotus, where the Four Ladies resided. The Quarters, I heard, encompassed many pavilions, courtyards with painted roofs, man-made lakes, and scented arboretums with perennial flowers.

I wished to meet the Four Ladies and see what they looked like. The Noble Lady was the daughter of the late Sui Emperor, I remembered. I did not know anything about the Pure Lady, Lady Virtue, or Lady Obedience.

Jewel, to my dismay, had become the Emperor's Most Adored, and she had moved to the Quarters. I would perhaps run into her someday, but I wished with all my heart I would not have to see her again.

I was ordered to start etiquette training, which court protocol dictated that every titled woman must learn. The classroom, located in a wooded area near a hill, was decorated with five plaques written with Confucius's virtues: courtesy, tolerance, faith, wisdom, and filial piety. Training with me were twenty-six other girls: Beauties, Graces, and Talents. Later, I learned they were ordered to go there every six months to refresh their training, and I was the only one who was new.

Similar to what we had done in the Yeting Court, we began with a recital. "Obey your parents, for it is from their veins your body is formed; revere your elders, for it is from their blood your name is given; submit to your superiors, for it is from their mouths that your food is provided; vow to your emperor, for it is by his grace that you walk on the ground…"

The words popped out of my mouth like tasteless, uncooked rice, yet I was told to recite them again and again. Finally, we finished, and I was ordered to put on a pair of boat-shaped shoes with heels that measured a hand's length. Every titled lady must learn the "perfect walk," the etiquette teacher said. "You must take a step half of your foot length each time. No more, no less. Your upper body must remain at a slight angle, so you will be ready to bow at any moment. When you walk, your skirt shall ruffle to a pleasing rhythm, and your eyes, no matter where your feet lead, must always focus on the ground five paces ahead."

As I balanced myself on the boatlike shoes, she continued. "Remember, when you smile, you shall never reveal your teeth. Prior to speaking, you always bow, and when you are given permission to behold, you shall always set your gaze upon the other's shoulder, never at the eyes."

I recognized Rain, the teacher. She was the girl from Pheasant's haystacks. Her eyes lingered on me when she caught my gaze. Then she looked away.

I thought of Pheasant and how he had helped me escape. I hoped the Captain had been kind to him and did not punish him. Ever since I had parted with him, I often studied myself in the bronze mirror, and I always made sure my hair was neat before leaving the chamber.

I wished to see Pheasant again and thank him. But it would be difficult to find him in the vast palace.

In the following days, I learned how to play *guzheng*, a rectangular instrument with eight cords. After the music lesson was my favorite calligraphy class, but I had learned four types of scripts since I was six: seal script, grass script, standard script, and running script. Seal script and standard script required the calligrapher to follow the rules of the square shapes and straight lines. Grass script emphasized free, unrestrained movement, and running script was a compromise between the standard script and grass script. I was best at grass script, for I loved to see the brush run freely on paper.

After those lessons came lectures for reception, rituals, visiting rites, and procession rules, and practices of bearing banners, practices of carrying wine vessels and holding parasols, and then tests that concerned the titles of the ladies and the contents of their monthly allowances. There were math lessons too—mainly counting. I had learned that when I was five.

I asked Teacher Rain when the training would end.

"When you receive an assignment." She gave me a long look.

"What assignment?"

"What else?" She lifted her triangular face. "You shall empty Most Adored's chamber pot, if you are fortunate."

I wished I had not asked her. She obviously resented me, and I hoped, with all my heart, that I would not serve Jewel.

When I had some leisure time, I went to the court's library, which collected Ban Zhao's *Lessons for Women* and rhapsodies from the Warring States period. I was disappointed. I missed the *Four Books and Five Classics*, Confucius's *Analects*, or even Lao Tzu's *Tao Te Ching*. But the book I missed most was Sun Tzu's *The Art of War*. I remembered what he said: "If you know the enemy and know yourself, you need not fear the result of a hundred battles. If you know yourself but not the enemy, for every victory gained, you will also suffer a defeat. If you know neither the enemy nor yourself, you will succumb in every battle."

I had known Jewel. Did I know myself? I thought so. Then I did not need to be afraid.

And since I was right beside the Emperor, I would fend off Jewel's swords and advance with the master's shield of wisdom, and very soon, I would win the Emperor's heart.

Jewel caught me on my way to the classroom one afternoon. "How good it is to see you, Mei. It has been a long time."

She strutted in a stunning pale blue gown, her white hair adorned with a long, iridescent kingfisher feather that almost reached the top of the willow tree near the trail. Two girls wearing garlands of peonies scattered rose petals on the path for her to tread on, and behind her, a train of servants followed.

Anger rushed to my tongue, but I bit my lips and bowed. "Most Adored."

"I must say I was surprised by what you did, Mei. How courageous you were to save the Emperor's life, and now you're a Talent. Look how far you have come. How is your training going?"

Her voice was gentle, but I knew what kind of woman she was. I would never trust a word of hers again. "As to be expected, Most Adored," I said. "If you will pardon me, I must take my leave now."

She walked closer to me, treading on the petals. "Don't hate me, Mei. Truthfully, you cannot blame me."

Would she say the same thing if I had betrayed her? I looked away.

"If you wish, Mei, come and visit me. We shall have a nice talk."

I shook my head and turned to a path near the willow. I did not like the fact that Jewel knew everything about me. And I was worried. I did not believe she had run into me by accident. She must have been planning something, but I did not know what.

✦ ✦

"Do you wish to know their secrets?" a girl with buck teeth said to me when I was having the midday meal in a loud dining hall, where the middle-ranking and lower-ranking ladies sat at low tables and many eunuchs threaded through the crowd to deliver trays.

Her name was Plum, one of my Talent roommates. She was always busy talking at bedtime, and during the lesson, she had paid no attention to Teacher Rain, so busy was she whispering to the others.

"Whose secret?" I asked.

"That girl." She pointed at a glum-looking girl sitting in a corner. "She is a Grace. Look at her, she's scratching her head again. Don't go near her; she has lice. And that girl in the green-and-white gown over there, she has terrible body odor. You know what I am talking about, don't you? The stink of a fox. She's never going to be favored, I tell you now."

I hesitated, unsure whether I should trust her. But I liked her. She had an innocent look on her face despite her talkativeness, and she was definitely different from Jewel. "Those are big secrets."

Smiling, she nudged me with her elbow. "Now tell me yours."

I slowly chewed a piece of pork belly. After I swallowed, she was still staring at me, almost nose to nose. "Fine. What do you want to know?"

The other Talents near us finished their food and moved away. There were only the two of us. Plum licked her lips. "You were very brave, saving the Emperor's life," she said. "How did you do it?"

"I ran," I said. "I was not brave. I was frightened to death."

"I know it. Anyone would be frightened." Plum grinned. "So do you like the training? I hate the 'perfect walk,' by the way. It gave me blisters, and when they popped, the fluid stuck to the inside of my clogs. I cried every day when I first came here. If you saved all my tears in a barrel, they'd flood the whole court."

"It must be a very big barrel." I smiled. I liked the fact that she knew many things about the girls. She would be the perfect supplier of resources, and perhaps a good spy. "How long have you been in the Inner Court, Plum?"

"About three years."

I finished my food and stacked the bowl and saucers on the tray. "Have you met the Four Ladies?"

"Of course. They're like four gods ruling the four directions of the court." Plum looked around and cupped her hand at my ear. "But to tell you the truth, the only lady we love is the Noble Lady. You've heard of her, right? She's very powerful. She oversees the Imperial Silkworm Workshops, and she is a weaver herself, most kind and generous."

"She is also the daughter of Emperor Yang from the Sui Dynasty," I said, recalling Father's story.

"So you do know."

"Why did the Emperor not make her the Empress?" After all, it had been almost three years since Empress Wende's death, and the Noble Lady had a son, Prince Ke, who was one year younger than the Crown Prince. She would be a good candidate for the crown.

"That's a long story." Plum sighed. "The Pure Lady would like to be the Empress herself, and she is gathering support for her son, Prince Yo."

I placed his name among the list of the princes. He was the fourth living son of the Emperor, after Taizi and Prince Ke. "What kind of support?"

Plum glanced around as though to see if anyone were eaves-dropping. Then she cupped her hand over my ear again. "One thing you need to know is the Pure Lady is ruthless. You must make sure you never offend her."

"I have yet to meet her." Laughter burst out, interrupting us. I turned to see a group of Graces in a corner, their heads gathered together. "So I hear I will receive an assignment after the training."

"Yes. We all have duties. Some weave, some clean, some do laundry, some serve the Ladies. Only the Ladies can sit on their stools and draw their beauty marks all day."

"What about the Emperor?" I asked. "When will we see him?"

He was wounded, but he would recover.

"We go to see him on the tenth day and the twenty-first day of every month."

The bedding schedule. I remembered what Jewel had told me during the bath. "Why those days?"

"Oh, according to the bedding schedule, the lowest-ranking ladies go to see the Emperor on the first nine days of the moon, then the middle-ranking ladies on the next three nights, followed by the high-ranking, and the Empress on the fifteenth and the sixteenth days of the moon, the full moon nights."

"Why on full moon nights?"

Plum licked her lips. "Because the full moon nights are considered most favorable to conceive a child. So the high-ranking ladies have this privilege. After the sixteenth night of the moon, the cycle completes, and we do it in the reverse order."

So the Emperor would have women serving him every night. "But there are nine Talents." I still did not understand. "Who among us gets to go on those designated days?"

"Oh, I forgot to tell you." She made a face. "We will all go together."

I would need to lie with the Emperor together with eight other Talents? "Really? No one told me that."

"It's true." She made a face again. "Each time when we go to see the Emperor, we go in a group of nine. There are twenty-seven seventh-degree ladies, so they are divided into three groups, the same with the eighth-degree ladies and the ninth-degree ladies. So they have nine nights total. We have nine Talents, and we have one night with the Emperor. So do the Beauties and Graces. The Emperor spends the night alone only with the Empress, who used to see him on the full moon nights. But since our Empress has died, the Emperor summons whomever he pleases on those nights."

I swallowed hard. "So the Emperor always follows the schedule?"

She shrugged. "He does as he pleases. Do you know Jewel, our new Most Adored? He's been calling her every cycle, ignoring the bedding schedule. Twice around the full moon! Even the Ladies lost their nights. They say he has grown rather attached to her."

That was bad news. "But he's wounded. Shouldn't he get some rest?"

93

"You are right about that." Plum stuck out her tongue. "It looks like we all need to wait until he recovers."

"Ah." I played with the eating sticks. Should I ask her? "Do you see anyone other than the female ministers here? I mean—" A eunuch holding a tray walked by me. I paused. When he passed, I continued, carefully. "Did you ever see the Emperor, Taizi, or his horses?"

I regretted asking. Of course, neither the Emperor nor Taizi would come visit the etiquette school.

"I saw them once."

"You did? How?"

"On the polo field. It's down the hill, not far from here."

"Did you see Taizi and his groom?"

"Groom? The heir has a dozen of them. Which one?"

"Never mind." I smiled. "We should go back to the classroom."

Later that month when I had free time, I wandered to the polo field behind the school. It was a vast area near a hill surrounded by groves of mulberry trees. The silkworm farming season had already ended, and no one was picking leaves, but the ladders were still scattered around. I passed the ladders and hid behind the tree branches.

In the field, a dozen riders pranced, holding mallets with curved ends. Taizi was there, his chest bare. Looking like a mountain on his ride, he pursued a scarlet ball near the net at the end of the field.

I studied the grooms around the field. Some ran back and forth with buckets of water; some groomed the horses with brushes. I did not see Pheasant. Disappointed, I turned away.

A whistle came from behind me.

I jumped, and there he was, standing beside me. The sunlight sifted through the thick mulberry leaves and lit up his chiseled face.

"Sorry." He smiled brilliantly. "I saw you coming, so I thought to give you a surprise."

He remembered me. "I was just passing by."

He grinned, and I could not tell if he knew I was lying. "And good timing too. I happen to be free."

"Well, I hope the Captain did not thrash you the other day," I said. "I also would like to tell you how grateful I am for your help."

"Don't mention it. I know many hideouts in the palace. If you wish to know, I will show you."

"Perhaps some other day," I said. "What are you doing here? Were you playing polo?" Would Taizi allow his groom to play a nobleman's game?

He shook his head. "Not today. The Emperor forbids it. He'll spank me if he catches me with a mallet. He worries about accidents. Taizi was knocked off his horse and nearly killed a month ago. Do you like polo?"

"Never played it before." He should know that it would be impossible for me to ever play polo. "It's not for a girl."

He shrugged. "Who makes rules like that? I shall teach you next time, if you like. But you need to be careful so the mallet doesn't smack your face."

I felt as if I had found a conspirator who agreed to steal a jug of honey and share it with me. I stared at him, unable to hold back my smile. "Smack my face? Sounds dangerous."

"Do you still want to try?"

"More than ever."

He grinned. "You are different," he said.

"Different? Is this your phrase for all the girls?" I was never happier, however.

"You wouldn't believe me if I told you no, would you?" He thrust his head to one side. "Come with me. I have a surprise for you."

"What surprise?"

"You'll see."

He pushed the branches aside and walked to a trail that led to the other side of the hill. It had to be the back of the court. The woods were dense, the buildings looked dusty, and there were few servants loitering about. We were, as far as I could see, completely alone.

I liked the way he walked, the way his arms swung and he held his head. He looked like a stallion enjoying a run in the breeze. He was also more attractive than I remembered: the profile of his nose was perfect, and the line of his jaw curved slightly. He still wore the same white tunic and a pair of white trousers he had worn on the day we met. They did not carry any embroidery works on the hem or any patterns that a noble boy's clothes would have. But he looked clean and well-groomed, and he smelled of hay and fresh fruit.

He did not let me trail behind him as custom dictated; instead, he waited for me to catch up with him, and together, we walked side by side.

Once or twice, his arm brushed mine, and he attempted to hold my hand. I giggled and hid my hands in my sleeves. When he stopped trying, however, I regretted it with all my heart.

After a while, we arrived at a tangerine grove, where yellow-orange fruits drooped among thick, green leaves. In the air floated a sweet, lemony fragrance mixed with an earthy smell. I stood under a tree, my foot poking at the ground. Part of me was worried. What if someone caught us? Part of me was excited. I had never been alone with a boy before. What were we going to do?

"Here we are." He plucked the fruit from a branch. "First batch of the season. Do you want a tangerine? This one looks ripe. Do you like tangerines?"

Of course I enjoyed delicious tangerines. But if I said I liked them sweet, would he think I was too predictable?

"Only if they're sour."

"I should have known." Chuckling, he dug his thumb into the depressed navel of the citrus. A plume of mist burst out, and the zesty scent flew to my nose. My mouth watered, yet I cast my gaze low. He was so close to me. If I tripped over something, I would fall into his arms.

He was concentrating on the fruit in his hand. Carefully, he peeled off the rind and arranged the pieces around the fruit like petals of a blooming flower. Then he picked up the threadlike pith and removed it until there was nothing on the reddish flesh. He held a segment between his fingers. "Open your mouth."

It would be rude to decline, wouldn't it? I felt the soft tangerine on my tongue and bit down.

"How does it taste?"

"Good." Actually, it tasted sour, with a hint of bitterness. But it did not matter.

His finger brushed my lips. "So you like it?"

I would have liked it if he had put a rock in my mouth. All I knew was his smooth skin and the tang of the citrus on his finger. No one had ever touched me like that before. "Yes."

"Just the way you like it?" His finger lingered.

My heart pounded, and my cheeks warmed. I wanted to lift my head and look into his eyes, but I was worried he would know my thoughts. "Yes."

"I'm glad." I stole a look at him. He was grinning. His eyes, shielded by a thick fence of eyelashes, sparkled. "I thought I would never see you again."

A sweet sensation rose from the bottom of my heart and spread to my limbs, but I said, "Why? Were you worried I would tell about you and Teacher Rain?"

He put his hand on my shoulder. "You know what I mean."

I could feel the warmth from his hand and his breath on my forehead. He was so close to me. His eyes, those pools of amber, danced with light, reminding me of how the rays of the sun sparkled on a summer field. Yes. I knew exactly what he meant, and that knowledge sent a ripple of happiness to my heart.

"Who is there?" a male voice called from the grove.

We froze. Pheasant grabbed my hand and pulled me to run. We dashed out of the grove, raced down the trails through the woods, and finally, turned onto the path leading to the polo field.

"That was close," he said as we stopped to catch our breath.

"Did he see us? Who was he?" I asked, my heart pounding from running, and I was nervous too.

"Perhaps a gardener. Don't worry."

A servant holding a tray appeared down the hill. I stepped away from him. "I think it's time for me to leave."

"Wait! Can I see you again?"

"I don't know." I smiled and walked quickly down the hill.

It was near supper hour. Time had gone fast. I had not known I had spent almost the whole afternoon with Pheasant. On the horizon, the sun shone brightly like a sweet tangerine, and the air smelled fragrant, intoxicating with its scent.

O

AD 641

the Fifteenth Year *of*

Emperor Taizong's Reign

of Peaceful Prospect

AUTUMN

11

I WAS READING IN THE LIBRARY WHEN TEACHER RAIN
snatched the scroll of poems from my hand. "Follow me," she said.

I walked behind her. She seemed ill-tempered, and I was wary.
"May I ask where we're going?"

She did not answer, and I followed behind her as we passed a
gate, a vast courtyard, then another gate, and another courtyard.
The ladies in the corridors raised their heads from *weiqi* tables and
studied me. Maids leaned over brooms and glanced at me. I did not
look at them, but I grew uneasy inwardly.

Where was she taking me?

She walked down a corridor and stopped in front of a building
with three bays. "This is the Emperor's wardrobe chamber," she said,
pushing open the center door. "You're to tend to it from now on."

My heart sang. I had been given an assignment in the imperial
wardrobe! Not emptying Jewel's chamber pot, embroidering, or
doing other onerous, menial work. Most importantly, I was closer
to the Emperor, and I could run into him at any moment. I wondered what Jewel would think when she found out.

I picked up my skirt and stepped inside.

Twelve tall wardrobes, engraved with elaborate flowery designs
and lacquered in shiny red, stood before me. Along the walls, rows of
shelves contained large chests, each the size of a writing table, stacked

to the ceiling. I could not tell how many there were. Hundreds, perhaps. A strong odor of mold slapped my face like a soiled rag, but I did not mind. It smelled better than any exotic perfume, and my heart swelled like a storehouse full of treasure and riches.

"What should I do?" I walked between the rows of chests with leather buckles. My clogs struck the wood floor, the clear sound echoing in my ears like sweet music.

Rain stuffed a scroll into my hand. "This will tell you everything."

I glanced at the document, which contained a list of my daily duties—preparing garments for the Emperor in the morning, organizing garments, counting linens, mending the seams, etc. "Where are the other caretakers?" Surely there were other helpers in the Emperor's wardrobe chamber; even my father had two maids dusting his garments.

"You are the only one. More will come when the Emperor approves the assignments."

I was surprised. "What about the previous maids?"

"Gone." She headed to the door.

"Gone where? Did something happen to them?"

"Hanged." The door swung shut behind her.

I wondered what they had done to deserve such a terrible fate. I studied the chamber again. It seemed different, the air filled with sinister threat. I must be careful. I could not make any mistakes.

I began to examine the chests. None of them were labeled. The former caretakers of the wardrobe were either too lazy to write the Chinese characters, or they were illiterate.

I opened the tall wardrobes. Inside were many extravagant sets of regalia. Red robes made of smooth silk, indigo robes interwoven with gold and silver threads, maroon robes embroidered with intricate designs of cranes, dragons, phoenixes, evergreens, and mountains, and multicolored gowns edged with fur and embellished with sparkling jewels. I was familiar with beautiful robes, but these touted finery I had never seen before.

"Sort out the garments according to the occasions the One Above All must attend…" I read from the list. "Important occasions include the audience on the first day of the moon, audience on the fifteenth day of the moon, days of receiving foreign ambassadors, worshipping Heaven and Earth, making sacrifices to ancestors, sacrifices to divinities of seas and mountains, offerings to the deities of grain and soil, offerings to the ancestors on their death anniversaries…"

But how would I know which robe was for which occasion? I knew enough not to dress him in red for his ancestors' death anniversaries, but I also understood the wrong embroidery, wrong patterns, wrong fabric could cause insult when none was intended.

I went on to examine the chests. I could not lift the ones stacked high, so I started with the ones on the ground near the wardrobes. One by one, I opened them. Inside lay the Emperor's casual outfits—long yellow robes; knee-length orange robes; tunics with wide sleeves; tunics with narrow sleeves; dresses embroidered with the sun, the moon, and stars; dresses stitched with paired deer and cranes; and many more.

"And the occasions are"—I checked the list—"court days, hunting, polo competitions, picnics, spring outings, admiring the full moon, spring outing, stargazing, feasting…"

So many occasions. I rubbed my eyes and moved on to the chests along the wall, which amassed an array of dazzling accessories, such as mortarboards, bejeweled girdles, jade clasps, beaded seal pouches, silk slippers with curled tips, jade pendants, leather boots, silk undergarments, even breastplates and capes.

In another container, I found red sable coats, black mink hats, spotted leopard vests, dyed leather gloves, and many crimson fur capes.

How could one man wear all these?

I started to sweat, but I had finished reviewing only half of the chests. Many accessories were tangled together and mismatched; to simply put everything in order would take days.

A girl dressed in a white tunic came to the chamber. She said she was the Emperor's dress maid and her name was Daisy. Playing with her long braids, she said simply, "Need polo suit."

"Polo, polo." I wished she could be more helpful, but she seemed rather distracted, her face blank, and when I asked her again, she only stared. I paced between the chests, remembering seeing a tunic with a picture of men riding. After half an hour, I finally found it at the bottom of the third container near the fourth wardrobe.

Over the next few days, I carefully sorted out the accessories, organized compartments for shoes and girdles, folded the garments, paired them with underclothes and belts, and labeled the chests according to the seasons. When it was sunny, I spread out the winter garments and fur coats and capes in the courtyard to rid them of dust, moth eggs, and tiny insects. Before the fur and fabric could get warm, I swiftly took them inside and stored them to prevent the color from fading.

Every day, I rose on the fourth crowing of roosters and arrived at the wardrobe chamber before dawn broke. By the time I returned to my bedchamber, the last ray of the sun had faded. After twenty-five days, I stretched my aching back and scanned the neat assortments with satisfaction. There it was. Orderly fashion.

Plum, along with four Beauties, came to the chamber several weeks later. Taking care of the garments became easier with their help, and Plum seemed to know the answer to every question I asked her.

"Those previous maids before us," she answered, smoothing some stubborn wrinkles of a picnic tunic, "they were hanged because they dressed the Emperor in mourning regalia on the fifteenth day of the moon."

I stopped sweeping the floor, shocked that such a small error would cost people's lives. "We must not make mistakes like that," I said. "I wish we could know what kind of clothing the Emperor would wear the next day, then we could prepare them ahead of time."

She shook her head. "It's not possible."

Only the imperial Taoist astrologer, who consulted the Emperor's personal almanac daily, kept the ruler's schedule. A sixth-degree Talent like myself certainly would not have the privilege of knowing it. Neither was I, nor any lady, allowed to keep a calendar, which required the monitoring of Heaven and thus was considered sacred. Again, only the Emperor's astrologer was allowed to create and keep a calendar, and if anyone else possessed one without permission, it was a severe crime, punishable by death.

AD 641

the Fifteenth Year *of*

Emperor Taizong's Reign

of Peaceful Prospect

WINTER

12

I RATHER LIKED MY ROUTINE. EACH MORNING, I PREPARED
the Emperor's clothing for the day, dusted the chamber, and
changed the mothballs in the chests. At noon, I counted the garments and linen sheets the laundry ladies delivered and finished
dusting the chamber. After that, I strolled through the courtyard
and went to walk around a small garden at the back. My bedchamber was located on the other side of the wardrobe chamber,
and it required half an hour's walking from one side to the other.
Usually, when I returned to my bedchamber, it was already dark,
time for bed.

One day, while waiting for the laundry women to deliver clean
linens, I made a mortuary tablet for Father out of a piece of wood
I found near the lake. I had always wanted to honor him with my
silent thoughts, as I was unable to visit his grave in Wenshui each
year on the Day of Qingming. It had been three years since he'd
died. He must have learned of my new title in the other world, and
I wished to tell him I would restore my family's fortune and perhaps
even make his dream for my destiny come true.

I put the tablet at the bottom of a chest and covered it with
my clothes.

I thought of Mother. How I missed her. It had been more than
two years since I'd left her. I prayed she stayed healthy. I wished I

could tell her how close I was to the Emperor, and soon, very soon, I would meet him and tell him about my family's situation.

A month after my appointment in the wardrobe chamber, I received my first allowance as a Talent, which contained ten *jin* of rice and two boxes of facial tincture and rouge. I did not use the beauty products. When I received the second allowance, I saved them as well. Once I saved enough of them, I would trade them to the other Talents for a silver ingot and send it to Mother. She needed money. I did not know if Qing offered her food or warm clothes. With the silver I sent, she would at least have one good meal. She would also understand that I had not forgotten her, and she would be greatly comforted. And even if Qing stole the money, it would be all right. At least he would know I was doing well in the palace. With his greedy nature, he would hope I could do something good for him in the future, and then at least he would treat Mother more kindly.

I also befriended Daisy, the Emperor's dress maid, although she was hard to talk to at first. People often joked that she had a rock where her brain was supposed to be, but Daisy failed to comprehend even that. Words seemed to reach her in delayed echoes, and she always responded a few moments slower than normal.

I made excuses to visit her in the Emperor's bedchamber, which was located far away in Ganlu Hall. Every time I went there, I hoped he would notice me, but he was always surrounded by an array of physicians, guards, and servants. They ordered me to stay one hundred paces away from the Emperor.

His recovery had been slow, even with the help of the great physician, Sun Simiao. The physician had famously declined the invitation of the Sui Court but now accepted the task of overseeing the Emperor's health. He suggested *citragandha*, a wonder drug that contained tamarisk manna, pine resin, and licorice, and had the Emperor take it with grape wine at noon and two hours before bedtime. He also prescribed drugs such as mica and cinnabar, which were said to be two important ingredients of Taoist's elixir, with careful doses administered by a team of physicians and food provosts.

The Duke, the man who suspected me of assisting the killer

in the Altar House, was always around, sniffing, frowning, inspecting the medicines before they were delivered to the Emperor. He was the Emperor's most trusted man, clearly, and I thought it best to stay out of his sight.

The rumor of Heaven's withdrawal from the Emperor died off slowly as he recovered. In time, I believed, the appearance of the comet would become a distant memory to everyone.

Day and night, the thick fragrances of the Emperor's medicinal herbs floated in the Inner Court, sometimes even drowning out the scent of plum flowers. But I breathed it in. As long as the Emperor was in good health, I would see him soon.

✦ ✦

Despite my preoccupation with the Emperor, I thought of Pheasant more and more. His face came into my mind when I swept the chamber or folded tunics. I knew I should stop thinking of him, and that Father would not have approved. But the more I tried, the harder it was to rid my mind of Pheasant. I could still feel his finger on my lips. What if I met him once more? Just once?

There were watchful eyes everywhere though. A few times, I caught two maids peering at me through the wardrobe chamber. I had never seen them before, and when I went to confront them, they pretended they were only passing by. I wondered if they had been sent by Jewel. Who else would be spying on me?

One time, Jewel visited before midday mealtime. "I'm helping the Emperor pick up his outfit," she said, strolling between the rows of chests. But she did not seem to be interested in the Emperor's garments. Instead, her hands flipped through the piles of the late Empress's belongings, her old clothes and her jewelry. Jewel did not take anything in the end and left without a word.

I was wary. After she left, I moved those chests to a far corner.

In time, the opportunity to see Pheasant came. I made certain no one was around and slipped out of the court. I did not know where to find him, so I went to the polo field again. He was there with Taizi, and when he saw me, he gestured to the mulberry groves, where I waited until he could join me. Then we went to a beautiful wooded area behind a vast lake and a long corridor, named A-Thousand-Step Corridor. I admired the intricate lattice works on the sideboards near the bridge, while he whistled and told me about his horses, and then we climbed atop the garden rocks and watched the falcons fly by. Afterward, we raced each other down the hill. The time dribbled like honey flowing from a secret comb, lazily but full of flavor.

One day when I went to see him again, he was in the mulberry grove waiting for me. Together, we went to the back of the Inner Court again and arrived at a garden with high walls. Thick bushes and twisty vines had overgrown the front gate, and a pair of heavy, rusty locks barred the arched entrance.

Light as a lark, Pheasant flipped over the wall with ease. A moment later, his voice wafted from the other side of the garden. "Are you coming?"

I looked around to make sure we were alone and climbed onto a rock. My feet slipped, and my skirt caught my foot. I freed myself, grabbed the bricks on the top of the wall, and heaved. After a few failed attempts, I landed on the other side of the garden.

"Are you all right?" Pheasant looked at me from the grass-covered path. Behind him was a pavilion with a broken roof and moss-covered pillars.

"I'm fine." I looked down at my dress. An ugly patch of mud had stained the back hem. I groaned; the last thing I wanted was untidiness. "You seem to know the palace so well. What is this place?"

"It's abandoned. No one comes here anymore. Come." He went to sit on the pavilion's windowsill and leaned against the latticed panel. The woodwork on the panel was broken, and the pavilion's ground was covered with fallen leaves. "I want to show you something."

I sat across from him, keeping my distance, although I yearned to be close to him.

"Here." He took my hand and left something in my palm. Carved out of opaque green jade, the beautiful piece had onyx eyes, minute gold feet, an elegantly curved back, and a smooth, supple belly.

"Silkworm!" My eyes widened. Silkworms were precious enough, but a jade silkworm was priceless. "Where did you get this?"

"It's my gift to you. Do you like it?"

I adored it. Stroking its smooth surface, I could not take my eyes off it. It was true what people said about jade. It calmed the nerves and brought tranquillity to the bearer. "Why do you want to give me a gift?"

"It was my mother's. She loved silkworms. She said the jade silkworm would bring skillful weavers good fortune. If you were a weaver with poor skills, it would transform you into a capable one."

His mother must have been a weaver in the silkworm nursery. The palace often recruited weavers, as well as their family members who possessed certain skills. That was, perhaps, how Pheasant ended up working in the stable. "Are you certain about this? It's your mother's."

"Yes, it's worth a lot of money." He grinned.

He had a knack for making me smile. "You know I don't mean that. Why do you want to give it to me?"

"Because I like you."

Did he mean that? Happiness bloomed in my heart. "But what about your mother?" I stroked the silkworm. "She'll be mad if she discovers it went missing."

"She died years ago." His head drooped, and a cloud of sadness covered his face.

I reached for his hand. His mother had died, and mine remained unreachable. In a way, we suffered the same hollowness, where the absence of motherly affection settled in our hearts like a wound.

"I cannot accept this." I returned the jade silkworm to his hand.

"What's wrong, sweet face?"

"A Talent is not allowed to possess precious gifts, you know that."

"But you won't tell anyone."

Of course I would not, and I would keep it close to my heart and never let it leave my sight. "But I still think you should keep it yourself."

"If my mother were alive, she would be happy I gave this to you."

"Why?"

He shrugged. "This is the silkworm; only the most worthy should keep it. If anyone should have it, it's you. Besides"—he stuffed the jade silkworm back in my hand—"I stopped seeing Rain. Well, I'll see her in the court. I can't avoid her. It's just you won't catch me with her in the haystacks anymore. And"—he hesitated—"I never cared for her. She came to me."

I closed my fingers on the jade, my heart swelling with delight. He had given me the precious jade as a token of his promise.

But even if he had given me a rock, it would have been more valuable than any gem. But I could not let him know that.

"I don't want to lie to you." I opened my scent pouch and placed the silkworm there, my fingers lingering on the pouch's opening as if it were a gate to happiness. "I can fetch a nice gown with this."

He looked dismayed and then realized I was teasing him. He caught my arms. "If I see this silkworm anywhere other than your pouch, I swear I'll never talk to you again, you sour girl."

I struggled to free myself, but he was stronger than I thought. "Get away from me." I giggled. "I'm not your girl, or one of your girls."

"If you say so."

He lowered his head, and his chin brushed my forehead. It pricked me with a strange sensation. I met his gaze. His arms, so hard and solid, were like nothing I had ever touched. I wished to stay there forever, to be close to him and feel his heart beating next to mine, but I also felt like a fish caught in a net, terrified about what awaited me.

His lips fell on mine. Gentle, like a breeze. Soft, like smooth silk. Sweet, like a summer's dream.

"Will you come here next time?" he whispered.

I thought of Father and Mother. And the Emperor, who had hanged the maids for putting him in the wrong dress. Would he whip me to threads if he knew about Pheasant and me?

But I whispered back. "Yes," I said. "Yes."

AD 642

the Sixteenth Year *of*

Emperor Taizong's Reign

of Peaceful Prospect

EARLY SPRING

13

I WAS ORDERED TO GO TO THE CHENGXIANG HALL TO receive my apples, the first fruit allowance of the year. I was excited. I had not tasted fresh fruit for months, as Talents did not have a fruit allowance in the winter. The ladies of third degree and above, however, received fruit every month, which came from the imperial ice pits where many fresh fruits—pears, melons, oranges, and berries—were stored.

But I was also excited because I would finally meet the Four Ladies, who would distribute the apples to us.

I waited in the corner of a corridor with Plum and the other Talents. On the other side of the corridor stood the seventh-degree ladies, the eighth-degree ladies, and the ninth-degree ladies. The Ladies-in-Waiting, Beauties, and Graces were ahead of us in the courtyard. I looked around. I did not see Jewel. I wondered why she was absent. Being Most Adored, she could have anything she wanted.

The courtyard became quiet when four ladies in splendid gowns appeared near the gates, followed by a group of eunuchs carrying barrels of apples. They placed the barrels in the center of the yard, and the ladies sat on the arranged stools in front of the barrels.

I identified the Noble Lady right away. She was in her thirties and carried an air of confidence and loftiness that none of the others had. She wore a golden phoenix headdress and a necklace with pearls as big as quail eggs. She was also plump. Her cheeks bulged like ripened apples, and when she nodded, every part of her body seemed to shake, the layers under her chin, the long, golden tail of her phoenix headdress, as well as the two strings of jade earrings dangling from her thick earlobes.

"Remember what I said about her?" Plum whispered to me as a eunuch called the Ladies-in-Waiting, who knelt before the Four Ladies to receive their apples.

I nodded. The Noble Lady was clearly the one in charge. The eunuchs picked up apples, turned to her for consent, and then bowed and put the apples in the basket. "People revere her."

"They do."

"Who's the lady with pale skin on the right?" That lady appeared to be obsessed with her looks. Sitting on the stool, she did nothing except stare into a bronze mirror held by her servant. Even with all the noise and confusion around her, she did not seem distracted.

"She's Lady Virtue. She was Most Adored once."

"I see." She was undoubtedly the most beautiful of the four ladies.

"The Emperor grew tired of her. She likes to eat chickens' feet and pork skin because she believes they improve her complexion. They are her beauty diet. She also drinks only morning dew because it's purest and won't tarnish her fair skin."

That sounded extreme to me. "Who is the one next to her?"

"Lady Obedience. She's a dancer."

No wonder she wore a dancer's costume, a low-cut red dress that exposed her bosom and a shawl that draped to the floor. Only a dancer would walk around in an immodest gown like that.

"She doesn't have a chance to compete with the others. She's also sick."

The Ladies-in-Waiting bowed and left with their baskets of apples, and the Beauties moved to the courtyard to take their place. The people ahead of us began to step forward in the corridor. I moved forward as well. "What kind of sickness? Anything serious?"

"Hemorrhoids."

I stifled a laugh. But perhaps having hemorrhoids was deadly when one's business was to attract the Emperor. I stared at the last lady, who was stroking a white cat in her lap. She was very thin, wearing a silver gown, and like the Noble Lady, she looked to be in her thirties. "And that's the Pure Lady?"

As if hearing me, the lady looked in my direction. Her stare was cold, unfriendly, sending a chill down my back. I lowered my head instinctively. Just then the Beauties left and the Graces walked to the courtyard. I was relieved to follow them.

"I just heard this." Plum cupped her hand around my ear, and her voice was so faint I strained hard to hear. "Remember the assassination plot? It is rumored she planned it."

I sucked in air and looked around, glad no one was behind me. The three groups of seventh-degree ladies, eighth-degree ladies, and ninth-degree ladies were on the other side of the corridor and whispered among themselves. But a eunuch in the courtyard turned around and glanced at me. I lowered my head. Plum and I fell silent.

"She? This can't be true," I said when the eunuch looked away. "Why would she do that?"

"The Emperor wasn't the target." Plum's breath moistened my earlobe. "The target was Taizi, but for some reason he left the Altar House early, and the killer stumbled on the Emperor."

The Pure Lady wished to murder Taizi so her son would replace him? I could hardly believe it. "Where did you hear this?"

Plum shielded her mouth with her hand and coughed as though to dislodge something in her throat. "Where? Many people are gossiping about this. Remember the court recorder? He was poisoned, dead, when the Gold Bird Guards tried to interrogate him."

"You think she ordered that?" I dared not lift my head in the Pure Lady's direction.

"That's what people say."

I thought hard. "Does the Emperor know this?"

Plum shook her head. "No. He believes Taizi plotted it."

Of course. If the Emperor died, Taizi would have his throne. "So the prince is in trouble then."

"That's why the Emperor is sending him away."

"Where is he going?"

The crowd moved again, and we walked toward the barrels, but I lagged behind to widen our distance from the other Talents.

"One of the Four Garrisons on the western border." Plum shrugged. "The Emperor said the assassination plot spurred revolts from other peaceful tribes. Even the Eastern Turks are getting restless. But it is just an excuse to send Taizi away."

"It may not be." With the war against the Western Turks, the Emperor needed a strong man to boost his army's morale. Taizi, with his muscles and his history in the military camp, was a good candidate.

"Well, the real reason is," she said, "the Emperor dislikes Taizi now. He does not trust him, and the Pure Lady thinks this is a good opportunity to further weaken the heir so her son, Prince Yo, can gain the Emperor's favor."

"I see." According to the traditional rule of succession, Prince Yo, the fourth son, could not take precedence over Taizi, whose mother, Empress Wende, was the legitimate wife. But if Taizi lost his right to inherit the throne because of the assassination plot, and if the Pure Lady became the Empress, then everything would change. "But I don't think Prince Yo has a chance."

"You don't think so? The Pure Lady invited some ministers to the court for the Lantern Festival months ago. Even the Chancellor joined. I am telling you she is working hard to gain support and win the Emperor's trust."

I glanced at the Noble Lady. Her cheeks shining like two red apples, she was smiling kindly at a Grace. "What about the Noble Lady?"

She had two sons. Her older son, Prince Ke, was only a year younger than Taizi. If Taizi fell into disgrace, Prince Ke, senior of Prince Yo, was more eligible.

Plum sighed. "I would rather she becomes the Empress, Mei.

You see, she has been managing the Imperial Silkworm Workshops since Empress Wende's death, and the silk has been very productive. I also heard she is kind to her maids. One time her maid broke her jade comb. The maid was worried to death, but the lady did not even raise her voice to her..."

Two servants came to stand behind me, eyeing us furtively. I could not tell whose servants they were, perhaps the Pure Lady's. I tugged Plum's sleeve, and she shut her mouth.

The eunuch called me, and I bowed to the ladies. Perhaps it was my imagination, but I felt the Pure Lady's cold gaze on my back. Did she really plan the assassination? Did she want to be the Empress that badly?

In haste, I received the apples and left with Plum. I told her to take my basket to our bedchamber, and I hurried to the wardrobe chamber. There was no laundry delivery scheduled that afternoon. I just wanted to make sure everything was in order before I went to meet Pheasant. I went down the corridor and pushed open the doors.

The sight inside sent a jolt through me. For a while I was unable to process what had happened. Then my knees weakened, and I almost collapsed.

All the wardrobes and the chests were wide open. Piles of robes, capes, bejeweled girdles, and silk slippers were scattered across the floor.

14

WALKING THROUGH THE DISARRAY, I FELT AS IF I WERE
treading on waves of water. I needed to gather them up: the robes,
capes, slippers, belts, all of them. I had to smooth out the wrinkles,
one by one, fold them, and store them back in the chests or wardrobes, yet I could hardly find the strength.

Who had done it? Why would someone ransack the wardrobe
chamber and give me trouble?

I sank down onto a chest, my leg brushing against something
hard and sharp. I looked down. I was sitting on a chest with metal
clasps. I could not understand. All the Emperor's chests used leather
belts. Only the late Empress's jewelry chests had metal clasps, which
I had hidden in a corner.

I looked again. It was indeed the late Empress's jewelry chest.
Someone had moved it.

A premonition seized me. I opened the lid. It was empty. All the
hairpins and crowns were gone.

I gasped. It was my duty to care for the items in the chamber
and my fault if anything went missing, and they were the late
Empress's jewelry! I should report the theft to the supervisors of
the Inner Court. But they would blame me, perhaps charge me
with dereliction.

What should I do?

"What happened here?" Daisy leaned against the door with her usual dazed look.

"I—" I quickly picked up a robe imprinted with a pair of stags and folded it. Then I undid it and folded it again. "I'm looking for something."

Daisy twirled the end of her braid with her forefinger. "It's cold in here."

I wished she would leave. Pushing my hair out of my eyes, I tried to remain calm. "Is the Emperor's morning audience over?"

"Morning audience?" Daisy glanced at the sky, looking confused. "I'm waiting for my supper."

I had forgotten the time. "Right. I was so busy."

"What are you looking for?" Daisy walked toward the jewelry chest.

"No!" I nearly tripped over the piles of garments on the floor. "I'll put everything back. You should leave."

"Do you think I'm clumsy too? I only wish to help."

"Clumsy? No. I was just—"

She pulled up her sleeve to show a bruise on her arm. "Look at what Most Adored did to me. She twisted me so hard. I was only trying to help her with her quilt."

My body tensed. "What are you talking about?"

"She brought her quilt here. The one with the peony pattern. Very pretty. But she dropped her crown."

"Crown?"

"Yes. She dropped it, so I handed it back. She looked mad."

I took a deep breath to calm down. So it was Jewel. She had stolen the crowns and all the hairpins. "You said she dropped a crown. Do you truly believe it was a crown?"

Daisy chewed on her braid. "I told you, Mei. I saw it. It was the late Empress's coronation crown. Everyone knows it. But Most Adored told me the crown was just a pillow. Well, was it a pillow or a crown? I thought I saw a crown, but why did she want me to say it was a pillow? I don't know…"

Jewel was clever. She must have wrapped the jewelry inside the quilt. "When did you see her?"

"After I received the apples." Daisy was of fifth degree, so she had received the apples before me. "Before you arrived. Um…Mei, you are not going to tell Most Adored about this, are you? She said she'd break my head if I told anyone."

"She won't break your head, Daisy. I won't let her, I promise." I stuffed a pile of garments into the wardrobe. "Can you do me a favor? Would you stay here until I come back?"

"All right." Daisy chewed on her braid again. "Where are you going?"

I gave her a gentle squeeze on her arm. I could not express how grateful I was for her help. "It's a secret."

I went straight to the east side of the Inner Court where the Quarters of the Pure Lotus were located, the residences of the Four Ladies and Most Adored. How long had I fancied to visit there, and even dwell there someday, but now I went ready to fall on my knees.

The five houses, with their blue eaves and red pillars, sat in a discreet circle connected by five corridors walled with elaborate lattice fences. In the center was a vast courtyard, where garden stones were stacked to shape a small mountain as high as a one-story building. Three goblets, bottoms up, were moored in a shallow pool near the mountain. The scene was reminiscent of the ancient custom of the Third Day of the Third Month, when nobles celebrated by drinking ale from goblets and composing poems. Jewel enjoyed entertaining these days. I wished she had choked on the wine.

Standing near the shallow pool, I studied each house. Which one belonged to her? I was about to knock on the door near me when a maid with freckles stepped out of a house facing the south. Jewel's maid. I walked to that building.

How to greet her, a woman who deceived, cheated, and stole? I did not know. But I had to do it. I had to get all the jewelry back. Inhaling deeply, I stopped in front of the building and raised my hand.

The doors swung open.

Jewel opened her arms. "Finally, you came, Mei. I have been expecting you. Do you like my new chamber?"

"Greetings, Most Adored." The sight of her angered me. Trying to keep my composure, I folded my hands across my stomach and gave Jewel a bow as custom required.

She looked me up and down. "You've changed, Mei. How graceful and elegant you look now. The training has brought out the best in you."

She was smiling, but I knew what hid underneath her skin. "I thank you, Most Adored. If I have your permission, I would like to ask a favor."

"Why in such a hurry? I want to show you this." She twirled to the painted screens near her bed. "Have you heard this used to be the late Empress's room? Very spacious, isn't it? Come and look at the murals; everything is newly painted. This one, the picture of 'The Beauty Wang Zhaojun Leaving Her Home,' is most exquisite. Do you like it?"

"I did not come here to admire a mural, Most Adored." I tried to speak calmly.

"Oh, right. Let me show you my new gowns. Would you like to take a look?"

The charade was getting tiresome. "Most Adored, you should know I would not come here if it wasn't most urgent."

"Well." She cupped her chin with her right hand. "Let me see. Why are you here?"

Faint footsteps came from the corridor outside. My back stiffened. Too many ears in the compound. I had to choose my words carefully. "You leave me no choice, Most Adored. Would you prefer me to report it?"

"You won't do that." Jewel's catlike eyes searched mine. "Your eyes tell me you won't. But let's be candid, for friendship's sake. Why do you think I dropped the crown in front of the stupid maid?"

I frowned. She had done it on purpose? "What do you want?"

"A friendly conversation. That's all. Let's start with the Pure Lady," she said. "I assume you have met her?"

"Yes," I said carefully.

"The truth is, she doesn't like you."

"Why?"

"You're young, beautiful, and a Talent. You take care of the Emperor's wardrobe, and soon, you'll be promoted and dress him every morning in his chamber. The Pure Lady, as well as the other Ladies, cannot see the Emperor unless he summons her. Do you understand now? You have all the chances that she does not." Jewel went to sit in front of her dresser, where she had spread out the bejeweled hairpins, jade combs, and colored boxes of tinctures.

"Do you expect me to believe that? She's a Lady. She has no reason to be jealous of me."

"What I'm trying to tell you is you must never offend her. Whatever you've heard about her, she is more." Jewel took a long, gold hairpin out of her white hair and began to comb it. "She stings her adversary like a hornet, and when she turns away—when you think you have survived the sting—she attacks like a scorpion that thrusts its venomous tail."

I understood why she had said that. "You are friends with her now."

She put down the comb. "You see, Mei. That's what I like about you. You're very intelligent."

I frowned. She still did not tell me why she had stolen the late Empress's jewelry.

"You do understand what's going on right now, don't you?" She picked up a makeup brush and dipped it into a colored tincture box. "The Noble Lady wants to be the empress, but so does the Pure Lady. The Noble Lady hopes her older son, Prince Ke, will replace Taizi. If Ke inherits the throne, then she's the indisputable empress. But the Pure Lady is the Noble Lady's equal in many ways. Do you see the predicament?"

The princes again. Why was Jewel telling me that? I felt as though she had spread a snare before me while I sauntered around the edge of it like an ignorant bird. "I need to go back soon, Most Adored."

"Do not be afraid, Mei. This is why you are here. You will help us."

"Help you with what?" That was why Jewel stole the jewelry. She wanted to hold me hostage and force me to do her bidding.

She began to draw something between her eyebrows. "Destroy the Noble Lady."

I wanted to laugh. How absurd!

"You've heard about her, haven't you? She keeps spiders as pets," Jewel said.

"She's a weaver," I said.

The way Jewel spoke, it sounded as if the Noble Lady was a witch of some sort, but in truth, all weavers liked spiders for their spinning ability. Once a year, before the silkworm farming season started, the weavers locked a spider in a chest overnight. If the spider produced a tight web the next morning, it indicated good luck for the weaver; if the web was loose or incomplete, it predicted the weaver's poor skill and a poor year ahead. As head of the Imperial Silkworm Workshops, the Noble Lady certainly watched closely the signs from spiders.

"That's the problem," Jewel said. "A second-degree Lady is not obligated to do chores, but she carries her spindle wheel everywhere. Who knows how much she weaves every day? Her intention is clear. She just wants people to believe she's the paradigm of goodness and a perfect candidate for the empress's seat." She turned to face me. "The Noble Lady is a crafty woman. Never be fooled by how good a facade she paints."

I said nothing. I had to tread carefully.

"Do you understand what I am saying?" She tilted her head.

I replied, hoping my voice was mild and docile. "Most Adored, there is nothing I can do to help you."

"Come." She beckoned me to approach and then cupped her hand at my ear. Her voice was soft. "I'll return the crowns and everything else I put in the quilt, once you extinguish the fire in the silkworm workshops. Very simple, isn't it?"

I pulled away. Although I was not very familiar with the process of silkworm farming, I knew how important the warmth was for the eggs. A delicate species, they relied on heat to hatch, and the nurseries must keep a dozen fires in pits to keep them warm. "The silkworm eggs will perish in the cold."

"They have countless batches of eggs in various stages of maturity. One night's cold won't kill them all."

Even so, the Noble Lady's reputation would be tarnished, and she would fall into disgrace, which was what Jewel and the Pure Lady wanted. But how could I bear the guilt if I froze even one egg? It was the silkworm. The most treasured creature of the kingdom. I thought of Pheasant's jade silkworm in my pouch.

"You must be mad. Really mad, Jewel. What do you think the Noble Lady's downfall will give you?"

"Everything a woman dreams to have. When the Pure Lady and I put our great minds together, we make good plans."

"So you are aiding her in becoming the Empress?" Then Jewel would take the Pure Lady's place, perhaps.

"I knew you would understand."

I raised my chin. I would not be blackmailed. "I am not your pawn."

She peered at me, a phoenix beauty mark painted between her eyebrows. "I would hate to hear something unfortunate happened to you, Mei."

I stood firmly. "Don't be so certain. You would be punished too if the Emperor knew of your stealing."

"My stealing?"

"You give me no choice, Most Adored." I would tell the Emperor the truth, even if he would punish me for my negligence.

"You do not understand, do you, Mei?" She sighed. "How will he think it's me, if he finds the crowns in someone else's chamber, say, a Talent's?"

I faltered. "You would not dare to do that!"

She picked up a piece of red paper near the colored boxes. "Of course not, Mei. It will not happen. I will not do that. I give you my promise. As long as you give me yours."

I bit my lip, unable to speak.

She sighed, staring at the red paper in front of her. "But such is our life in the court, Mei. I'm certain you know it as well as I. The gate to the Yeting Court is perpetually open, but the path to return to the Inner Court is long and tortuous."

I could not raise my head. It had taken me so long and so much pain to get to where I was. My Talent title, my duty in the wardrobe chamber. I was so close to the Emperor, who would summon me any day. And Mother. I had not yet saved enough silver to send to her. If Jewel succeeded in accusing me of stealing the jewelry, everything—my dream to take care of Mother, my title, even my life—would be ruined.

"I'm glad you understand this now. You may leave, Mei." Jewel's hand flicked in the air. "When I hear the news of the fire, I'll return the items to you."

I wrung my hands. "I do not trust you."

"What other choices do you have, Mei?"

"But…but…" I could not move. "What if the silkworms die? All of them?"

She laid the red paper between her lips and smacked. Perfectly red lips appeared in the mirror. "Then I'll wear my old gowns."

"But the workshops are guarded," I said, desperate. "There is no way I can get in."

She smiled wickedly. "You're a clever girl, Mei. And a clever girl will always find a way."

15

THE IMPERIAL SILKWORM WORKSHOPS, A SITE ALMOST AS sacred as the family shrine, was accessible to only a few skillful weavers and workers who had special permission granted by the Noble Lady. Fiercely guarded, it was where silk—the bargain for peace offerings, the gift to a woman's heart—was made in secret.

How could I enter the workshops?

I thought of Sun Tzu, belatedly, after I left Jewel's chamber. "The clever combatant imposes his will on the enemy but does not allow the enemy's will to be imposed on him." I wished I had remembered that while I had been in Jewel's chamber.

I made my way to the workshops, housed in a walled building behind the Archery Hall on the east side of the palace. When I came to the front of the gate, where two guards stood, I told them I would like to speak to the Noble Lady.

They looked me over suspiciously. "Wait here," one said, and the other went inside the workshops.

I paced in front of the gate.

Every year, the silk farming started in early spring, and many bolts of silk would be produced and brought to the markets throughout the kingdom. The Imperial Silkworm Workshops produced half of the kingdom's silk. The other half came from the silk farms in the south, where the weather was warmer and the temperature was easier to control. Everyone in the kingdom, young or old, understood that silk was our promise of prosperity and that silkworms were Heaven's gifts to us.

And I had been ordered to destroy them.

I thought of the powerful Lady at the apple distribution, whom the eunuchs had to consult before giving away the apples. Would I bring her ruin? Or would she destroy me first?

A plump figure in a splendid yellow gown came to the building's threshold, and my hands began to sweat. I had hoped the Noble Lady would send a maid to fetch me. Once inside, I would find an excuse to slip away, locate the nursery, put out the fire, and leave.

But she had come to greet me. Personally. Outside the walls of the workshops. I wanted to flee, but it was too late. I lowered my head and gave her a deep bow, thankful that etiquette mandated I avoid making eye contact.

Hoping my voice was calm, I said, "May I be allowed to give my utmost respect to the Noble Lady, the one and only, the kindest of all."

"So you are the girl they were talking about. I was hoping to speak to you during the apple distribution but did not have the chance." The Noble Lady had a pleasant voice, strong but not too loud, confident but not haughty, as if she was accustomed to speaking to a group of women. "Mei, isn't it? You have exceptional courage, I've heard. If you had not been there in the Altar House, the One Above All would have been seriously harmed in the attack. I see goodness and bravery in you."

I lowered my eyes to show my respect. But I was surprised. Her courteousness toward a low grader like me was unexpected.

"Would you raise your head so I will have a good look at you?"

I obliged and fixed my gaze on her shoulders.

"What an exquisite face. So young, graceful, and delicate, like a summer peach." She took my hand and patted it.

I did not know what to think. A lady held another's hand only when they were equals, but the gap in social standing between us was as vast as the Yellow River. "I'm honored to be in your presence, my Noble Lady."

She put something in my hand. A pearl necklace. "A gift. I would like to reward you for your courage."

All the phrases I had prepared earlier evaporated like mists under the sun. "My Noble Lady…" I forgot the etiquette and stared at her in astonishment. "This honor is too great for me. I do not deserve it. Besides, a Talent is not allowed to possess any expensive gifts." I had Pheasant's present, of course, but no one needed to know that.

She sighed. "I forgot. In this case, tell me, what would you like to have as a gift?"

"I… I… " I bit my lip. "I do not desire any treasure, my Noble Lady. If I must accept the honor, I shall be bold. For my entire life, I've been curious about silkworms, yet I have never seen one."

"Silkworms." She hesitated. "I see." She waved at the two guards at the gate. "She has my permission to enter."

The guards exchanged glances, hesitated, but stepped aside to let me enter.

"Come." The Noble Lady waved at me to follow her inside the building.

I took a deep breath and crossed the threshold. I could not face her, afraid that she would read my mind. She led me to the front parlor, a small, rectangular reception room with a tiled roof. The area had a square table, two painted stools, and a vase containing a sprig of plum blossom. On the wall hung a painting of a mountain and a waterfall. Everything seemed tranquil and graceful, as if we were in a home, not in a workshop.

After passing the parlor, we came to the front courtyard. A loud clatter rose. Startled, I froze. In front of me stood three looms, each the size of a small house. They clacked busily as female weavers pushed the front movable bars of the frames to tighten the wefts. Between two curtains of threads, shuttles flew back and forth, like swift fish in a pool of a waterfall. Each time the shuttles reached the end, the weavers stepped on the pedals and pulled the front bars of the looms. *Clack. Clack.*

I had heard the noise when I'd waited outside the walls, but I had been too preoccupied to notice. So close, the sound was sharp and piercing.

"The Imperial Workshops include five courtyards this size." The Noble Lady ascended a raised terrace, where some female workers rolled the finished silk from the looms and some measured the silk into bolts. "The dyers work there." She pointed at a wide space below the terrace, where some workers pulled silk through buckets of dyes.

"I have never seen anything like this," I said, careful not to rouse the lady's suspicion. But I could not help being curious. I scanned the area. There was no fire or nursery to be found.

"We shall see the silkworms soon." She led me down a walkway near the terrace, and then I entered another world.

The place looked like it had come from a painting. White spring lilies were tucked among the green grass like opaque pearls, blue water lotus flowered in the shiny ponds like lapis lazuli, and a field of red azalea spread near the wooden bridge like a thick carpet. In the distance, groups of willow trees stood, their long branches drooping, like crowns of exquisite silk threads.

"Beautiful!" I blurted out.

"As it should be." The Noble Lady slowed down, and I could see she was not used to so much walking, but she continued until we arrived at another courtyard, where a score of workers sat before rows of steamy vats. Inside the vats, the cocoons dipped and rose in the bubbling water like eyeballs. Holding pairs of long chopsticks, the workers poked the cocoons to unfurl the silk threads.

Ahead of me, a wide hall came into view. The Noble Lady turned to face me, her plump face blossoming with pride. "Do you hear that?"

There was a loud *swish* somewhere. It sounded like the steady rhythm of drizzle, but there were no raindrops.

"Yes." I nodded, confused. "What is it?"

She led me to the hall and nodded to a servant at the door, who hurried to open it. "Here we are."

The swishing sound rushed to my ears as the hall opened before me. She walked in first, and I followed.

Rows of bamboo shelves spread from wall to wall. On the

shelves were many large trays holding green mulberry leaves. Between the rows traveled many workers, their hair tied in head wraps and their arms carrying trays.

The nursery.

My heart raced faster. I walked down the aisle after the Noble Lady, and when she pulled out a tray, I looked over her shoulder. The tray was covered with tender red leaves, and under the leaves squirmed numerous white worms covered with tiny spots.

"Silkworms," I whispered.

The most diligent workers, the most cherished pets, and the most precious of all creatures. The kingdom feverishly guarded them because of the threads they provided, and I stood in front of them, bearing an ugly secret.

"Take this one." The Noble Lady placed a small silkworm in my hand. Her voice was raised slightly so I could hear her above the swishing, the sound of the silkworms nibbling the leaves. "This baby silkworm was hatched yesterday. Be gentle. Let it like you. It thrives in quiet, warmth, and goodness."

I coughed, my face heating up, and the silkworm wriggled, tickling me. I tensed, praying it would not grow stiff and suddenly die in my hand.

"How many silkworms do you have here, my Noble Lady?"

"Do you think I would know?" She scanned the trays. "Thousands. The divine Goddess of Silkworms sees to it that they multiply by thousands."

"This one is so small."

"In three weeks, it'll grow as big as your little finger and spill silk threads. It has a big appetite. Four feedings a day, four feedings a night. After a week, the silkworm baby eats ten times a day." She handed me a mulberry leaf. "It's hungry. Feed it."

I held the leaf in front of the silkworm. It nibbled the stem, devoured the whole leaf, and squirmed, as if asking for more. I was fascinated. What a miraculous creature. Gingerly, I put it back in the tray and peered down at another tray underneath.

Thousands of tiny specks.

Silkworm eggs.

I tensed. They looked like white sesame seeds. But unlike those oval seeds, solid and lackluster, the silkworm eggs were round, supple, and opaque, as if imbued with an invisible force within.

"The eggs will hatch any day now. Everyone is waiting impatiently to see the baby silkworms. This spring is unusually cool. We must keep the fire on during the day and the night."

"Where is the—" I caught myself. Just then a soft chanting rose in the room.

"Come. It's time to pray."

She went to the hall's entrance, where workers knelt before a statue of a maiden with a hairstyle formed like two wheels. The Silkworm Goddess. Softly, they chanted. Their prayers were a soothing hymn to my ears but a reproachful song to my heart. I hesitated and knelt to join them. I wanted to raise my head and searched for the fire, but I was facing the courtyard with my back to the nursery, and I dared not attract attention by twisting my head back too many times. When the praying finished and the group dispersed, I rose and turned around. There, I saw it. At the end of the shelf, near the corner of the nursery, was a bronze brazier. In fact, there were four of them, one in each corner.

The Noble Lady stood beside me. "Do you like your reward, Mei?"

My heart was beating faster, but I tried to keep calm. "I don't deserve to see this."

She smiled and headed out of the nursery.

I followed her to the corridor. "Do you need help here, my Noble Lady?"

"We're always busy."

"I can help pick leaves," I said. "I would like to help."

"I shall keep you in mind." She went to sit on a stool in front of a small spindle wheel. Her left hand twisting three yarns, she spun the handle with her right hand.

I stood beside her. Workers came and went around me, their steps agile, their faces content, and the heavy swishing echoed in my ears. I remembered the silkworms' small mouths, their tiny bodies squirmy with life. The place resembled a tight cocoon with hope and vibrancy. "This is a wonderful place, my Noble Lady."

She smiled. "It's because of the silkworms. They are lovely creatures. I often come here and work when I can't sleep. The sounds of the looms and the silkworms nibbling leaves calm me. They bring me memories of a special lullaby."

Her wheel spun. *Squeak. Squeak.* The sound gnawed at my insides like a rodent trying to break through the shell of my feigned kindness. I felt smaller than the silkworms and slighter than the delicate silk threads.

I could not remember how I left the workshops.

16

A WEEK PASSED. THE NOBLE LADY DID NOT ASK ME TO help pick leaves.

I grew frantic.

When I counted the sheets in the wardrobe chamber, I got the wrong number. When Daisy came, I gave her the robes with mismatching belts, and whenever the Emperor's other dress maids' footsteps echoed in the corridor, I grew nervous that they would ask for the Empress's crowns, discover they had gone missing, and then report it to the Emperor. I knew I was paranoid, but I could not help worrying.

I went to the polo field to look for Pheasant. He was my only comfort, and I hoped to talk to him about the silkworms. But the field was crowded with grooms, horse trainers, horse inspectors, and polo players holding mallets. It seemed they were preparing for an important match, and Pheasant was with some riders, who nodded vigorously as he talked. When he caught a glimpse of me, he held up two fingers.

I would need to wait for two days until we could meet in private. I returned to the wardrobe chamber. Jewel's maid, the one with freckles, was waiting in the corridor.

"You have until tomorrow," she said.

"What do you mean?" I swallowed.

"That's what she wanted me to tell you."

"Then what?"

She shrugged and left.

Sitting on the floor, I hugged my knees. The night fell, but I did not want to move. She had given me one day. One day, and then my life would be ruined.

I did not know what to do. I liked the Noble Lady. All the good things Plum had said about her were true. I could not imagine repaying her kindness with treachery. And the silkworms. I could not harm them.

But I needed to retrieve the jewelry, and the only way to get it was to do as Jewel had asked. I could not fight off Jewel and the Pure Lady. They were ruthless, and they would destroy me if the Emperor believed I had stolen the jewelry.

I did not have a choice. I had to obey them.

In fact, it might not be as difficult as I had imagined. The Noble Lady liked me, and she would allow me to enter the workshops. Perhaps I could go there during the night when there were not many people and smother the fire without anyone knowing.

I breathed hard. Yes. I could do it when no one was around.

Quickly, I tidied up the room, ate my supper in my bedchamber, and put on a black robe. By the time I went to the workshops, it was near midnight. To my relief, the guards on duty were the two I had seen before.

They frowned as I approached them. "Did the Noble Lady call for you? At this hour?"

"Oh, no. She did not call for me. I came myself. She does not know," I said pleasantly.

"I'll let her know you've come."

She was still working at this hour? I did not expect that. "It's all right... I can wait to see her."

"Then get out of here."

"I will... I will... You see... I don't know what to do about this..." I fished in my pocket and took out the silkworm Pheasant had given me. "I found this near the wall. I don't know who this belongs to. But it looks valuable. Whoever lost it must be anxious. I don't know who I should give it to..."

The guards peered at the silkworm. "Leave it to us. We'll give it to the Noble Lady."

"Of course, of course." I put my hand out then took it back. "It's not that I do not trust you... It's just I would like to give it to the lady myself. She is so kind to me. Please?"

They hesitated but finally waved me through. I dashed inside as fast as possible and crossed the courtyards. The whole building was quiet, only lanterns illuminating under the eaves. Some workers were still there on night duty. I could hear their footsteps behind the doors. When I reached the nursery, a lantern shone in the corridor, where the Noble Lady sat at her spindle wheel. Lights from the nursery shone on her plump face. She looked like a Buddhist statue. I hid behind a pillar, waiting.

The sound of swishing echoed steadily in the nursery, and a few night workers paced inside. They must have been changing the leaves or checking the fire in the braziers. After a while, the Noble Lady rose, rubbed her chest as though tired, and instructed the night workers to get some sleep. "It'll be another good four hours until our babies need to feed again," she said, and they nodded and spread out pallets in the corridor. With four braziers in the nursery, it was too hot to sleep there.

Four hours. That would give me plenty of time. I waited until the lady left and the workers fell asleep. They were obviously exhausted, and their snores rose instantly. I waited a bit longer and then tiptoed past them.

Once inside the nursery, I snatched a broom and began at the brazier in the far corner. The heat from the fire burned my cheeks, and my hands trembled. I had no choice, I reminded myself. I was like a baby silkworm too, cocooned in the threads of my enemies' conspiracies. And if I did not obey them, I could not transform to become the moth that flew on my own wishes and pursued my own light.

I stabbed the flames with the broom, and they died off without resistance. I repeated the action with the second brazier. The nursery darkened. It became cooler. I moved to the next corner and stirred. The fire shot up fiercely, as though fighting me, but dimmed, and gradually, the red color faded from the embers. At the same time I could hear the swishing sound of the nursery became fainter, as though the silkworms had lost their breaths. Had any baby silkworms stopped hatching because of me? Were any silkworms freezing to death right now because of me?

One more.

I held the broom tight and moved to the brazier near the corridor. Afterward, I could go to Jewel's chamber and get the jewelry back.

"Mei!"

I jerked around. In the corridor stood the Noble Lady. She had returned. Why had she returned?

She was trembling, her whole face shaking. "What are you doing? What are you doing?"

I dropped the broom and fell to my knees. "I… I… Forgive me, my Noble Lady!" The workers had awakened. They hurried to restart the fires. "I can explain… Please… I can explain!"

"Yes. You have much to explain."

I could not hold up my head. She would report my crime to the Emperor, who could throw me in prison, exile me, behead me, or execute my family. Destroying the kingdom's silkworms was a felony, after all. I wished I had not been so foolish. "It's Most Adored, my Noble Lady! And the Pure Lady. They stole the late Empress's crowns and blackmailed me! I did not want to extinguish the fire. I would never harm a silkworm. Please believe me, my Noble Lady! Please forgive me!"

She sighed. "I forgot my handkerchief. That was why I came back. I did not expect to see you here. All of you"—she waved at the workers—"make sure the silkworms are not harmed. Mei, you come with me." She went to the corridor and sank onto the stool before her spindle wheel. "Sit down. Look at me, and tell me. Tell me everything."

I perched on the edge of the stool, mortified. Slowly, I told her everything. How Jewel had stolen the jewelry from the chamber and how she had asked me to destroy the silkworm eggs.

The Noble Lady seemed to have a difficult time understanding me. Then she stood and paced in the corridor, breathing hard. "She is Most Adored. Why does she resent me so?"

"She befriends the Pure Lady." I stood too, not knowing what else to do.

"The Pure Lady! She's always planning something. Last year, she roasted a dozen mother silkworms. Mother silkworms! I didn't tell the Emperor. Fortunately, the harvest of eggs was good, and the silk production was not affected. Now she wishes to extinguish the fire and freeze the eggs. This is unacceptable. We would suffer a great loss."

I glanced at the nursery. The fires shone through the window, and the swishing was heavy and steady again. I breathed out. I hoped she had caught me in time. "I am so sorry, my Noble Lady. I was stupid to do as she asked."

A worker whispered in the Noble Lady's ear, and she nodded, looking relieved. It seemed the damage to the silkworms was minimal, and the workers went back to the nursery.

"It's because of the upcoming polo game, isn't it?" She began to spin the wheel.

"What polo game?"

"You haven't heard? It's a competition between the Imperial Team and the Tibetans, a major event of the year. The whole court has been preparing for it."

Was that why the polo field was crowded and Pheasant had been busy? "Why the Tibetans?" Those haughty mountain horsemen were not known as our kingdom's allies.

"You've heard of the wars on the border, haven't you?"

I nodded.

"Well, the Emperor's garrisons lost the last five battles and are retreating to a fort near the Jade Gate in the north. But the Western Turks are not stopping. They have allied with Qu Wentai, King of Gaochang, a powerful tribe in the northwest. Once they attack, they will kill thousands. The Tibetan king, Srongtsan Gampo, grows restless too. The Emperor is worried he will join the Western Turks and Qu Wentai."

If the three powerful tribes joined forces, the map of our kingdom's western border would never be the same. The neighboring towns near Lake Kokonor, and even the towns near Dunhuang, would fall into our enemies' hands.

"I thought the trouble of the comet was over," I said.

"Over?" She shook her head. "The comet has given permission for everyone to doubt the Emperor. This is simply the beginning."

"So the Emperor invited the Tibetans for a friendly game?" The Tibetans were superior players of polo, I had learned, who had introduced the Persian game to our kingdom.

"He proposes a marriage to seal the alliance." She nodded. "The competition is to show the goodwill between us. All the important lords and vassals will attend, and"—she stopped in front of the spindle wheel—"by protocol, the Empress needs to be present. Because of Wende's death, the Emperor has requested I attend the reception where the vassals swear their fealty to the One Above All."

And Jewel and the Pure Lady had plotted to disgrace her so they could take the honored seat next to the Emperor.

"I—" I dropped my head in shame. "I am so sorry, my Noble Lady. I did not wish to dishonor you in any way."

"I understand, Mei." She sighed. "Fortunately, Silkworm Goddess bless us, nothing has happened to our babies. It's late. Go to your chamber, and go to sleep. Forget about what happened tonight."

I felt like crying in gratitude. "Why, my Noble Lady? I don't deserve your kindness."

She waved her hand, looking sad. "I grew up in the palace, Mei. I understand how life is, and all these years living under the Emperor…" Something in her voice tugged at my heart, and I remembered the story Father had told me. The Emperor, who was a duke then, had killed the Sui Emperor, the Noble Lady's father. "You are a courageous girl. You are different from them, better than them. I can see that. I would like to give you another chance."

I bowed deeply to her. "I will never forget your kindness, my Noble Lady. I shall leave at this instant..." I could not finish. The late Empress's crowns...

"I'll see you tomorrow, Mei." She began to spin the wheel.

I turned to the stone stairs. The light from the hall failed to reach there, and I could see a valley of darkness lurking under the stairs, reminding me of what awaited if I left now. I felt ashamed of asking the Noble Lady to help me retrieve the crowns. After all, she was a peaceful, honorable woman, and she had no reason to confront Jewel because of me. Yet she was my only hope. "My Noble Lady, what do you think Jewel and the Pure Lady will do when they learn they have failed?"

She stopped spinning, looking thoughtful.

"I do not mean to upset you, my Noble Lady." I walked to her. I needed an ally, and I had to persuade her to be on my side. "But you should know by now that the Pure Lady is a persistent woman. This time she plotted to extinguish the fire. Next time she will plan something else. She will not stop until she succeeds."

Holding the spindle wheel with two hands, she hesitated.

I seized my chance. "I have a suggestion, my Noble Lady. If you'll bear to listen to me."

"What do you suggest? Report to the Emperor?"

"Why not?"

"Do you think he will let me come off without blame? If I could, I would have done that last year. I know what kind of man he is. I might as well ask for my own disgrace."

"I am not asking you to explain, my Noble Lady. I would never put you in harm's way," I said softly. "I would explain to him."

She gazed at me. "You?"

I nodded.

"You're accountable for the loss of the crowns."

"I know."

"Are you not afraid?"

"I think the most important thing is I tell the truth," I said with conviction and hoped she would not hear the fear in my voice. "This is the best solution."

She did not speak. But her plump face looked serene, and I knew she was considering my suggestion.

"Yet I have one request, my Noble Lady." I held my hands tightly. "Would you agree to come with me?"

She looked pensive. Whether she would become my ally depended on her answer. If she agreed, I would have support in the court from that moment on. If not...

"I shall be glad to go with you." She nodded.

I let out a sigh of relief.

The Emperor swung his mallet, grimaced, and then swung again. A ball bounced in the courtyard in the early morning light. A servant ran in haste to catch it and put it near his feet. He cursed, touching his chest.

Nearly a year had passed since the assassination attempt. His wound had healed, and the physician Sun Simiao had suggested it was time to strengthen his *qi* and nurture his vital organs. He prescribed food recipes that contained fungus, such as ginseng, musk, and oyster, and some tonics mixed with *realgar*, rhinoceros horn, and deer velvet. The Emperor had taken short walks every day. Soon he would be able to ride a horse, and within a few months, even play polo.

But Daisy told me he had changed somehow. He slept fitfully at night and often fell asleep after drinking jugs of herbal wine. Several times, he slipped off his stool, and if it were not for Daisy and the other night attendants, he would have injured himself.

He also appeared bad tempered in the morning, and when he dined, he would be angry when served a lamb stew, even though he had asked for it in the first place. He had not officially resumed the bedding schedule yet, only summoning the Ladies, sometimes the Ladies-in-Waiting, and always, the conniving Jewel. But he was not interested in bedding them, Plum had whispered to me. One time he summoned Lady Virtue, but he let her sit on the floor, naked, for hours, without touching her, and then kicked her out, blaming her for staring at the mirror and not him.

He looked morose, his face hard and his lips pursed tight. He did not appear to notice me kneeling in the corner or how long I had waited. Perhaps that was a good thing. I ran through the phrases again in my mind and glanced at the Noble Lady, standing under the apricot tree. I was ready.

Then two figures scurried to hide behind a pillar in the corridor, one holding a fan and the other stroking a white cat in her arms.

Jewel and the Pure Lady.

The words in my mind turned to dust.

The mallet touched my chin. The Emperor stood before me. He was breathing faster than usual, his whiskers leaping up and down.

"I remember you," he finally said.

"The One Above All." I lowered my gaze to the front of his robe where a golden dragon, soaring in the clouds, glared at me. I remembered folding that robe. "Forgive my insolence. I should not have come—"

"What's the matter?"

"I can't locate the crowns that belonged to the late Empress. I asked the Noble Lady, who has kindly offered to help me, but it seems the items inside the chest were all misplaced."

"Were they taken or were they misplaced?"

I swallowed.

"Where were you?" The dragon seemed to come alive as his chest rose and fell.

"I...I was receiving the apples in the courtyard."

"Receiving apples?" he asked. "Not flirting with some groom?"

Was he talking about Pheasant? Did he know us? My hands trembled. But it was not possible. He could not know. We had been very careful, and I had not seen anyone around us when we had met.

"No, the One Above All. I would not dare."

He did not speak, and my heart pounded. Could it be possible that someone had reported to him that I was not in the wardrobe chamber all the time?

"The Noble Lady?" he said.

"Yes, the One Above All." The Noble Lady folded her hands across her abdomen and bowed.

"You know about this?"

"She is telling the truth, the One Above All."

"Have you searched?"

"Only in the wardrobe chamber, the One Above All."

"Search again, and ask the other ladies too. Report to me when you find them. You have my order."

"Yes, the One Above All."

"And let all know that if any mischief happens in the future, all of you Ladies will be held accountable. Now go."

The Noble Lady bowed deeply and left. I wanted to leave with her. I wanted to get out of there as fast as possible.

"I haven't dismissed you yet." His mallet pushed harder against my chin.

I stiffened. He wanted to punish me after all. "Yes, the One Above All."

"Have you seen a polo game?"

"What? Polo? No."

"Then get yourself ready. Join me at the competition." The mallet withdrew. The dragon turned around. Facing me, on the back of his robe, was another dragon coiled in a medallion. "Now, get me my morning audience robe."

Relief washing over me, I rose and hurried out of the court-yard. In the corridor, the Pure Lady stood alone and watched me, her eyes narrowing. Jewel was not there.

When I arrived at the wardrobe chamber, the Noble Lady beck-oned to me. "Look, Mei." She pointed at a chest near the wardrobe.

I ran to open it. Inside were the stolen crowns and hairpins. After counting everything to ensure all the items were in place, I sat on the chest and sighed. Tomorrow, I would ask for locks to be put on all the chests.

"Have you received all of the missing items, Mei?" the Noble Lady asked and tilted her head to listen as one of her maids whispered to her.

"Yes. She was fast." I eyed the maid, wondering what message she had brought.

"She should be."

"Do you think the Emperor knows it was Jewel?"

"He might. He is not a stranger to the household conflicts." She waved away her maid and fingered the pearls around her neck. "But I don't think we should worry about Most Adored right now. We shall talk about the honor he has bestowed upon you."

"Honor?"

"You didn't hear her?" She pointed at her maid, who had whispered to her. "He's given you the honor to sit next to him at the polo game. This was his way of rewarding you, I imagine."

"He ordered me to join him, but not sit next to him."

She smiled. "Had he not meant that, he'd not ask you to come to the game, and I assume you would sit with him as he receives the vassals' vow of allegiance after the game as well."

That was an ultimate honor I never ever had dreamed of. "But you are supposed to…"

"I suppose he has changed his mind."

A flood of sublime euphoria overwhelmed me. "But what about you? I'm sorry, my Noble Lady."

"Don't be." She strolled to the door. "This is the best outcome I could have imagined. The Pure Lady has her warning, and I keep my duty in the workshops. And the best of all—" She turned around to give me a meaningful stare. "You are part of the game now, my friend. Play well."

"I thank you, my Noble Lady." I gave her a deep bow, for she was the vital force that helped me spring forth and, because of her, a true ally, I slipped out of the door of treachery and leaped into a window of opportunity. I would never forget that. "I shall not disappoint you."

Yes. I would play well. I had to.

AD 642

the Sixteenth Year *of*

Emperor Taizong's Reign

of Peaceful Prospect

LATE SPRING

17

I SENSED A CHANGE IN THE AIR THAT AFTERNOON. VERY subtle. Like the wind shifting its direction. People glanced at me curiously when I passed and whispered among themselves, and later that day, some eunuchs came to my bedchamber to deliver a bolt of fine silk, a pair of exquisite silver figurines playing *pipa*, a pair of jade combs carved with deer, and four boxes of fresh fragrances: cassia, camphor, musk, and rose mallow. Soon a gaggle of seamstresses arrived to take my measurements.

"What an honor you have received! They are treating you as if you are already Most Adored," Plum said after the seamstresses left. She picked up the boxes of fragrances, eyes filled with envy. These were my bestowals from the Emperor, the token of his favor. No one could take them away from me, and I could do with them as I pleased.

"He has yet to summon me for the night, Plum."

"I know, but this is the beginning of his favor, Mei. More will come after you watch the polo game with him. You will have so many gifts that your eyes will get blurry."

I smiled. "Then I should do something to take care of my eyes, shouldn't I?" I handed her the boxes of musk and rose mallow. I knew they were her favorite.

Her eyes widened. "You're giving them to me?"

I nodded.

"You don't like them?"

"I do. Very much."

Plum looked at the boxes. "But how will you please the Emperor without divine fragrances?"

"I don't know." I smiled. I gave the jade combs to Daisy and the rest of the silk and fragrances to the other Talents. For a moment, the chamber was filled with joyful shouts and giggles. Watching their faces, pink with excitement, I knew I had done the right thing. The Emperor's favor had given me great joy, but it was more satisfying to see the others, the forgotten ones, happy.

I saved only the silver figurines. Then I went to look for Eunuch Ming, the eunuch who had conspired with Jewel to steal my summons.

I found him near the gate outside the Yeting Court. From behind a stone statue, I beckoned to him.

He glanced at the female guards near the gate and coughed. Finally, he walked to me. "I know you."

I did not want to frighten him away. "Let's forget about what happened between us." I gave him one of the silver figurines. "I'm not here to scold you."

"What is this?" He stared at the precious metal in his hand.

"The Emperor's gift," I said. "Now it's yours."

He clenched the figurine. "What do you want?"

"I hear you have connections." I watched him. Plum once said eunuchs were a different species, and she was right. Eunuch Ming was slippery like water, and his face changed faster than the light. He had been castrated when he was young and had served in the palace for a long time. I did not like him. He was ugly, with a face shaped like a goat's. And his eyes, beady and narrow, like a rat's, always seemed to look for gold. I would never trust a man like him, but I had no choice but to ask for his help.

"What connections?"

"Don't worry. I wish only to ask a small favor." I handed him a small pouch. It contained the other silver figurine from the Emperor's bestowals and some coppers I had saved from my monthly allowances. "Would you deliver this to my mother?"

Ming's eyes flicked from the figurine in his right hand to the pouch in his left. He looked hesitant, and I began to worry if my bribe was persuasive enough.

"I don't know where she lives."

He wanted more money. But I was not certain the Emperor would send me more bestowals, and my Talent's allowances would not be due until the last day of the month.

"I see," I said. "Perhaps you haven't heard who has the honor to sit next to the Emperor during the polo game."

He looked at me, a flicker of interest in his eyes. It was all over the Inner Court that I would replace the Noble Lady in the game, and I was confident he knew too.

"So?" I lifted my chin.

He scratched the corner of his mouth. "It'll probably take a few months."

"I can wait." I smiled.

◆ ◆

The polo field was more crowded than last time. Five groups of men poured buckets of sunflower oil on the ground, and behind them, another five groups of men pushed tables, legs up, to flatten the surface. Around the edge of the field, the Gold Bird Guards planted banners, while the eunuchs arranged platforms and benches in the audience section.

Behind the mulberry branches, I searched among the grooms who gathered with the horses. I could hear them talk about the fifteen dragon horses, the newest gifts from the snowy valleys of Kashmir. Pheasant was among them. He knelt over a piebald, his hand tracing something on its neck.

I tried to contain my excitement. What would Pheasant say when I told him about my great honor? Would he be happy for me?

A man with shaggy hair came to him. Pheasant pointed at the

characters branded on the horse's neck. "Inspector, this brand is wrong. This horse should be 'flying,' not 'wind.'"

The characters were the horses' identifications, as all the imperial horses must be branded according to their type, agility, speed, the origin of their birth, and the grade within their species, to discourage stealing. Sometimes, the number of the identifications were so many the horses would be covered with characters from their tails to their mouths. Pheasant had once complained to me about the cruel method of branding, but there was nothing he could do to change the practice.

But I was surprised. He could read. How had a low-born groom like him learned to read?

The inspector peered at the characters. "Good observation." He nodded. "Someone has made a mistake."

A shirtless rider with bulging muscles like rocks trotted close. Taizi. He pulled his horse to stop before Pheasant and slapped Pheasant's shoulder. Pheasant straightened. He did not bow or shout. He only smiled.

It was a smile I was familiar with. I could see his teeth shining in the sunlight. But something struck me then. I took out the jade silkworm and stared. The green color was rich, and the eyes of black onyx gleamed, blinding me.

Why had I never thought of that? A weaver would not possess something precious like this silkworm. Only a woman of high position would. And then suddenly many things, many things that had been whispered in my ear but I had not paused to think about, made sense.

He'd looked familiar when I had first met him. He knew every corner in the Inner Court. He was always beside Taizi. And his plain white robe. He wore that not because of his base birth, but to mourn his mother.

Pheasant was not Taizi's groom. He was his brother, the youngest of the late Empress's three sons, the Emperor's eighth living son, formally known as Li Zhi.

✦ ✦

"You didn't tell me who you are," I said to Pheasant when I came to the abandoned garden that night. I wished I had known his identity before. But when we were together, we were always alone. There was no way to know who he was from the way other people treated him, and because I kept him a secret, I had no way of learning who he was from anyone else.

"My brothers call me Pheasant." He stood beside me.

"But you know what I mean. You should have told me whose son you truly are." The night was chill. The wind bent the branches. They sprang back and forth, like my mind, swaying.

"I'm sorry, Mei. You caught me with Rain," he said. "It was not a good time to tell you. I forgot it later, when we were together."

Pheasant was not trying to deceive me, I understood. But that did not make the situation all right.

"Would it make a difference?" His face was sober, too sober. He almost looked grave. He was worried.

I did not know. Perhaps I would still go out and see him. We would still laugh and share tangerines together. But yes. In a way, it made a vast difference. He was the love of my heart, but also the son of the man whose bed I wished to share.

"He won't know. I promise you."

"But—"

He held my shoulders. "Don't worry, sweet face. He won't care. He never cares."

He drew me closer to a tree trunk and pushed me against it. His hand slipped under my robe. A cool touch, but sparked with passion. I shivered. It was the first time a man had touched me. The eunuch had scrubbed me, like laundry, and the Emperor had seen me unclothed but had not bothered to look at me.

"You're beautiful."

His voice sounded like a dream. I did not know what I was anymore. I was sixteen. I had grown taller. My body had begun to show a woman's shape: my waist was thinner, and my breasts had grown supple, like Jewel's. When I walked, I could feel the rhythm of my body, singing like grass greeting the spring wind, and deep within me, a murmur grew, enticing me, like a star glinting in the distant sky.

"But what if he finds out? What if someone finds out?" Pheasant's hands were hot, leaving a trail of fire on my naked skin.

"We'll be careful."

He beheld me like a flame eating the edge of a paper. Slowly but eagerly, he consumed me. My hair. My limbs. My breasts. My stomach. Until there was nothing left but my insides—like the center of the paper surrounded by flame—and slowly, they diminished and finally were charred with desire.

"Pheasant, Pheasant," I whispered. "You're ruining me."

"I will not do that." He pulled away, his hands at his sides. "I swear it."

I sighed, leaning toward him.

"Would you like to sit?" He pulled me down, and I slid to the ground, almost falling on him. He laughed and put his arm behind me as a cushion.

Leaning against the tree, I pulled his hand under my chin. He was the Emperor's eighth son. His chance of inheriting the throne was almost nonexistent. Perhaps that was a good thing? "I'm going to sit next to the Emperor during the polo game."

The thought had originally given me much joy, but now I did not know what to think.

"It's a great honor." He did not sound troubled.

I relaxed. "Are you going to the game?"

"Me? Of course. I won't miss it."

"You probably shouldn't go. I do not wish the Emperor to discover us." Pheasant, one of the younger princes, did not need to be present. Only the heir was required to be there.

He protested. "It's the grandest polo match. Everyone wants to go."

"Please."

"I swear I will not talk to you, and he won't suspect a thing."

"Pheasant."

He groaned. "Fine. I won't go. If this is what you wish."

My heart sweetened. As long as we stayed secret, no one would know. I tilted my head. The dark sky was a vast blanket stitched with silvery stars. "Where did the moon go?"

"Here." He touched my chest.

He tickled me. "I'm talking about the moon."

"You're my moon. The most brilliant and sweetest of all."

I smiled. "So you have heard the story?"

"Chang E?"

"That's it." I nodded, happy he was familiar with the folklore. Of course he would know. He must have learned as many classics as I did. The clouds drifted, and the silver bowl shone above the cobweb of shadowy tree branches. "That's why some people believe the moon brings tears."

"Well, tell me about her. I'd like to hear it from you."

"Once upon a time there was a young couple who lived near the foothills of a mountain. The husband, Hou Yi, was a respected archer, and the wife, Chang E, was the most beautiful girl of the village. Every day, Hou Yi went into the woods and hunted for food. He was a good man, and each time, he shared his game with his fellow villagers. The gods in Heaven heard of his good deeds and decided to reward him with a pill of immortality. Hou Yi came home and showed his wife the pill. Chang E was excited, for she had not told her husband that she was unhappy. She did not like living in the village. She wanted to see the palace where the gods live, to touch treasure and live in grandeur. She wanted to become immortal herself. So when Hou Yi was not looking, Chang E took the pill. And you know the ending."

"She flew to the moon."

"Where she found an empty, heavenly palace with a cinnamon tree and a black rabbit."

"She was foolish. No wonder she weeps by the cinnamon tree every night."

"Foolish?"

"What good is immortality if you live in loneliness?"

I stared at the moon. I could make out the shadow of a slender figure of a woman, a black rabbit in her lap, waiting under the tree. She must have been peering at her husband, or us.

If I were Chang E, would I choose the pleasure of a celestial palace or the humble home of Pheasant's arms?

"I can assure you she misses her parents," I said, thinking of Father and Mother.

"No more talking, sweet face." He lowered his head to kiss me.

I smiled and nestled my head in his arms, and there we sat in silence.

The wind swept the treetops, singing a soothing melody. Before us, a pair of rocks, almost as tall as the trees, stood peacefully in the night's shade. They faced each other, like a couple of lovers whispering.

It was still spring, and we had the whole summer to ourselves. But the windy days would arrive, followed by the frosty winter—it would come eventually—and we would not be able to meet in the deserted garden.

But until then…

18

A FEW DAYS LATER, I WENT TO THE POLO FIELD WITH THE
Noble Lady to watch the Imperial Team practice. The Emperor's
three older sons—Taizi; Prince Ke, the Noble Lady's son; and
Prince Yo, the Pure Lady's son—were said to be among the team.
I had heard so much about them, and I thought it was a good
opportunity to observe them.

Wearing my new gown the seamstresses had made, I stood
under a pine tree at the end of the field with the Noble Lady. The
Emperor was sitting on a bench placed on a high platform near the
edge of the field. Because he had not invited us to the practice, we
could not disturb him.

Shouting constantly, he appeared engrossed in the game. "Rout
the Tibetans!" He stood, waving his hands as the players dashed
across the field.

He wanted to win. If we lost, the Tibetans would lose respect
for him, and perhaps even make more demands than just a
Chinese princess.

And all the members of the team seemed to know the high
stakes, and they looked eager to please him. Mallets raised high
above their heads, they galloped across the field, competing
against one another.

Taizi was the most imposing figure of all. Dressed in a single loincloth and nothing else, he perched on top of his mount like a statue. He was undoubtedly the most powerful player, the ball spinning at high speed each time he struck it. His hits were hard and deadly, but his horse ran slowly, burdened by the prince's weight. After two chukkas, his mount panted foam, and he had to switch horses.

Prince Ke was the opposite image of the heir. One year younger, he possessed the delicate features of a young maiden. He had pale skin, scarlet lips, rosy cheeks, and the willowy waist of a dancer. I feared for his life each time the heir roared past him, but he was resilient, like the willow. I hoped, for his mother's sake, he would play a good game and impress the Emperor.

Prince Yo bore no resemblance to either of his half brothers. His suntanned face was covered with layers of dust, and his slanted eyes were alert like a hound's. But the most prominent feature on his face was his eyebrows. Long and thick, they looked as if a calligrapher had lost control when he drew them.

He looked angry and impatient, and he played polo like someone who was racing against time. Quickly and precisely, he ran through the field like an unsheathed sword.

They all had much at stake. If Taizi disappointed the Emperor, he might be forced to leave the court again, or face something worse. If Prince Yo scored more, he would greatly please the Emperor, and his mother, the Pure Lady, would rise with him. The same went for Prince Ke.

"Do you think we will win?" I asked the Noble Lady.

"I just hope Ke will be safe." The lady's gaze followed her son, who spurted forward and struck the ball but missed. "Polo is a dangerous game."

I did not speak, but I thought she would have wished more than that.

"I would like to tell you, the workshops are no longer my responsibility," she said. "The Emperor ordered the Pure Lady to replace me."

Surprised, I turned to her. Had Jewel whispered something in his ear? "He should not have done that."

Prince Ke had another reason to win the game—to compel the Emperor to reconsider his mother's duty in the workshops.

The Noble Lady shook her head. "Never question him, Mei, for your own sake, and remember that we shall always obey him and respect his decision, no matter what it is."

"But—"

"Look." She turned, and I followed her gaze. Four female porters, carrying a sedan chair, were heading toward the Emperor. Sitting on the chair was an obese scholar with massive girth that seemed to spill onto the porters.

It was Prince Wei, Taizi's younger brother. He was only nineteen but larger than the four women combined. His enormous weight apparently took a toll on the porters, who doubled over, their faces raining perspiration. But he seemed oblivious. Holding a calligraphy brush, he gestured as though composing an important poem in the air.

"And that's Prince Zhi," the Noble Lady said, looking behind the porters.

My body tensed, but I kept still. Pheasant was holding the reins of a piebald horse, his head turning toward the men on the polo field. He cupped his free hand around his mouth and shouted something, and Taizi waved his mallet as a response. Grinning, Pheasant went to the Emperor, who gestured for him to sit beside him. They lowered their heads together, nodding, pointing at the men on the field, and then both raised their heads, laughing.

"He's his favorite," the Noble Lady said.

"Prince Zhi?"

"Yes," she said. "The Emperor gave him the nickname Pheasant when they went out hunting together. The Emperor saw a large pheasant with a magnificent tussock of tail feathers that none of them had seen before. Everyone vowed to shoot it and give it to the Emperor as a gift. But Prince Zhi stopped them. He said to leave the bird alone. The bird would be happier to be with its family in the wild, he said. The Emperor was touched by his kindness. He praised him and has called him Pheasant ever since. He was only five at the time."

What a beautiful story. My heart sweetened.

"But later, the Emperor told me something else. Prince Zhi had too much love, he said. A ruler does not rule the kingdom by love."

I was quiet. But perhaps it did not matter. Pheasant did not have a chance to ascend to the throne anyway.

"Here he comes." She waved at her son, who dismounted and walked to her. The practice was over. "I shall go." The sunlight gleamed on her golden headdress. She turned to face me. "I'm happy for you, Mei. The game is your chance. When everyone sees you next to the Emperor, you will be luminous, rising like a new moon in this court."

I bowed. "I thank you. I shall do my best."

The Noble Lady smiled and left to meet Prince Ke. Ever an affectionate mother, she kissed her son's forehead and smoothed his robe.

I stood alone under the tree, chewing her words. She was right. My fate would change after the game.

Her servants came to me to ask their leave. Deeply, they bowed. I nodded, acknowledged them, and left as well, but I was surprised by their obsequious manner. Nearby, all the servants, some I did not know, turned and dipped their heads to pay me respect.

I held my long sleeves tightly in my hands.

I was eager for the game to start.

When I returned to my bedchamber that night, I took out Father's mortuary tablet, which was tucked under my clothes. I wished I could tell him of my progress in the court, and I promised him, as soon as I could, I would ask the Emperor to return our family's fortune to us.

I thought of the day Father died and how my life had changed.

Those images swirled in my mind again: the yellow, bulbous eyes, the whirling leaves, and the desperate cries echoing in the sky. "Mei, Mei!"

I could hear it was Father calling my name, and there, I sensed it too, a bright orange figure, silent and sinister, looming a few feet beside me. What was it? I wanted to see, I wanted to know, but my neck was stiff, and I could not turn. And suddenly, a gust of wind swept around me, and all the memories vanished. I held the tablet tight. Mother had told me Father fell off a cliff and died. I did not believe it. Something else must have happened.

What really happened to him? Why could I not remember?

AD 642

the Sixteenth Year *of*

Emperor Taizong's Reign

of Peaceful Prospect

SUMMER

19

THE MUSIC OF DRUMS, FIFES, AND FLUTES SWELLED, AND A scarlet ball vaulted into the sky. Along the edge of the polo field, the flag bearers waved their flags frantically. Men shouted from the benches. Horses whinnied, their hooves pounding across the vast field. The competition between the Chinese Imperial Team and the Tibetan Team raged on.

I sat next to the Emperor on a raised platform, a black veil draped over my face. I wore a lavishly embroidered red gown suitable for an empress, and even though I could not see myself, I knew I looked like one.

I felt like one too, in fact. After all, today would be most marvelous and memorable. All I had to do was watch the game, entertain the Emperor, and then after the game, I would go to the banquet hall with the Emperor as he accepted the vassals' vow of allegiance. They would bow to me too, and I would greet them, gracefully and magnificently. And then, as the Noble Lady had said, I would become the rising moon of the palace. Everyone would know I was in favor, and then the Emperor would love me, keeping me by his side, and soon I would wear the crown of Most Adored, and Jewel would don the hat of Most Abhorred. And Mother... I would be able to take care of her. I would ask the Emperor to give our house back and also to bestow many riches on her...

I tried not to look at Jewel, who was sitting on a bench near the platform. She was veiled as well, but I could feel the sting of her glare. Around her, arranged in the law of *feng shui* and the order of seniority, were the Noble Lady, who smiled at me kindly, the Pure Lady, holding her cat, Lady Obedience, and Lady Virtue, who gazed into the mirror held by her maid. I was relieved she was more interested in her looks than in me, but on the other side of the platform, some high-ranking ministers were eyeing me appraisingly, and behind them, the Emperor's vassals—the chieftains of various tribes on the northern border—shouted something in my direction. I wondered if they were talking about me too.

"Wine." The Emperor knocked on the table.

"Yes, the One Above All." Holding my wide sleeves back with my left hand, I poured the wine from the jug. He was a different person today, content and warm, like a wise and benevolent ruler. It seemed each time I met him, he looked different.

"Your thoughts about the game?"

I hesitated. I had not paid much attention to the game. The veil obscured my view, and every time the horses sped across the field, a cloud of yellow dust blanketed me. But I should not tell him that.

"I've never seen anything like it," I said.

He nodded, looking happy with my answer. "I shall give you a reward if you guess who will win."

That was an unexpected surprise. I lifted the veil to get a clear view of the field. "Let me see—"

A deafening roar shook the field. Taizi, in his usual loincloth, sped up to pass three horses and struck the ball. He missed the net. Another rider in a black tunic with a red belt, Prince Yo, intercepted the ball. He struck. The ball dipped into the net; the whole field roared.

The Emperor shot to his feet. "Well done!"

I applauded too, reluctantly, and glanced at the Noble Lady. She looked worried, gazing at her son at the other side of the field, who swung his mallet idly. But the Pure Lady smiled wickedly and stroked her cat.

"So, have you picked a winner?" The Emperor stroked his whiskers.

"I daresay, the One Above All, the Tibetans will be routed."

"Are you willing to bet on that, Talent?" the Duke said, leaning forward from his bench.

I did not like him interrupting us; I did not like him at all. He was the one who had interrogated me and nearly had me beaten for intruding into the Altar House. I would like to have glared at his long face and told him to go away. But he was the Duke, and I had to show respect. "Why, I thought our Grand Duke should devote himself to a virtue." Rather than the vice of gambling.

"Right now, my virtue is to assure proper attention is devoted to the game." He snorted. "A maiden like you probably doesn't even care for the scores."

"This is the third chukka," the Emperor's uncle said near us. I was not certain if he was trying to help me or not. "We won the first two. One more, and we will win."

"I'm asking the maiden," the Duke said curtly. The Uncle's face turned red; he looked insulted. It was disrespectful for the Duke to speak to him in such a manner.

"What bet do you have in mind, Wuji?" the Emperor asked, using the Duke's given name.

"If your Talent wins, the One Above All will grant her any reward, and I will give up my house and present it to her. If she loses"—the Duke smirked—"she'll lose her title of Talent."

Who cared about his den filled with aristocratic filth? I would rather keep my newly earned title and stay out of it. I lowered my head to rearrange the goblets on the table.

"It looks like your Talent is rather frightened." The Duke's tone was condescending and laced with contempt.

I raised my chin. "I'm not frightened."

"A bet then?"

I could not reply. The Emperor tilted his head toward me. I should not disappoint him. Yet to risk my title? I took a deep breath, determined to decline, when I saw the Emperor smile. Not at me, but at someone among the ladies on the bench. Jewel stood up and bowed.

"It's a bet," I said.

"Done!" The Duke slammed the platform with his fist.

"I shall be glad to offer my Talent a reward." The Emperor fingered his whiskers. "You're going to lose, Wuji."

It was too late to rescind it. I faced the field, biting my lip. Taizi dashed toward the ball. A Tibetan vanguard clicked his tongue, making a loud *di-di-di* noise, but he was too late. Taizi snatched the ball with the crescent top of his mallet and scored.

"Third chukka score: Imperial Team 4, the Tibetans 3," someone shouted.

I wiped the perspiration off my forehead. One more point, and the Imperial Team would win the third chukka. And the game. Then I could ask any reward from the Emperor and even keep the Duke's residence. Drink to that, Duke.

"You see," the Emperor said. "My Talent has foresight to match her courage."

I had just smiled when a Tibetan got the ball. He struck. The ball shot into the air and bounced on the field. The vanguard raced to it and directed it to the net. Fortunately, he missed, but another Tibetan horseman dashed to it and struck. He scored.

My heart sank. It was a draw.

The horses galloped again, and mallets crossed in the air. Prince Ke steered his steed toward the ball, but Prince Yo slid his mallet under the horse's belly, and the ball flew. Prince Ke forged ahead. He was about to touch the ball when Prince Yo's mallet appeared, aiming at his head. I gasped and stood up. If Prince Yo wounded Prince Ke, we would lose a valuable player. I could not imagine why Prince Yo would take such a big risk. Around me murmurs arose, but when I raised my head at the field again, the situation had changed. Prince Ke withdrew to the back, and a Tibetan stole the ball and scored. They won the third chukka.

The score: Imperial 2—Tibetan 1.

My throat was dry. I should not have gotten lured into the bet. The Duke was evil. Had he allied with Jewel to dishonor me?

"A break," the Emperor ordered.

I sighed inwardly but felt no relief.

"Heavenly Khan," one of the Emperor's vassals, a chieftain, shouted at the Emperor from his bench, his mouth full of meat. "The Tibetans are no match for your men." He grabbed a wine pot and poured the wine directly into his mouth. "Teach them a lesson! Kick them back to Tibet!"

Near him, another chieftain, whose eyes had been darting constantly from the Emperor to the ministers, said, "Of course our Heavenly Khan will win, my dear khan."

Of all the spectators, the Emperor's vassals did not fit in with us. They wore knee-length pants, exposing a good portion of their hairy legs, and they had not bothered to wear hats.

"Khan of Tuyuhun, Khan of Eastern Turks." The Emperor beckoned at them and the other chieftains close to him. "I hear you made inquiries about my health. Here, I invite you and all my vassals to see I, your Heavenly Khan, can still rip apart whoever stands in my way."

I filled the Emperor's goblet with wine. I wondered why he had brought up the subject of his health; after all, it had been a year since the assassination attempt. Some shouts came from the field. I raised my head. The Tibetans broke into a strange dance to celebrate their gain, their shoulders tipping to one side and their legs swinging high. Near them, Taizi kicked in the stirrups, shouting, "You putrid fly eaters! Stop singing like women!"

"We're honored to see our Heavenly Khan strong as a lion. This is a great victory to us all, and we shall return home with joy," the chieftain with quick eyes, Khan of Tuyuhun, said.

"But I can't let my vassals return empty-handed." The Emperor drained his goblet. "I have a special present for you all." He pointed to a chest behind me. It was rather large, the size of a writing table, wrapped with a piece of black cloth. "It's in the box."

I heard whimpering from inside. Perhaps it was a precious animal, but it was strange the Emperor would bring it to the polo field.

"And I shall show you, all of you"—he struck the table with his fist, suddenly looking murderous—"what is a traitor's fate."

No one dared to speak. The chieftains lowered their heads and returned to their benches, looking smaller than before.

The drums began to beat urgently on the field. The fourth chukka had started.

I turned to the field, watching every strike of the mallets and every prancing of the horses with great concentration. Halfway through the chukka, Taizi broke the Tibetans' defense and seized the ball. Before he struck it, he switched the mallet to his left hand and shook his right hand.

Taizi was injured.

My heart wrenched in panic.

Taizi missed two more strikes, and the Imperial Team slowed. The Tibetans seized the chance and tore through Taizi's side of line like a spear. The Imperial Team lost the fourth chukka.

The Duke leered. "Imperial 2, Tibetans 2."

"Break!" the Emperor shouted.

I poured him more wine, but I could barely see the liquid or hear what he said to his vassals and ministers. On the field, Taizi was shouting again, this time to Prince Yo and the other imperial players, who laid their mallets across their laps and lowered their heads.

A bitter taste lingered on my tongue. My bet was doomed.

The fifth chukka—my last opportunity! The crowd shouted, and the sound of the drums deafened. I could barely breathe. My eyes darted here and there. Each time a Tibetan scored, the Duke hit his fist against his palm in victory. I wanted to punch him.

Taizi held the ball again. Hooves pounding, he sailed through the Tibetan defense and struck the ball. It soared in the air, and he forged ahead to add a decisive hit. But the Tibetan vanguard broke through the right wing from nowhere. Their steeds pranced as they met muzzle to muzzle. Cursing, Taizi yanked his horse to the left, where another Imperial player galloped forward and plowed into him with a thunderous crash.

I stood up, shocked. Screams pierced my ears. People rushed toward the field. But I could not see anything through the cloud of dust.

"He's under the horse!" someone yelled.

"He's dead!" another voice cried out. "He's dead!"

Taizi was dead? I raced to the field and forced my way through the crowd. Then I saw him. A man lay on the ground; the imprint of a hoof dented his chest. Blood and dirt plastered his face, while his head was cracked opened like a shattered watermelon.

It was not Taizi, but all the same, my stomach churned. The polo match had been a gamble for me, but it had been a battle for that man's life.

"What the hell are you all standing here for?" Taizi bawled, leaning against a brown horse. "Drummers! Restart the game! I shall send the Tibetans home with their heads between their legs."

"Why did you turn left?" Prince Yo, his face red, dove toward the heir and pummeled his chest.

"My horse was startled." Taizi blocked another blow.

"That was not part of our strategy." Prince Yo's thick eyebrows knotted tightly. A fire of resentment burned on his face. "You ruined the game. You ruined everything, you idiot."

"Swine! You think you're better than me?" Taizi cursed.

"What's wrong with you? Have you lost your mind? Where is your brain? Is it sitting on your cock?"

"Fuck," Taizi spat. "Stupid horseshit. Fuck." He lurched forward as though to punch Prince Yo but collapsed on the ground. My heart sank. The heir's leg was broken.

"Get them out of here. Both of them!" the Emperor ordered.

Several ministers raced to take Prince Yo aside, and the Duke and other guards carried Taizi, still fighting, out of the field.

"Now, let me see..." The Emperor turned to look at the net at the end of the field.

I glanced at him in surprise. Taizi had broken his leg, but the Emperor did not spare him a glance. The rumor of him deposing the heir must have been true.

"Shall we cancel the game, my Heavenly Khan?" the Tibetan ambassador asked.

I was glad to hear that, and the Captain, who had patrolled the grounds sullenly, ordered to remove the carcass of the horse.

"No, the game must continue." The Emperor rolled up his sleeve. "I will take my son's place. When you go home, tell your king a wager is a wager."

Protests instantly rose from the ministers. The Emperor was still recovering, and it was unwise for him to lead the team on a polo field.

"Father." Prince Ke, his eyes timid, glanced at his mother, who nodded slightly, and cleared his throat. "I can replace the heir. I know how to play Taizi's position."

The Emperor did not seem to hear him. "Anyone else?"

"Let me try." A clear, feminine voice came from beside me. I had not turned when Jewel, wearing her veiled hat, sauntered to my side.

What was she doing? A noble lady, even if permitted to play the sport, did not mingle with a group of foreign men.

But nobody objected. Then a wave of laughter spread.

"Go do your needlework. Only wild women from the steppes fight with men," the Emperor said.

I did not like it. He should have been angry at her interruption, but he was not. Instead, he looked amused.

Jewel put her left hand on her waist and thrust out her hip to make a pretty show of her womanly figure. "The One Above All, I do have my reasons. Please allow me to explain. Legend says that when you were ten years old, the Western Turks raided a northern village. You asked to fight the raiders, but your father's troops told you to stay in the camp. Instead, you led your men, attacked the enemies, and the rest is history." She smiled. "Isn't it so that women, like young boys, may surprise others with what they can do?"

I frowned. It was a clever speech of flattery, but the Emperor would not fall for it.

But he laughed. "What do you want? I shall grant you any wish other than this," he said.

I could not believe what I had heard. Any wish?

Jewel drew her round fan from her girdle and fanned herself, despite the morning breeze. "Why, the One Above All, my wishes? I wish I had one. I have the adoration of my Emperor. I am the envy of all women. *I* am the wish all women dream of." She walked past me. "Is there any wish that would make me happier? Truly, are there any women here, ladies or maids, with titles or without, luckier than me?"

Certainly, no woman in the kingdom could have been more shameless than her.

The Emperor laughed again, his whiskers shaking. It was terrible to see him like that. "From now on, I pronounce you the Lady-in-Waiting, a third-degree lady. Now, go…"

Shock and disbelief overwhelmed me. I could not hear the rest of his words. Jewel had stolen my moment again, and perhaps my reward. That title must have been what the Emperor had had in mind for me.

I raised my head and met the Noble Lady's gaze. The sense of defeat filled the space between us. I dropped my head, unable to face her.

"Now, if you have objections to me playing, may I request the khans finish the game?" The Emperor faced his vassals, who looked at one another in surprise. They were not familiar with the sport, I could tell. But they stood, pulling up their sleeves.

The drums beat again, and the men raced to the field. But the signs of their defeat were everywhere, the Khan of Tuyuhun lost his mallet the moment he struck, and the Khan of the Eastern Turks gave the ball to the Tibetans.

The Tibetan players scored. Again and again.

Everything was over. First Jewel's trickery, and now the loss of my title.

"My vassals, come," the Emperor called out. "I do hope you have entertained yourself. Now I have a surprise for you. You all are aware that a crime was plotted against me last year. Against me! Your Heavenly Khan and the Emperor of Great China!" he bellowed, his face dark, and his forefinger stabbing his chest. "Today, I will show you the fate of a traitor if anyone else dares to plan such an abomination!"

He dropped his hand, and behind me, the Duke pulled aside the veil covering the box. Inside crouched a girl with a slight frame like a monkey. Wearing a sheer white skirt and a triangular red bandeau, she raised her face, and the bright sunlight illuminated her green eyes.

She could not have been older than me—probably younger, even.

I could not understand why the Emperor said she would have the fate of a traitor. She looked innocent, and I could not imagine how she had betrayed him.

"Now I command you all to look at this slave, and look closely. Remember her face, and never forget her fate, for if you, any of you, dare betray me, you shall suffer the same death"—the Emperor's voice grew louder—"the death under the hooves of horses!"

I was stunned, and around me, the ministers, the vassals, and the ladies looked shocked as well, their mouths open wide, their eyes glittering with fear. But I understood what the Emperor was doing. I had heard enough stories from Father to know that emperors often showed the fate of one person in order to warn the others. It was called "killing a hen in order to frighten the monkeys."

"Take her!"

A guard pulled the girl out, threw her on his back, and raced to the field. The bystanders rushed to the side, clearing a path for him. He reached the edge and dropped the girl before the horses and the players. A horn blew, and the drummers began to drum. The horses pranced, and the players raised their mallets.

They sped across the field. Behind them the clotted turf swarmed like hungry flies. So fast the horses galloped toward the slight figure. Closer. And closer...

A scream. Long, piercing, and heartrending.

But the drumming grew louder and louder. *Boom. Boom. Boom.* The fifes joined. Wailing, long and sharp. And the horse hooves pounded. *Clop. Clop. Clop.*

Something loud cracked, like a hard object suddenly splitting open, and the shriek rose even higher, rattling the platform I was standing on, shaking my black veil, shaking the sleeves of my new gown, and through the maze of the yellow clouds, I could see black speckles—perhaps turf, or blood, or bits of broken bones—flying into the air like useless, deflated polo balls, and plummeted like birds pierced with arrows.

Then all the sounds died.

I retched. And retched again.

Sometime later, the Tibetans danced on the field. They had won. The Emperor walked to them, followed by the ministers. Their heads lowered, the ministers looked grim, and hard as they tried, they could not hide the fear on their faces.

It was time for the feast. The men exited the field, heading to the banquet hall. The Ladies and Jewel left as well. I lowered my head and lined up behind the Talents. When I passed the bloody smudge in the field, I could not help but look away, and there I caught the sight of the Emperor ahead of the procession. He seemed benevolent, smiling, but his gaze no longer warmed me; instead, it stabbed me like an icicle, and long after his disappearance, the iciness chilled my heart.

20

I WAS NOT REQUESTED TO ATTEND THE BANQUET AFTER
the polo game. Jewel took my place, sitting next to the Emperor
and receiving the vassals' fealty. I lingered in the courtyard outside,
listening to the people feasting and drinking.

I returned to my bedchamber alone.

In the days after, I settled back into my routine. The servants
passed me without greeting. The Beauties and Graces walked by
me without turning their heads. Occasionally, some people peered
at me with contemptuous smiles.

There was no meat in my meals. I ladled the bland yellow bean
soup, ate a shallow bowl of millet porridge, and chewed pickled
radish. I could not taste anything.

News came to me that the Emperor had arranged a marriage
between a princess and the Tibetan king Srongtsan Gampo after
the polo game, and the vassals also appeared obedient. They ral-
lied behind the Emperor as he launched an attack against the King
of Gaochang, while the Tibetan king's army cut off the Western
Turks as they tried to aid their ally. The King of Gaochang died
on the battlefield, the Western Turks retreated, and the border
appeared to be quiet again.

Plum told me the girl who was sacrificed had belonged to the
Rourou tribe from the northwest region. She had been captured as

a child, fed only milk, and thus considered pure. Because she also had rare green eyes and pale skin, she made a much prized pleasure toy whom the Emperor kept for years. But the fact that he would discard her like that frightened me.

I had never before felt like that, fear seeping into my skin and drilling into my bones. What if the Emperor wanted to throw me under the horse's hooves? I thought of Mother, who would not know what had happened to me. She would still call for me, not knowing I could not hear, not knowing my ears rotted under the ground. Or perhaps, she would raise her head, her eyes filled with love, searching for me, unaware that my hands no longer felt the breeze and my bones had turned to dust.

Or worse, he would make my family, Mother or Big Sister, suffer such a death too.

I tried not to think like that. But the saying was right: "Accompanying an emperor is like accompanying a tiger." I never wanted to be near him again.

And yet, how could I stay away? My family, and their future, depended on me.

◆ ◆

"You're late." Under the starlit sky, Pheasant appeared, treading on the path of wild grass near the pavilion.

"You're early." I smiled.

How good it was to see him. The night garden felt like a home, with the glittering sky for the ceiling, the bushes our rug, and the dilapidated pavilion our bed. Pheasant lit up the place like a heart-warming hearth fire. He was the walls of my sanctuary, the food for my eyes, the scent of a home. He was everything. I wanted to stay there, with him, for eternity.

"I've been thinking of you." He pulled me close in his arms. "What a horrifying game."

"Were you there?"

"At a distance. He wasn't always like this, I hope you know. He changed after my mother's death."

We went to sit on the low windowsill of the pavilion. "Did he love your mother?" Many people had said they loved each other, and Empress Wende was a wise woman, a subject of court ministers' praises.

He shook his head. "They had disagreements."

"About what?"

Pheasant swallowed. "My mother did not agree with some things he did to his brothers... I don't know what happened, but Mother mentioned them sometimes. She never said anything to his face, however...but when he was not around, she would let us play in yurts and ask us to put on Turkic clothing, and she would sing us Turkic songs. She believed my father owed this kingdom to her."

Empress Wende was a prominent descendant of a Xiongnu tribe, one of the nomads in the north. She was perhaps right that the Emperor owed his kingdom to her. But she was still the Empress of our kingdom. To openly declare and worship her own heritage was scandalous and would certainly have undermined the Emperor's rule over the Han people. But the Emperor's own mother, in fact, was also a member of a nomadic tribe, although the Emperor did not allow anyone to mention it.

"Father also kept too many concubines. Mother was not happy with that either, and there was one particular concubine... She did not like the way he treated her... But Mother died..."

His voice dropped lower, and I changed the subject. "Taizi's leg was broken during the game. How is he doing?"

"He will be fine. Can't stand. The physicians ordered him to lie in bed. He is angry, threatening to wring their necks when he's well."

"He certainly is capable of doing that."

"He's a good man." His voice was guarded. "Whatever you've heard about him is not true."

Pheasant did not understand I was jesting. "What are you saying?"

"Forget what I just said. I know you don't mean it. I'm tired of people's gossip, that's all. There are people who do not wish

Taizi to be the emperor. They spread rumors and say he is unfit for a ruler."

"I heard he's a champion wrestler?"

"The best kind. No one is better than he."

I was quiet for a moment. "What do people say about him?"

"Many things. Some hold it against him that he did what my mother liked, acting like a Turk."

I understood why Pheasant felt the need to protect him. Of course, the heir of the kingdom must remember whom he would rule in the future. "Who is against him?" Pheasant did not look like he wanted to talk about it, so I said, "You trust me, don't you, Pheasant?"

"It's my great uncle. He delivered a speech in the Audience Hall, saying my brother had night parties in a yurt, doing Turkic funeral dances. He said he was out of control, and there are also the other princes…"

Prince Yo. I touched Pheasant's hand. "They cannot harm him. He is the heir, your brother. No one can change that."

Pheasant breathed out. "I know. That's what I have been telling myself. I don't like those gossips at all. Why do people fuss about what my brother does and what he likes? He's the best man I know! But I'm glad I talked to you, Mei. I'm glad."

I was relieved. Together we stood and listened to the song of our heartbeats. The night was too short, and I did not wish it to end.

Near the hour of midnight, we agreed on when to meet again and also agreed on our secret signal—a small rock. When the rock leaned against the wall, we would see each other; when it lay flat on the ground, it meant one of us could not come that night. Then I left first.

I climbed up the wall and landed on the other side of the garden. Carefully, I dusted the dirt off my skirt. I had gotten better at flipping over the wall but still needed to be careful to keep my skirt clean, or when I returned to my bedchamber, people might ask what had stained it.

Leaves rustled nearby, and I raised my head.

A hooded shadow dashed down the narrow path near the grove. I froze.

"Who's there?"

I ran after it, but the shadow had already disappeared. Blood rushed to my head. Someone was spying on Pheasant and me.

✦ ✦

At the end of the month, I did not receive my Talent's allowance.

I asked the distribution eunuch what happened, and he replied that Most Adored had decided to keep it for me. When I asked Jewel, she smiled and shook her head.

I knew what was going on. Jewel, knowing I had lost my bet, must have realized it was an opportunity to strip me of my title. I felt sick. The Emperor had not officially denounced me, and I had hoped he would forget about it. After all, he had more important things to do than deal with a low-ranking concubine. But Jewel would not let it go.

I went to visit the Noble Lady. She was examining a bolt of silk the Imperial Silkworm Workshops had delivered to her.

"If I were you, Mei, I would make sure Most Adored could not take what belongs to me," she said after I told her my problem.

"What do you suggest I do?"

She dismissed her maids. "Enchant him. Keep his eyes on you. Then his ears will turn to you too, and Jewel won't have her play."

She wanted me to seduce him, but I could still hear the slave's scream in my ears, and besides, I did not know how.

"You are young and beautiful. He will like you." The Noble Lady smiled. "You will succeed."

I felt my cheeks warm. "Well…"

"I shall do anything I could to help you, Mei." She picked up a piece of yellow cloth and fingered the silk, feeling its texture. "I hope you know that."

"I know…my lady."

She sighed. "He has long lost interest in me. He no longer

summons me for the night. The last time I was in his bedchamber was five years ago. I do not know what he likes now." She smoothed the silk imprinted with medallions. "And I heard he has changed since he was wounded."

"Changed?"

Her plump cheeks grew pink. "Well, I heard he summoned three women last week, all dancers. You know Lady Obedience? She was there, and they performed…indecently. He did things to them… Never mind that now. But he was still angry, kicking them out without bedding them."

"Why?" The Noble Lady kept clearing her throat, looking embarrassed. I felt my face heating up as well. I liked her, but I was not yet accustomed to discussing such intimate details with her. Yet I needed to know.

"You're too young, Mei. You'll understand better when you're older."

"I wish to know, my Noble Lady. Is something happening to the Emperor?"

"I suppose you can say that… He has difficulties to do his duty, but really, he is not to be blamed. He was rather a vigorous man when he was young, a skillful man good at plucking flowers," she said, using a euphemism. "He fathered thirteen sons—although three died in infancy. But even an old lion falters and loses his appetite, and his claws, which always sank into whomever he wanted, wherever he wanted, have lost their sharpness."

Now I understood. "Then why does he still summon us? And the new Selects every year?"

"Because even if a lion cannot eat, it doesn't mean it doesn't wish to."

"What about Jewel?" He still summoned her, I heard, and she was Most Adored and a Lady-in-Waiting.

"I don't know, but she seems to know many tricks. I hear she keeps some white horses' penises steeped in wine and honey in a jar. I wish I knew more…" She rubbed her chest, her plump face growing pink again. "You do wish to keep your title, don't you?"

I thought of Mother. She must have received the silver figurine from Eunuch Ming, and she would be very pleased. I could not stop my quest to win the Emperor's favor. I had to do more to take care of her. "Yes."

"Then you need to win him back."

"I shall think about it." But I hesitated. I wished I had more courage to tell the Noble Lady I did not know the secrets of the bedroom affair, but she already looked embarrassed.

"And, when you decide to do so, you will need to be summoned."

Of course, that would be another obstacle I had to solve. I watched her measure the fabrics and divide them into different piles that would be distributed to the other Ladies. I liked the silk's pattern and its color, and I would like to have some of it. But as a Talent, I received only leftover silk from last year.

I bid her good day and turned to leave.

"Wait." The Noble Lady went to a chest near her dresser, and when she returned, there was a scroll tied with a red silk ribbon in her hands. "Here." She placed it in my hands, her face reddening like ripened autumn apples. "I don't know if you have seen this or not… Some ladies here have them, I hear… Anyway, I am an old woman. I do not need this anymore. You are still young…"

The scroll was light, almost transparent. I could see the colors, red and black, through the fine silk. "What is it?"

"Paintings…" She cleared her throat.

"What kind of paintings?"

"You will know. Go read it in your bedchamber. Not here." She waved, turning away, and I could see how embarrassed she was. "Read it when you're alone."

The bedroom affair! It must be. "I—"

"Go. Go now."

She waved again, and I stumbled out, blushing. In the corridor, her maids were embroidering something, and I hid the scroll in my sleeve, lowered my head, and passed them without speaking.

As soon as I left the Quarters, I regretted taking the scroll. I should not have taken it. I would never have the courage to stand before the Emperor again. He had treated me like a maid the first time, and this time, he would perhaps kick me like a slave.

But I was also curious. What did those paintings look like? I wished to see them and understand the true meaning of the bedding affair. After all, I was sixteen years old, and many women my age had already borne two or three children.

I picked up my pace, eager to get to my bedchamber.

◆ ◆

By the time I reached my bedchamber, it was supper time. The court bustled with servants carrying trays. I stepped aside to let the carriers pass as they came behind me. The fragrance of the meal wafted past me, and I inhaled deeply. Could I have some meat in my bowl tonight? A succulent duck quarter glazed with honey or a piece of pork belly seasoned with five spices? But I knew what I would see: tofu blocks, bamboo shoots, and a spare amount of rice, most likely. The food could barely fill me, and I was always hungry.

Plum was talking with the other Talents around the table. "And now, she says it is just a pickled radish that will not stand, even if you use chopsticks," Plum said, and the girls covered their mouths, giggling.

"What are you talking about?" I sat near her, tucking my feet under me. The scroll's bamboo spine rubbed against my arm, and suddenly, I was conscious of the secret in my pocket. I cleared my throat.

"Lady Obedience," Plum said, and the Talents burst out laughing again. "She went to see the Emperor last night."

"Oh." I looked down at my tray—barley soup, fried bean curds with mushrooms, and some rice. Just as I had expected. "What are you laughing about?"

"You did not hear us?" Plum asked.

"I did." I blinked, unable to fathom her joke. "Why is it funny?"

The others laughed again, and Plum leaned over me, her face near the bowl on my tray. "Never mind that. Is something wrong?"

"What? Nothing."

"You look different."

I waved to dismiss her. "I'm tired, that's all."

"Tired?" Plum drew back. "After supper, we're going to play *weiqi*. Do you want to join us?"

"Maybe next time." I pushed some rice into my mouth. That was good news. When they were gone, I could view the paintings.

"You're not afraid of me beating you, are you?"

"You beat me? You're joking, right? You never pay attention to where the stones go. How many games have you won so far? Zero?" *Weiqi*, a two-person board game that used 361 pieces of stones, was getting popular those days in the palace. The goal was to capture the most stones and cover the most territory on the board.

"But I never cared about the stones."

"Now you're telling the truth."

The Talents laughed, and Plum waved her eating sticks, pretending to strike me. I ducked my head. She rose to pursue me. I leaped behind the other girls, keeping out of her reach. For a moment, we played hide-and-seek, laughing and taunting each other. Finally, we grew tired and sat to finish our meal. While I cleaned up the trays, Plum went to the courtyard with the others to play *weiqi*. A few Beauties next door also joined, and some started to play jump rope. The courtyard was alive with motion and laughter.

I closed the doors, made sure no one was going to enter, and placed the scroll on the table. My heart racing faster, I unfurled the scroll and read the opening paragraph, titled "The Dreams of the Spring."

"A thousand years ago, things were different. Men and women were free and happy. Every spring they came to a river and made merry, with any mates they wished. They called it the Rites of Spring, described in the song 'Joy of the Mulberry Groves.' When dynasties were founded, women were no longer free. They were bound by the wishes of their fathers, their husbands, and their emperors. Their own wishes were no longer important, forgotten, discarded like rotten roots. And this is why the pictures must be kept, to remind us of the ancient joy."

Oh, how perverse the words were, but very interesting. I unfurled the scroll farther.

A picture. Rather idyllic, with parasol-like green trees, crimson peonies, and porous garden rocks. On the rock sat a man, and on the man sat a woman, whose arms wound around his neck while his hands pushed her skirt up to her waist, uncovering her legs, lower abdomen, and everything in between.

Well… The two were dallying right there. I wanted to avert my eyes. But I could not resist it. I straightened and unrolled more.

Another man and woman. In a study, where brushes, ink stones, and papers were spread neatly on a writing table. A bejeweled, pretty woman sat on it too, and in front of her stood a man, his buttocks bare. He was so close to her—almost touching her—while the woman leaned back, supporting herself with her arms. There were splashes of pink on her cheeks and somewhere else…

Holy ancestors of nine generations!

I rolled up the scroll, my face burning. So that was the secret of the bedroom affair. I knew it now, even though the events were unrelated to the locale. Would I do that with the Emperor? Bare myself like that? I felt as if my skin had been peeled off, like a skinned rabbit waiting to be roasted.

But the woman. Her face … It was as if she were sailing to a place she longed for…and her body…I had never seen anything so revealing, vivid, and…exquisite. Did I look like her? I bit my lip. Hesitating, I slipped my hand into my loose pants…

Ah…the true meaning of being a woman…

I perspired. More…

I moved to the third picture.

Two women. On a bed. One wearing a pink bandeau, one with a blue shawl. One was lying down, and one was sitting…

I almost dropped the scroll. Women!

Footsteps came from outside. Hastily, I rolled it up.

Plum entered the chamber with her friends. My heart throbbing, I turned my back to her and tucked the scroll under my mat. I sat on it, straightened, and pretended nothing had happened. But

I kept thinking about the scroll, its round and long shape, like a certain part in the painting.

The chamber became stuffy, and the air smelled hot and sweaty. I fanned myself with my hand. The images of the painting floated before my eyes, but all I thought of was Pheasant.

By the time we were ready to sleep, I was certain it would require eighteen horses to ever drag me to the Emperor's chamber.

✦ ✦

A few short weeks later, I had already forgotten about seducing the Emperor when Heaven's intention once again disrupted our routine.

I awoke one morning to a commotion in the courtyard. Shooting stars had appeared during the night. For the whole morning, I saw people gathering in corners, whispering, their faces pale.

It had been two years since the appearance of the comet, which had brought us the assassination plot against the Emperor and changed our relationship with the tribes at the border. And now, we had shooting stars.

"The Emperor is having a meeting with his astrologer," Plum whispered to me while we walked to the wardrobe chamber. The corridors were quieter than usual. "The two have been locked in his library since dawn. Do you know what they are discussing?"

"I don't." I reached the wardrobe chamber and pushed the door open. "Do you?"

The astrologer, a Taoist who claimed to be the listener of Heaven's murmurs, was an important man. The Emperor often consulted him regarding many matters such as calendar, harvest, drought, worship, crowning, war, or even dreams. Once, the astrologer had climbed the ladder of blades to reach the door of Heaven. The blades, all honed and whetted as thin as a maple leaf, could have sliced a man's feet, but he ascended barefoot, his hands holding nothing but a scroll and a brush, and reached the top without shedding a single drop of blood. It was rumored that he drank only rainwater and ate ginseng shaped like an infant. On the drought days, the Emperor summoned him to call the rain. After each performance, the rain always came.

He was, no doubt, also a dangerous man.

Plum cupped her hand around my ear. "You will not believe what I am going to tell you, Mei. They said the astrologer interpreted the signs and revealed a prophecy."

"A prophecy?" I remembered the Buddhist monk, Tripitaka, had predicted my future by reading my face. That had been a long time ago. The Taoists also made predictions, but they often observed Heaven's signs to reach their conclusions. "About what?"

I did not want to tell Plum, but I was worried. If the imperial astrologer revealed a prophecy, then all the sign watchers on the street would certainly know about it and talk about it, and then the rebels and those who harbored hatred toward the Emperor would use the words to revolt. The Western Turks had kept quiet after the demise of the King of Gaochang, but who knew what else would happen if more rebels rose to plot against the Emperor?

"This is what I heard." She went to close the chamber's door. Fortunately, the Beauties had not arrived yet, and we could speak freely. "The astrologer said a certain man would end the Emperor's reign, and he is coming."

I was shocked. "Are you certain? Who is the man?"

She made a face. "I would be an astrologer too, if I knew."

I peered at the sky. It was still early. The sun had just come out. I wished I could listen to the astrologer as he spoke to the Emperor. But the Emperor's library was located inside the Outer Palace, and I was not allowed to wander there without permission. The Beauties arrived, and Plum and I busied ourselves with our tasks. Later, when I delivered laundry to the laundry women on the other side of the Inner Court, I heard some men's voices from the street outside. I stopped at the entrance of the Inner Court and peered out from behind the gate.

The Emperor was returning from the library with the astrologer and other ministers. He nodded grimly as the astrologer, dressed in a white robe embroidered with moons and stars that many Taoist priests donned, said something. He was an old man, with a long, silvery beard that reached his knees and long, gray hair speckled with black dots like sesames. He wore no hat or boots.

The Emperor came closer, and I hurried to leave, thinking about what Plum had told me. If it was true the astrologer believed a man would end the Emperor's reign, then whoever that man was, he was doomed. The Emperor would not let him live.

✦ ✦

A few days later, I went to the garden to meet Pheasant at night. The rock near the garden's entrance lay flat. I turned around. Pheasant was busy tonight. For the next few weeks, we were unable to meet. The Gold Bird Guards had tightened their patrols around the palace, as a thief had been caught stealing a horse in an imperial stable at midnight. He was killed instantly, penetrated by an arrow. Later he was identified as a palace guard nicknamed Black Boy. I remembered him. He was one of the two Palace Escorts who had brought me to the palace a few years before.

I wondered why a palace guard would risk his life stealing a horse. It did not make sense to me. No one with a brain would attempt to steal an imperial horse inside the palace. Many people gossiped about it too, including some guards, but then, for some reason, the gossip seemed to die overnight, as though there never had been a horse thief.

It was clear to me someone had ordered the cease of gossip, and I could not get it out of my mind. I wondered if it had something to do with the prophecy.

AD 642

the Sixteenth Year *of*

Emperor Taizong's Reign

of Peaceful Prospect

AUTUMN

21

I HAD JUST COLLECTED THE EMPEROR'S ROBES FROM THE seamstress when Eunuch Ming beckoned to me from behind a cinnamon tree.

"What is it?" I looked around to ensure we were alone. "Did you give the money to my mother?"

"I couldn't find her."

"I gave you the ward's name." I frowned. With the names of the ward and my family, he should not have had trouble locating Qing's house.

"Your mother has disappeared."

"What do you mean?"

"Your half brother banished her."

I gasped. "What? Why?"

He shrugged. "They said she left the house a year ago."

I bit my lip so hard I tasted the saltiness of my blood. "Do you know where she is now?" She had no one to rely on in the capital. The only places for her would be streets, ditches, corners of grave-yards, and the Northern District, where unfortunate women were forced to sell their bodies for a living.

"They didn't tell me."

"But there's nowhere she could go!"

"That's what I heard, and now I'm telling you."

My hands trembled, and I almost dropped the robes. "Why? Why did he banish my mother?"

That heartless gambler. How could he do that?

When I raised my head again, the eunuch had left. Whether he had pocketed the money for himself or gave it to Qing, I did not know or care. The most important thing was Mother.

Where was she? Where would she sleep? What would she do when it rained and snowed?

A sweeper appeared in front of the tree and peered to see what I was doing. I left the shade and went to the wardrobe chamber. But I could not concentrate on folding a single garment. I told Plum I did not feel well and returned to my chamber.

The only person who could help me was the Emperor. He could issue an imperial notice and have it posted on the wall in the Western Market. Then everyone would help find Mother.

How could I get his attention again? I had reviewed the paintings. I knew more about bedroom secrets. I could seduce him, persuade him...

But Pheasant... What would he think if he knew I had gone to his father's bed?

I slept fitfully that night. One moment I seemed to swim in a cloud of rain and mist with Pheasant but soon plunged into a pool of tears that Mother shed. I called for her, swam to her, but somehow the pool transformed into a dark cave filled with echoes. Before dawn broke, I got up from my mat and stepped into the courtyard. No one was up yet at that hour, and it was unusually quiet.

The air smelled fresh. I sat on a stone bench under the oak tree. I tried to think—I had to—and I had to think fast. But I was cold, my mind thick, hard, like the walls surrounding me.

Strings of daylight spun in my eyes. A golden oriole flitted around a pear tree and then settled to perch on a branch. White petals and fine nectar showered to the ground. The bird stretched its neck, trying to swallow something, a seed or perhaps a grain of rice.

"A woman is not a bag of grain to be weighed and passed around by whoever wishes to purchase it," Mother had said once when

Father was teaching me Confucius. I could not remember what made her say that, but her voice, so clear and dignified, stayed with me.

Would I be a bag of grain if I used my body to get what I needed? And what would Pheasant say if he knew? But I had to make a decision, and I would not tell him what I would do, because nothing outweighed my desire to care for Mother.

I had to win over the Emperor so he could help me.

✦ ✦

I walked down the trails leading to the Quarters of the Pure Lotus and came to Jewel's bedchamber. I composed myself and then knocked on her door.

She was eating lychees, the rare fruit with a scaly shell and jellylike pulp that every lady coveted. It was not lychee season, and she must have received them from the imperial ice pits. "Oh, Mei, there you are." She waved away her maids. "You don't look like you slept well. Or have you been crying?"

My eyes lingered on the fruit. They looked plump and juicy, and I knew they were incredibly rare and precious. "It's a windy day. The sand got in my eyes, and I rubbed them too hard. You haven't gone out?"

"Is it so? It must be a strong wind; otherwise, it wouldn't bring you here."

There was no point dancing around the subject. I folded my hands across my stomach. "I have come to ask a favor, Most Adored."

She picked up a lychee. "Want one?"

I had always loved them. But if I accepted it, I would owe her a favor. Besides, I could not eat anything. "No."

"They're delicious. Everyone loves them. Try one."

I ignored her extended hand. "You would still be in the Yeting Court if not for me. You owe me, Jewel."

"I knew you'd ask for something. What do you wish for? And I am deeply sorry for what happened on the polo field. I asked for you after the feast. My maid said you refused to see me."

She was trying to change the subject. I bit my lip. "I am here now, Most Adored."

She sighed, peeling back the thin, red shell on the lychee. "You know I would be glad to help you, Mei. I'm not your enemy, I assure you. But it's not that simple. The Emperor is the Emperor. He won't listen to me."

"I'm not asking you to beg for me."

"I know you are better than that. You're an honorable woman, Mei. I've always admired your courage."

"Really? Then give me one of your nights with him. We'll be even."

The thin shell fell on the table, and Jewel held the white pulp to her lips, juice flowing down her fingers. "One night?"

I nodded firmly. "One night."

Slowly, she ate the fruit, relishing it—I could tell—and spat out the tiny pit. "One night with the Emperor. What a fine idea. If you bear him a son, you will ride a shortcut to his heart." She peered at me. "Even if you have a girl, you will stay in the court as the mother of an imperial princess."

What she said was true, but I did not care about that. All I wanted was his forgiveness, and then he would agree to search for Mother. "That would be ideal, except it does not happen very often. How long have you been bedding the Emperor?" I reminded her. She had yet to bear a child, and in fact, none of the Emperor's concubines had conceived any since my arrival in the Inner Court.

"You are young."

"You're a mare who knows its way."

Jewel picked up another lychee. "Very well. I shall return the favor I owe you. But on one condition."

"What?"

"I want to be there."

I could see a trap spread in the air like an invisible ladder waiting for me to climb. "Why?"

"In case you need my assistance." She smiled. "I remember you don't know much about the bedroom affair."

"I know now."

"Then I promise I will not disturb you."

I studied her hard to detect any signs of trickery. I did not find any. Anyway, did I have another option?

"Come to his bedchamber tomorrow night."

I was relieved. "I thank you." I bowed and took my leave.

When I stepped into the courtyard, a group of women gathered around a birdcage glanced at me. From the way they tilted their heads and whispered, I could tell they had heard our conversation. They were the Pure Lady's servants, and I was certain they would report to her the moment I left.

I knocked on the Noble Lady's door. She was inside, working on her spindle wheel. Near the wheel was a desk where a few boxes sat. I knew what was inside without looking—spiders.

I explained my plan to win the Emperor's affection.

"This is good news, Mei," she said, smiling. "And you must be very persuasive to ask a night from Most Adored. Did she tell you why she wished to be there?"

I shook my head. The Noble Lady did not ask me if I had reviewed the scroll, and I did not tell her I had. It was better to leave it that way.

"I wish you the best of fortune, Mei. If you please him, you could keep your title and allowances, and perhaps much more."

"I thank you for your kindness, my Noble Lady. I am already fortunate to have your help."

"When are you going to see him?"

"Jewel says her night will be tomorrow."

She nodded. "Good luck, Mei."

I thanked her and left.

22

THE NEXT DAY, SUNLIGHT DIMMED ON THE PEAR TREE'S branches. The last patch of gold lost its luster and melted into a pool of murky gray. A temporary tranquillity mixed with an eerie silence descended on the courtyard, and gradually the tree's sprawling branches thickened and joined the night's darkness.

I tucked the scroll under my mat, dusted the dirt from my skirt, and walked to the Emperor's bedchamber. I was ready. Well, not entirely. But I could not hesitate, because I might never be ready.

The Emperor's candleholder, a dwarf, opened the door, a scroll in his hand. The fresh scent of ink wafted to my nose. The Emperor had composed a new poem, it seemed. Any other time I would have liked to know what it was about, but not at that moment.

I ignored the smirk at the corner of the dwarf's mouth and went into the bedchamber. I coughed, to let Jewel know I was there.

"Is that you, Mei?" Jewel called from behind the screen.

"Yes, Most Adored." I paused. The arrangement of the furniture looked different from what I remembered. The screens had been moved from near the brazier to shield half of the bed.

"Come."

The Emperor seemed to be dozing on the oversize bed while Jewel lay beside him, her right hand supporting her head. The dim firelight flickered on her body. She was barely dressed, her breasts and long legs exposed in the candlelight.

"I'm glad you came. Would you read a poem for us?" she said.

I spoke, hoping my voice was calm. "Where is it?"

"There." Jewel gestured with her foot to a futon near the bed.

I found the scroll, which reminded me of the paintings the Noble Lady had given me, and for a moment my face grew hot. I took a deep breath, sat down, and unfurled the scroll. Then I began to read by the light coming from the brazier. The poem was something about the strength of the grass would be known when the gale assaulted, and the loyalty of a minister would be tested during uncertainty. When I finished reading, the Emperor was still asleep. I did not know what to do. Would he sleep forever?

Then he groaned and sat upright.

My hands trembled, but I managed to sit still.

Jewel covered her mouth, tittering. "Don't worry. I made him drunk. He's most agreeable in this state. Believe me, you'll be glad I did." She lowered her voice. "You know what to do to make him happy, do you?"

"I know."

"You should thank me." Jewel cupped her hand around my ear. "See the front of his pants?" It was stained. "I used pistachio nut oil for you."

The aphrodisiac? I was surprised Jewel would help me. "Thank you, Most Adored…"

An arm pulled me, and I was in his grip. He smelled of strong kumiss, fermented from mare's milk, the only drink he indulged in within the chamber, I had learned. "Take it off," he said gruffly.

I untied my robe, aware that Jewel, smiling, was watching me. After the robe fell, I reached for the strings of my bandeau. My hands shook. I had trouble untying it. Jewel went behind me and loosened the strings. The bandeau dropped to the floor, and I pulled down my skirt and loose trousers underneath.

Even though I did not look at myself, I knew I was as beautiful as Jewel. When I had bathed with her years ago, I was just a girl, but now I had developed an attractive, womanly landscape: slender arms, supple slopes, and smooth curves, just like her. And the candlelight shone on my skin, bathing me with a warm golden hue.

"Lovely, lovely indeed." He nodded, turning me around.

Remembering the paintings, I wanted to fold my arms across my chest but feared he would view it as unwillingness. So I stood with my arms at my sides. I was so close to him, like I was with Pheasant, and there was nothing between the Emperor and me.

I felt dizzy. Jewel peered at me, her eyes gleaming. I could not tell whether she was jealous, but the sight of her, so close, startled me. I stepped back, my hand sweeping a brush on a stool near the bed. A trail of black ink dotted my white tunic on the floor.

How clumsy I was! I reached out. "I'm sorry!"

"Stop!" His big hand blocked me. "What are you doing?"

"I—" I froze. "I—"

He went behind me. A squeeze on my buttock. Then he came before me. A pinch on my nipple. Coughing, he parted his legs and stood solemnly. His night robe slipped off his shoulders, but he did not seem to notice. "Well?"

This was it. I stumbled to the bed and pushed the crimson quilt aside. The silk felt cold, like a dead man's skin. But that was not all. There was something else soft touching my fingers. A piece of gilded paper.

I squinted at the words. I could not make it out at first, and when I did, I could not believe it. The paper announced Jewel's crowning as Empress.

I froze. There lay her true intention. She had not given me her night for free. She had prepared the ink and wanted to slip the scroll to the Emperor when the time was right. I did not know when or how, but if he signed it, it would give her the dream of a lifetime.

I straightened and faced the Emperor. The candlelight radiated above his shoulder and blinded my eyes. But my mind had never been clearer. I must take control. I must be the master of my night.

I gave the Emperor a deep bow. "Allow me to serve you, the One Above All. It is the privilege of which I have only dreamed."

"I don't need your service." His voice sounded ominous.

I must do better. I slid my hand across the bed's smooth redwood frame. "If you don't mind, the One Above All, I would like to share some inspiring paintings I viewed today. The paintings portray the joy of fish swimming in the water." The phrase was a common expression for the bedroom affair in the painting. "Or would you like me to describe them to you?"

"No paintings."

Jewel snickered. I must not be distracted. But she reminded me the Emperor often summoned her. I put on Jewel's smile, the one that was coy and seductive. "Then perhaps there are other ideas the One Above All might find interesting. If I may suggest—"

"You don't make a suggestion unless I ask you."

My heart pounded frantically, but I continued to smile. "How disrespectful I was, the One Above All. I beg your forgiveness!" I tilted my head, and with my eyes half open, I parted my lips and then my legs. "Whatever the One Above All has in mind, I will be happy to oblige."

There was silence, and at the corner of my eyes, I saw him fingering his whiskers while his eyes flicked to my chest and below.

I could not stop. I walked to him, my back straight, my hips swaying, slowly, one pace at a time, and when I neared him, I kissed his hand.

"What is your name?" He lifted my face, his voice gentler.

"My parents called me Mei." Meaning *little sister*, it was only an informal name used among my family, but then, none of the women in China were given official names, even the noble ones, as was the tradition. Men, however, had at least three official names: a given name, a noble calling, and a title.

"Stand straight. Arms at your sides."

I felt cold, even as the candlelight shed its golden sheen on my skin, but I did not hesitate. I gave him a dip of my head, let my arms drop naturally, and straightened my back.

He put his hands on my chest. "Good." He nodded and then increased the pressure. I tried not to grimace. His fingers felt like iron tongs. "Perfect."

He was still again, as though considering his next move. Then, suddenly, he grabbed the brush on the stool and flexed his arms. His face grave, his eyes unwavering, like a general on a battlefield ready to send an attack signal to his army, he threw his right hand upward and swung his hand with great energy. The wet goat hair licked my skin like a dragon's fiery tongue.

"There." He puffed out, and in his authoritative voice, he said, "I do believe you deserve it. I now formally name you Mei Niang."

I could barely identify the sprawling strokes and vertical lines of my new name. The ink flowed from my breasts, converged in my cleavage, and snaked toward my navel. It tickled terribly.

But Mei Niang, the seductively beautiful girl. He had honored me greatly by bestowing on me a formal name, and I would be the first woman in the kingdom to bear an official name.

"I am honored." I lowered my head.

"Precisely. So beautiful and seductive," Jewel said, but her face suggested otherwise.

I had surprised her. I had earned myself a name and his attention. "Thank you, Most Adored."

"Go." The Emperor prodded me with the end of his brush. "Walk to the door and show me the living calligraphy."

I took one step, my heart filled with happiness. The ink flowed down my thigh, but it no longer bothered me. My hand on my waist, I held my head high, strutted to the screen, and paused there. When I turned around, the Emperor nodded, stroking his whiskers, his eyes alight with mirth.

"This is the seductive girl I want to keep." He squeezed my buttocks when I returned. "Should I deal with you now?"

"How about one more round to the door?" Jewel's voice came suddenly.

She did not wish him to bed me. But even if she got her wish tonight, she had already lost. I smiled. "Would you like me to walk again, the One Above All?"

"Go now."

I swung my arms and swayed my hips, treading on the ground of triumph. The scent from the brazier was fragrant, and the yellow candlelight danced. Everything in the chamber—the shiny crimson bedding, the carved posts of the bed, and the green balls of the dragons on the top of the posts—seemed to brighten.

When I stopped at the screen, a lean figure appeared at the door.

"Father!" he called.

I dashed behind the screen to hide my nakedness.

"Who is there?" The Emperor stood. Jewel gave him a robe, and they both went to the door, where they talked rapidly. It sounded as though Taizi was hurt, and the Emperor had to leave.

"We must go now, or they'll kill themselves, Father," the informer said.

The voice sounded anxious and concerned but familiar. Too familiar. I froze.

Pheasant! Why had he come? Why had he come then? I pressed myself against the wall. My heart pounded. If only I could slip into another chamber. If only the wall could dissolve. If only I could dissolve.

"Mei Niang!" the Emperor called out. "Come."

Blood rushed to my head. I did not wish to go anywhere. I just wanted to stay at the corner of the bedchamber and not be seen. But I could not disobey him. He would know something was wrong if I refused.

"Yes, the One Above All." I scrambled to put on my bandeau. But I could not find my trousers. Hastily, I grabbed my robe and put it on, and then I stepped from behind the screen to greet the Emperor and my lover.

23

TWO FIGURES STOOD NEAR THE DOOR: ONE OLD, THE OTHER young. One had his back to the fire, and the other's face was bathed in light. Both stared at me.

The candlelight was too bright. It glared on my naked face like daylight, scalding me. I lowered my head.

"Here you are. Come with me." The Emperor turned around, pulling his cape around him.

"Mei Niang?" Pheasant said. There was a thick current of confusion in his voice, and something else, a tremor, like that of a wounded animal.

My throat tightened. Did he believe I had betrayed him? Did he believe I no longer loved him? I could explain. I could tell him I was pleasing the Emperor only to help my family. I could tell him it had nothing to do with how I felt about him. Would he understand?

"Prince Zhi." I bowed and prayed he would not say anything to expose us.

The smoke drifted from the brazier and stood between us. It smelled scorched, like that of a pyre.

"That's the formal name the Emperor bestowed on her," Jewel said.

"I see." Pheasant sounded as though something had caught in his throat. There was silence again, and then I realized he was staring at my naked legs. Awkwardly, I covered them with the sleeves of my robe.

"Shall we go now, Father?"

The Emperor waved and left with Pheasant. I went back to the bed to look for my trousers and girdle. I was still shaken. The Emperor did not suspect anything between Pheasant and me. We were fortunate. But Pheasant... I thought of him and how his voice had changed when he saw my bare legs.

"We should follow them quickly," Jewel said, returning. "Where is my girdle? Mei?"

I composed myself and pulled up my trousers. "Yes, your girdle is near the futon."

She took it and wrapped it around her. "It's a great honor to have the Emperor bestow a name upon you."

"I know. I'm honored. Shall we go now? Where are we going?"

"To the Eastern Palace." She stuffed the unsigned golden paper in her pocket. "If you don't wish to go, you could stay here."

I wanted nothing other than to hide in a corner, but if I stayed, Jewel would suspect something was wrong.

She cocked her head toward me, her catlike eyes glinting. "Are you all right?"

I could not arouse her suspicion. I squeezed out a smile. "Of course. I am disappointed, that's all."

"Disappointed?" She arched her painted eyebrows. "Are you blaming me for ruining your night?"

"No. I'm not."

She nodded and walked toward the door. "Did you see how Prince Zhi stared at you?"

My hands froze on the ties of the skirt. "How did he stare at me?"

She chuckled but did not answer. I could not understand whether she was fishing for clues or simply testing me. I tidied up my skirt and tucked my hair behind my back. When I was ready, I folded my hands across my abdomen and followed her out.

We soon caught up with the Emperor, who was riding on a

sedan carried by four porters, and Pheasant, who walked behind him with a number of servants holding lanterns. The Eastern Palace, separated from the Inner Court by a tall wall, had one entrance, Tongxun Gate, which opened to the Inner Court. It required a long walk from the Emperor's chamber, and we would need to pass the back of the Imperial Silkworm Workshops before reaching it.

I walked slowly behind them, putting some distance between Pheasant and me. Pheasant's gait looked stiff, and he nodded while the Emperor talked.

"So what happened, Prince Zhi?" Jewel asked, walking near the Emperor.

"Taizi and Yo had a wrestling match near dusk. Yo lost. He insulted Taizi." Pheasant turned sideways and glanced at me.

I stumbled, my face burning and my heart racing faster. *Look away, look away, Pheasant.*

"I'm certain it didn't mean anything," Jewel said. "Brothers banter with each other all the time."

"He cursed Taizi's women too and said they were barren."

"That was thoughtless of him." Jewel sighed. "However, he does have a point. The heir is a grown man and has twenty concubines. But he has not fathered a child. Shouldn't he have a son by now?"

Neither Pheasant nor the Emperor answered as they ascended the stairs to enter a gate. I lifted my skirt to walk easier, gazing at the light dancing before me. I prayed Jewel would keep focusing on the heir so she would not pay attention to me or Pheasant.

"And I suppose Taizi insulted him back?" Jewel asked as we left the gate and entered a corridor.

Pheasant cleared his throat but did not speak.

"Nothing? That's unlike the heir."

"He pissed on Yo."

"Pissed! How inappropriate! I certainly would not have imagined that. Did you hear that, the One Above All?"

The Emperor grunted. We finally reached the Tongxun Gate.

"What do you think about the heir, Mei?" Jewel turned to me while we waited for the guards to open the gates.

She would not leave me alone. I felt the Emperor's gaze on me, and Pheasant's too. My heart pounded. "I... Most Adored...I'm afraid...I don't know."

"Don't know? What does that mean?" Jewel asked.

"Enough talk," the Emperor said.

The gate opened. He entered the passage under the archway, his back red in the lantern's light. Fortunately, Jewel said no more and we entered the Eastern Palace, heading toward the heir's stable, where many shadowy figures were gathered.

"Halt!" The Emperor got off the sedan and went straight to them. Pheasant followed. The crowd parted, and a clamor arose as the men shouted.

"Father, this swine insulted me!"

"Father, he pissed on me!"

"I think this is the moment," Jewel said, standing close to me. A group of ladies came before us, blocking our view. I stood on tiptoe, watching the two princes, their faces lit by the bonfire in front of the stable.

"What moment?" I asked.

"What kind of Emperor would he be if he gives his kingdom to an uncouth heir like Taizi? He's finished. The Emperor will depose him."

Of course Jewel wished Taizi to be deposed so the Pure Lady and her son could rise. I could not stand her tone. "This is rather hasty, in my opinion. Taizi is a good man."

She tilted her head at me, and I looked away, afraid she could read my mind.

"We'll see." She faced the Emperor.

Some guards held Taizi and Prince Yo apart, but they still argued with fists and spittle. Their arms thrust violently, and their heads jerked this way and that. Pheasant stood between them, pushing them apart. Poor Pheasant. It must have been hard on him to see Taizi suffer such a disgrace.

"Has he met you before?" Jewel said, her voice smooth.

My heart tightened. "Who?"

"You know whom I'm talking about. Empress Wende's youngest son," Jewel said. "He has grown up to be such a handsome man. So delightful and charming. Do you know he lives in the Eastern Palace with Taizi, and the Emperor allows it?"

Only Taizi was supposed to live there, and the other princes, those older than fifteen, lived in the wards outside the palace. I said honestly, "I did not know." After all, I had thought he was a groom of Taizi, who was always surrounded by many men.

"Wouldn't you say he is a man of many girls' dreams?"

There was something in her voice that made me pause. Suddenly, I recalled that Jewel used to live in the Inner Court. So she must have known Pheasant when he was young. I looked at her levelly. "Well, you seem to like him, Jewel, very much. Is there something I should know?"

"Oh, Mei. How clever you are." She chuckled. "Certainly I like him. Without a doubt. He's the Emperor's son! Everyone likes him. He has the softest heart and is the gentlest soul of all. Even his half brother, Prince Yo, doesn't complain about him. Can you imagine that?"

"I certainly can't." I cleared my throat, thinking about what she had told me when we bathed together a few years ago. "But, Most Adored, I wish to ask you, you never did tell me who exiled you to the Yeting Court. If you had done nothing wrong, like what you have said, why were you exiled?"

The smile on her face faded. "Exiled?" Her voice was suddenly stiff. "Where did you hear that?"

She was going to deny it? She had told me herself.

A cry came from the crowd. I raised my head, searching. Howling, Prince Yo hurled something into the air. A dark shadow hit the Emperor. He staggered back, covering his face.

The crowd quieted in shock.

"What's this?" The Emperor wiped his face. His voice was shocked. "You threw horse dung at me?"

"I told you he's crazy! Why don't you listen to me?" Prince Yo shouted.

"Do not question me!"

"You're blind. He pissed on me. He did it first. Why did you not say anything about that? Why do you blame only me, not him?"

I sucked in air and heard the crowd gasp as well. Prince Yo had gone too far. He needed to stop. But he fumed, his thick eyebrows twisted dangerously. He looked ready to throw himself at the Emperor.

"He's a freak," the prince shouted again. "Like his dead mother. Can't you see it? I'm better than him!"

The Emperor pointed at Prince Yo, his hand shaking. "Out of my sight. Out! I don't want to see you again."

Prince Yo was not finished. "I have had enough of his shit. A champion wrestler. So what? Give me two years. I'll make him weep like a girl. I beat him in the polo game. Didn't you see that?"

"I said out, now!"

Prince Yo spat. "Fine. I'm going."

"Stop," the Emperor roared, his whole body trembling. I had never seen him so angry. "That way." He jabbed to his right. "That way you go. Do not come back."

"Where?"

"Shandong Prefecture."

Gasps rose around me. Shandong Prefecture was one thousand *li* away from Chang'an City. The Emperor was exiling the prince.

"Yes. You go. Go! Take him. Take him now!" The Emperor was fuming with anger.

"He's drunk," Jewel said, her voice faint as though she had lost all her strength.

I was too shocked to speak. I had no sympathy for Prince Yo or his brash behavior, but to ruin his life by banishing him, a mere twenty-year-old, to a remote land, separated from his mother and the rest of his family, was most harsh and unforgiving.

"Father." Pheasant stepped up to him. "Let's not rush into decisions."

"This has nothing to do with you, Pheasant."

"I brought you here." He looked chagrined. "I shouldn't have."

"He hit me with horse dung and spat at me." The Emperor turned to Prince Yo again. "You will leave by dawn's light."

Pheasant looked as though he would speak more, but two guards had already wrung Prince Yo's arms from behind.

"The One Above All." The Pure Lady rushed out of nowhere. Her cat leaped from her arms, and she dropped to her knees. "May I plead on behalf of my son, his impudence and stupidity—"

The Emperor threw up his hand to silence her. "Take him."

"You can't do this to me," Prince Yo screamed. "You can't!"

The guards dragged him away, and he disappeared into the night's darkness. The Pure Lady rose stiffly, her tall frame sharp and unbending like a spear. She had enjoyed much attention and esteem with the ascendancy of Prince Yo in the court these days, but in a moment, she had lost her son and her hope of becoming the Empress.

And Jewel looked as though she had been struck dumb. Her carefully chosen ally had fallen. I wondered what the Noble Lady would say when she heard about it. She would probably sigh, but out of relief rather than sadness.

"Come!" the Emperor shouted, walking toward the stable's entrance.

I looked up. He was beckoning to me. But I did not wish to go. I wanted to see what Pheasant was doing. I wanted to talk to him, to explain, and to comfort him too. But the Emperor was waiting. Quickly, I moved toward the entrance, feeling Pheasant's eyes chasing me in the dark.

24

THE EMPEROR ASKED FOR ME WHEN HE HAD HIS MORNING meal, and I stood behind him while he dined. I accompanied him to the imperial library, where he reviewed the petitions—an honor only the second-degree Ladies and Most Adored would receive. While he made decisions and gave grants, I ground the ink chalks in the ink stone. Once, he was in an especially jovial mood and encouraged me to write. I showed off my calligraphy, quoting Tao Yuanming's "Song of a Serene Garden Life" and Wang Xizhi's "The Preface of Orchard Pavilion." He was delighted. He gave me a bolt of silk embroidered with exquisite patterns of thrushes and peach blossoms as a reward.

Everywhere he went, he took me with him. His five imperial stables, the feasting halls, the library, and the Archery Hall. More and more bestowals were sent to my bedchamber: a ceramic bowl with blue flowers, a toy horse with a red bridle, and a vase painted in yellow, green, and white. I shared all the gifts with Plum, Daisy, and the other Talents.

The Emperor liked me. He really liked me. I was his new favorite concubine, and everyone knew it. People in the Inner Court turned their attention to me again. They began to treat me more courteously, and chunks of meat filled my bowl. I was also given the chance to choose whatever color, whatever pattern of silk I liked for my silk stipend, a privilege of which I had never dreamed before.

I knew why he liked me. He liked the girl he had seen that night, the soft, feminine, tempting woman who swayed her hips and arms with charm. If I wanted to keep his attention, I must continue to give him that woman.

I practiced those steps more often. I studied Jewel, the way she smiled, pouted, nodded, and even frowned. I observed secretly how she gave in, how she made a request without making it sound like one, and how her eyes misted up one moment but then twinkled with laughter the next.

I could do all those and more.

I learned how to form my hair into many innovative shapes. One week I would braid my hair in ropes, the next I kept them straight and erect like a rabbit's ears, and another week I would build twin mounds wound with silk ribbons around my ears. In a month's time, my fashions were duplicated by the maids and even Lady Virtue.

Plum taught me how to apply makeup. She fussed around me, plucking my eyebrows, applying white cream to my face, and coloring my lips. When I stared at my image in a bronze mirror, I hardly recognized myself. A sheet of whiteness blanketed my face, a red dot smudged the center of my lips, and above my eyes were two lines, shaped like the wings of a fluttering moth—fragile, fleeting, and destined to die.

I looked foolish, like one of the Noble Lady's maids. But that was the style all the ladies worshipped, and my intention was to embellish rather than distinguish.

Plum asked what beauty marks I would like to paint on my cheeks. I paused to think. I could have a rabbit, a cherry, or a peony, like everyone else, but I decided on a bird. Like the pheasant.

But if someone asked, I would say it was a pigeon.

I also put my womanly figure on good show. I had an alluring body, I noticed, more pleasing than anyone else's. My bosoms had swelled, and my body was well proportioned. I was not too short like Lady Obedience or too tall like the Pure Lady. When I passed Lady Virtue, I felt her eyes linger on me with envy.

When the Emperor was around, I donned sheer gowns that complemented my curves. I revealed the inner wrist of my hands when I ground ink, and I wore gowns with wide collars that showed my bare shoulders and nape. When he looked in my direction, I let the shawls slip.

A few days later, while we were feasting in the garden, the Emperor asked us to entertain him. Lady Obedience danced, Lady Virtue played the zither, and Jewel, to my surprise, wrote a poem. She recited:

"Cutting the finest qi silk,
White as frosty snow.
I shape a pair of love fans,
round and round like the bright moon.
To go in and out of your sleeve,
and give you cool breeze as you move.
But often I worry the coming of autumn,
when cold draft drives out summer's heat.
And you toss me in the hamper,
your love and affection forever asunder."

It was actually Lady Ban Jieyu's work. The ancient court lady had written "The Sad Song of Round Fans" after she lost her emperor's favor. I doubted the Emperor knew Jewel had stolen the verse, but it did not matter. I had to do better than her.

I looked up at the night sky where a crescent moon hung. Words came to me:

"Like an unstrung bow,
The new moon stands by,
Don't say it's tiny as a moth brow,
When it's round, it shall illuminate the sky."

211

"Well said!" The Emperor clapped his hands, laughing. "I have never heard of a woman with such a fine spirit. Tell me, my fair Talent, what do you wish to have?"

I could not let the opportunity slip away. I leaned over and cupped my hand around his ear. With the fragrance of wine wafting from his breath and his whisker touching my cheek, I told him about Mother and said how much I would like to find her.

"The Secretary shall take care of that. Tomorrow. He will have the notices pasted all over Chang'an."

Happiness filled my heart. I bowed.

"But you deserve more than this. I have another announcement to make." He stroked my cheek. "You shall be my personal attendant from now on."

He had promoted me. Personal attendant. My hours at the wardrobe chamber would be reduced, and I would attend to him while he went to the Outer Palace, where he received foreign ambassadors and dealt with state affairs. I would see him in two courts, the Inner Court and the Outer Palace, a great honor and privilege. Jewel made an excuse to leave the table.

Sitting near the Emperor, I felt dizzy with happiness. Everything was perfect. Mother would be found, and she would be safe and sound, and my future, like the candles before me, finally glowed with radiance.

On my first day as the Emperor's personal attendant, I walked down the wide streets of the Outer Palace lined with maples and elms. In my right hand I carried a tray of apples. A few paces ahead of me, the Emperor sat on a sedan carried by four porters. Beside him were seven other attendants, holding parasols and banners.

I was eager to go to the Audience Hall to observe the audience, to listen to the details of state affairs, to learn how the Emperor governed, and most important of all, to find and forge an ally among the men who had the Emperor's ear. For it was with the support of the ministers that an empress would be born, and it was in the Audience Hall that an empress would reign.

The air was fresh in the dawn's light. We passed several buildings sitting on raised platforms, where many ministers and scribes knelt at the door, waiting for the Emperor's passing. In the distance, I could see many majestic buildings, the famous Cuiwei Hall with red corridors and white stone fences, the Zhengshi Hall, and the solemn Taiji Hall, where enthronements for emperors and empresses took place. It was a building with blue roofs and three bridges, each with a long, steep staircase.

We arrived at the vast yard in front of the Audience Hall, a wide, towering edifice. My legs were sore, and my arms had grown tired from holding the tray. But I was excited to see so many ministers waiting for the Emperor. There were also foreign messengers, some in high hats and boots, some in fisherman's sandals. They all crowded around the steep stairs that led to the hall, for our kingdom, the most prosperous and the most cultured, was also the most powerful under Heaven.

A loud gong sounded, and a court announcer's distinctive voice pierced the sky. "I hereby announce the Emperor of China, the One Above All, Emperor Taizong, the Conqueror of the North and the South, the great ruler of all land and the seven seas, has arrived!"

All the men kowtowed, heads bowed, backs arched, and hands flattened on the ground.

I followed the Emperor as he ascended the stairs and entered the Audience Hall. He went to his throne, threw his long sleeves behind him, and sat, his hands resting on his thighs. I went to an antechamber at the left of the hall with the other attendants. We would wait for the Emperor there, where he would have refreshments during the audience and change his formal attire at the end of the session. Behind us, the ministers holding their ivory tablets filed into the Audience Hall and lined up along the two sides.

The court announcer began to call out the names of the courtiers. First came the three most powerful men, the Duke,

Chancellor of the Shangshu Department; Wei Zheng, Chancellor of Menxia Department; and Secretary Fang Xuanling of Zhongshu Department, then the Emperor's uncle, then the second-degree courtiers, the third-degree courtiers, and many more. I remembered my grandfather had been one of the chancellors in Sui Dynasty, though I did not remember which department. As I listened to the men's names, I watched them through a gap between the screens that blocked off the hall, memorizing their faces.

Whom should I approach to win their support? The Duke was out of the question. What about the Emperor's uncle? Or the Secretary? The Chancellor? Or perhaps the other second-degree courtiers?

After the roll call, the ministers joined to recite the virtues of the Emperor, their voices rising high to the hall's ceiling. Then the Emperor ordered the foreign messengers to enter. One by one, they stepped into the hall, identified their kingdoms, presented their tributes, and stated their requests. The Emperor received their gifts and granted their wishes. Then a group of fishermen entered. The Japanese, the court announcer declared. They asked the ruler's permission to stay in the capital in order to study our culture, architecture, and even our clothes.

"Come here, Mei." Daisy beckoned, standing near many chests that contained the foreign gifts offered to the Emperor. Near her, the other attendants leaned against pillars and dozed. We had risen at the third crow of the rooster and were all tired.

"What is it, Daisy?" I moved away from the screen.

"Look at this." She held up a medallion and bit into it, denting the soft metal. "The messenger said it was made of real gold. See the man on this medallion? It's their king. What's the round bowl thing he's wearing?"

What else would the king put on his head? "I think it's a crown."

"A crown? Looks more like a chamber pot."

"Why would someone wear a chamber pot on his head?" It had to be a crown, even though it was unlike anything I had seen. I took the coin from her hand. It was inscribed with some squirmy letters like a child's scribble. They did not have the straight edges or corners of our characters.

"I don't understand. The king doesn't have jewels on his crown, but the coin is made of real gold." Daisy flipped another medallion in the air. "Do you think this kingdom has plenty of gold?"

"It's possible."

"It's from Byzantium. Have you heard of it? Such a funny name. It sounds like a name for a pagoda. Where is the kingdom, do you think?"

A book in the library had mentioned that shallots often thrived wherever a gold mine lay, that wild onions grew near silver deposits, ginger, and copper. Wherever Byzantium was, it must have grown lots of shallots. But I had no desire to explain, because the announcer had just introduced the kingdom's messenger. I returned to the screen and peeked out.

"The servant of our great Basileus, the King of Kings, Heraclius." A man in a white robe stepped toward the throne. "Hail to Your Majesty, from our kingdom, Byzantium, the most ancient civilization of the world."

He was accompanied by a man with long, grizzly hair and a thick, messy beard, who looked like a merchant and also served as a translator.

"Boast not, young man, boast not. No country is more ancient than mine. Byzantium, that's how you call it?" The Emperor's voice echoed in the hall. "It is young. Founded in the year 324? My country dates back to one thousand years ago."

"The glory of Your Majesty has reached to the heart of our realm. That is why our Basileus sent me here," the messenger said.

"What do you want? Trade, vassalage, or protection?"

"We are not here to seek vassalage, trade, or protection, Your Majesty." The messenger bowed. "Our Basileus, the King of Kings, Heraclius, offers Your Majesty an opportunity to rule half of the world. Heraclius, our Basileus, rules the West, and Your Majesty, the East."

I was intrigued. An offer of alliance? I pressed my eyes closer to the screen, trying to see the Emperor's reaction.

He looked contemplative. "I heard Khusro II, from the Sassanian Empire, had launched a massive campaign to battle you Byzantines. Isn't it so that your king lost the cities of Damascus, Jerusalem, and the city near a river, called Egypt?"

"That was twenty-five years ago." The messenger's voice was thick with an accent, but even so, I could hear the tinge of amusement in his tone. "Our Basileus crushed the Sassanids and recovered all the territories that Your Majesty is aware of. And by the grace of God, he returned the True Cross to the sacred land of Jerusalem."

"Do not talk about God with me. War is man's business, not God's," the Emperor bellowed.

The messenger coughed and spoke rapidly in a low voice. Gasps rose in the hall, and the ministers murmured, as if stunned by the message.

"So you say the Sassanian Emperor is no more?" The Emperor stood up.

"I'm afraid so, Your Majesty."

"Who destroyed them?"

"That is why I'm here, Your Majesty." The messenger handed a scroll to the Duke, who stood near the throne. He presented the scroll to the Emperor, who took it and unrolled it.

A map. I took a deep breath. Sun Tzu's *The Art of War* had mentioned that with a map, an army could drive through the enemy's territory as if it were their own backyard. I had never seen one before.

"The men on horses, the Kingdom of Circumcised Man," the messenger said. "My Basileus dreamed they would conquer vast lands in the west and east, bound by one prophecy."

"Who are they?"

"They are called the Arabs."

"A small tribe." The Emperor rolled up the map.

"Your Majesty may have nothing to fear, but what about your vassals? Will they be strong enough to hold against the Arabs' assault?"

That was a good point. As the Heavenly Khan, he had the duty to protect his vassals, or they would rescind their oaths and revolt. I waited for the Emperor's answer.

Silence befell the Audience Hall. After a moment, the Emperor spoke. "Any thoughts, my counselors?"

A resounding mix of voices filled the hall as the ministers argued.

"The Arabs are nothing," the Duke said, holding his ivory tablet.

"Their emperor had a dream!" the Emperor's uncle countered. His voice was angrier than usual. Earlier, when they were lining up before the throne, I had noticed he kept a great distance from the Duke, eyeing him in disgust. I remembered the friction between the two. Perhaps I could seek the Uncle's support?

"I say we consider their emperor's offer of alliance now and attack the Arabs," said another voice. It was the Chancellor, Wei Zheng. "We can send the men from the Four Garrisons to the west. There is a good saying: you kill the animal when it's a cub; you don't wait until it grows to be a lion."

"Unwise! We shall defeat them when they come!" the Duke said.

"Only a coward will wait!" the Uncle said, raising his voice. "A true warrior will not wait for a war."

"And you're an old man. You can hardly see the stairs ahead of you, let alone find the right path," the Duke said, raising his voice too.

I heard gasps rise in the hall, and the Emperor's voice came. "Counselors! Shall I remind you this is a moment for consultation? Consultation! Anyone?"

A moment of silence, and then a wave of murmurs followed.

I pulled away from the screens. If the two most prominent officials would argue like children in front of foreign guests, the rift between them must have been unsealable. Perhaps it was not a bad thing. I remembered clearly that Sun Tzu had mentioned that division bred weakness, and weakness provided opportunity.

The Emperor appeared in the antechamber. I took a tray of apples and went to him. He shook his head and asked for an empty tray. When I returned with one, he took off his bejeweled mortarboard crown and placed it on the tray. Daisy and the other attendants bowed and asked whether he needed any sweetmeat for a snack.

Carrying the tray, I stepped back, studying the crown. What a brilliant piece. There were thousands of pearls strung together to form two curtains in the front and back.

I was so close to the crown, however, that after a moment, the pearls turned dewy with my breath.

25

IT WAS DARK WHEN I REACHED THE GARDEN. THE SMALL rock was leaning against the wall, and I could hear Pheasant's whistle coming from inside. I hesitated. I was the Emperor's favorite, and soon I might be Most Adored. But the other night, when Pheasant burst into the Emperor's chamber, we had nearly exposed ourselves.

But I could not resist it. I had to see Pheasant. I put my hands on the wall and pulled myself up. I heard rustling behind me. I jerked around.

A shadow ran down the trail. I leaped off the wall and ran after it.

"Wait, wait!" I followed the shadow as it dashed to a grove. "I know it's you, Rain!"

The shadow slowed and turned to face me.

"How did you know it was me?" she asked.

I stopped a few paces away, panting. My throat was tight, and I could hardly breathe. "You've been following me, haven't you?" And if she told the Emperor about me seeing Pheasant...

"Now I know your secret."

Her voice was hard, brittle, filled with resentment. I swallowed. "I know your secret too, Rain."

"Well, what will you do, Talent? You cannot harm me."

It was true. She was not the Emperor's concubine, like me. "But you don't know that, do you, Rain? If the Emperor believes you seduced Pheasant, he might grow angry and expel you from the court. Then you will be disgraced. But I want to tell you I never thought to expose your secret. I wish you would understand."

"Of course you will say that. What else would you say?"

"I mean it." She looked hesitant, and I hurried to continue. "What would you gain by hurting me? How do you think the Emperor would reward you if you told him? He may punish me, yes, but what about you? Pheasant will not forgive you. He'll never forgive you."

She came closer to me, her shadow slithering on the ground like a sinister beast. "You want my silence."

"I…I wish…we could be friends." I knew I sounded dubious, but I would not be the first woman in the court who put up a pretense to get a reconciliation.

"Friends? You stole him from me."

"I…I'm sorry."

"So we're even now," she said slowly.

Relieved, I breathed out. "Yes, we—"

"But we are not finished." She slapped me.

When I raised my head again, she had turned and walked away. Her pace was assured and steady, reminding me I should not underestimate her.

I turned around and ran back to tell Pheasant about Rain. I could not stay after that. I walked back to my chamber, my mind in disarray.

I dreamed of Father that night. We were at our family's grave site, constructing his coffin. I was so small, not yet five then. He cut the planks and hammered the nails while I sealed the seams with fresh pine resin and coated the wood with thick lacquer. Together, we also selected golden grave goods, fifty-five of them, to match his governor's status. That was my favorite moment from childhood. Then suddenly, he looked into my eyes. I thought he was going to smile, but he frowned.

I awoke. He knew I was seeing Pheasant. He was warning me. Even though he did not speak a word, I could hear him saying, "You're so close, Mei. So close. You must do what is the best for your family, not for yourself. Don't lose yourself, Mei."

A slab of heaviness pressed to my heart. I put my chin on my knees. Had I been in the palace for so long that I had forgotten about why I had wanted to come to the palace? Forgotten about my father?

He was a prudent man who was most concerned about his heir, who would be responsible for his burial rite and carry his name after his death. When Little Sister was born, with Mother in her forties, he realized he would not have a male heir. To ensure he would receive a proper burial when he died, he devoted his time to preparing for his afterlife himself. He selected the best cypress for his coffin, constructed it with me, and when he finished it, he draped the oiled cloth over the coffin to prevent it from decay and placed it on the ceiling joists in our reception hall. He also made his white silk funeral garment, stitched with clouds and pines, symbols of eternal life in Heaven, and purchased white silk slippers padded with goose feathers.

But after the monk's prophecy, he knew I could still carry his name and, even better, I could bring his legacy to a height even a boy could not achieve.

Would I disappoint him?

I could not let my passion ruin my dream, my father's dream. Especially since Rain knew my secret.

I had to stop seeing Pheasant.

I sensed him before I saw him, standing on the other side of the bridge in the garden. Gripping the basket of clean laundry, I paused on the trail leading to the wooden bridge. It was not a coincidence

Pheasant had found me. I had stopped coming to the garden, and when I came across him with the Emperor in the Outer Palace, I had avoided him.

"So this is what everyone is talking about," Plum said, walking beside me and Daisy. She did not notice Pheasant, nor was she aware that I had fallen behind them. "And it's serious. Even the Emperor cannot stop the gossip. Who do you think is the king-dom's foe, Mei?"

"I don't know." I shook my head. The prophecy had spread all over Chang'an, and everywhere, people whispered.

"Look, it's Prince Zhi," Plum whispered to me. "He's looking at us."

Daisy's bosoms rose and fell dramatically. "So handsome. I think I am going to faint."

"I forgot to bring the sheets from the laundry. I'll go get them," I said. "You can go without me."

"Are you certain?" Plum asked, unsuspecting. I had not told her about Pheasant and me. I trusted her, but for her own sake, it was better that she did not know.

I nodded and, to make my lie appear real, I retraced the path to the servants' quarters with my basket.

Giggling, Plum and Daisy passed Pheasant, their hands covering their mouths. They walked to a path near the bamboo grove and disappeared. I stood where I was for a moment and then walked to the bridge.

"Where are you going, sweet face?" He was still standing there, not moving. He looked pale, and the stubble on his chin had grown thick, like a dark cloud. His white tunic was crumpled. He looked as though he had not slept well for weeks.

A pang rose in my chest. "To the wardrobe chamber." I reached for the wooden rail for support.

He coughed, looking awkward, nothing like the fellow who used to leap off haystacks with grace. "I saw you at the imperial stable a moment ago with my father. They were branding horses. You probably didn't notice me."

His voice was hoarse, and each word hit me like a hammer. Of course I had noticed him. But I could not tell him that. I turned to look at the pond under the bridge, where a goldfish leaped, and the water rippled. I dug my nails into the rail. "There were many people there, and the Kashmir horses were of superb quality."

"Right," he said, his voice low. "I don't like branding horses."

I knew it, but I said, "The Emperor does. He told me the horses needed to be branded for their age, speed, breed, and condition, even their agility and stamina." Pheasant had been the one who had told me that. I bit my lip.

He thrust his head back and ran his fingers through his long, loose hair. "I wanted to tell you. I talked to Rain. She promised she would not tell my father about us. So will you come again?"

"I'm afraid not."

"I know it's risky. But I told her if she dared to tell my father about us, I would tell him she had seen me too."

So Rain could not harm me after all, thanks to Pheasant. "It is still dangerous, Pheasant," I said slowly. "And that night in his bedchamber…"

"I did not say anything, did I?"

"What if it happens again?"

"I swear I would not say a word."

A raindrop fell on my sleeve and vanished on the surface of the fine silk gown the Emperor had given me. Before me, the bamboos swayed near the bridge, and the sky darkened. It would rain soon. Should I tell Pheasant the real reason I could not see him again? "I don't know…"

"Besides, have I told you I am not like my brothers? I can choose whom I marry. Before my mother died, she made my father promise my wife would be my choice, not his."

Wouldn't it be wonderful if Pheasant chose me? Wouldn't it be beautiful if we could be together? I wanted nothing other than to stay with him. He was the one I wanted. But he was not for me. Nor was I for him. "You could never marry me, Pheasant."

"Why not?"

Because I had a destiny, and he was not part of it. And I was so close… "I'm not worthy of you. Can you not see it?"

"What are you talking about?" He took a step toward me.

I closed my eyes. "Do you remember the story of the girl who flew to the moon?"

"The moon girl?" His eyes grew bright. Too bright. "I thought you were different from the others. You never cared. You did not even know who I was."

"You are wrong." My heart wrenched, but I forced myself to continue. "I'm no different from the other girls." The girls who wished to be an empress. Or Chang E, who wanted her immortality. I put down the basket of laundry and, my hands trembling, I took out the jade silkworm from the scent pouch. "You should keep this. Or give it to Rain."

He held it in his hand, gazing at the silkworm. I thought he would fly into a rage, lash his anger at me, shout at me, or strike me. I would have felt much better if he had. But he closed his hand over the silkworm. His fist remained clenched for a long time, and when he raised his head, a deluge of anguish had flooded his eyes.

I wanted to wrap my arms around him and tell him I was sorry. I wanted to tell him to forget about what I had said and that I would not leave him. I did neither. Instead, I descended the stone stairs of the bridge and passed him.

And the rain fell on my face like a shower of ashes.

The Emperor summoned me that night. I painted my eyebrows and beauty marks, whitened my skin with some creamy tincture, and dabbed fragrance under my armpits to make me smell pleasant. Then I put on a transparent silk veil and draped it around me.

It was my night. There would be no Jewel, and he would be all mine. If he continued to summon me for a month, I would replace Jewel. I would be known as Most Adored.

He waited, wearing a loose white tunic and a pair of night

trousers with gold threads on the hem. He did not sit on the bed or the stool, but rather on a floor mat surrounded by candles. He seemed to be performing a ritual, one I had never seen before. His hand was shaking, and the flames flickered on his shrunken face—was it lopsided somehow? But that must be the light... I was certain though, he looked haggard, uncertain, even...fearful.

I sat at the outer circle of candles, keeping a discreet distance from him. Daisy had told me he was different at night, but I had not expected to see him act so strangely. In fact, had I not seen him in his elaborate formal regalia and crown in court, had I not seen how calm he was when he gave the order to throw the slave under the horses at the polo match, I would not have believed he was the Emperor of China.

"Wine!" he ordered, handing me a small jug.

I hurried to a table and poured the wine. He took it from my hand and dismissed the other servants who waited in the corridor. "Go!" He gestured me to the bed.

A wave of nervous heat rushed through me, but I did not hesitate. I lay down.

He came close. "Hold this." He pushed the wine jug into my hands, as if he were asking his groom to hold his belongings before he headed out for hunting. Then he pulled up his robe.

I could not understand why he had given me the jug, but I obeyed, held tight to it as his cold fingers scratched my thigh. I should not complain. I had asked for this. Many maidens had looked forward to this moment. I should have been glad, should have felt privileged and honored that I would become the Emperor's woman. Emperor's woman...like Jewel... I wondered how she felt when she came to serve him.

The liquid in the jug swished, wetting my palm as he pushed at me. He seemed to be having trouble, however, grunting and cursing. I stared at the ceiling. The bedposts seemed to shake, and the green balls in the dragons' mouths appeared as if they would fall out any moment. There were two reflections, the Emperor's back and my head. We looked small, like insects crawling...

His cursing grew louder, and his breath became heavier. I tensed, worried. I hoped he was not upset with me.

"Turn around!" he barked. A force smacked me, and his hands clamped down on the sides of my face. My ear was rubbed raw, and my jaw was nearly crushed.

What would it be like to do it with Pheasant? Would he hurt me too? I should have been ashamed. I should not have thought of him while I was in his father's bed...

A loud sound exploded. It was the jug. I looked at my empty hands. The Emperor had snatched it from me and smashed it.

"Useless, useless!" he bellowed, flinging his arm wildly. Another crash. Then another. He breathed hard, his face crimson as though he were about to kill someone. "Get up. I said get up!"

He would not take me. I was too shocked to stand up. He did not like me? Was there something wrong with me? Was I too ugly?

"Wine! Wine!"

I jolted. Quickly putting on my gown, I went to a nearby table. There I found another jug and filled it with wine.

He drained the whole thing and tossed it away. "More!"

I gave him another, and he drank again, streams of wine trickling down his chin. I had never seen him drink in such haste and without grace.

"You, all of you, are useless," he said. His voice was as hoarse as though a fire had burned his throat, but the fire had died, and there were only blisters and scars.

I remembered the Noble Lady had mentioned that he had trouble doing his duty. So perhaps it was not my fault after all. But I still had something to do with it. I had failed to please him. If I were more skillful, if I were like Jewel, he could have taken me. I could not hold up my head.

"Tell me," he said, wiping his mouth. "Are you a good liar?"

I wondered what he meant, and carefully, I said, "The One Above All, when I was a child, I studied Lao Tzu. He said that Heaven and Earth encompass all things in between, like a bellows, and nourish them with their abundance, whereas a man's utterances would sound full and pleasing, but they would soon be spent."

"Nonsense. Say what is in your mind!"

"It is better not to lie, and a man could always avoid it by keeping silent." And if I must lie, I would lie only to my enemies, not to myself.

"Silent? I am asking you now." He waved his arm, and beads of wine flew to my face. "Do you lie?"

There was fury in his voice, and I knew the fire would return if I did not comply. "It depends."

He nodded. "This sounds more like you. Go on. Why do you lie?"

Because it was convenient and it provided protection, I wanted to tell him, but I said, "I don't know, the One Above All. I only know that truth does not die, and we can't live without it."

He shook his head. "You don't know what you're talking about."

"Yes, the One Above All."

"When you're older, you will know not to talk to your emperor like this."

"Yes, the One Above All."

"We always lie. We lie to our servants, we lie to friends, we lie to enemies, and we lie to ourselves. Lies are like this jug of wine. We drink it constantly to keep our essence and to fight. Who daresay it's not good for health?" He raised the jug. A drop of wine fell on a candle, and the flame spluttered. He did not seem to notice. "And truth, who cares?"

I did not know what to answer.

"If we lie well, if we get everyone to agree to it, if we lie until our death, if we lie for a hundred years, would you not say the lies are the truth?"

That argument sounded perverted, and I did not like it, but I had to agree. Truth had value only when people cared to know, but if people were fooled for centuries, if they thought they knew, who would ask to hear the truth? Likewise, if a person pretended for his whole life, putting on a kind face and hiding his darkest secrets until his death, would people not think they had known the kind person all along?

"The hard part would be the moment when you awake from wine. Then you see his eyes." He pointed at no one in particular. "His dead eyes."

He froze, his head cocked to one side, his eyes distant. It looked as though he was lost in an old memory. There was sadness—yes, I was certain of it—in his eyes, and his mouth twitched as though he could not bear the pain of it, as though he were about to cry. Then he punched the air, and his face changed. There was no sadness, only hardness and coldness spreading over his face like a mask.

"But he punishes me. He is trying to make me weak! It's him! I know it's him!" he bellowed. "He stares at me. He even calls out my name. 'Shimin, Shimin.' How many years have passed? I don't remember, but I remember the truth I made." He stabbed his chest. "My truth, and everyone believes in it."

I was confused. So confused. What was he talking about? Whom was he talking about?

"Do not lie to your emperor."

"Never, the One Above All."

"Liars, all of you." He drank more. "I did what was necessary. He couldn't blame it on me. He deserved it. He would have done the same. What can he do now? He's dead! What harm can he do to me? He was no brother of mine. No, not anymore."

His brother. The heir who was supposed to inherit the throne? Emperor Gaozu had three sons. The oldest son, Li Jiancheng, was the heir to the throne, but he died, and the youngest son died as well, leaving only the Emperor to inherit the throne.

The Emperor rose. The hem of his night trousers licked the flames. I gasped and dashed to smother the fire.

He swirled around. "What is it?"

"The flame—"

He staggered backward, his head turning left and right. "Where? Do you see him? I know he's here. I know it!"

His voice changed again. It was cracked, broken, like a bone fractured under pressure. "Tell him to leave. This is my bedchamber. Tell him to leave. He's screaming at me. Do you hear him?"

He was shivering. He looked frightened. I was alarmed. "No... the One Above All...I don't hear anything."

The flame caught the hem of his robe. I was about to cry out, warning him, when he dropped to his feet, smothering the flame. "You're lying," he said. Smoke drifted near his feet, and he buried his head between his knees. "You hear him. He mocks me, threatens me. 'Sooner or later,' he says, 'sooner or later, Shimin...'"

I did not know what to make of it, and how swiftly his mood had changed. "I...I'll get more candles."

"Go. Go. Get out!"

I could not move. I had come to bed him, but he did not seem interested, and he was angry at me.

"No. Stay. Don't leave." He lay down on the floor. "Don't leave."

Relieved, I went back to the candles. He mumbled, waving his hands. Finally he quieted, and with his feet curled up, his arms tucked close to his chest, he fell asleep. I waited for a moment and then gingerly took the broken candle near his feet and put it on a table. Then I sat, hugging my knees.

The candle's light glowed. It lit up the bedchamber, creating a bright ring of light, like the shining edge of the sun near eclipse, and inside the ring, darkness had spread to swallow the Emperor.

I could not understand what had happened to him or why he was so tormented. But he needed me. I was still his favorite, and that was good enough.

O

AD 642

the Sixteenth Year *of*

Emperor Taizong's Reign

of Peaceful Prospect

WINTER

26

FINALLY! SECRETARY FANG GAVE THE EMPEROR THE
report of his search for Mother.

The Gold Bird Guards had pasted many bulletins in the capital,
and in a month's time, they had received many messages regarding
Mother, the Secretary said carefully. But it turned out people had
misidentified Mother and most information was false, and all the
clues led to nothing. It was his belief that because she had disap
peared too many months ago, all traces of her had been lost. He
paused and said no more, but from the way he bowed, I could sense
what he was thinking—Mother was dead, and we might never find
out what happened to her.

I wept, but I implored the Emperor to keep searching. Mother
was still alive. I could feel her. And I would never give up on her.

A few days later, I came to the Audience Hall again.

"The One Above All." Secretary Fang, in his purple robe, spoke
first. "Forgive me that I must bring up this subject again. It has been
more than four years since our beloved Empress Wende's passing.
The people are eager to pay their respects to the next empress,
whose grace shall bring fortune to our kingdom." I peeked farther

out around the screen shielding the men. The Secretary had a square face and short legs. He was a taciturn man and frowned perpetually, as if he were unhappy in the court.

My heart raced faster when I realized what he was going to say next—his proposal for the new Empress. His strategy made sense. If the lady he suggested became the Empress, he would gain great control and fortune in the court.

"Let me restate this. Until another son is born, there will be no Empress." The Emperor waved.

So the rumor was true. The Emperor considered it a punishment from Heaven that he had begotten no son after the Empress's death.

The ministers near the Secretary shook their heads in disappointment. I moved near the screen so I could see their faces behind their ivory tablets. I wondered who they would ally with. With the Pure Lady's son in exile, she was in disgrace, and none of them would support her. Then Secretary Fang had to ally with one of the three other Ladies or Jewel. But the Secretary did not know Jewel very well, so she would not be a likely choice. Perhaps he wanted the Noble Lady. The thought gave me great hope, and I was happy for her.

I was sad too. None of them would speak for me.

"I beg the One Above All to reconsider." The Uncle, holding his ivory tablet, stepped next to the Secretary. "A kingdom without an heir can't prosper, and likewise, the palace without an empress won't have peace." His voice was loud, assured, and full of authority.

"The One Above All." The Duke came in front of the throne. "I beg to differ. The matter is of utmost importance, and we must not decide on impulse. The candidate for the crown must meet many conditions, such as family background of nobility, her pedigree, her title, and the number of children to whom she gives birth. Although it has been a while since the Empress's death, sufficient time and careful examination are needed in order to make a proper evaluation."

I was not surprised. The Duke did not want a new Empress,

because the late Empress had been his sister. Anyone who replaced her would reduce his power and influence in the court.

"This is only your excuse." The Uncle pointed his cane at the Duke accusatorily. "You will bring our kingdom to ruin, and your selfish ambition will bring our people to ruin! I only hope the One Above All will see that—"

"I did not ask for your tirade, Uncle." The Emperor's voice was threaded with warning.

The Uncle's face turned red. It was the first time I had heard the Emperor openly reprimand him to side with the Duke.

After a moment of silence, the Secretary bowed again. "If I may be allowed to speak, the One Above All." He cleared his throat. "By the glory of the One Above All, there is a woman who meets all your criteria. With her impeccable nobility, her pedigree, and her title, she has captured the heart of our Emperor and will make the whole kingdom rejoice."

The Duke raised his head. "My esteemed Secretary, I am afraid there is no such woman."

The Emperor looked interested. He leaned forward. "Let me hear you, Secretary. Whom do you suggest?"

I held my breath. Did he support the Noble Lady?

"I suggest no one other than the Lady-in-Waiting, whose wit has stunned those of us who have a chance to know her, our Most Adored."

Jewel.

I froze. What had she done to win his support? But how clever she was. Being a third-degree lady and still Most Adored, she had enough of the Emperor's affection and support to get what she wanted. And she had seized her chance to climb further since her former ally, the Pure Lady, was out of the picture.

"Ah." The Emperor nodded, his fingers drumming the throne's armrest.

I could not listen. Would he agree?

The Duke laughed. "Secretary, have you checked? She has borne no son."

"She's still in her twenties, young and fertile. She has plenty of time."

"What about the order of ranks and seniority? How can a third-degree lady surpass the second-degree ladies to become an empress?" That was ironic. I had never liked the Duke, but it seemed he was helping me.

"Are you suggesting that the One Above All must bow to the boundary he created, and he can't choose his favorite woman as his chief wife?"

"I'm concerned only that such an endeavor will subvert the social order and tradition we have so valued for hundreds of years!"

The Emperor held up his hand. "What are your thoughts, Grand Chancellor?"

I searched for the hunchbacked man, Wei Zheng. He had helped me when the Duke accused me after the assassination attempt, and the Pure Lady had sought his support once. He was undoubtedly an important man.

"May I suggest—" The Uncle stepped forward.

"I'm asking the Chancellor." The Emperor did not look in his direction.

The Uncle breathed hard. He looked humiliated. A few ministers glanced at him from behind their ivory tablets.

"Chancellor?"

"I read the signs on the chart today." The hunchbacked man seemed more bent. "Today is not a good day to discuss domestic affairs."

"Well, then." The Emperor straightened. "We shall devote the rest of the morning to discussing foreign affairs."

I went to sit in a corner. I had to tell the Noble Lady of the Secretary's proposal. How had Jewel won such support from a powerful ally? And most importantly, what should I do now?

After the Emperor finished the audience, we headed back to the Inner Court. I finished my midday meal quickly and went to the Noble Lady's bedchamber.

"I've heard." She nodded. "What a surprise. Most Adored has been busy making friends, and what a powerful ally she has obtained. You said the Emperor asked the other courtiers' opinions too?"

"Yes. Several."

"What did the Emperor look like when he listened to their suggestions?"

"He didn't seem to object to Jewel."

The Noble Lady rubbed her chest nervously. "So we must stop her."

"We need more time." The Emperor liked me, but I was not Most Adored yet. I would need to spend more nights with him to solidify my status. "Or we could forge alliances."

We needed a champion who would suggest the Noble Lady or even me. But I could not speak that thought openly, even with the Noble Lady. And we needed to find an ally fast. Secretary Fang would not stop pressing the Emperor until he succeeded, and we would not have the astrology chart to help us next time.

"The Duke has only his own welfare in mind," the Noble Lady said. "He will not agree to have his late sister's position replaced by another woman. Besides, he hates me." She sighed. "His late sister was not fond of me."

"How about the Uncle?"

He did not have the Emperor's favor, for the moment. But he was still influential in the court. Then I realized he must have been the one who was behind the empress proposal. He resented the Duke. If he succeeded in making another woman the empress, he would gain a powerful ally and possibly crush the Duke.

"He's from the older generation," the Noble Lady said. "Proud and conceited. He was the one who aided Emperor Gaozu during the war. I hardly know him."

"What about the Grand Chancellor?"

"It's difficult to say. He is a great statesman, a well-known historian, but also a traitor."

"Traitor?"

"He used to serve my father."

I frowned, feeling lost. The intricate court relationships were more complex than I had ever imagined. Everyone had a history, a purpose, and a stance to maintain, but I had no history, no supporters, and my purpose led me nowhere.

"Then why did the Secretary support Jewel? Could it be possible that she is a relative of his?" I asked.

The Noble Lady shook her head again. "I know him. He is not related to Most Adored."

"But she must have known him somewhere or some time ago," I said. "Is she meeting him in secret? How does she get to know him?" I wished I could ask her in person, but it had been a few months since I talked to her in the stable. Suddenly, I recalled Jewel's odd behavior there. It seemed she had known Pheasant when he was young, but she had denied she was exiled. She had been lying to me. She was trying to hiding her past. "My Noble Lady, are you aware that Jewel was exiled?"

"Exiled?" She looked at me in surprise. "Where did you hear that?"

"I met her in the Yeting Court years ago. She told me."

"I did not know. Why didn't you tell me before?"

"It did not seem important."

"I have never heard that she was exiled. I thought she was one of the old Selects from the Yeting Court. Are you certain?"

"She told me a few years ago, before she won the Emperor's favor, but then more recently, she tried to deny it."

The Noble Lady looked pensive. "If she had been in the Inner Court before, shouldn't I or someone else know her? When was she in the Inner Court?"

Jewel had waited in the Yeting Court for seven years, and it had been two years since she told me her past. "That would be at least nine years ago."

"Nine years ago? What was her title?"

"She didn't mention it so she could have been a minor concubine." I stared at the Noble Lady with hope.

"Nine years ago, a minor concubine named Jewel... Let me think... A minor concubine... I would not see her often." She shook her head. "I don't remember. But with her cunningness, and her returning to the Inner Court for the second time, she would certainly know how to manipulate the ministers."

"Including the Secretary." I sighed.

"Now I'm very curious." The Noble Lady stroked the box filled with spiders. "Why was our Most Adored exiled from the Inner Court?"

I had asked Jewel the same question, and I had heard no answer. But all the same I was excited. Jewel had a secret, and that would be her weakness. If I found out what it was, I would be able to strike back. I could even stop her from taking the crown.

I bid the Noble Lady a good day and then left her bedchamber.

The master's words came to me: "Let your plans be dark and impenetrable as night, and when you move, fall like a thunderbolt."

What was Jewel's secret?

✦ ✦

I began with Jewel's maids. I stopped in front of her house more often. To make myself less conspicuous, I dropped the things I carried, a candle or a handkerchief, so I could get an idea of the activities inside Jewel's house. But Jewel's maids noticed me and they drove me away. I changed my strategy, bribing them with my allowance, sending them sweet dates and rice cakes. The maids ate them but never had the grace to say thank you.

I began to talk to the food delivery eunuchs, the laundry ladies, and then the eunuchs working in the kitchen. None of them knew of Jewel's past.

Eunuch Ming. Would he know about Jewel's history? I found him near the entrance to the Yeting Court. He caught sight of me and followed me as I led him to a quiet bamboo grove near a pavilion.

I put out my palm, where a gold ingot sat. I had five of them, which I had saved for moments like this. "Tell me about Most Adored. Why was she exiled?"

His small rat eyes fixed on the gold. "Exiled? I did not hear of that."

I closed my fingers on the gold. "Well then, I will give this to someone else who will be more helpful."

"Well, it must have happened many years ago. Who would remember?"

I turned.

"Wait, wait! Come back! I don't know why she was exiled, but I know she is not who she claims to be."

"What?" I turned around.

"She is not called Jewel. I remember some old eunuch mentioned it once. He died years ago. A sick man, you know what I mean. Yes, Most Adored. She was in the Yeting Court for years, always alone too. She had a different name then, but somehow she told people her name was Jewel. No one really cared then…"

She had changed her name? How clever! It was easy to do in that forgotten court where no one knew her. "What is her real name?"

He frowned, scratching his head. "It's…Slender Willow? No… Silver Lotus? Wait…Snow Blossom!"

I handed the gold ingot to him.

My heart racing with excitement, I walked fast to tell the Noble Lady. She would be shocked, and pleased, to hear Jewel's real name.

"Snow Blossom?" The Noble Lady's eyes were wide. "Her real name is Snow Blossom?"

I nodded. That was why few people remembered her. She had been a minor concubine in the Inner Court nine years before, and she had changed her name. After so many years, with her white hair just like the other old Selects in the Yeting Court, everyone just assumed she was one of them.

But why was she banished? What was she trying to hide?

"Mei, there you are!" Plum put down a handful of roasted sunflower seeds on the table and pulled me to the corner as I entered our bedchamber. "I must tell you something. Most important news! Very shocking indeed."

"What news?" I asked.

"They found a body this afternoon, buried in the leaves under a bridge near the Archery Hall. A body! A guard's body!"

"Who's the guard?"

Plum popped a sunflower seed into her mouth and spat out the shell. "He was the head of the ninth Gold Bird Guards division. His nickname was Fifth Girl."

Traditionally, when a boy was born, his parents addressed him as a girl to avoid evil spirits snatching his life, and that nickname usually stayed with the person well into adulthood.

"How did he die?"

"Some said he was drunk and involved in a brawl, so he was killed by accident," Plum said, her face pink with excitement. "But some people also said there was no brawl, and Fifth Girl was not drunk, because he never drank, so they said he was killed for no reason."

I frowned. "So how did he really get himself killed?"

She went to the door to make sure that no one was coming to our chamber and lowered her voice. "It is because of the prophecy, Mei. Everyone is talking about it."

"Are you certain?"

"Yes! You should listen to them! No one has ever died in the palace before, they said, but ever since the shooting stars, two guards"—she put up two fingers—"not one, died without a reason. What else could it be?"

She reminded me of the other guard, nicknamed Black Boy, who was shot for stealing horses. Something told me that what Plum said was true, but I did not want her to keep talking and get into trouble.

I picked up a handful of seeds from the table. "These smell good. How do they taste? "

Plum did not appear to hear me. She looked around to assure no one was eavesdropping on us, even though we were alone. Her face pink with excitement again, she said, "Here's another thing, Mei. Have you heard of the ballad?"

"What ballad?"

"They said the children on the streets are singing this, and the grocery eunuchs heard it. It goes:

"This morning, a crooked branch grows on my mulberry tree,
It dips low to my well and begins to sing a story, that I must tell thee.
Once upon a time a phoenix shed hot tears in the mountain of flame,
the fire burns a young crane that flies over, leaving no name.
Now the old dragon shuts his eyes and sleeps under a stone,
and the crow sings on his throne."

I sucked in air. Of course. That was why the Emperor made those cryptic comments about lies and truths when he'd summoned me that night.

"You said the children on the streets are singing this?"

She nodded. "If the Emperor finds out who started it, he will—" She made a gesture of slashing her neck with her hand.

My mouth was dry. Whoever started the ballad could also be the man predicted in the prophecy, the man who would end the dynasty's reign.

"So do you think the Emperor knows who his foe is, Mei?"

I shook my head. He did not. If he had known, there would have been only one death, not two.

"You don't think Fifth Girl is the one?"

"He could be."

"I don't understand, Mei."

"Me neither." I sighed. "I just hope this will be over soon."

Or was that only the beginning? I thought of the reports of violence that had broken out on the street lately. In one particular case, a group of rebels had stolen two transportation boats that carried grains from the Grand Canal. The Emperor's uncle went to arrest the rebels, but when the Gold Bird Guards arrived, the rebels had all fled. The Duke, who took advantage of the Uncle's failure, accused him of letting the rebels escape deliberately. The Uncle was furious and claimed the Duke had planted a spy among his men and sabotaged his mission.

In any case, the damage was done, and the outlaws from nearby towns, even those in the south, were encouraged by the rebels' success and attacked the imperial delegations that transferred horses, grain, silk, and gold.

Plum popped three sunflower seeds in her mouth. Her mouth wiggled for a while, and then she spat out all the shells and swallowed the kernels. I watched her, fascinated by her skill.

"How long have you been in the court now, Plum?" I put a seed between my teeth and cracked it open.

"Almost five years."

So Jewel had arrived in the palace before Plum. There was no way she would know Jewel's true identity.

"Why did you ask, Mei?"

"Perhaps it's time to prepare for your five-year anniversary," I said, carefully picking out the small, cream-colored kernel with two fingers.

"What are you not telling me?" She stood nose to nose with me. "I heard the Secretary's proposal in the Audience Hall. It doesn't look good for the Noble Lady, does it?"

"I don't wish to drag you into this."

"What do you need to know?"

I did not speak.

She nudged me with her shoulder. "Out with it."

I chewed the kernel. "Do you know that Most Adored's name, Jewel, is not her real name?"

Her eyes widened. "Then what is her real name?"

"Snow Blossom."

"Why did she change her name? I thought she was a lady from the Yeting Court, an old Select."

"No. She is not a Select either. She was exiled to the court years ago."

Plum raised her pained eyebrows. "Are you certain? Why was she exiled?"

243

"You tell me."

"Well, well, well." She smiled, showing her bucktooth. "It's my skill to unearth the hidden secrets. I'll let you know as soon as possible."

27

THE NEXT DAY, WHEN THE EMPEROR CAME TO THE Audience Hall, I waited in the antechamber. Secretary Fang championed Jewel again. Just as I feared, the Duke and Wei Zheng could not find another excuse to stop the discussion, and the Uncle remained quiet. The Emperor appeared to consider Jewel seriously. The following day, she appeared in front of the advisers during a meeting and gave them bolts of silk and lavish gifts. When they took a break between meetings, she brought out trays of delicacies for them: roasted quail, poached pig ears, and stewed bear paws as their snacks. The ministers looked pleased. They devoured the food and soon sang a song of praise to Jewel.

"Indeed, Most Adored is the most virtuous woman I have ever seen," they said.

The Emperor laughed. He walked together with Jewel and the ministers while I trailed behind. None of the men noticed me.

Despair grew inside me like a spring seed. I needed to work harder and quicker.

But Plum found nothing, and I still did not know the reason why Jewel had been exiled.

✦ ✦

The Noble Lady raised her head as I entered her bedchamber. "Sit, sit," she said, fingering her necklace as she went to a painted stool near the window.

"You wished to see me, my Noble Lady?"

"I don't know how to begin, Mei. But I believe you must know this." Her hand left the necklace, and she faced me. "There is a rumor that you sold the Emperor's night robe for money."

"What? I did not." I clenched my fist. "You don't believe that, do you?"

"Of course I don't. You would never do such a thing. I talked to some eunuchs and paid them to quiet the rumor. I assure you this won't get to the Emperor's ears."

"It's Jewel's trick again," I said. "She should have played something new."

"You're wrong about this, Mei." She shook her head. "The sources said it was not from her, but she definitely heard it and fanned the rumor."

"Who started it then?"

"They said it was a female minister."

I inhaled deeply. Rain. I had almost forgotten about her.

"Do you know who she is?"

I nodded.

"Is there anything I should know, Mei?"

I could not lie to her. "Teacher Rain had an affair with Prince Zhi. She thinks the prince is interested in me."

"Prince Zhi."

I glanced at her, uncertain if she was angry with me.

"The Emperor adores him, I told you before, and when Wende lived, Zhi stayed in her bedchamber, and she raised him like a pearl. People still treat him differently. The girls lose their heads when they see him. I don't understand why the Emperor keeps him in the Eastern Palace. Perhaps he doesn't know about Zhi's dalliances. But Prince Zhi is trouble. You'll stay away from him, won't you?"

"I will."

"Good. I have faith in you. You're not like other girls, who are easily fooled by him." She went to her spindle wheel. "I'm happy you discovered Most Adored's real name, Mei. You did excellent work. Have you found out anything else about her?"

I shook my head. Plum had bribed the eunuchs, the teachers from the etiquette schools, and even the scribes from the Outer Palace. Soon, she said, she would hear something about Jewel. But by then, it might be too late.

We did not have much time. Since the ministers had approved of Jewel, it depended on the Emperor. Once he decided, she would become the Empress. He could announce his decision any moment.

"She hasn't come out of her bedchamber," the Noble Lady said, beginning to spin her spindle wheel.

"Why?" I asked.

"I don't know."

Doors squeaked open in the courtyard. I looked through the latticed window. Jewel's maid, the one with freckles, came out of her bedchamber with a tray of food.

"What is it?" the Noble Lady asked.

"It looks like she didn't like the meal." The food was untouched, and I could see a plateful of chicken. "She didn't eat it."

"My maid said she has had a poor appetite lately."

"Perhaps she's sick." I hoped.

"I don't know." The Noble Lady shook her head. "I don't know." She had never sounded more worried.

My heart heavy, I bid the Noble Lady my leave and stepped into the corridor. People were busy in the compound, and I paused to look at them. In the center of the courtyard, a group of maids were crouched over a board, playing *weiqi*. Near the small mountain, some maids were embroidering, some were sweeping the ground. I turned to look at the lady's chambers. At my right was Lady Obedience's chamber, where she was swaying her hips, fluttering her arms, dancing to the rhythms of a waist drum. At my left side was Lady Virtue's house, where a few seamstresses, carrying bolts of cloth in red, indigo, and green, gathered in front of the corridor. The Pure Lady's chamber was shut. I wondered what she was doing. I had not seen her since her son, the hot-tempered Prince Yo, was exiled last year. She did not attend the feasts, fruit distributions, or other gatherings, and most of the time, she shut herself in her chamber. But I would be a fool to think she had decided to become a recluse. The Pure Lady was the type of woman who would grab something to go down with her if she were drowning.

I looked at Jewel's house. There were some shadows floating around inside, but I could not tell what it was. Why was she not eating?

I decided to return to my chamber. When I passed the knobby pine trees near the small mountain, I noticed a blanket of frost had capped the mountain's peaks and covered the crevices of the stones. The whiteness had not covered the rocks completely, and there were speckles of black tips poking through the frosty sheet like spiders' feet. In the pond, the water was still but not frozen, and a piece of thin floe hung near the edge.

I pulled my sheep coat tighter around me. I did not like the frost or the snow. I preferred storms and thunder, and the furious power of the two joined to wash away the grime and dust.

It had been so cold at night lately that I had not slept well. Often I lay in bed, staring at the moonlight that shone through my windows. It printed pretty black patterns on the ground. Sometimes Pheasant came to my mind, and I shut my eyes to stop thinking of him.

"I hear you're spying on me." Jewel's voice came from behind me. She stood under the eaves of her house near the end of the corridor.

I lowered my head to bow. She was still Most Adored. "You came out." Should I call her by her real name? I should not. I could not alert her.

"Of course I did. I wish to ask you a big favor, Mei. You will indulge me, won't you?"

I smiled charmingly. "As you wish, Most Adored."

She pulled her red fur cape around her. Her white hair cascaded down her back. On her cheeks, beauty marks of pink peonies bloomed. "I knew you would say that."

"What's the favor?"

"When he summoned you a month ago, I heard he talked to you, and he slept in a circle of candles."

Who was her spy?

"Yes." I expected her to ask how my service to the Emperor was, but she did not speak.

She looked up at the sky for a moment. The wind swept her white hair like invisible fingers. "Have you been sleeping well, Mei? It is so cold lately I couldn't sleep. Last night, the moonlight shone through my windows and left patterns like black plum flowers. I wish you could have seen it. I would like to paint it, but I haven't painted for a while."

How odd. We had noticed the same thing. But she was my enemy and she had gained the Secretary's support. "You have been busy."

Her shoulders rose as though the wind had touched her neck and she was cold. For a moment I could not see her lips, only her catlike eyes as she peered above the red fur. "What did he tell you?"

"Many things, but nothing about you."

"That's not a surprise. But were you frightened when he mentioned the dead?"

She knew more details than I had supposed. I kept a straight face. "What dead?"

She stared at me, her eyes still as the frozen pond. Then she looked away. But a glimmer flew across her eyes, and I caught it—a glimmer of unease, or perhaps even of pain. It was faint, subtle, fleeting, and it died the moment it was lit. I had a feeling she had found what she had been looking for, but I did not know what it was or what I had done or said to give it away. I was disappointed.

"I bid you good day, Mei."

"How did you make Secretary Fang speak for you, Jewel?"

She shook her head. "Better luck next time, Mei."

I did not expect anything from her anyway. I turned to leave. But how did she know what the Emperor said on my night? And why did she look troubled after she heard my answer? I paused and looked back. She was still there, standing under the eaves, staring at me.

But she was no longer alone. Beside her stood a slim figure with a sharp, triangular face.

Rain.

My heart dropped. I hurried on.

AD 643

the Seventeenth Year *of*

Emperor Taizong's Reign

of Peaceful Prospect

SPRING

28

THERE WAS A FEAST TONIGHT, I WAS TOLD, EVEN THOUGH it was not a festival occasion. Following behind the other ladies, I went to the feast hall. The moment I walked in, I knew something was awry.

The ministers had come, and the musicians lined up at the door. On the tables sat many bouquets of flowers carved out of watermelons, oranges, and pears. Next to the Emperor sat Jewel, cloaked in a red damask gown printed with patterns of peach blossoms, vermilion birds, and parrots.

I took my seat among the Talents as the servants brought trays of food to the table. Bird's nest soup in ceramic bowls painted with bamboo leaves. Broiled camel humps in rectangular plates. Stewed bear's paws in small pots. Steamed, silver-striped mullets from the Po Sea with tangy ginger sauce. And many of the Emperor's favorite foods and rare delicacies I had only heard of. Jewel covered her nose and waved the fish away. I frowned, and my eyes caught her other hand stroking her stomach. My heart sank.

How had I missed it?

Jewel was pregnant.

"Heaven be blessed! Finally! My blood. My progeny!" The Emperor's voice shook the hall. "I have a great announcement to make!"

The servants behind me asked me something, but I was so shocked that I hardly heard them. They removed the food from my table and brought out small saucers containing bites of meats.

"Heaven promises me another child! Let it be a son, who shall be a witness to the halcyon kingdom I have created." The Emperor's whiskers shook as he shouted. He looked in high spirits. "Counselors! Listen up. I shall bestow the crown on this woman, who brings me honor and pride. Yes, this is my woman, and she will be the next empress of this kingdom!"

I could no longer see people's faces or hear the waves of deafening praise. The only sound I heard came from inside me.

Jewel. Empress.

In the corner, someone strummed a lute, the sound a deep groan like a dying wolf. The voluptuous Lady Obedience rose and moved to the center of the tables. She clapped her hands, signaling the musicians to play music, and swung her arms like graceful wings. The sound of *guzheng*, jovial flutes, and the clear tinkling of bells filled the hall. It was the song of "Towering Mountains and Trickling Streams."

The ministers lined up before the feast table to deliver their praises. The Ladies followed. The Noble Lady toasted first. Slowly, she walked, her face ghastly pale and her eyes teary, as though she were in a funeral procession. But what a remarkable lady she was. As soon as she approached the table, she smoothed her gown and bowed deeply.

I could not watch. Jewel did not deserve the Noble Lady's bow. She did not deserve anything.

Lady Virtue, her eyes also red from crying, looked away from her bronze mirror and came to bow too, and then Lady Obedience. The Pure Lady was absent as usual.

Next came the Ladies-in-Waiting. Beauties. Graces.

My turn came. I gave Jewel a bow and held out the cup to toast her. "*Gong xi.*" Congratulations.

"I shall accept your good wishes from the bottom of my heart," she said.

I bit my lip.

"After the coronation, I shall need some personal attendants." She sipped her wine.

"There are many girls in the Inner Court for you to choose from," I said.

She shook her head. "Not them. They're too pretty and clever." She gazed at me, her catlike eyes glinting. "Clever girls are troublesome. They'll distract me and the Emperor. I will not allow that. I think they need to step aside, and I will summon some new maidens from the kingdom. I need to have new faces around me."

She wanted to get rid of me. I felt my face chill. "Of course you can do anything you wish. You will be the empress."

She sighed. "I am so sorry, Mei. I like you. Truly. I do. It is not my wish to harm you, but I made a promise to a friend."

Rain. My hand shook, and the liquid spilled on my fingers.

I did not know how I returned to my table. Sitting there, I stared at the trays of food in front of me. There were plates of duck, quail, mutton, pigs' feet, cows' tongues. They were either stewed, roasted, or fried—animals dead, cooked, and sliced.

A woman I had never seen before stood in front of the wardrobe chamber. "Most Adored wished me to tell you," she said, "that I would take care of the Emperor's wardrobe from now on."

"It's my duty." I tried to control my temper. "She cannot overturn the Emperor's order."

"If you wish to ask the Emperor, you may do so."

"Where is he?"

"In Most Adored's bedchamber."

Desperate, I went straight to the Quarters of the Pure Lotus. But when I reached the courtyard, I turned back. I would only make myself look pitiful if I confronted him. Besides, I could not find any reason that he would side with me.

I felt desperate. Jewel had started to push me aside, and she was not even the empress yet.

And Plum told me nothing that I did not already know. Everyone had thought Jewel was only an old Select, and no one could recall the name of Snow Blossom.

✦ ✦

The imperial astrologers gathered in the Emperor's library to discuss which day was most auspicious for the coronation. Among them was the barefoot astrologer. I stood behind the other maids and lowered my head. I did not like the astrologer, and I was glad he did not notice me.

With the incense lit, he chanted with the others, crouching over a ball instrument held by a tripod with toads for legs. A famous instrument built three hundred years ago, it was said to be able to detect Heaven's intention. The men pointed their fingers here and there, frowning, nodding, and murmuring. There were some days good for weddings, fishing, traveling, riding outdoors, and some days we should wear wooden ornaments rather than jade, don garments of plain colors instead of red, avoid the topic of snakes, or refrain from lighting fire and cooking.

"For coronation"—they studied the instrument together—"let's see…"

I hoped they would never find an auspicious day for that occasion in the next two hundred years. But after a while, they clapped their hands and shouted. "The twentieth day of the third month!"

Only one month away.

Suddenly, the court was crowded with seamstresses, musicians, jewelry makers, wine specialists, and eunuchs who reviewed lists of specialties around the kingdom for the banquet. Jewel pranced around. Her maids supported her arms as she walked, as if they were worried she would trip and kill herself, while the nutrition provosts trailed behind, instructing her on what food would fatten her and the fetus. My ears hurt from listening.

✦ ✦

Too soon, the third month of the year came.

"Still didn't find anything?" the Noble Lady asked when I came to her bedchamber.

I shook my head. Plum was talking to an old laundry woman, but that would surely lead nowhere.

"I'm sorry to hear that. I've spoken to the Chancellor about the Emperor's intention. He said it was up to the Emperor to make the decision about the Empress."

I rubbed my forehead, disappointed.

"I knew he would not support me. I was asking too much from him." She sat on a stool near her bed, her hands on a metal warmer. "I also asked the Emperor's uncle. The old man received me and asked me what I thought of the Duke. He gave me a tirade about his foe, telling me how unworthy he was and how the Emperor had wronged him. I'm afraid he is growing angry and senile."

There was nothing to stop Jewel now.

On the eighteenth day of the month, two nights before Jewel's crowning, I stood in the courtyard of my chamber, watching the night sky. There was no moon, only stars, scattered like frozen sunflower seeds. I thought of Father. I was sorry. I could not fulfill his dream after all.

Then I heard a piercing howl from the east side of the Inner Court, the Quarters of the Pure Lotus. It was Jewel's scream. Without thinking, I dashed to the quarters.

All over the court, many servants scuttled around. Near Jewel's chamber, her maids rushed out with bedding stained with blood.

She had lost her baby.

Heaven help me! Perhaps Jewel would not be the empress now.

From the Noble Lady's chamber, I watched women who came to visit Jewel. It was protocol for the Ladies to offer condolences, even though we all knew it was sheer pretense. When the Noble

Lady returned from Jewel's chamber, I asked her, "Is the Emperor going to delay the coronation now?"

"I don't think so." She shook her head.

"But she has a cold womb." A fetus could not thrive in a cold womb, I had heard.

"I thought so too. But Most Adored claims that is not the case."

"What else could have happened then?"

"She said someone put aconite in her wine."

I was shocked. Aconite was a poisonous herb that aborted an unwanted fetus. "Who would do that?"

She sighed. "No one would be so heartless to do that. But she is angry. That's the reason. You should be careful. Don't let her see you. You don't want any attention right now."

My heart sank. Would Jewel accuse me of poisoning her?

That night, when I lay on the mat, I could not sleep. Would I be sleeping on the cold floor in the Yeting Court tomorrow? Or worse?

✦ ✦

The night before Jewel's coronation, the Emperor summoned the Talents to serve him. The other eight Talents and I arrived in our silk gowns and waited on a large mat in a corner. The Emperor sat inside the ring of candles, drinking. The news of Jewel's miscarriage had shaken him, I could tell, and he looked sad, his eyes bleary, his whiskers sagging. He did not ask us to take off our clothes or approach him. Soon, the other Talents grew tired of waiting and began to whisper about tomorrow's coronation.

"Mei," Plum whispered in my ear as he leaned over me on the mat. "I found out why Jewel was banished."

"You did?" I almost bolted upright. The Emperor, holding a jug with his left hand, was trying to grab his sword with his right. He seemed to have trouble doing it. "Why did he banish her?"

"Not the Emperor. It was the late Empress. She was jealous, because Jewel was beautiful and the Emperor liked her. The

Empress made an excuse, killed all of Jewel's family, and banished her to the Yeting Court."

"Really?" I glanced at the other Talents, who were growing quiet and turned around to sleep.

"That's not all. Here's the best part," Plum said. "Jewel was the Emperor's older brother's concubine before she became the Emperor's."

I sat up. "The Emperor's older brother?"

"Yes."

"Are you certain?"

"No doubt about it. I came across an old woman with a bad hip at a eunuch's burial. She told me. She was in the Emperor's brother's household many years ago. She did not recognize Jewel at first. But when I mentioned Snow Blossom, she remembered."

"Did the Noble Lady see her when she was in the court nine years ago?"

Plum peered at the Emperor. He had grabbed the sword, but his hand shook, and he dropped it. He cursed. "Oh, no, I do not think any of the ladies did. The Emperor put her in a special hall, hiding her from the Empress. That was why it angered her."

No wonder no one had heard of her. What would the Noble Lady think when she heard of that scandal? She would be surprised, for sure, but Jewel's coronation was tomorrow. It was too late. We could not stop her even if we worked up the gossip overnight.

"I wish I had known this sooner. She'll be crowned tomorrow."

"There's something else." Plum cupped her hand around my ear. "Jewel keeps a special handkerchief."

"Special?" It was common to keep a handkerchief, of course. Everybody had one.

"It belonged to a man."

"The Emperor?"

She made a face. "If it belonged to him, it wouldn't be special."

"Then to whom did it belong?"

"Wine!" The Emperor's loud voice echoed in the chamber, startling me.

Plum rose. "Wait for me. When I return, I'll tell you."

The hem of her skirt brushed my knee as she passed me.

I gnawed my knuckles. Finally! I knew Jewel's secret. What an interesting past she had, and she had kept a man's handkerchief?

"Tell me, Plum," I urged when she padded back. "Whose handkerchief is it?"

"All I can say is it has a man's name stitched on it."

My heart pounded. "What kind of name?"

"It says *Jiancheng*, or something like it. I can't be certain. Jewel keeps it close to her."

I knew that name. Emperor Gaozu's firstborn, the Emperor's older brother. So Jewel had indeed been his concubine. "How did you find out about it?"

"A laundry woman mentioned it a few days ago. But I couldn't prove it. It was chaotic today, with her losing the baby this morning. Many people came and left her chamber. I slipped in and took a peek. Swiftly. It has a pair of love ducks and that man's name."

The Noble Lady would be pleased to hear that. I glanced at the Emperor, who had gotten a good hold on his sword and stood up, as though trying to perform a sword dance. I turned to Plum and said in a low voice, "Do you swear by it, Plum?"

She shrugged. "I can't. I may be wrong."

"A handkerchief," I repeated in a low voice. "Wait here, Plum. I'll be right back."

Yet I could not leave immediately. The Emperor turned toward me, thrust his sword, and shouted. Anxious, I bit my nail and waited. Finally, he spun around.

I slipped out of the chamber and ran to the Quarters of the Pure Lotus.

◆ ◆

The Noble Lady's hand flew to her chest as I finished my words. "Are you certain about that? She was his brother's concubine?"

"And she still keeps his handkerchief. With his name embroidered on it," I added. "It has to be from him. It can't be from anyone else. But why does she still keep it, after all these years?"

"Only she can answer that." The Noble Lady looked pensive. "Now, if we had the handkerchief in our hands, we could show it to the Emperor."

"You think we should steal it?"

"No, no." She sat on a stool near her bed. Her cheeks flushed. "We should never commit a crime like that. I refuse to sacrifice my pride for her."

I was surprised to hear that. I would not mind stealing the hand-kerchief if it could save my life. "What do you suggest we do?"

She paced before me, her eyes thoughtful and her phoenix headdress quivering. Finally, she stopped. "Even if we wanted to, she would not leave it in the open so we could take it. I'm so sorry. I was almost certain that with the handkerchief we could destroy her. But I think I'm wrong. There is no way. If the Emperor's brother were not dead, this would have been the downfall of Most Adored."

"So we just let it go and watch her be crowned tomorrow?"

"I'm afraid so." She sighed again. "Go to sleep, and get ready for tomorrow."

Disappointed, I dragged my feet to the door. "The Emperor once asked me about his brother. He seemed to think his brother was watching him. It's strange, isn't it?"

She stopped me. "You didn't mention this to me before. Tell me. What did he say?"

"He was sitting in a circle of candles. He looked afraid." I took a deep breath. "I think he was even haunted. But I don't understand. Why is he afraid of his brother?"

Her eyes sparked in the candlelight. "We are not supposed to gossip about this, Mei. That is why you didn't know. The Emperor murdered his family."

I was shocked. So the phoenix ballad was true.

"That was how he ascended to the throne," she said. "There was a gruesome battle at the Xuanwu Gate, during which the

Emperor slew his older brother, the rightful heir, and murdered his younger brother. He even enslaved their women, slaughtered the young children, imprisoned his father, Emperor Gaozu, and then proclaimed himself the One Above All."

I stared at her. So that was the truth! "You said the Emperor slew the heir? And enslaved the women?"

"I suppose he kept Jewel for himself." She sighed. "He was the second son, Mei. He would never have had the chance to ascend to the throne."

I remembered what Pheasant had told me. *There was a concubine… My mother was not happy with the way he treated her…* It made sense. "And the children?"

She sighed. "The oldest was seven. The firstborn of the Li family. Seven boys and five girls. And the women, servants, courtiers who supported them…"

I shivered. I could hear the children's screams and their small feet running, helplessly, away from the blades. I could see those small faces streaked with tears of fright and their bodies saturated in blood. And all those people… "So the Emperor believes his brother's ghost is haunting him?"

The Noble Lady did not answer, staring at the candle's flame. Her plump face shaking, she gripped my shoulders tightly. "Mei, I believe we just found a way to defeat Most Adored."

There was a tremble in her voice that I never thought to hear from the Noble Lady. It was not fear. It was excitement. Her breathing quickened, and I could see how hard she was trying to control herself.

"How?"

She went to open the door and called out for her maids, who stood outside the chamber. "Prepare my lanterns."

I swallowed, knowing where she was going. But I wanted to make sure. "Where are we going, my Noble Lady?"

She waved. "Follow me, Mei."

29

I WAS OUT OF BREATH WHEN WE REACHED THE EMPEROR'S bedchamber. It looked busier than when I had left it. Shadows rushed in and out—Jewel's servants, perhaps making the last arrangements before the coronation.

Standing near an immense kylin statue with the Noble Lady, I dabbed the perspiration off my forehead.

"All the better she's here," she said, waiting for a eunuch to announce her arrival.

When the Emperor was ready to see us, the Noble Lady walked into the bedchamber, and I followed. Plum and the other Talents were nowhere to be seen.

I glanced at Jewel, who sat on a stool next to the Emperor. I had not seen her lately and did not expect to see her like that. Her white hair tumbled to her chest in disarray. The peony beauty marks on her face were smudged, her lips appeared cracked, and the candlelight revealed deep lines etched around the corners of her eyes. She was wearing a long pink skirt and a white robe that looked like a nightgown. On the stool near her were the yellow regalia and a phoenix headdress she would don tomorrow.

"What is your business, Noble Lady?" the Emperor asked.

His voice sounded slurred. He was drunk, swaying, and his sword lay on the oversize bed.

The Noble Lady knelt before him. I hesitated and then knelt beside her.

"The One Above All," she said. "Forgive me, I should not bother you at this late hour, but I fear I must speak for the interest of the Inner Court, even though I might offend the ears of our most superior."

"Speak."

"This spring, I went to pay my respect to our ancestors in the Altar House on the Day of Qingming," she said. "I perhaps shouldn't say this, but I happened to hear the prayers the Most Adored said in a corner after you left."

I was not sure what the Noble Lady had in mind. The Day of Qingming was when people gathered their families to pay respect to the deceased. Most families went to the graves to sweep the ground, light incense, and offer fruits and meat. On that day, the Noble Lady and the other ladies had lit the incense in the Altar House after they visited Emperor Gaozu's mausoleum, while I had offered my prayers to Father in front of the tablet I made, since I was unable to travel to Wenshui.

"What is this? It was a long time ago. Why do you bring it up?" Jewel interrupted, as if sensing something ominous. "Besides, the One Above All, I left with you. Do you recall?"

The Emperor ignored her. "If this is what you came to say, Noble Lady, I've heard it."

"The One Above All, allow me to speak more. I shall not repeat the details here. I happened to hear Most Adored express her undying thoughts and affection to the deceased. But her prayer was not offered to Emperor Gaozu."

The Emperor straightened. "To whom did she offer?"

"I'd rather not speak his name."

"Noble Lady, I wasn't aware you were capable of spinning vicious lies as well as silk," Jewel said. "Do you think our most sage ruler will believe such a despicable tale?"

"The dead are powerful, Most Adored, and both you and I understand their vengeance can expel the fruit of love that we try to conceive."

She was clever to weave the Emperor's fear of the dead into Jewel's tragedy. The Emperor shook slightly. Jewel rose and stepped close to the Noble Lady.

"You should watch your tongue, Noble Lady." Her eyes narrowed, but her face was stark white.

"Alas, Most Adored, we fear them, worship them, and yet we are still unable to be rid of them." The lady kept her perfect, serene demeanor. "And most astonishing of all, we keep a token from them, hoping to preserve a piece of the past."

My heart stopped. It was risky. What if there was no handkerchief? What if it turned out to be a gift from the Emperor?

Her eyes pouring hatred, Jewel leaned over. "Shame on you, Noble Lady. How can you lose your sense of honor and accuse the innocent?"

The Noble Lady did not flinch. "If Most Adored claims no affection for the dead, then why have you never parted with his handkerchief?"

"Handkerchief?" Jewel faltered. "How...how..."

"What handkerchief?" The Emperor shot to his feet.

Jewel stepped back, her hands clutching her gown. "I don't know what she's talking about."

"Where is the handkerchief? Give it to me."

Jewel looked as if she was going to flee. The Emperor grabbed her. "Where is it?"

Before I realized what was going to happen, he ripped the gown off her with one yank. He kept tearing, cursing, slapping, until a piece of fabric dropped onto the ground.

I stared at it, my mouth open. The handkerchief was made of fine, transparent silk, beautifully embroidered with a pair of nestling love ducks. But what was most astonishing was the stitched inscription: *To My Most Beloved, I send you my undying love.* Jiancheng.

Screaming, the Emperor threw it on the floor and stomped on it. "You have his handkerchief. And his name! His name!" He grabbed Jewel's neck, choking her. "How dare you! How dare you show his name before me!"

"I...I...would...be honored...to...explain." Jewel's face turned crimson.

"There...is...nothing...to...explain!" he bellowed, thrusting Jewel aside. And Jewel's pink skirt flying before me, she crashed near the door.

It all happened so fast. Before I could blink, the Emperor roared, and many servants rushed in the chamber and dragged Jewel out to the courtyard. A deafening uproar shook around me. Jewel screamed, the men shouted, footsteps pounded, and the maids and eunuchs gasped. I scrambled to my feet and ran to the door. From the corridor flooded many men holding their clubs and swords. I winced, my back knocking into the door. Guards usually were not allowed inside the Inner Court, let alone guards carrying weapons.

The Emperor shouted something, and they dove at Jewel. Her skirt was torn with a sharp rip, followed by a hysterical shriek that resonated in the sky.

I could not see her. There were so many shadows, so many clubs, and so many feet. I stumbled closer to a pillar and finally found Jewel near the stone stairs. At first, she covered her head, her body recoiling from one fist or another. Then she collapsed to the ground. Rods clobbered her back. Powerful kicks were aimed at her abdomen where a life had been nourished, and a hard sheath rammed into her right eye. She thrashed, twisted, trembled, and wallowed on the blood-drenched earth.

I closed my eyes, my bones aching from watching her. When I opened my eyes again, before me was a naked thing, wearing nothing but blood. Her trembling fingers dug into the ground, and her body heaved, but she slumped again.

I should have felt joyous and relieved. My rival for all these years, my worst enemy—the conniving, deceiving Jewel, who had sabotaged my chances and ruined my life—had finally fallen, with no way to return.

But my face was chilled, my hands numb. Why did it have to be like that? Why so many men and so many clubs?

"She deserved it," the Noble Lady said beside me.

"She didn't moan," I said. "Not one moan."

Nor had she cried. Not a tear.

"Would it help if she had?"

I did not know what to say, and I wanted to look away.

"Hold her!" the Emperor hollered. A guard clamped his arms around Jewel's shoulder, and the Emperor cut her face with his sword. One line, another, and then another. A character, bleeding thick blood, formed on her cheek. *Nu.*

Slave.

"I here denounce you." His voice was filled with venom. "You shall be stripped of your title, imprisoned in the Yeting Court, and dwell in the darkest room infested with mold and rodents for the rest of your life. You shall clean chamber pots and rake muck in the garden from sunrise to sunset. Captain! Take her!"

The Captain answered. He picked up Jewel's limp body and hurled her in a wheelbarrow. The Emperor shouted again, fuming, and finally stormed away. Beckoning to the guards, the Captain pushed the wheelbarrow to leave. It squeaked past me, the single apricot tree in the courtyard, and finally reached the immense stone statue of kylin, the mythical unicorn that guarded the entrance of the compound.

It stopped, and inside the wheelbarrow, a shadow rose.

I went to her. I did not know why. The Noble Lady was still standing behind me, and she perhaps wondered what I was doing. But I could not help it. I just wanted to look at her. One last look.

She was struggling to hold on to the statue, which sat on a raised pedestal, trying to climb it. The statue was too tall for her, and if she had been standing on the ground, she only would have been able to touch its belly. But there she was, standing in the wheelbarrow, heaving, her arms flinging over the back of the mythical animal. When she took hold of it, she swung over, lying on its massive back. Then one hand pushing against the statue, she raised her head toward me. Her white hair, matted and bloody, spread around her face like poisonous vines, and her eyes, her catlike eyes, gazed at me with an expression I had never seen on any living face.

I wanted to say something, but I did not know what.

"There you are, Mei," she said, her voice hoarse, indistinct. "How interesting this turns out. I would never have expected it. But don't feel pity for me. Don't. Because I should have known."

I tore my gaze away. "I…I didn't know they would treat you like this—"

"You did what you had to do. I can't blame you. In fact…it's me… I should be the one…" Blood trickled down her cheek, but she did not wipe it off. "I wish to apologize for all the foolish things I have done. Tricking you, setting you up…"

"I—"

"But it's all right. You don't need to say anything. Just forget everything. Forget all, and forget me."

She flung her arms out, and something wet dropped on my neck, scalding me, like a droplet of burning oil. I cringed.

"You'll come back. You always do," I said.

She shook her head. "Not this time."

"You're a fighter. You'll fight, Jewel."

She turned away. She seemed to be struggling to rise, to stand on the statue, but her legs wobbled, and she kept slipping. Finally, she stood, her body swaying and her long, matted hair sticking to her back like a stained white cape. "I am tired, Mei. I am so tired." Her voice was weaker, barely audible, as though all the climbing had drained her energy. "I shall go now. Farewell, my friend."

She leaped into the air. Her arms spread wide, her head down, and her hair swept through the air and arched like a colorless rainbow.

Then she plunged. Her head crashed against the wall. There was a dull thud, and thousands of tiny droplets raced through the air like heavy beads. Abruptly, they halted and finally transformed into a shower of black rain.

For a long time, I stared at the darkness, unable to move. Sometime later, there was movement around me. The Emperor ordered everyone to leave. He had returned to the courtyard at some time, but I did not know when or whether he had watched Jewel jump. Shouting, he threw his sleeves behind him and left the courtyard. The Noble Lady called for me. I did not answer, and soon, she left too.

Jewel lay still near the wall. A black pool had formed around her; a shimmering river grew from her head, trickled to the stairs and into the courtyard. The Captain picked her up and tossed her in the wheelbarrow. The crowd dispersed and retreated into the dark.

Something round lay at the foot of the statue. Jewel's fan.

I picked it up. It was painted on both sides, perhaps by Jewel herself. On one side, she had drawn a lady, her head drooping, gazing at a peony; on the other side another lady, her head raised, admiring the moon. I did not know why, but they reminded me of Jewel and me.

In truth, we were similar. Like two sides of a fan, we were at odds with each other, we competed with each other, but our fates similarly rested in the hands of the Emperor—the holder, the commander, the manipulator of our destinies.

And there was nothing we could do about it, because we were simply a whim in his mind, a fancy in his bed, an accessory beside his pillow, nothing more. We provided threads for his rapture but never the fabric of his happiness.

O

AD 643

the Seventeenth Year *of*

Emperor Taizong's Reign

of Peaceful Prospect

SUMMER

I NO LONGER NEEDED TO FEAR THAT JEWEL WOULD SEND me to the Yeting Court or set traps to ensnare me, and when I walked behind the Emperor, I did not need to glance sideways to look for Jewel's catlike eyes, although I did so anyway. Soon, I was also given back my duty in the wardrobe chamber, where I was promoted to oversee the other five wardrobe maids and twenty-nine seamstresses.

The Noble Lady believed she could even promote me to the Lady-in-Waiting, the position Jewel had held. "I shall do my best to put in a good word for you in front of the Emperor," she said.

After Jewel's death, the Noble Lady was again the most powerful lady in the Inner Court. The Emperor restored her duty over the Imperial Silkworm Workshops. She received Jewel's extravagant gowns, fur coats, and jewelry and was also in charge of dispensing with Jewel's maids. When I became a Lady-in-Waiting, the Noble Lady said, we would rule the Inner Court together.

I was not sure, however. There was something in the dust of the victory that unsettled me. I dreamed of Jewel, her death, and the violence of it. When I woke, I rubbed my neck as if I could still feel the droplets of Jewel's blood there.

Without telling anyone, I went to see Jewel when they buried her. I followed the two eunuchs who pushed the ox cart bearing her coffin as they took her to the cemetery for disgraced women. None of her maids came. I formed the entire funeral procession. When we arrived at a small mound near a grove of dead trees, I asked to open the pine coffin. Inside, Jewel curled awkwardly, her arms outstretched as if trying to hold on to the crown she had lost. Her cheeks were black and swollen, her hair matted with encrusted blood. One of her catlike eyes was frozen in stillness; the other was gone.

I did not recognize that woman. It was Jewel, but it could have been any of the disgraced women who had died in the past. Or it could have been me, in the future.

✦ ✦

I did not speak to anyone of Jewel's death and her funeral, but I thought of Pheasant more and more. He would have understood me. He would have understood how I felt. I missed him more than ever.

I went to look for him near the polo field. Standing under a mulberry tree, I remembered how I had stood at that exact spot two years before. He had found me, taken me to the tangerine grove, and started our adventure. Once again I was there under the trees, but he would not come for me again.

He was riding a black stallion on the polo field, his back straight and his strikes graceful. His shoulders were broad, and he had grown muscles like the heir. He was not yet eighteen, and already he looked like a man. In a year or two, he would perhaps be as imposing as the Crown Prince.

He paused on his horse and turned to face the tree where I hid. He was too far away to spot me, but was he at least thinking of me?

"He's a man in many maidens' dreams," Jewel had said.

In my dreams, but not in my destiny. Why must it be so? Why could he not be my dream and my destiny?

I left in tears.

✦ ✦

"I heard you went to the polo field," the Noble Lady said to me, while we inspected the piles of Jewel's gowns in her chamber.

"I was taking a walk." I kept my head low.

"Shouldn't you be busy preparing for tomorrow?" She examined the stitches on a sleeve. The next day was the annual hunting day. Every year, the Emperor hosted the hunting game in the Forbidden Park. Many ministers and imperial family members would come. "And I have been thinking this will be a good time to ask the Emperor about giving you Jewel's title."

I bowed. "I am grateful for your help, my Noble Lady."

"You are doing well, Mei. Jewel is dead. The Pure Lady does not bother you. No other girl can compete with you. Soon, you will take over the title of Most Adored and you can have anything you wish. You must not ruin your chance."

I wondered if she knew the true reason why I went to the polo field. My cheeks grew hot. "No, I won't, my Noble Lady."

"Do you like this one?" She handed me a long, indigo gown with patterns of sea waves and mountains.

I eyed the yellow gown next to it. I could not ask for that, however. Yellow was the color for the Emperor and the Empress. "It's precious."

"You should wear this. It'll look good on you. Here"—she took off her bangle and put it around my wrist—"it looks better with this bangle. Do you like it?"

"I do." I tried to slip it off. "But it's yours."

"Keep it. You can borrow it. Tomorrow is an important day. You should make a good impression." She patted my hand and then added, as if it was almost an afterthought, "Prince Zhi is Wende's youngest, and the eighth prince. He doesn't have a chance."

"I understand, my Noble Lady."

She nodded, and I was relieved she did not speak more.

✦ ✦

That afternoon, the Emperor left early to prepare for his hunting.

I put away the ink and scrolls in the library with Plum, who had come to help, as one of the Emperor's personal attendants had become ill. We were ready to step out into the courtyard when I saw the barefoot astrologer conversing with a group of men wearing the robes of stars and moons, the formal Taoist robes. They had held a meeting with the Emperor earlier, but I had not realized they were still there.

The astrologer caught sight of me and beckoned. "Come."

I stopped sharply. I had a feeling that we were like cat and mouse, and I had inadvertently stepped on the trap he had set.

He pattered to me instead, his bare feet slapping against the ground. "You look familiar. We have met before. Not here in the palace. Somewhere else."

His voice had the strange undertone of a priest performing a sacrifice. My forehead moistened. I lowered my head to bow. "I do not believe I have had that honor, my astrologer."

He frowned, and the rest of the Taoist priests walked to me too. They looked cautious, their eyes unblinking. "Who are you?" one asked.

They were dangerous men. I stepped back.

"What is your father's name?" the astrologer asked.

I elbowed Plum, and together we hastened to leave, ignoring his shouts behind me.

My heart was still beating fast when I reached the entrance of the Inner Court. I felt as though I had almost tripped and fallen from a cliff.

The next morning when I came to the Forbidden Park, the hunting had already started. The men stayed near the Emperor and his team at the edge of a clearing, while the Four Ladies sat under an ancient ginkgo tree, their servants standing behind. There were other titled ladies and ministers scattered on the other side of the clearing. It was a hunt for the Emperor, but a holiday for all of us in the palace, since we did not need to attend to our daily duties.

The Noble Lady, sitting in the front where she could watch the hunting closely, nodded at me. I went to her. The Pure Lady, who had been absent on many social occasions, sat to the distant right, her white cat perched in her lap. She narrowed her eyes when she saw me. I looked away.

She was cursing. Perhaps at me, but perhaps at someone else. It did not matter, because I could tell she hated everyone, especially the other Ladies. I had heard that when Lady Virtue was bitten by mosquitoes in her garden several days before, the Pure Lady had sent her a cup of juice from pounded leeks—a common cure for the bites, but the liquid turned out to be something else, not leek juice, and soon Lady Virtue's skin had become infected.

I wondered if the Pure Lady blamed me for Jewel's downfall. Most likely she did, and perhaps she would give me a cup of poison if she had the chance.

"There's no reason why he would refuse," the Noble Lady said to me as I came beside her. Her voice was low, as if she was worried about being heard by the Pure Lady. "He's rather fond of you, as it is plain to see."

"When will you speak to him, my lady?" I asked, watching the Emperor on his favorite horse, Brown Grizzle. He raised the bow, and behind him, the bystanders chanted, "Shoot, shoot! That antelope! Antelope!"

I could not understand why men were fond of hunting. It was such a cruel sport. It was not even real hunting, more like shooting, because the hunting party did not take the trouble of walking through the woods. Instead, the herders, with hounds and leopards on their leashes, drove wild boar and antelopes, which had been captured the night before, to the center of the clearing. Then the Emperor and his team, standing at the outer circle of the clearing, walled by more hounds and dogs, began to aim and shoot.

The goal was to kill the animal with one arrow, and whoever killed the most would win the top prize—sitting next to the

Emperor during the celebration party afterward. If the shooter wounded an animal rather than kill it, the score turned negative.

I wished the hunt would end as quickly as possible so the Noble Lady could talk to the Emperor and request Jewel's title for me.

"After this, they will have some refreshments. Then I shall walk to him," the Noble Lady said. "You will come with me."

"I shall be glad." The Emperor turned the bow slowly, looking for a target. Then an arrow flew into the air. A whimper came from the clearing. The Emperor groaned in disappointment. He had missed.

I stifled a yawn. What was the fun about hunting if the animals were already trapped? Shielding my eyes with my hands, I craned my neck, pretending to have a better look at the Emperor's next shot, but I searched among the imperial members quickly. Pheasant was not there, and neither was his older brother, Taizi.

I could not remember the last time I had seen the heir. Was it the night he fought with Prince Yo? I did remember, however, after Prince Yo's exile, Taizi was also in dishonor. Rumor said the Emperor was irate at his inclination to violence and doubted his ability to reign. Taizi was thus disciplined. He was not allowed to hold any wrestling bouts, and his allowance and the number of his retinue had also been reduced.

"Are you looking for someone?" The Noble Lady shielded her eyes too.

"Oh, no," I said quickly. "Taizi did not come." Pheasant's other brother, Prince Wei, was present. He was obviously too fat to pull a bow. Sitting in a sedan carried by four sweltering women porters, the obese prince looked like an elephant riding a lily pad, a peculiar sight among the adroit riders.

"It appears the Emperor did not invite many important people." The Noble Lady licked her lip, the shadow of the ginkgo branches spreading a dark cover over her gold necklace. "The Emperor's uncle is not here either."

I scanned the sweaty faces of the ministers. She was right. "Why was the Uncle not invited to the hunt, my Noble Lady?"

"It's getting worse between the Uncle and the Duke. Two days ago, the Duke suggested a promotion of a minister. The Uncle disagreed, saying the man was incompetent and the Duke has taken his bribe. The Emperor told his uncle to shut up and promoted the man the Duke chose."

"I see—"

A shriek came from my right. "You spilled wine on me." The Pure Lady, her hand on a maid's ear, was gritting her teeth. "You clumsy maid!"

"Don't look at her," the Noble Lady said to me. "She is looking for trouble. Could you serve me some wine?"

I went to fetch the wine jug from a tray behind me. "I imagine the Emperor's uncle is very upset to be excluded from this important event."

The Noble Lady nodded. "I heard the Uncle lost his temper during the audience. He said the Emperor was unwise and ungrateful and many other things. The Emperor was angry. He ordered his yearly allowance taken away and suspended his duty in the court for a month."

That would be a blow for an old man who was used to his power. I filled her cup. "I suspect he did not take it very well."

"I only hope he will come to his senses somehow. There is no peace in the court if he continues to quibble with the Duke. Who is that etiquette teacher?"

"Who?" I followed her gaze. Rain had appeared next to the Pure Lady. She bent low and whispered into her ear. The Pure Lady jerked up her head and fixed her gaze on me. If her gaze could kill, I would have been dead ten times over. "Remember a female minister spread the rumor that I sold the Emperor's night robe for money?"

"That's her?"

I nodded.

"What is she doing with the Pure Lady?"

"I don't know." Rain was not to be underestimated. She had teamed up with Jewel, but because I had already stopped seeing

Pheasant, they could not harm me. What were she and the Pure Lady conspiring about? "I wonder what she's telling the Pure Lady."

"Don't worry about her." The Noble Lady turned to stare at the Emperor, who was taking a break from shooting, and Prince Ke and the other princes mounted their horses, ready for their turns.

"Shall we go to the Emperor?" I asked with hope.

"Not yet." The Noble Lady shook her head. "Have some wine, Mei."

I nodded and took a sip from a cup. The wine tasted bitter but smelled fragrant, reminding me that, at home, Mother, Father, Big Sister, and I used to sit under a ginkgo tree and drink ale during the Moon Festival.

"My Noble Lady, do you think of your mother?" The Emperor had agreed to continue to search for my mother, but sometimes, I could not help thinking that they would never find her, and she was already gone…

She faced me. "My mother?"

"I'm sorry." I regretted it immediately. I might have offended her. The Noble Lady's mother, the Empress of the Sui Dynasty, had died in the rebellion that overthrew the dynasty. It was a violent and gruesome death, many had whispered.

"No, no. No need to apologize. I think of my mother all the time, and I can tell you"—she turned to face the clearing, where her son pulled his bow to shoot—"children are birds, and a mother is the tree. No matter how far the birds fly, they always long for the tree to rest on."

I stared at her. "But a tree will fall…"

"Even if it falls or dies, its roots delve deep into a child's heart and nourish it with her eternal thoughts."

Her eloquent speech warmed me. I was hopeful. Perhaps they would find Mother. Perhaps I would see her again someday. "Your son is doing well."

"He's doing his best." Prince Ke had the most shots so far. Perhaps soon he would win the prize to sit next to the Emperor.

"I hope he wins," I said.

"I should hope so." The shadow of the tree swayed to the side, and her gold necklace glittered in the sun. She looked proud, and rightly so. Jewel's death had made the Emperor realize how valuable the Noble Lady was, and if ever he deposed Taizi, Prince Ke would no doubt become the heir. "Have you prepared what to say when the One Above All comes?"

Before I replied, a white shape landed on my shoulder. A furry paw with claws swiped at my face. I gasped, flinging my arms. Those claws. They had attacked me before... Not the same ones... but similar.

And there was a deafening growl, followed by a heartrending shriek, and the sky seemed to spin, while a storm of leaves blasted around me... "Mei!" Father's voice!

"Mei?"

I jerked. It was only the Noble Lady. But I could not understand. Those images. Where did they come from? But wait! The beast was still perched on my shoulder, growling. I cried out in fear.

"Go away," the Noble Lady said, waving her hand, and the weight left my shoulder. "Are you all right?" She held my shoulder, and I panted in relief. "Are you all right, Mei? Did it frighten you? It's only a cat."

I tried hard not to tremble. "I know, my lady...I know."

The Noble Lady turned to the Pure Lady, who was stroking that cat. "Did you see what your cat just did, Pure Lady? You should be more careful," she said. It was the first time I had heard her speak to the Pure Lady in a disapproving tone.

The Pure Lady shot to her feet and dashed toward us. "Now you would chide me over my cat? My cat? You're very proud of yourself, aren't you, Noble Lady? Everything works out for you. My son is exiled, and yours stays here shooting animals. What else will you do to me?"

"How could you say that, Pure Lady—"

"And look at you, wearing all this gold and jewelry, looking so splendid and superior. You think you're better than me? You're nothing without your son, and you don't deserve to wear this." She yanked the gold necklace off the Noble Lady.

The Noble Lady gasped, her hands flying to her neck. "You can't blame me for your son's exile, Pure Lady."

"Is that what you think? But you must pay." She thrust her head back, and her long arm lashed out to point at me and then the others. "You, and all of you." She stormed away.

"You're bleeding, my Noble Lady." I held her arms. The necklace had cut deeply into her skin, and two gashes had appeared on either side of her neck, so it looked as though she had been wounded by two swords crossing under her chin. I felt terrible for involving her in this.

She did not seem to hear me. "Did you hear her? Did you hear what she said?"

"I did."

"She said she would make us pay, but what did we do? It was not my fault her son was exiled."

"She was angry." Blood was trickling down her neck. "Would you like to go see the physicians, my lady?"

"Physicians?" Her plump cheeks had turned pale. She looked as though she would faint. "Oh, yes. Take me to the physicians."

We would need to talk to the Emperor some other time. Hurriedly, I left the shade of the ginkgo with the Noble Lady and her maids. Behind me, Rain made a sound like she was suppressing a chuckle. My heart tightened. I could not explain it, but I felt the worst was yet to come.

AD 643

the Seventeenth Year *of*

Emperor Taizong's Reign

of Peaceful Prospect

WINTER

31

"RISE." A HAND SHOOK MY SHOULDER.

It was the Emperor. I rose from my mat and rubbed my eyes. Around me, the other Talents were still sleeping. The night before, we had gone to the Emperor's bedchamber, but as usual, he had not favored us; instead, he had passed the night drinking in the circle of candles. According to the protocol, we were supposed to leave once he finished with us, but lately, he always ordered us to stay. I could not understand why, but at least he still followed the bedding schedule.

"Follow me." He woke Daisy too, who had recently been demoted to a Talent for her clumsiness, and then the three of us, with Daisy and me holding lanterns, left the compound.

I wished to know where we were going and why we had to leave the bedchamber on the cold night. I would rather have gone back and slept, but he needed us to hold the lanterns for him. Shivering, I walked in front of the Emperor, holding the lantern with my right hand and wrapping my coat around me with my left.

It was very early in the morning. The sky was dark as ink. Snow drifted. The court was quiet, and most servants were still asleep.

We walked until we reached the Xuanwu Gate at the back of the Inner Court, where a group of guards were waiting for us. The Emperor beckoned them to follow, and together we passed the

Gate and went into the woodland that was part of the Forbidden Park. For hours, we trudged through the snow-sodden, knee-high thickets. I had never set my foot on that part of the Forbidden Park before. The area was vast and hilly, challenging to climb.

The dawn's light appeared, and the trees and hills revealed themselves. Daisy and I extinguished the lights inside the lanterns. When we reached a clearing near a valley, the Emperor stopped under a poplar near a giant rock with a steep front and a pointy tip. He ordered the guards to spread out nearby. "And do not approach unless I give you an order."

The guards left, and Daisy and I stood close together, waiting for him to dismiss us too. But he did not say anything, his head raised at the sky where two hawks soared.

Why did he want to come here in the early morning?

The warmth quickly escaped me, and the chilly morning air plunged savagely into my throat. My nose was runny; my face was chilled. I rubbed my hands and looked around. The frozen land, covered with towering trees and thorny bushes, stretched endlessly before me, while at my left, a deep valley, its rugged surface sprinkled with white, cut through a grove of fallen trees and disappeared behind snow-dusted spruce.

I shivered. The frosty sheet buried the tracks ahead of me but could not hide the crackling bark of the trees and the stark barrenness of the land. There was no man or animal as far as I could see, and the only sound I heard was water gurgling in the distance near the valley, perhaps from the canal that ran through the palace.

The Emperor was still standing there, his hands crossed behind his back. I stamped my feet to keep warm. If we stayed any longer, we would miss our morning meal.

A faint screech came from the sky. A hawk, or something similar, plunged.

"Stay here," the Emperor ordered us. He walked along a trail near a steep rock and disappeared behind it.

"Where is he going?" I asked Daisy, tucking my hands under my arms.

She shook her head, her face buried in her scarf, her breath puffing near her ears. For a long time, we simply wrapped our arms around our bodies and jumped to keep warm. I kept checking the rock, hoping to see the Emperor return.

"Ah…" A faint voice, guttural and masculine.

I stopped jumping. "What was that?"

Daisy shook her head before lowering it farther into her coat.

I hesitated. It sounded like it had come from where the Emperor had gone.

"Ah…" Another cry.

I made up my mind. "I'm going to take a look. I'll be right back, Daisy."

"What?" She stared at me, her face bearing the usual look of confusion.

"It could be the Emperor."

"Don't leave me alone." She looked around, the flaps of her hat shaking like two ears. "Wolves will come. Nobody comes here but wolves. And snakes! I'm afraid of snakes."

"Follow me then. I won't go too far."

We went to the steep rock, following the Emperor's trail. Behind it was the valley, where the woods were dense and the tree branches were laden with layers of snow. I paused, searching. A gentle slope with tall reeds and dead trees rose ahead of us, and I glimpsed some water in a distant section of the canal that ran through the palace. There was no Emperor, and the faint cries had vanished. I was about to turn back when I saw a boat appear in the canal. Inside it stood a hooded figure.

The Duke. Rather than wearing his usual ornate court regalia, he had donned a black tunic like a monk's stole. The tunic clung to his legs and chest, looking wet, as if he had waded through water. Some black animals, small, like dogs, were wriggling near his feet. He lowered his head and kicked them.

I frowned. Did the Emperor come here to meet the Duke? Where was the Emperor? I stood on tiptoe, searching hard. I found him, standing below a jutted rock some distance before me. His back facing me, he waved at the Duke in the boat, as though giving him a signal.

I raised my head toward the Duke, but his boat had moved out of my sight.

"I don't see anything," Daisy said. "Let's go back."

"Wait," I said. Those black animals in the boat must have been important or the Emperor would not have ventured out in the cold to see them. And the Duke. He looked furtive, dressed in a hooded black tunic. What were those animals?

"I want to go, Mei."

"Just a moment, Daisy." I wanted to take a closer look, but I dared not walk too close. So I waded through the snow to my left and tried to climb a tree. The trunk was slippery with frost, but eventually I grabbed a thick branch over my head and found a firm footing. I hoisted up and peered at the canal. There, I got a better view of the canal and the Duke, and I could see clearly that those animals—there were at least twenty of them—were not dogs but men with their heads covered in some black cloth. Their arms and legs trussed, they struggled frantically. Some boulders were attached to their necks and feet, and a rope wound around their waists, tying them together. My heart raced faster. What was the Duke going to do with these men?

"Get down, Mei! Why are you climbing on a tree?"

"Be quiet, Daisy," I whispered, hoping she would lower her voice. The Emperor and the Duke would kill me if they found out I was watching them.

"I'm leaving, Mei. Are you coming?"

I could not reply, because at that moment, the Duke kicked a man near him and shoved him to the edge of the boat. The man cried out, his voice muffled, but the Duke continued to shove until he dropped into the canal. He sank into the water instantly, weighed down by the boulders tied to his body. The rope, linked to another man, pulled him to the edge of the boat as well. Sensing danger, the man struggled, his body twisting. The Duke unsheathed his sword and thrust it into his chest. The man slumped and fell into the water.

I lost my grip on the branch and dropped to the ground. My face was chilled, and my teeth were chattering. I wanted to call out for Daisy, but I could not find my voice. My hands trembling, I climbed the tree again. But my legs were too weak, and I could not pull myself up. I could hear, however, the desperate cries and the loud splashing coming from the canal. When I was able to hold on to a branch again, I peered at the canal.

The men were all gone, and the Duke was alone in the boat. On the surface of the water, some black cloths popped like bubbles and sank slowly as I watched, and a carpet of broken floes, thick heaps of algae, dead leaves, and grass floated over to cover the spot where the men had sunk.

And the Emperor nodded as though he was greatly pleased.

"D–Daisy? Did you...did you see that?" I whispered. "Daisy?"

I did not hear her answer. She had already gone ahead of me, but she turned around and came back to me. "What? A snake? Did you say a snake? Where?"

I slipped off the tree. "No. Not snake."

"Then what is it? We better go, Mei. The guards will find us gone. Are you coming?"

"Yes, yes, but..." I swallowed the rest of my words. From behind, the Emperor's voice drifted toward me.

"How many left?"

"About one hundred and fifty." The Duke's voice.

"You will take care of them?"

"I shall be honored, the One Above All."

There was heavy breathing as the Emperor climbed uphill. "...so that should take care of the prophecy..."

I stumbled. My hand swept a branch, a shower of snow raining down on my head. Shivering, I hurried to catch up with Daisy.

AD 644

the Eighteenth Year *of*

Emperor Taizong's Reign

of Peaceful Prospect

SPRING

THE EMPEROR WAS DESPERATE. THE DEMEANING BALLAD was sung in many corners of the kingdom, rumor said, and still the Emperor had not captured the man who had spread it.

And he was running out of time. Revolts from many regions of the kingdom were reported, each claiming their leader was the man in the prophecy. The peasants in the south, led by a woman general, were said to be most threatening.

Every week, messages sent by horse relay were placed on the Emperor's table, indicating the progress of the thousands of peasants who had joined to attack the local *yamen* and officials. Every day, the woman general gained more support. The army overtook Yangzhou and controlled the Grand Canal. The Emperor dispatched five thousand men to quench the revolt but failed. The peasant army was marching north to Jingzhou. In two months' time, the army, if not stopped, would reach Chang'an.

The Emperor gathered the cavalry from the west border and sent them to the south, leaving the border towns vulnerable to the Western Turks, who seized the chance and attacked, rampaging from one town to another. While our people on the border writhed in fire and smoke, it was Taizi who saved them. He led his cavalry and drove through the Turks' yurts in the moonlight. With the camp in disarray, the heir captured their leader and asked to wrestle him. If the Turkish leader won, they would stay; if they lost, they would return to their territory for good. The Turks agreed, and the wrestling started with men's shouts. But it ended quickly, as Taizi threw the Turkish leader off the ring after only three shoves. Forced to honor their bet, the Turks withdrew in shame.

Taizi did not stop there. He continued south and vowed to crush the peasant army. The slight-framed southerners, who had never seen a man of such a stature, believed they had seen a god. They scattered with their hoes and rakes as the prince galloped toward them. In that strange manner, the rebels were defeated, and Taizi returned home, where the Emperor accepted him with a much-softened face.

✦ ✦

Sickness ravaged me after my return from the park that morning. For weeks, I lay in bed. My limbs felt wasted, my joints hurt, and I was hot and cold intermittently. The imperial physicians said my vital force, *qi*, was disturbed. "An evil wind has attacked your body and enfeebled your mind. Once you regain the balance of your yin and yang, your *qi* shall be restored." They advised me to keep the chamber's door closed and remain inside. They also prescribed drinking hot water steeped with ginger and cane sugar. "That will increase the flow of your jade liquid, which will help stimulate your internal organs and facilitate *qi* to travel through the rest of your body."

Jade liquid was saliva, one of the three vital elements, the physicians believed. I did not understand the importance of the elements, but I was glad to see the dryness in my throat went away after a few days. A few weeks later, my strength returned, and my head was clear again.

But I was unable to rid my mind of the sight in the canal.

✦ ✦

Sitting in front of a bronze mirror, I drew the shape of moth wings on my eyebrows with a kohl stick. The line looked squiggly. I wiped it away and began to draw again, slower that time.

When I finished, I stared at my face in the mirror. The sickness had sharpened my chin. My oval face had lost its softness, and my cheekbones protruded. Around my eyes, the skin looked brittle, like cracked ice, and some creases had appeared.

Had I grown old?

I was only eighteen, but I felt more like an old woman on her feeble march to her grave. The dreadful feeling crept over me like mists enveloping the woods. Life was meaningless. When I walked in the garden, the trees looked pale, the grass silvery, and the flowers blanched. The birds swung in a sad motion, and the winds moaned poignant melodies. I missed Pheasant. I wished I could hold his hand and talk to him again.

I put down the kohl stick, dipped a brush in red cream, and began to draw the beauty mark. Should I try a hawk or a kite? But why bother? A different bird might appear on my face, but the only bird of my affection would not leave my heart.

Urgent footsteps pounded in the corridor. The doors swung open.

"Plum?" I raised my head. "What's wrong?"

I had not told her about what had happened in the canal, although I really wished to. But for her own safety, it was better she did not know.

"Mei, something happened in the Eastern Palace. The Noble Lady asked you to go there." She was panting, pulling at my sleeve.

"Let me finish."

"There's no time. You must hurry."

I put down the brush and draped a shawl on my shoulders. "What is it? Why are you so frantic?"

She wiped her face. "I don't know, but she said it was urgent. You must go there now."

"Is she there too?" I asked as we scurried down the courtyard.

"Yes. She sent me to fetch you."

We left our compound and went down the path that led to the

east side of the court. Many servants were also headed toward the Tongxun Gate, the only entrance to the Eastern Palace.

When we arrived at the palace, many ministers had already gathered there. Some shook their heads, whispering, while the others surrounded the Emperor's uncle, who stood in the corridor of the library.

"Disgrace! May our ancestors forgive us," he shouted, waving his fists at the people around him. His position in the court had been resumed, but the ministers looked reserved. They only nodded politely. The Uncle turned to the hunchback man, Wei Zheng. "I warned you, Chancellor. He can't be trusted. What would you say now?"

The Chancellor only leaned over his cane and rubbed his eyes, his jade pendants clinking at his belt.

What could the matter be? Had Taizi hurt anyone? He was a hero after his victory, and the Emperor seemed to accept the fact that he would make a decent heir. He had ordered Taizi to study classical music and learn how to govern. The heir had obeyed. He had dispersed his wrestlers, hired troupes of musicians, and spent mornings playing music and afternoons reading Confucius and even books by Han Feizi, who drew up the legal system that our kingdom had adopted eight hundred years ago. He even accompanied the Emperor to the morning audiences and attended discussions on how to restore peace to the south. None of his brothers, even Prince Ke, could find any fault with him.

"Mei," the Noble Lady called to me from under a cinnamon tree. When Plum and I approached, she studied my face and nodded. "You painted only one beauty mark. Other than that, you are groomed well."

I was surprised she still cared about my appearance. "I didn't have time for more, my Noble Lady. What's going on?"

"The Emperor had a meeting with his advisers a while ago, and then he decided to visit Taizi during his music lesson."

"And?"

"He found out the heir was not learning music."

"So what was he doing?"

She paused. "Something unspeakable."

Something in her voice forced me to stare at her. She sounded uneasy, rubbing her plump cheeks. What event in Taizi's residence could upset the Noble Lady like that?

She turned around, and I followed as she went down the trail in a garden and led me to the private residence of the heir. We had just passed the building that housed the imperial academy when two ladies in indigo gowns, members of Taizi's household, rushed from the building on the left. Their faces stark white, they tripped over the stairs and looked back in fear, as if running away from something.

Almost at the same time, the Emperor's voice rang out. "Who are you?" His voice was laced with danger. "Who are you? Halt! Who are you?"

"Who is the Emperor shouting at, my Noble Lady?" I whispered.

"A flutist. I shall take my leave now." She hesitated, then turned to leave.

A lady of her rank could not come to the heir's bedchamber without an invitation, I understood. But if I were she, I would have let the rule of propriety slip once and stayed to see what would happen next. "I shall report to you once I know more, my Noble Lady."

Nodding, she left, and I entered the prince's private building. Plum, already ahead of me, raced toward the corridor near the front parlor and squeezed through a crowd that had gathered there to get to the front. I followed her and stood next to her.

The courtyard before me was empty and quiet, but the prince's bedchamber across from us, which people were staring at, was open, and the Emperor was roaring from inside.

"All these days you said you were studying classical music, you were fiddling with this thing? This horrid thing?"

A boy, disheveled, bolted out of the bedchamber and pressed himself against a pillar. I could not believe my eyes.

"Who's that?" Plum's mouth was open. She did not seem to understand either.

"Is he the flutist?"

"I don't know."

I stared at the flutist in shock. The boy and Taizi, a mighty wrestler? How could that be possible?

"Where is he? Where is the flutist?" The Emperor appeared in the corridor outside the bedchamber, his sword in hand.

Behind him, Taizi emerged. He looked his usual self, shirtless, his body covered only by a piece of loincloth. "Father."

"And you? Who are you? A sodomist?" The Emperor was shaking. He looked terrifying.

"Father!"

Was that why the heir had never fathered a child?

"You make a fool of me for this horrid thing? I can't stand it! Get out of my face. Get out of my palace. Get out. Get out!"

The boy bolted toward me. The floor of the corridor vibrated under my feet. He had a young face, distorted like a melted silver cup. His robe hung loose on his bare chest, and his underpants slipped down to his hips.

"Run, you want to run? You want to run away from me?" The Emperor unsheathed his sword. "Guard the door, Captain! He's not going anywhere!"

The Captain answered and came to the parlor. The boy stopped, gulping in fear. Then he leaped into the courtyard and ran to the other side of the corridor.

"So you think you can run? I'll run with you." A shoe smacked the flutist's back. In a moment, the Emperor ran down the corridor too.

The boy yelled shrilly and slowed.

"Run, run again. Do you want to keep running? Do you think you can run away from me?" The Emperor caught him and stabbed his shoulder with his sword.

The boy fell off the stairs to the courtyard. Rolling on the ground, he groaned, blood spurting from his wound. My stomach clenched, and I covered my mouth.

"I order you, now." The Emperor's voice sounded like venom as he stepped into the courtyard. "Get up. Run until the last drop of blood drains out of you."

"Father." Taizi stomped across to the courtyard. He was so tall, his head nearly reaching the eaves of the building behind him. He had always been a towering, terrifying presence each time I saw him, but now he drooped his head, looking small and pitiful.

"You're going to kill him, Father." He balled his fists and loosened them. Again and again. The muscles of his bare chest and shoulders bulged. He looked as though he had just stepped off a wrestling ring, but there was something different in his eyes. Those were not the eyes of a fighter but an injured man.

"I will kill him." The Emperor pointed at the boy. "This thing shames me. What he did in my court, under my nose. I shall kill him a thousand times; still, a thousand deaths of this thing doesn't make me feel better. I do not feel better." He pointed his sword at his son. "I shall kill you too, so nobody knows what an ignominy you are. You are my son, my heir, yet you're an abomination—you shame me."

Taizi's bloodshot eyes remained fixed on the figure on the ground.

"Confess now. Why did you do this to me? Why?"

The heir did not answer.

"Did he tell you to do this to me?"

"No one told me, Father."

"He." The Emperor breathed hard and waved wildly, pointing at something in the air. "He! Did he tell you to do this to me? He said this would happen. He said he would shame me!"

The Emperor was trembling, the skin on the right side of his face stretching longer, and suddenly the corner of his mouth twitched, and his whole face contorted. So familiar... He looked just like that when he had talked to me in the ring of candles...and I could even hear a thread of fear in his voice that I had never before heard during the daytime.

"It has nothing to do with anyone. It's my fault, Father. Let him go."

The Emperor stood perfectly still. Then, *clang*. His sword slipped to the ground. His shoulders slumped, and his head drooped. He looked as if he had aged ten years.

"Wake him up, Chengqian." He picked up his sword, calling Taizi's given name. "He's losing consciousness."

He sounded resigned. I breathed out in relief.

Casting a grateful look at his father, Taizi tore a strip of cloth off the boy's pants, knelt down one knee, and wound it around his shoulder. There was tenderness in Taizi's eyes that I had never expected to see from him, the mountain-size wrestler.

"Look into his eyes, call his name, make certain he sees you and knows it's you." The Emperor tossed his sword to the heir. "Then kill him."

I shuddered, and the stark light reflected off the blade and pierced my eyes. I shielded them with my sleeves. When I put down my sleeves again, Taizi, his hands trembling, was still winding the strip of cloth, his movement slow and broken.

"Do it."

"Father—" Taizi's voice cracked.

He would not do it, I was sure of it. He would plead with the Emperor and make him change his mind. I did not know what the heir would say, but he had to.

"Do it! Or you are no longer my son."

Taizi lowered his head. The muscles on his back swelled to form round mounds, those on his shoulders hardened, his skin glittered, and his eyes were still like death.

Then he picked up the sword and slid it through his lover's heart.

There was a moment of silence, so long that it seemed it would never end. Taizi howled, pounding his chest. The crowd murmured. Plum whispered something. I turned away and wiped my face, pushing back the moisture welling in my eyes. I might never understand why the heir loved a boy, and I might never know how it felt to kill a beloved person—I hoped I would never have to do that—but his helplessness and anguish thrust deep inside me like that sword.

I could not watch anymore. Straightening, I glanced at Taizi one last time before I took a step back, but I froze. Pheasant was there, standing next to him.

"Go away, go away!" Taizi hollered. "It's all your fault!"

Pheasant's shoulders slumped. He murmured something and tried to hold his brother's shoulders, but he pushed him aside. "You're a traitor. Traitor! I hate you. I hate you. Stay away from me!"

Pheasant's hands dropped, tears mapping his handsome face.

Then he ran.

My heart wrenched. I turned around, searching for him. His head appeared and disappeared above the crowd around me, and I shifted behind the people to keep track of him. Finally, I pushed aside the servants, eunuchs, and ladies, ignored their frowns, and ran after him.

I found him in a garden at the back of the bedchamber, where he held a branch and slashed at the air like a madman.

"Pheasant," I called.

"What?" He threw away the branch. "What are you doing here?"

"What's going on?" I walked closer to him.

He sat down on a rock. "He saw me come in with Father. He thought I had betrayed him. I didn't! I was trying to stop Father!"

"Perhaps you can explain to him later."

"He wouldn't listen to me. I tried to warn him when Father came, but he didn't hear. He's never going to forgive me, and now..." He buried his head in his hands. "Now his favorite boy is dead. Do you think I wanted that?"

His voice was hoarse, and his shoulders trembled. I could not stand to watch him like that.

I put a hand on his arm. "I'm so sorry, Pheasant."

He buried his head in my gown. I wrapped my arms around him and held him close. I could feel his frustration, his helplessness, and his sadness rise to touch me, tap my own well of grief, and make me part of him. I held him tighter. I wanted to tell him that tomorrow things would be fine and that tomorrow Taizi would forgive him. I even wanted to tell him I would like to meet him in the garden again.

Footsteps sounded behind me. I raised my head. The Emperor's golden regalia. I dropped my arms and shrank from Pheasant.

It was too late.

He lunged toward me and slapped me. The force sent me spinning. I tried to grab the stone lamp near the tree, but I slipped and crashed against something behind me. Blackness cloaked me, and for a long moment, I could not see. I heard only voices. Many voices. Men's. Women's. Shouts. Gasps. Groans. Arguments.

"Father!" Pheasant's voice was loud and desperate. "What are you doing?"

"Vile woman. How dare she seduce you!"

"It's not what you think."

"I saw her with my own eyes!" the Emperor bellowed. "She put her hands on you. What a wanton woman! She deserves to die!"

"You can't!"

"Don't you dare protect her!"

"It's not what you think. It's not! She didn't seduce me. I did! I seduced her. She was unwilling. She didn't wish to betray you."

"You!"

"I am to blame. It is my fault. All mine! Punish me. Punish me, not her!"

I groaned. Pain erupted in my head, but I pushed against the ground, trying to rise. A group of women stepped away from me to stand beside the Emperor. I could not see their faces. Or were they women? They wavered before me like empty gowns.

"Guards!" The Emperor's voice stabbed my heart. "Lash him. Twenty rods!"

Many legs flashed before me. They lengthened and transformed into full figures, hazy but menacing, and they rushed toward Pheasant and shoved him to the ground. Their arms raised high, their rods long and thick, they struck. A thud. Followed by a heavy groan. Another thud. Then another groan.

"Stop it, stop it," I said.

But the awful sound continued, echoing, drowning out my voice, and there were waves of groans—thick, lingering, and painful—stabbing my heart. Then nothing.

"He passed out!" someone shouted.

I jerked. There. Pheasant, lying on the ground, the back of his white robe a splash of crushed rose petals.

"Take him to the physicians." The Emperor's golden robe stood before me. I shrank in fear. But I would have liked to follow Pheasant, to see him and hold his hands. I would have liked to call his name and let him know I was there. "Kneel."

I struggled to rise. I could not feel my hands, feet, or knees. A salty taste burst in my mouth, and something wet dripped on my hand. I did not wipe it away. The Emperor was going to punish me. He would never forgive me. Everything was over.

"You shall never rise again."

He strode away. Behind him trailed a group of women. One stopped, the corner of her small mouth pulled up. I blinked a few times before I realized who she was.

Rain.

This time, she had succeeded. She had followed me and chosen the perfect time to expose me and Pheasant. What else could I say? I had been careless. I had forgotten what kind of court I lived in.

Soon she left too.

At first, I could hear the whispers of Plum and the other attendants and the gasps of the servants. But soon, all faded. I was alone.

The sun, crawling to the middle of the heavenly dome, grasped me with its talons of brutal heat. By late afternoon, my vision blurred, and my knees felt ready to snap off my body. A harsh voice, from a eunuch who watched me, scolded me every time I slouched. Countless times, I collapsed sideways, and each time the voice berated me and forced me to keep my position.

The moon replaced the sun, and the sun returned. Still I knelt.

33

"MEI, MEI!"

Father's voice. Faint but urgent.

I lifted my head. And there it was, its yellow, bulbous eyes locked on me. It had a striped torso, lean and majestic, its flinty paws clawing the grass. It stared at me from near the pine branch a few paces from me.

A tiger.

Time slowed. For a moment I looked into its eyes, unable to speak or move. How beautiful they were, the eyes of the powerful. It looked complacent, content, and arrogant, the epitome of beauty and supremacy. It did not appear to care about me, the forest, the sky, or anything around it. It was an animal that was used to killing and knew it could do it easily. It was a king who could always have his wish, a king who could never be defied. And it wanted me.

"Run, run now!"

Father's voice tore through the forest and hit my ears. I turned around.

It was already before me, so fast I did not have time to scream. But then Father appeared, blocking me, his arms outstretched, a branch in his right hand. "Run! Now!"

I flew in the air instead, and a storm of tree branches, leaves, rocks, and clods of dirt whipped my face. Father's voice chased me, followed by a deafening roar that shook the mountain. And then the ground slammed against me, all the sounds vanished, and the sky darkened. When I awoke, I went home alone, unable to recall anything.

Later, people found Father. He was caught on a pine tree on a cliff near my family's grave site, a branch pierced through his chest. No one knew about the tiger or what happened to him, so Mother assumed that he had tripped, that it was an accident.

But kneeling there, I saw how Father really died. And I remembered everything.

✦ ✦

The sky seemed to spin, and roof tiles fell like raindrops. A piece landed in my mouth. It tasted like dirt but smelled like fresh pine resin. I looked up.

Staring at me with yellow eyes, the tiger opened its mouth. "Caw, caw."

My heart leaped to my throat. It had returned. I lurched forward to grab something but could not move my feet. It strutted toward me. One step. I shivered. Two. I wanted to scream.

Then it flapped its black wings and vanished above the tiled roof of a distant hall.

A crow.

Trembling, I closed my eyes.

✦ ✦

"Calm down, Mei. Calm down," a soft female voice said, and arms embraced me.

I tried to raise my head, but it felt so heavy. "Who is there?"

"Drink it." A spoon touched my lips. A plump hand held my shoulder. The Noble Lady.

"My father...my father died to protect me, he died to protect me..." I said. I knew it, deep in my heart. All these years, I could not remember, but I had always known something was there, some unanswered question. Had he not died, my family would still be happy and thriving... I was responsible for Father's death, for what happened to my family's fortune, for Mother's disappearance...

"What are you saying, Mei? Don't talk, Mei. Don't talk. Now, listen to me. Drink this. Slowly, yes. You'll feel better. Look, you're burning hot."

I coughed. The liquid scalded my tongue. It tasted hard and bitter, like a piece of bark I chewed once in the woods with Father. We had spent so much time there, looking at our land, talking, feeling the breeze on our faces... I shook my head and pushed the spoon away.

"It's rice porridge. It's good for you. I'll feed you. You can't stay like this without food." She patted my back.

Her touch was gentle, and I lowered my head obediently and sipped. It did not taste so bad, and soon the sweet flavor of rice porridge spread in my mouth.

"You must stay strong, Mei. You must hold yourself together. Do not give up. Hang on." She squeezed my hand.

Then I remembered where I was and that I was being punished. "How long have I been here, my Noble Lady?"

My voice sounded coarse and old, like a sick, elderly woman who had not spoken for a hundred years.

She fed me another spoonful. "Today is the second day."

It felt longer than that. "How is Pheasant?"

"He is well now. The physicians applied ointment to his back and bandaged him. They also gave him medicine so he could sleep. I think he'll recover soon." She lowered her head to study me. "Plum wanted to come and see you, but she is not allowed. What happened there?"

"I don't remember."

"I told you, Mei, to stay away from him."

"I'm sorry." I had failed her. I was so close, and I had failed. Again.

"I'm sorry too." She put the spoon in the bowl. "You were doing so well. I wish I could do more. I pleaded with him, but he wouldn't listen to me."

Hopelessly, I gazed at her. Did the Emperor really want me to kneel until my last breath?

"I'm afraid I ought to leave." She dusted off her gown and rose.

"But..." I reached out to stop her, then my hand dropped in midair. I could not burden her. "That's right...my Noble Lady. You must not make him angry with you."

She sighed, waved to her servants, and left.

It was only me again. I slumped, staring at the ground. My eyes burned, my lips cracked and bled, and my back became hard and brittle, ready to snap. The ground seemed to do strange things. One moment it looked like a pile of white bones. Then it sank into a dark pit, and then again, it raced ahead like a wicked sandstorm.

The night would come soon. It would be the second night I had knelt. Would I ever see the morning light again?

So it was true. I had caused Father's death, and that was why I had to do whatever I could to fulfill his wish. And indeed, I had had my chances. It was unlikely now...

After a while, I heard a man's voice.

"Up now," he said. "He pardoned you."

I jolted upright. No more kneeling? "Why?"

"Don't know." He stood a few paces away. It was the Captain, the man with a patch of purple birthmark covering half of his face, who always did the Emperor's bidding.

Waves of relief washed over me. I struggled to rise, but I was too weak. More determined, I pushed against the ground and hoisted myself up. I fell sideways. Panting, I steadied myself again and continued to struggle. But no matter how hard I tried, my knees would not straighten.

I could not stand.

I scratched my kneecaps. Nothing. I pinched my leg and twisted the skin hard. Nothing. I dug my fingernails into my skin. Nothing but a long, bloody trail on my leg.

I wanted to cry. "What's wrong with me?"

"Let me help you." He stepped closer.

"No." I clenched my hands together. "May I borrow your sword?"

"A guard never parts with his sword."

"Then stab me." I pointed to my legs. "I cannot feel anything."

He frowned. "It's probably bad blood."

"Bad blood?"

"You'll never walk again."

I glared at him. A sword man should be allowed to use only his sword, not words. Who did he think he was? Only a callous killer, that's all he was.

"I'll show you." He took his dagger from his boot, squatted before me, and struck my kneecap with the end of the hilt.

I should have felt pain, and my leg should have responded.

But nothing. No pain. No response.

"See? Bad blood."

I covered my face with my hands. He said something more, but I did not understand. A thought sprouted in my mind like a malicious weed. Unuttered, tenacious, and shapeless, it rooted in my head and grew bitter fruits of destruction.

I was a cripple.

Furiously, I clawed my skin and beat my legs.

"If your bad blood travels to your heart, you will not see the full moon this month," he said. He sounded like he cared for me, but his voice was cold as usual.

"Go away."

"I'll give you a clean cut." He put his hand on his sword. "You don't need to be afraid."

"Go away!"

"You must decide fast."

I would rather die than live as a cripple. With all the strength I could muster, I dragged myself to the edge of the garden. The stones on the ground rubbed against my raw skin, but I could not feel it. I continued to crawl. Finally, I sat in a corner and buried my head in my sleeves.

So quiet. Like death. I closed my eyes. Would I see Father soon? "I ruined everything," I would confess when we met. "You were wrong about me."

I drifted into sleep. When I awoke, night had descended. But there was no light from a candle or a lantern nearby. I looked around. I was alone, curled up in the corner like a forgotten cat.

A pair of arms lifted me. Bewildered, I raised my head. My hand swept a chiseled jaw.

"Pheasant?"

"There you are." It was him. "I've been looking all over for you. What are you doing here?"

His familiar voice almost drove me to tears. "I can't walk," I said.

He settled me against his chest. "Let's get out of here."

His arms were strong, his skin warm, and his heart beat steadily against my chest. I clung to him like a cicada grasping its leafy home.

He passed a dark building, moving gingerly, and turned right toward an entrance to another garden. Once we entered it, he crossed a bridge.

"Where is everyone?" I whispered. It was quiet. We were alone. I liked that.

"At the other side of the garden with Taizi." He looked around the small area surrounded by many trees. "They're burying the flutist."

"And you?" I touched his arm.

"I'm fine."

But his pace was slower than usual. "You lost consciousness."

"That's nothing."

"Did he forgive you?"

He nodded, and we did not speak for a while.

"You shouldn't have said that to the Emperor, Pheasant."

He shook his head and walked toward a stone bench. Then he put me down and put a finger to his lips. There were faint lights coming from my left. Some murmurs drifted to my ears. The night was so quiet, I could hear someone reciting the end of a burial text nearby.

Finally, voices urged the heir to return to his bedchamber. Their footsteps rose and soon faded. I leaned against the tree next to the bench and stared at the sky, where a round moon hung like a shattered plate. A sprawling branch over my head poked my shoulder. I sat still, recalling what the Captain had told me. I was a cripple, broken, like a table without legs, an abomination, like the heir.

I felt the bench's hard surface against me. "The Captain recommended he cut off my legs. He said it was bad blood."

"What?" He lowered himself to the ground to stay at my eye level, looking stiff.

I turned to Pheasant. The pale moonlight draped on his head like a luminescent net. "I can't walk."

He turned his face away from me. "He must be crazy," he said, his voice hoarse. "Don't listen to him."

"What if he's right?"

He turned around and cradled my face in his hands. I could not believe how much he had changed. All traces of that easy manner of his were gone. He looked different, intense and melancholic.

My heart poured out for him. "Oh, poor Pheasant." I held him. It just occurred to me that he could not sit because he still hurt from being whipped. "What have I done to you?"

He stroked my hair. "Don't say that. I would do anything for you."

My eyes moistened. As long as I had him, I did not care what happened to me. I could have held him and died at that moment, and I would have had no regrets.

"I need to tell you something," he said.

"What?"

"He promised to leave you alone."

"He forgives me?"

"Yes. He won't beat you, demote you, or expel you from the court."

I searched his face. I should have known that Pheasant would protect me, that he would convince the Emperor to spare me. "What did you do, Pheasant?"

He did not answer.

I held the front of his robe. "You promised you'd never see me again?"

He looked away.

My hands trembled. "Is he going to send you away?"

"To study classics."

"And?"

"Remember what I told you? Before my mother's deathbed, my father promised I could marry any woman I wished, any woman of my choice."

I remembered. He was her youngest son, her most beloved son. She wished him to be happy, not a pawn of the throne.

"Now, he has chosen one for me," Pheasant said. "And I agreed."

My hands slipped, and I faced the emptiness of the night. So vast and open. I felt the weightlessness surround me as if I were falling into a void, like a leaf blown into a gorge.

"Take care, my love." He stood up, stretching out his hand as if to touch me. "I promise I will not see you again."

"Wait." I clutched his sleeve. Our gazes locked, and his eyes glittered in the moonlight. "Just a moment longer, all right?"

He nodded.

"When do you leave?"

"At dawn."

So soon. Next time I saw him, he would belong to someone else. "Can I see where they struck you?"

He reached for his belt and untied his robe. Around his waist and back were bandages, beneath which flowed the blood that had bled for me. I did not touch it. I only stared. "Pheasant, have I told you about my father?"

He shook his head.

"He died to save me. I was twelve years old. He took me to my family's grave site and showed me our family's land. We were talking so merrily. He loved me, Pheasant. I was his favorite. But a tiger attacked us. No. Attacked me. He pushed me away to save me. For years I could not remember, but now I do."

He squeezed my hand.

"He wanted so much for me. He raised me like a son. He believed in me, believed in some prediction, and then he died to protect me. I wanted to make him happy, to make him proud of me. I wanted to walk the path he chose for me. I couldn't be with you"—I raised my head—"even if I wanted to."

He stroked my head. Once, his tenderness would have crushed me, pained me. Not anymore. I traced his skin near the bandages. He cringed. "But I think there is nothing I can do. I have to disappoint him."

I had to make a choice, my own choice. It was neither a right one nor a good one. Because with the choice, I would banish my father's dream to the court's shadowy corner, where it would wander like a homeless ghost, and because of it, I would bring my family no fame or glory.

I untied my robe and let it fall off my shoulders. Then I took Pheasant's hand and kissed him.

He swallowed hard. "I can't now."

"Why?"

"You were right. I will ruin you. I have been selfish. This will bring you danger and dishonor. I will not do that to you."

"I don't care." I undid the cords of my bandeau and dropped it too. Cool air swept across my naked chest, but I did not feel cold.

"Mei..." His voice was faint.

I did not stop. I pulled down my skirt and trousers, lifting my bottom to remove them. When there was not a thread left on me, I raised my arms to loop around his neck and pressed against him.

We both trembled.

"I still can't—" His warm breath touched my lips like a delicate brush. His heart beat the same fierce rhythm as mine.

"Kiss me."

"Mei..." He was struggling. His breath quickened.

I leaned closer to him, stroking his chest. He breathed fast but still would not hold me. I moved down. He stilled. Then suddenly, I was beneath him on the stone bench.

How strange I felt. I was there but not there. I was high but also low. I was soft but also hard. I was less but also more. I drifted, I flew, I leaped to a world distant and unknown. I transformed into water, I turned into gold, and I relived as fire. Every part of my body seemed to evolve, but I did not know what I would become. I only knew, however, that I was stronger.

Then something deep within me emerged, pulsating, its beats persistent but subtle, like a butterfly's flutters. It grew stronger and stronger and swept my breath away like the powerful wings of an eagle.

"You all right?" he asked.

"Yes," I whispered.

We stopped to breathe, my face resting in the nook of his neck. We were so close. I could feel his soul next to me, and the seed of sweetness flowered within me.

He brushed my hair aside. "What are we going to do now?"

I squeezed his hand. "You have a safe journey tomorrow."

His arms circled me tight.

"We don't have a choice, Pheasant."

His grip became tighter. I let him hold me, my eyes closed. I would want nothing more than to rest with him and stay with him, but that was not a fate we could have. Slowly, I pried open his fingers, one by one, and I took his hand off my waist. I picked up my clothing and dressed.

"I'll talk to my brother, Prince Wei. He'll look after you when I'm gone." He stood beside me.

"I'll be fine." I slipped off the bench and froze.

"What's wrong?"

"I..." I could not finish the sentence, my heart pounding with joy. "Look, look!"

We both looked down. A carpet of luminous light veiled the ground. There was nothing else there, except for the dark tip of my clogs poking under my long skirt.

"I'm standing!" I held on to Pheasant's shoulders. "I'm on my feet again. I feel my feet!" A wave of painful sensation struck my feet and legs, and I wobbled. "Do you see that? The Captain was wrong!" My knees gave way, and I lurched forward.

Pheasant caught me. "I knew it!" His face beamed with such

brilliance and happiness, as if he were the one regaining his strength. "I told you he was crazy. Do you believe me now?"

Joy radiated through my limbs. "Yes, I believe you." Gazing at him, I cupped his chin with my two hands. "Always."

He lowered his head. Lingeringly, we kissed.

Somewhere, a night bird cooed. Its soft lilt echoed in the darkness and settled in my heart like a nest.

I wished to stay there a bit longer. I wished the night would never end. But then came the servants' voices, brusque and strident, tearing the night's silence. I gave Pheasant one last glance and limped away.

AD 644

the Eighteenth Year *of*

Emperor Taizong's Reign

of Peaceful Prospect

AUTUMN

34

I OFTEN THOUGHT OF THAT NIGHT AS THE NIGHT MY LIFE was forever altered, and I also realized I was a terrible student. I had memorized Sun Tzu's lines of how to succeed in the Nine Situations, how to attack by fire and water, how to cultivate tactical dispositions, and how to use spies to excavate the enemy's deep secrets. But I had failed, tragically, to understand myself.

Yet I did not have regrets, and if Father had been alive, I would have knelt before him and begged for his forgiveness. I could not fulfill his wish, no matter how splendid the vision was, and no matter how perfectly my destiny had been designed. I was only an ordinary woman, saddled by an ordinary woman's weaknesses and tears.

I knew now: love and destiny were two wild horses that could not be curbed. They galloped in different directions and ran down different paths where streams of desire and hope would not converge. To follow one was to betray the other. To make one happy was to break the other's heart. Yet I supposed that was part of life, a lesson we had to learn. To grow up was also to give up, and to build the future was to dissolve the past. The only thing we could do was hope for the best, to believe that the horse we chose would find us a safe destination.

✦ ✦

On the surface, everything remained the same. I tended the ward-robe chamber, gave instructions to my helpers who delivered the garments, and slept on the mat in the Emperor's chamber with Plum, Daisy, and the other Talents on our nights. On occasion, I followed the Emperor to the Audience Hall. He did not dismiss or scold me.

But something had changed. He strolled past me as if I did not exist. His gaze swept the faces of the attendants, but he did not see me. When he ordered wine, he never turned in my direction as I bowed to present my tray. He did not call me to keep him company when he sat alone in the ring of candles. It seemed he had banished me to an invisible corner where he would not set his sight.

After the New Year, I would be nineteen, but I had ruined the chance of a lifetime.

Sometimes, I wondered what would have happened if I had not run after Pheasant. I also wondered what would have happened if I had never met Pheasant or fallen in love with him in the first place. I would perhaps have become Most Adored a long time ago.

Pheasant moved out of the palace a few days after we said good-bye. The Emperor had given him a house outside the palace. The servants whispered about the woman the Emperor had chosen for him. She was from the prestigious Wang family and had a love for animals. Many believed she was a good choice.

And, to my great dismay, the shameless Rain, more wicked than anyone I knew, even Jewel, gave birth to a baby boy, for she had lain with Pheasant after I left him last year. I did not sleep well after hearing the news. I hoped the Emperor would punish her severely for having an illicit relationship with Pheasant, but he did not. Because she bore a precious son, the Emperor not only forgave her, but also ordered the celebration of the birth with great pomp. He even decreed that Rain serve Pheasant from now on and become an official member of his household. She was to be his concubine.

Suddenly, Pheasant, my Pheasant, the love of my heart, was a husband of another woman, a father with a newborn son.

On the night when the palace celebrated Pheasant's son, the

Emperor danced, laughing, spilling too much wine. I stayed in a corner while Pheasant drank with the others. When court protocol forced me to toast to him, I approached his table, knelt before him, and congratulated him.

He raised his head, his eyes two deep wells of anguish. But there was nothing we could say, with Rain sitting at his right, holding her newborn. I held my head low and poured wine into his cup.

The amber stream cascaded like a waterfall of tears.

✦ ✦

The Emperor retracted Taizi's allowances and forbade his activities in the Archery Hall, the imperial stables, the libraries, even the parks. Neither was he welcome at any formal gatherings. The heir retreated to his residence and spent all his time hosting wrestling tournaments. Sometimes, when I woke in the night, I heard the men's boisterous laughter and drunken shouts echo in the distance. I thought about how tenderly Taizi had bound his lover with the strip of cloth and how his hands had trembled when he'd heard the Emperor's order. I understood the hollowness in his voice, and I knew his pain was as real as mine.

And the Emperor, oh, he had changed as well. He even lost the last vestige of handsomeness. His cheeks sagged, and the right side of his face seemed somehow longer than the left side. He could not hold his sword anymore. The blade lay at his fingertips, but he simply could not reach out and hold it.

Still, he summoned us to his chamber, following the bedding schedule, but when I, together with the other Talents, went to his chamber, he always sat in the circle of candles, holding the goblet with his good left hand. As always, he did not trouble to bed us or ask us to seduce him. Rather he ordered us to stay in a corner far from his stool. Walking in front of him was forbidden. When someone did, he would hold his head and cry out, "Shadows, shadows!" as if they gave him a terrible headache.

He also ordered his dress maids—not me, never me—to read

poems or summoned his musicians to play percussion and windpipe music until dawn. But he listened to none of these—his snore was louder than the music. And as soon as their recitals stopped, he woke with a start. It seemed he was afraid of going to sleep.

His nights with other ladies went worse than mine, I heard. He cursed, kicked, threw things, and when the ladies begged him to stop, he would jerk back, as though suddenly awake, and then he would weep. Sometimes, in his exhaustion, he would curl up in his oversize bed and doze, and then in the morning, when I received the linen sheets from his chambermaids, they were often soiled and stained with his essence.

Why had he changed so? Was it because of the ghost of his brother? I would never know, perhaps, and I was careful not to talk about the Emperor with Plum or Daisy.

✦ ✦

"Perhaps, the One Above All, it is time to revisit the Art of Bedchamber." The Taoist astrologer's voice resonated through the Audience Hall as I waited in the antechamber.

I wished the audience would end quickly. I had lost interest in the Emperor's governing strategies and the events happening in our kingdom. When I listened, I felt a thick, lethargic stupor clouding my head. It seemed to me the Emperor was not interested in audiences either. These days, he did not come to the audience very often. When he did, it was short and tedious, and his ministers had to wait outside in the corridor rather than inside.

The Emperor's meeting with the astrologer was unplanned. He had complained of an ache on his face, or inside his mouth, which he did not seem to be sure. So he had consulted with imperial physicians, and the physician Sun Simiao had prescribed him pills for a toothache. But the Emperor had also summoned the astrologer for his opinion.

"The cure of a man by a woman is the true cure in the universe. Many practice it, but few succeed," the astrologer said. "The essence escapes, a man's spirit weakens, and a woman, in return, is strengthened."

"I have no sickness other than a toothache," the Emperor replied. His voice was low and weak, carrying a slur with which I had become familiar. "Tell me a good remedy for it."

"Yes, the One Above All. May I elaborate? If the essence is contained, a man enjoys good health and a strong mind. Woman's yin, thus, succumbs to man's yang." The astrologer droned on, and even though I could not see him, I could imagine his sesame-speckled beard shaking as he spoke. "Suppose a man copulates with ten women without losing his essence. His mind is greatly strengthened, and all sorts of dreams—of woman, of demon, or of any forbidden vision—shall be expelled, and thus the curses of the roaming ghosts shall be dissolved."

"What did you say?"

The sharpness in the Emperor's voice made me raise my head. Around me, the other attendants glanced at one another. The voices from the corridor dimmed somewhat, as though the ministers, who waited outside for their turn, were alerted as well.

"The One Above All, dreams of all sorts are curses of those ghosts who roam on the dark side. They strive to break into the mind's barrier, enticing man with their secret wishes."

"You exaggerate." His voice was still slurred, but now it had turned hard.

"When a man's mind is weak, his defense is lowered. The ghost succeeds when a man releases his essence in a dream. That, the One Above All, is the ultimate calamity to a man."

If he had seen the sheets I had collected, he would not have said that. But it was too late.

"I think your calamity befalls rather sooner than you think." The Emperor roared, "Captain!"

Outside the Audience Hall, the Captain answered.

"Stitch up this man's lips, so he can never utter another word in his life again."

Some footsteps pounded on the other side, and soon, a prolonged scream pierced the hall. I covered my mouth, as if the needle had pierced my own lips. Another hysterical cry. Then a string of heart-rending wails. The ministers waiting in the corridor murmured, but none of them dared to object or enter as the astrologer's screams slowly succumbed to whimpers. I went to the antechamber's door and peered out. The poor man, stumbling, stepped over the hall's threshold and rolled into the corridor. A pitiful thing, like a sacrificial animal, saturated in blood.

"Resume the audience!" the Emperor ordered, and the ministers trickled into the hall. One by one, they presented their individual cases, as if they had seen none of the blood, as if they had not heard the astrologer whimper nearby.

The usual solemnity, though thicker than ever, descended on the other side of the hall, and I leaned against the pillar behind me, wondering what the astrologer would do with his lips stitched. By now, I was sure, words of his punishment were already flying. And by the time the audience finished, all the people, the ministers, the scribes, the servants, the guards, the ladies, and even the people in the kingdom would question the Emperor's sanity.

And that would not be the end of it. From now on, nothing would be the same, because even though we could not speak of it, we could feel it, the moodiness of the Emperor, hanging above our heads like an invisible sword suspended in the air and threatening to drop when we least expected it.

A sudden scream rose in the hall. I jolted and rushed to the side of the screen and peered through the gap of the folds. I could not believe my eyes.

The Emperor was trembling, violently, not just his hands or his arms, but his whole body, as though someone we could not see was angry at him and shaking him. White foam gushed from his mouth, and his eyes rolled upward to the ceiling. Then, as the ministers cried out frantically, he stood up and threw out his arms as though trying to order people to calm down, but a spasm ran through him, his legs buckled, and his head snapped to one side. He tumbled from the throne.

✦ ✦

The court physicians were quickly summoned. The Emperor was swiftly removed and carried to his bedchamber. By dusk, everyone in the palace was whispering.

"The Emperor is haunted!"

"He is poisoned!"

"He is dying!"

"He is dead!"

If I had not accompanied him to his bedchamber, I would have believed them. But it was true. The Emperor looked dead. He did not respond to our cries or the probing touches of the physicians. He did not open his eyes, or his mouth, or wave his arms. He simply lay there, his face contorted, his hands bent, and his breath faint.

Day and night, the court physician Sun Simiao paced around him, feeling his pulse, examining his eyes, and listening to his breathing. Occasionally, the Emperor's arm jerked and his mouth twitched. But he would not open his eyes.

The Duke asked the physician if someone had poisoned the Emperor. Sun Simiao shook his head, looking adamant. "This is not poisoning," he said. What was it? He would not give an answer.

But all the same, rumor shook the palace like a great storm. The Emperor would not live to the end of the moon, it said, and something restless, something ominous, began to drift in the air. It hung low on the servants' lips, the guards' arched eyebrows, and the ministers' uneasy coughs. It followed me, haunted me, like a stench that refused to dispel.

One day, I went back to the Audience Hall to fetch the Emperor's belt, which I had forgotten, when I heard whispers from a corner in the adjacent corridor. I stopped to listen. Ever since the Emperor's mysterious sickness, the Hall had been almost abandoned. Who would be meeting there?

"All morning, a flock of crows cawed on a pine tree in the Western Market, and all the fowl nearby died mysteriously."

The voice sounded familiar. I peered through the gap of the

doors. A minister with a stooped back, Chancellor Wei Zheng, was talking to a man holding a cane. The Emperor's uncle.

"It's Heaven's sign!" The Uncle's eyes grew as large as polo balls. "He's not going to make it. He is going to die! I talked to a fortune watcher too. He predicts his days are numbered."

"No, no. It's only a rumor... He is only forty-six, a man of great strength—"

"A sick man on the verge of dying, my old friend, and it is his due." The Uncle shook his head. "We should not have supported him when he conspired to kill his brother. Now the ghost heir is punishing him. Next will be us! We must do something, or we are all condemned!"

I could not leave. I had to listen.

"My old friend, do not work yourself up. This is a dark moment. It shall pass. We must stay calm," Wei Zheng said.

The Uncle knocked his cane against the ground. "We're only fooling ourselves, my friend, you know better than this. We shall take this opportunity to right what we have wronged. This is our moment. We will make history again, just like the old times. We will choose our own emperor and kick out the Turkic clown. What do you say?"

A moment of silence.

"I would not have risked speaking to you if I were not confident. All the ministers resent him. He ordered the stitching of an astrologer's lips, remember? Our reverend astrologer! The man who watches Heaven's signs! I'm telling you, my nephew has lost us! Listen, my friend, I'm going to tell you something very important. We have received everything we need. The khans are with us. The khans! You know well they dislike him and his arrogance. They have agreed this is the time. They will attack the borders at our signal. Yes, on our signal they will surround him, just like the old times."

The Emperor's vassals, the Eastern Turks and the people in Tuyuhun, had remained silent after the polo game, but the prophecy and the rebellions within the kingdom had surely reached their ears too.

"The khans? It's unlikely. Didn't Taizi quiet them all when he defeated the Western Turks?"

"That's true. The vassals respect the heir. They do not like how the Emperor treats his own son. That is why they will join us."

A sigh. "Which khan?"

"All of them! They are displeased with the yearly tributes demanded by the Emperor. It is too much. They cannot afford it. Have you seen last year's breed? A poor batch of skinny horses! Besides…" He cupped his hand over Wei Zheng's ear and whispered.

"What? She is part of this?"

Who was she? I pushed closer to the door.

"Yes! The Pure Lady—and what an extraordinary woman she is!—has hired mercenaries, bought the rebels on the borders, and even recruited men near Chang'an. She has prepared everything…"

Blood rushed to my head. I could not believe my ears.

"But why? Why will she take such a huge risk… Yes, I know, I know… Of course I know about the prophecy… What?"

"It is true, old friend."

"I… This…this is hard to believe…"

"There is no denying it, my friend. Prince Yo is the man. He is the one who will destroy this dynasty. Remember the sign that says my nephew's dynasty will end and his foe is coming?"

"Yes, yes. But how can he be the man in the prophecy?" Wei Zheng's jade pendants clinked against each other as he leaned closer to the Uncle. "How can you be certain?"

"Think about it! Recite the prophecy."

"He comes when the stone turns flesh, the animal weeps, the birds cry thrice from Heaven. Then the Wu Man comes…"

The Wu Man? What did it mean? The sound "Wu" contained numerous homonyms. Depending on the tones, each sound indicated different meanings. Of course, my family's name was Wu too, but I was not a man…

"Think about his rank in the birth order!"

A pause. "He's the fourth son…"

"Yes, and now add the infant boy who died before him!"

Wei Zheng had a sharp intake of breath. "He would be the fifth…"

The word *fifth* was pronounced as "Wu." I covered my mouth, nearly gasping. So the Wu Man in the prophecy meant the Fifth Man, and the Uncle believed Prince Yo, the exiled prince, was the real man in the prophecy.

"Do you understand what I'm talking about, my old friend?"

"That…that is…unexpected… But…but the Emperor told me he had eliminated the threat. He drowned two hundred men whose surname bore that sound of 'Wu.'"

His words struck me. The trip to the Forbidden Park, the two dead guards, the Black Boy—black was also pronounced "Wu"—and Fifth Girl. The Emperor had killed them, believing they were his foes.

"He drowned the wrong ones! Now the augury says his rival is coming, upon three signs! If it's not Prince Yo, who could it be?"

"I don't know. I don't know." Wei Zheng's pendants jingled.

The Uncle stepped closer to him. "This is Heaven's design. He exiled him, and now he can't touch him. He's protected. All we need is a signal from the lady. A signal! Then everything will change. What are you waiting for, my old friend?"

"Let me think it over. Let me, my friend."

Wei Zheng reached for the lion's head on the railing and shuffled to the stairs. Together, they descended.

I pressed against the door, my heart pounding. The belt was wrinkled in my grip, and my underrobe was soaked with perspiration. If they knew I had been eavesdropping, the Uncle and the Chancellor would not let me walk out alive. But planning a revolt! The Uncle and the Pure Lady must have been insane. But perhaps I was wrong. They had chosen a good time after all, now that the Emperor was unconscious…

I had to tell the Noble Lady as soon as possible. It seemed the Uncle would put everything in motion soon…

Taking a deep breath, I stepped from the antechamber.

"What are you doing here?"

Startled, I twirled around. The Captain stood behind me, frowning. My heart pounding, I scurried down the stairs.

"Come here!" he shouted. "I need to talk to you."

I ran as fast as I could. When he was out of sight, I slowed down, in case other people grew suspicious of me. It was not until I arrived at the Inner Court that I began to worry he would report my eavesdropping to the ministers.

35

"THE UNCLE?" THE NOBLE LADY ASKED AFTER I TOLD HER
what I had heard.

I nodded. "With the Chancellor." We were in a dire situation
indeed. The physician Sun Simiao could not tell us when the
Emperor would awake, or if he would awake at all. If Prince Yo
attacked the palace, no one would be able to lead the Gold Bird
Guards and defend us...

"I never would have imagined this. I thought the old man
would have accepted his fall from favor by now. How could he
plot such an abominable crime? With the Pure Lady?" She stroked
her neck. She was wearing another gold necklace, and I could see a
scar had formed around her neck where the Pure Lady had yanked
her necklace off.

"He must be desperate. Did the Emperor suspend his duty in
the court again?"

The Noble Lady sighed. "Worse than that. He wanted him to retire."

"Retire?" That was no different from exile.

"The Emperor had drafted the edict, but he fell sick, so he did
not announce it. The Duke has decided to follow through with
the Emperor's decision. The Uncle's retirement will be official next
month. He must have sensed something, or perhaps a scribe told him."

Since the Emperor's sickness, the Duke had taken charge of

collecting all petitions and state matters. When there were some urgent matters, he had made decisions on behalf of the Emperor.

"Of course, the Duke hates the Uncle." And the Uncle would not be squeezed out easily; after all, he had made considerable contributions to founding the dynasty.

The Noble Lady nodded. "I didn't tell you about this, Mei. A few weeks ago, I caught the Pure Lady conversing with the Emperor's uncle during a gathering in the Outer Palace. She handed him a piece of paper. The old man read it rapidly and then spat on the paper and smeared the words with his forefinger. He nodded, agreeing with her about something."

"Did you hear anything they said?" I asked.

"I did not. I didn't give it much thought, but the way he smeared the words was peculiar, and I could not forget that afterward." She paced in her room, looking thoughtful.

They must have been plotting then. "What should we do, my lady?"

"I know the Pure Lady never forgets a grudge. But planning a rebellion?" The Noble Lady seemed immersed in her own thoughts. "How clever she is to choose the Emperor's uncle. The old man is bringing about his own doom because of his feud with the Duke. Now he hates the Emperor too."

"He's still powerful in the court." Even the Chancellor seemed to side with him.

"That is why this is unthinkable." Still in deep contemplation, she stroked the box that contained her spiders. It was not spring yet, and the weavers were not working for the season. "Did he say when they would revolt?"

I shook my head. "He said they'd send a signal."

"What kind of signal?"

I shook my head again. Whatever the signal was, we had to find it before it was sent out.

"We need proof."

That would be the challenging part.

"We must act quickly. I will talk to Ke. You must not tell anyone about your discovery."

Since Taizi had been dishonored; Prince Ke was the most favored. If he proved the Pure Lady's treachery, no doubt the Emperor would claim him as the heir.

I nodded. "I won't."

"It's for your own safety."

"I understand."

"Meanwhile, you must keep an eye on who the Emperor's uncle contacts and listen to their conversations if possible. You may learn more details about his plan."

I was not certain I would do better spying this time. "What are you going to do now, my Noble Lady?" I would have liked to hear her thoughts, and if she could lay out her plans with me, that would have been even better.

"We must not waste a single moment," she said, ignoring my question.

One afternoon, the Duke, who had come to see the Emperor in his bedchamber, ordered me to go to the Emperor's library to fetch some ink and calligraphy paper. As soon as I turned onto the path near the building, I knew I was being followed. I walked faster. The large figure behind me walked faster too. I stopped and spun around.

The Captain.

My heart jumped to my throat. Had he seen me eavesdropping on the Uncle and the Chancellor? Had they ordered him to arrest me?

"Stop right there." He stood before me, the purple patch spreading on his cheek like a shadow. He did not look as menacing as I had expected, but his voice was emotionless. "I have a message for you."

I stiffened. "What message?"

He took out a roll of paper as small as my finger from his pocket. "It's from your mother."

"What?" I snatched it and unfurled the roll.

It was Mother's handwriting. She was well. She had sought shelter in a Buddhist monastery. I covered my mouth, relief washing over me. "She's safe! She's in a monastery. A Buddhist monastery."

I wondered where the monastery was. In China, the nobles studied Confucianism and worshipped Taoism, and Buddhism was a foreign religion that was looked down upon and appealed mostly to women, outcasts, and the lower class. There was no official Buddhist temples or monasteries in Chang'an, and the religion did not receive support from the Emperor or the palace. Relying mostly on themselves, the temples and monasteries were often located in remote places and remained isolated.

"Destroy it. Before anyone else sees it."

"I will." I composed myself. Secretary Fang had searched for Mother but found no trace of her. The Captain, the man in charge of the Gold Bird Guards, had nothing to do with the search. "How did you find her? Why are you helping me?"

"Not helping you," he said, turning to leave. "Your mother found me. I knew your father. We went to war together. He was a good man."

"Wait!" I followed him. "How can I see her?"

"You can't," he replied without looking back. "Leaving the palace without permission is against the Emperor's law. I'm his captain. Don't forget."

But I had to see her, and I could not wait any longer. She was already at the age of Knowing Heaven's Mission. If I delayed, I might never see her again.

How could I leave the palace? I could not ask the Emperor, who was still unconscious, and even if he were awake, I would not dare to ask him. Who could help me? I gnawed my knuckles.

I went to look for Eunuch Ming. I could not find him. "He died," one eunuch told me when I inquired. "Stomach ulcer. Died two months ago."

I passed the bustling servants who delivered hot water to the other ladies, and I paused. Of course. I could ask for their help. The servants who purchased the groceries in the market had the freedom to leave and enter the palace every morning. They used an exclusive entrance near the kitchen on the west side of the court, where neither ladies nor guards would set foot.

"I'M NOT GOING TO THE MARKET TOMORROW." THE POCKMARKED
eunuch shook his head as he shuffled in front of a stove. "I can't
help you."

"Perhaps I didn't make it clear," I persisted. "I won't get you
into trouble. I'll wear kitchen staff's livery when we leave. On our
return, you can pile the vegetables on top of me. No one at the
gate will know."

"I'm too busy."

"I'll make it worthwhile, I promise." I took out two silver
ingots. He peered at me. I added one more in desperation.

"Come here at the hour of *chou* tomorrow." He snatched the
silver from me and stuffed a greasy robe into my hands. "Don't
be late. It's a long drive to the monastery you want to go to, even
with my mules."

We left the palace three hours after midnight. By the time we
reached the mountain outside the city wall, the dawn's pale light
shone on the edge of the horizon. I climbed out of the grocery cart.

The mountain was so immense, I could not see its top where
the thick fog floated. Some steep, narrow stairs, covered with green

moss, wound around the mountain and vanished behind towering junipers. And there, high on a cliff, perched a small building: the Buddhist monastery.

I climbed the stairs, imagining my reunion with Mother. We would embrace, we would laugh, we would cry, but most of all, we would be ourselves—a daughter and a mother. I thought of her tenderness and wisdom, and my limbs became alive with energy, and my heart pumped with happiness. Oh, how I missed her. Mother! My tree. My mountain. I should never part with her again.

I reached the monastery. It looked worse than it had in the distance. It had mud walls, a thatched roof, and the front door was a thin, wooden board where many termites crawled.

A nun with her hair wrapped in a skintight cap answered the door when I knocked. She was the abbess, she said, and she gestured to the back of the building when I told her I was there for Lady Yang, Mother's maiden name. I passed the small courtyard and reached the kitchen door. There, I composed myself and then pushed it open.

Facing me was a small dining table, but no stools. Near it, a sliver of sparkling sunlight lit up a neat trail of dust on the dirt floor. In the corner, water bubbled in a pot. Its sonorous simmering almost soothed my nerves. Almost. Stooping under the low doorway, I held the door frame, my heart racing faster than when I had climbed the steep stairs.

I did not see Mother.

"May I be of service?" a voice asked near the cooking pit. A Buddhist nun put down a handful of dried mushrooms and walked to me.

"I'm looking for my mother. The abbess told me she was in the kitchen," I replied, disappointed.

"We are all Buddha's children," the nun said.

Out of courtesy, I nodded, although I was in no mood for the religious talk. Behind the kitchen, someone dropped a bucket into a well. Perhaps Mother was fetching water. She must have worked as a kitchen helper while she sought refuge in the temple. Hardly containing my excitement, I bowed to take my leave.

"You've grown up to be a true gem, a woman with astounding beauty and grace," the nun said. "Your father would be so proud."

My head hit the door frame. "Mother?"

She looked shorter, and her long hair, into which I had often buried my face, was gone. Her face, which had refused to shed the tears of a hard life, looked leathery and bore marks of the sun and the wind. She looked so different from the graceful noblewoman I had remembered, but she was indeed my mother.

I threw my arms around her. I had been lost, and now I was home.

"It has been so long." Mother patted my back. "Five years, isn't it?"

"Yes." I nodded. So many things I yearned to ask her. Why had Qing banished her? How had she come to the temple? Had she heard anything from Big Sister? "I was so worried about you, Mother. What are you doing here? Why are you dressed like this?"

"I have found profound comfort and solace in following the path of Buddha. Five years of solitude draws me closer to nature and far from the human world. I did not expect to see you again."

"I didn't think I'd see you again either, Mother." I touched her cheek. "You've lost weight."

"And you have grown."

"I know." I gazed at her, preparing for her next question. She would ask me about how I was doing at the palace. "Everything is fine," I would say. But she did not ask. Instead, she went to a small niche above the stove where families prayed to their ancestors. Her hands pressed together, she closed her eyes and murmured.

I stared at the small figurine sitting in the niche. Tears blurred my vision. Mother had not forgotten Father; she kept his altar in the temple's kitchen.

"I must confess something to you, Mother." I went behind her.

She would be disappointed, but she had to know: I would not become the empress.

"To him, the true warrior for all souls." Mother pointed at the white figurine in the niche.

It was not Father, but rather a monk, sitting underneath a tree with leaves shaped like palms. "When he returns, he'll bring salvation and spread the true messages of Buddha. He shall deliver us all."

The pious tone of her voice stunned me. Mother had become a devout Buddhist nun. I bit my lip.

"Buddha returns?"

"No," Mother said. "The great monk. The warrior who broke the Tang's law to embark on a pilgrimage to India, the birthplace of Buddha. His only companion being a horse, he will return and bring us the true words of enlightenment and nirvana. I pray for that day to come."

I squeezed out a smile to please her. But in my heart, I wanted her to love me, not an unknown monk. "Don't you want to know how my life is in the court, Mother?"

"You don't remember him, do you?" she said, as if not hearing me, and her fingers busily pushed the wooden beads of her rosary. "You've met him. Tripitaka."

I remembered the name. "Yes."

"When he left for Buddha's land years ago, he passed by our home. Your father asked him to read our family's future. It was he who foretold your future and your father's death. Do you remember?"

Of course I did. I turned away to stare at the bubbling pot. "Did you know, Mother." I swallowed. "Father died because of me."

The beads stopped flowing.

"I could not remember it all these years, but now I do. It was not an accident. I was there when the beast came. Father died to protect me." I choked on my words. "It was my fault. If he had not died, we still would have lived in Wenshui. Little Sister would have been alive, and you, you would be home too."

"You were there?"

"Forgive me, Mother." I buried my face in her lap, unable to keep back my tears. "I brought down our family."

"So that was why he cried out for you."

"What?" I raised my head.

"Your father came to me in my dreams. Your name was the only one he mentioned. That's why I asked the Captain to deliver the message to you, so I could talk to you. I met him in the market. He and your father fought in the war together. He remembered me."

"What did Father say?"

"Father said not to blame you."

I gazed at her. "He...forgave me?"

"I did not understand that at first. Now I do."

I burst out in tears again. "That's all? Did he say anything else?" She shook her head.

I sniffed. A weight lifted off my shoulders. "He forgave me... just like that?"

Nodding, she stroked my hair. "Let all that was gone be gone. Worry no more, child."

Tightly, I hugged her. She was all I had, and I wanted to stay with her, sweep the floor with her, fetch water from the well, cook for her, eat with her, watch her hair grow, wash her stole, and talk to her until we fell asleep.

"You should return to the palace," she said gently.

"What about you?"

"I'm happy here."

I straightened and looked around the dirt floor and cracked walls.

As though reading my mind, she said, "When you're older, you will understand this—what happiness means. It is an illusion men promise to deceive themselves. I have learned so much from Buddha. All people lead a life of torment and suffering, from infancy to death, and after death, the souls suffer an eternity to make amends." Her fingers pushed the beads of her rosary. "It's true, child. Life has no worth, no meaning, no happiness."

I drew back. "What about family? They are not illusions. They mean something."

"What do they mean? Family, children, love, and honor. Where do they lead us?"

I could not find a word to say.

"They are only secular ties and deceiving vanities that pull us

337

like a yoke and force us to mill. Remember, in the end, nothing is important, and all return to dust."

"Dust?"

"I pray all shall come to peace. I pray all the lost shall be found." A chant came at the door. The abbess appeared, her hands pressed together. Mother rose and returned her a similar gesture.

I watched them. Their motions were smooth, their expressions calm and identical. Mother did not need me. She did not need my embraces, my love, or my protection. She was at peace, on her own terms. Or on Buddha's terms. It did not matter.

After a while, I bowed to Mother and the abbess. I wished them good health, promised I would visit again, and took my leave.

I stepped out of the monastery. The opaque mountain mists shifted around me. A falcon screeched over my head and vanished in the stands of mountain pines on a distant cliff. I thought of Father, his forgiveness, and Mother's retreating to the religious world, and slowly I walked toward the stairs.

Under my feet, only a few flights stretched, the rest hidden in the thick clouds of mists. A single misstep and I would plunge into the rocky depth.

But I understood it now. Somehow, sometime in our lives, we all needed to find a path through the clouds of our destinies and walk down. Alone.

Slowly, I descended the mountain stairs.

AD 644

the Eighteenth Year *of*

Emperor Taizong's Reign

of Peaceful Prospect

WINTER

37

SOON AFTER I RETURNED TO THE PALACE, THE EMPEROR finally opened his eyes. He was extremely weak and unable to speak. All of us, concubines ranked seventh degree and above, were relieved of our usual duties and ordered to stay with him day and night, caring for him. A month later, he was able to take some broth and herbal drinks and sit with assistance. Gradually, he uttered words, though with a thick and strange slur, and held his meetings in a hall adjacent to his bedchamber. He could not hold his calligraphy brush, so he met the Duke and dictated to him. The Uncle and the Chancellor were not summoned, so I did not need to spy on them.

The New Year came. The whole kingdom was immersed in celebrations, and the Emperor took an opportunity to rest, although he ordered the word spread that he was wholesome and riding horses, for fear of doubts over his health.

The Noble Lady planted trusted people to watch the Pure Lady and even her maids. Every day, their movements were reported to the Noble Lady and her son, who analyzed them carefully. "If she sends a signal, a letter, or a message, she'll go meet Jewel's spirit," she said confidently.

I was not sure. A letter would certainly incriminate the Pure Lady, but what if she did not send out a letter? What if it was something that we could not see?

The Pure Lady seemed to be aware she was being watched. She did nothing more than sit in the sun, play *weiqi* with her maids, or stroll in the open, her cat in her arms. When the weather was fine, she went to the Eastern Palace to admire the plum blossoms. Once, she stopped at the stable to watch a mare giving birth to a foal. I thought it strange she would go to the stable, Taizi's haunt, but she did not speak or spit at the heir, as I had expected she would do. She only watched the foal, they said.

Something was wrong, terribly wrong, but I did not know what.

The servants appeared at ease. Most of them believed the Emperor would live. Here and there, they greeted each other, even smiled at times, their cheeks red with holiday celebration and their stomachs sweetened by glutinous rice cakes, dried dates, and persimmons.

Plum mentioned Pheasant had wedded Lady Wang in his house outside the palace. I wished to hear more about the wedding, the bride, Pheasant, and how he thought of his new bride, but Plum did not elaborate other than saying Lady Wang was very tall.

Lantern Festival arrived. Lanterns carved in the shapes of deer, rabbits, and turtles paraded in the Inner Court and illuminated every corner. Paper artworks crafted as eagles, parrots, and swallows hung below the houses' eaves. Everywhere, the colors of red, mauve, indigo, green, and other iridescent hues greeted me. The last day of the long New Year holiday, the festival of lights, was supposed to bring us luck for the entire year.

I was hanging two paper cardinals in the garden when I glimpsed Pheasant at the gate. He put his hand on his left shoulder to attract my attention. I was surprised. Since he lived outside the palace and was married, I seldom saw him. Sometimes I would catch a glimpse of him gazing at me when he came to visit the Emperor, and that look would stay with me for days. I would walk in the corridors thinking of the intensity of his gaze and then go to sleep, pretending he was holding me, not his wife.

But when there were people around, he rarely looked in my direction, let alone asked to see me in private.

I nodded slightly to let him know that I had seen him and

then turned away, waiting for an opportunity. Finally, a group of eunuchs came over, carrying a tree decorated with gold leaves. People swarmed over to admire it. I slipped out.

I went down the bridge and found him behind a garden rock at the back of a hall.

He stood in the rock's shadow. The lanterns cast a pool of red light near his feet. He was the same Pheasant for whom I had waited in the pavilion. But he looked solemn, solitary, and much older. I was worried.

"What's wrong?" I walked to him.

He was not himself. He fidgeted, and his feet kept kicking the ground. At my voice, he straightened, turning around to make sure no one was watching us. "I'm sorry to put you at risk again. This is the last time I will ask you to meet me, I promise."

"Don't worry. No one saw me." The Emperor, his high-ranking ministers, and the Ladies were celebrating the festival in the feasting hall in the Outer Palace, and many servants were there as well.

He placed his hand on the rock. There was a pause before he said, "I came to warn you, Mei. It's not safe here."

I could not help myself. I stepped closer to him. "What's going on?"

"Something disastrous is going to happen. You must leave the hall. Now. Run to your chamber as fast as you can and bolt the door. Or"—he took off his hat and combed his hand through his hair—"go to our pavilion. Somewhere unknown and safe, and hide there until tomorrow night."

Was the Pure Lady about to take action? "Why?"

"It's my brother." He inhaled deeply. "I think he's out of his mind."

I was relieved it was not about the Pure Lady. "Taizi," I said. He was deeply unhappy; we all knew that. "What is happening with him?"

"I found weapons hidden away. Weapons. You know what I am saying, don't you? Lancers, swords, armors, bows, and arrows." He balled his hands in fists. "Bundles and bundles of them, in a stable."

I gasped, fully aware of its meaning. The law banned people from bearing arms, even princes. "Is he planning something? Why would he amass such a large amount of weapons?"

Pheasant's head drooped. "It's because of the flutist. I know it. Father should never have ordered Taizi to kill him."

"It's too late to say that. What is he going to do with all those weapons?"

A wave of laughter wafted in the night air. I could not tell where it came from. Both Pheasant and I stood still.

"It might be nothing. He likes to try weapons. Perhaps now he wants to become a swordsman."

His voice was raspy, and his chest heaved rapidly. I wanted to pull him into my arms and smooth his hair. I wanted to believe him, to tell him that was exactly why Taizi had bought the weapons and smuggled them into the palace. But the word *treason* pummeled my head, and I knew I could not indulge myself or Pheasant.

"Forget it." Pheasant kicked the ground again. "I'm just fooling myself. He's meeting a guard before dawn breaks."

"A guard?" My body tensed.

"The leader of his army." Pheasant smiled wryly. "I overheard him talking with his men in the stable. He arranged for his men to replace the guards posted in the Outer Palace so none of my father's army outside can enter the palace. He even bribed the sentries in the watchtower."

"He's going to revolt now?"

Pheasant wiped his face. The red light reflected in his tormented eyes. "I need to talk sense into him."

"What?"

"I'm his brother. I cannot watch him lose his head. He's the heir, for Heaven's sake. The kingdom is his no matter what. Why would he challenge our father?"

"Has Taizi forgiven you for the flutist?" He did not speak, and my heart sank. "He is still angry. Why do you think he'll listen to you? You cannot go, Pheasant. Taizi has lost his mind. Talking to him will not change anything."

"But if I don't talk to him, who will? What kind of brother am I? He can't revolt against my father. It's suicide."

Poor Pheasant. Caught between the stones of his father and brother. "Maybe you should tell the Emperor."

"My father?" Pheasant raised his head toward the direction of the Outer Palace, where the Emperor and his people feasted. He shook his head. "I can't! Do you remember what happened when Taizi had a fight with Prince Yo? He exiled Yo. What do you think my father will do if he knows about Taizi's weapons? He'll kill him!"

I grasped Pheasant's hand. "But you can't go, Pheasant. This is rebellion. Taizi wants revenge. He is not going to listen to you. If you tell him, if he knows you are aware of his plan, he'll kill you. It doesn't matter that you're his brother."

"I have no choice."

I looked into his eyes. "Listen to me. Don't rush into this. Let's think about it. Go to your room, drink some wine, and go to bed. Maybe nothing will happen. Maybe he'll forget this."

Pheasant faced me, and his hand swept aside my fallen hair. A shadow crossed his eyes, and the fence of his eyelashes trembled. For a moment, his square jaw seemed to melt, but his lips tightened and his immaculate face transformed into a perfect sculpture of resolution.

He cupped my face. "I want you, sweet face. I hope you know. Only you."

My heart softened. He loved me still, even though he had Lady Wang. "I do."

"I've never regretted it. Do you?"

I shook my head, pushing back my tears.

"I have to stop my brother. I have to save him."

I wanted to cry. "No..."

He dropped his hand and went down the corridor. His thin frame emerged into the pool of lantern light that bled like rivers of blood. Then the night's darkness swallowed him.

I walked back to the garden, where the eunuchs had set up the golden tree. I strung the lanterns in threes and fives and hung them on the golden branches, but I hardly saw them. What would happen to Pheasant? Would Taizi listen to him? Or would he kill him? I shivered. Of course he would. He would never let Pheasant reveal his secret.

I pushed the scattered lanterns away from my feet and ran to the Eastern Palace. Behind me, Daisy called out, asking what the hurry was, but I continued to run.

The east side of the Inner Court was deserted. Almost everyone was already in the feasting hall in the Outer Palace. I ran toward the vast area near the Tongxun Gate, passed the long, arched tunnel, and entered the Eastern Palace. I banged on the gate of Taizi's residence.

"Taizi!" I shouted.

Silence.

"Pheasant!"

No one answered.

I panicked, and with all my might, I banged and shouted. No one came. Something was terribly wrong. Even if Taizi was not inside, his servants should have answered the door.

I turned around.

I had to find help. I had to save Pheasant before it was too late.

38

I RACED TO THE OUTER PALACE AND BURST INTO THE feasting hall. Before me were heads of the ministers, colorful gowns of the ladies, and the bustling servants. The Duke was there, and so was the Chancellor. But the Emperor's uncle and the Pure Lady were absent. Where were they? Had they sent out their signal yet? But I could not think of their revolt right now.

The Emperor was seated at the feasting table at the end of the hall. He looked well enough, but he had never quite recovered completely from the spell that had weakened him. He was slouching, his right cheek hanging low, like a piece of wrinkled calligraphy paper glued to his face.

I had to tell him about Taizi's plot. Then he would take his men and break into the Eastern Palace and save Pheasant. I went behind the pillars, stepped away from the servants holding trays, passed the musicians playing lutes and zithers, and approached the center table. I slowed.

Would he believe me? What should I say when he asked me about the source? I would confess it was from Pheasant. But then he would understand Pheasant and I had met behind his back.

I hid behind a pillar and steadied myself. From behind a framed lantern, I peered at the tables where the ladies sat. The Noble Lady leaned over her son, Prince Ke, and said something to him.

Perhaps I should talk to her, so she could tell the Emperor about Taizi's plan. But then the Emperor would investigate further, and then it would come back to me and Pheasant.

I could not think of a way to save Pheasant without risking myself.

Catching sight of me, the Noble Lady raised her hand and waved, her golden necklace sparkling in the candlelight. I could not move. What would she tell me if she knew what I was going to do next? "Don't be foolish, Mei," she would probably say. "Are you asking for Jewel's fate?"

But I had to do it, or Pheasant would die. I took a deep breath and walked to the feast table. Near me, Lady Obedience twirled, her long, green sleeves encircling her like an emerald ring. Noises, heavy and thick, drummed in my ears.

I reached the feast table and knelt. "The One Above All," I said. "Forgive me that I must interrupt this halcyon moment. A terrible plot is unfolding in Taizi's residence. Pheasant is trying to persuade the heir to abandon his foolish idea. I fear he will not be successful."

The voices around me ceased, and Lady Obedience's feet scuttled away from me.

"What plot?" the Emperor asked.

His voice, more slurred than ever, clamped around my head like an iron ring. I did not flinch. "It involves weapons. It is said Taizi bought many of them and hid them in a stable. He is contemplating arming his men and revolting."

Gasps rose up behind me. I remained still.

"Revolting?"

I lowered my head.

"Who told you?"

I put my hands on the ground to support myself. "Your son, Pheasant."

Silence.

"Pheasant? Where is he?"

"He's in grave danger. He said he needed to stop the heir. He went to the Eastern Palace several moments ago."

The Emperor's feet appeared before me. Fear and dread crept

348

up my spine, yet I could not stop. Pheasant's life, and my own life, depended on that moment. "You must believe me, the One Above All. I speak the truth. I went to the Eastern Palace and knocked on the door. No one answered me. Please do something. Pheasant... You must save him."

A hand pushed up my chin. "Look at me."

No one was supposed to hold the Emperor's gaze, but I knew why he was ordering me to look at him. He wanted to peer into my soul and excavate the secrets of my heart. Yet for the first time since I entered the hall, I had no fear. I did not care if he would punish me. I did not care if I could win his affection. It was not important to me anymore. For now, I chose the wish of my own heart, and I had no regrets. I looked up.

Dark blots spread across his face like ominous shadows, and his eyes, now hooded, were sunk deep in the sockets, and his right eye especially, dragged down by the loose skin, was small and pitiful, like a burned hemp thread lying in a pool of melted candle wax.

But they were both flickering. Still bright, still frightening.

My hands jerked, but I did not look away.

"I shall deal with you later." He dropped his hand and shuffled to his feasting table. "Captain! Bring your men to the Eastern Palace. Break down the gates, check the stable, and bring me Taizi and Pheasant."

The Captain answered and left. In silence, we waited. I still knelt, my back bent and my hands on the ground. But I felt relieved. Pheasant would be safe. They would find him and rescue him.

It seemed I had been kneeling for ages when footfalls echoed outside the feasting hall. They had arrived! I turned around. But there was no Pheasant, no Taizi, no Captain. Only another guard.

"The One Above All!" the man shouted.

My heart pounded. Something was wrong. He had spoken before he was given permission.

"Emergency!" he shouted.

"What is it?" the Emperor asked. "Where's the Captain?"

"Taizi ambushed us with his men. We were surrounded." The

guard wiped his forehead. He was about to speak again when a bell tolled from outside. The strikes were loud and urgent, the warning for an approaching threat to the palace. The hall fell silent. All the ladies and ministers stood to listen, their faces ashen.

"What is it? Who is attacking the palace?" The Emperor was shaking.

Another guard raced into the hall and prostrated before him.

"The One Above All! It's Prince Yo's army! We're under attack!"

A sea of gasps rose around me, drowning me, and I shuddered with fear. Impossible! Taizi was revolting inside the palace, and now Prince Yo was striking from outside.

"Take me to the watchtower!" The Emperor stood, his hand on the table for support.

"There are too many of them. It's too dangerous," the guard said.

"Wuji!" Calling the Duke, the Emperor shuffled to the entrance. "Come with me. Let's squash them!"

The Duke hurried to join him. Behind them, the ministers jostled, looking frantic. Then they followed too. The Noble Lady's son, Prince Ke, ran after them. Soon they all left, leaving the hall filled with frightened ladies and fidgeting servants. I went to the Noble Lady and stood next to her.

"Prince Yo attacked. When did the Pure Lady send the signal? How did she do that with me watching her?" The Noble Lady looked shocked, but she sat demurely, her hands folded in her lap, as though she were giving instruction to her servants.

I shook my head. We were late, too late.

"And Taizi?" She rubbed her chest nervously. "Why would he rebel against his father?"

"I was surprised too," I said. Was it a coincidence that the two princes attacked on the same night? No, it could not be a coincidence. The princes must have conspired together. That was why the Pure Lady went to the Eastern Palace to watch the mare giving birth to a foal, and the plum blossoms. She must have passed her signal then.

But why would Taizi agree to conspire with Prince Yo? Taizi hated the prince. He must have been so grief stricken that he had lost his mind. Prince Yo, of course, would not have refused any help to break into the palace.

The Noble Lady gazed at the door. "I wish my son hadn't left us."

"If you wish, I will go after him." It was my excuse. I did not want to wait there. I wanted to follow the Emperor and search for Pheasant.

"It's better if we wait. I hope they will be back soon."

"But—"

"We wait."

"All right." I began to pace between the tables, slowly at first, then faster and faster. Around me, the women looked anxious. Some sobbed; some huddled together, shivering. It seemed as if they were breathing fear rather than air.

"Could you stop pacing? You're making me dizzy," the Noble Lady said.

I rubbed my hot face. "I'm sorry. I didn't know what I was doing."

She picked up a cup and sipped. "Would you like some wine?"

I shook my head. I did not have the stomach for anything.

"Fine wine—"

A clash of metal exploded outside. I froze.

Her cup crashed to the ground, and then, the hall turned silent like death.

"What is that? What is that?" someone asked frantically.

As though to answer her, heavy footsteps thundered outside and men cried out. I could not tell who those men were, but I could hear they were close to us.

"They are coming here! The rebels are coming!" someone else shouted near me.

Panic raced through the hall faster than a pack of hungry rats. The women screamed, jostling one another, knocking over the candles. The hall went dark.

Fear gripped my throat. "Are you all right, my Noble Lady?"

She did not answer. I stretched out my arms, searching for her. Something crashed onto my head. I fell to the ground.

I blinked rapidly, but it was too dark and I could not see any-thing. My knees grew weak, and I groped in the dark. Everywhere

I touched were people: their shoulders, their hair, and even their eyes. I murmured apologies, and desperate, I turned around like a blind man. My head knocked against a pillar. I slid to its bottom and leaned against it. It was comforting to know that something supported me.

Thunderous hooves drummed the ground outside. Metal clanged against metal. Heartrending cries rose, fell, and then were abruptly cut short.

The hall trembled. Dirt and dust showered from the ceiling. Something rolled against my hip. An apple, still in its silk wrappings.

Silence descended. Just when I thought the battle was over, another wave of shrieks ripped the ceiling, and more frantic rumblings and chaotic noises resonated.

"Mei?" The Noble Lady's voice came from somewhere. "Where are you, Mei?"

"Near the pillar, my Noble Lady."

The people around me shuffled, and the Noble Lady's fleshy hand touched my cheek. "Oh, you're here. I'm so glad I found you."

I held her hand and made room for her to sit. "Are you all right, my Noble Lady?"

"I am." She took a deep breath, but her hand was shaking. "This is ironic. I have gone through this before."

"What do you mean?"

"The Emperor invaded this place, the same palace, when it was still my home. I was ten years old then. I hid under a table in a dining hall, and when I came out"—her voice was faint and sad—"all my family members were dead."

Goose bumps prickled my arms. "I am sorry. I didn't know that."

"All except my mother, of course, and they held her...a sword under her chin... I've always wanted to be like her, to be an empress. I wanted to die with her then..."

I shuddered. "This time is different. The Emperor will win. He always wins."

"We shall hope for that. But sometimes, I would rather... He kept me. I do not know why. I never told anyone. But if I could...I would rather do something different. I would rather have a hand in my destiny..."

Her voice, thick with helplessness which I had never heard from her before, shook my heart. I felt like crying, for all the pain and sorrow she had suffered at a young age, for all she had endured these years, living under the command of the man who took her mother's life, but I did not wish her to continue, wary of the ears around us. "Let's not talk about this now, shall we? Soon, we will return to our chambers and rest, and in the morning, we will gather together and enjoy the warmth of the sun in the courtyard."

"Mei, you are too young. You don't understand, but I know how this will turn out. We will not survive."

"My Noble Lady—"

"This is life, Mei. All these years, I did not wish to remind myself of who I was, and all these years I fought and spied on the other ladies. Now they are gone. Jewel is dead, and her baby is dead too. No more fear or threat... I put aconite in her wine, Mei. It was me. I could not stand her. I had to..."

I could not believe what I had just heard. The Noble Lady, the lady known for her benevolence and kindness, would poison her rival and abort an innocent life? What other measures would a woman take to destroy her rival?

"Shh ... Someone is coming," a voice said.

A rider. Most likely armed. I heard metal clunking. It sounded as if the rider was searching the front court of the hall. Gasping, people shrank around me. I felt the Noble Lady shake beside me.

"Don't worry." I put my arms around her. My mouth was dry, and my heart pounded in fear, but I tried to comfort the Noble Lady. "It could be an imperial guard, or the Emperor himself."

"It could be anyone." She shook her head.

"Be quiet!" someone, perhaps Lady Obedience, snapped in a low voice. "They will find us."

They? The heavy hoofbeats pounded against the stones on the ground. It was true. It sounded like there were at least two riders. The women began to sob, pushing toward the back of the hall. I could not help it. I held on to the Noble Lady and moved to the back as well.

"Mei!" The Noble Lady's voice cracked. "The door…"

I looked at the entrance. I could not see it clearly. "It's bolted." I hoped. It would take at least five men to break in with the bolted door. But if it was not… My throat tightened, and I could not breathe. And the hoofbeats ceased outside. Had the riders left?

A thunderous crash shook the hall, and the doors blasted open. I jumped, my hair standing up on my nape. But no one burst through the door. No movement either. Only silence.

"What was that?" the Noble Lady asked, her voice quavering.

I shook my head. The night's wind rushed through the doors like a massive hand sweeping the top of my head. An animal howled in the distance. Or was it a man shrieking before his death?

"We need to close the door. Could someone please go shut the door?" It was Plum's voice.

No one moved. The women beside me trembled violently. The Noble Lady's eyes were closed, and with the faint light coming from outside, I could see her face was stark white.

I rose, and even though I felt no strength in my legs, I said, "I'll close it."

Holding my breath, I crept toward the entrance. I was going to die, I was sure of it. A sword was going to flash in the air and chop off my head before I could cry out.

When I made it to the threshold, my hands were shaking, and I could hardly breathe. But I did not see a sword or any rebels.

Outside, the lights from the lanterns under the eaves were extinguished, and the yellow moon hung low, like a water-stained round fan. No one was in the corridor or the yard. Perhaps the rebels had left. I reached for the door frame.

Something exploded above my head, and thousands of shattered pieces burst in the air. Covering my head, I fell on my back as a hoof thrust through the door frame. A beast bolted into the hall.

"A horse, a horse!" the Noble Lady shouted. The women screamed.

My heart pounded. The horse, a large war mount, twisted its head and puffed thick fumes. With powerful legs hitting the ground, it lowered its head and charged.

The women screamed louder. Some ran to the corners of the walls; some raced to the doors. I was squeezed tightly among them. An elbow knocked against my head. I fell again. Scrambling, I tried to stand, but another hand flung me aside.

"Mei, Mei!"

I raised my head. There. Among the frantic legs, I glimpsed the Noble Lady, her eyes closed, shivering on the ground. And the horse, its head bent, its powerful hooves pounding, charged in her direction. "Watch out, my Noble Lady!"

Her eyes flew open. For a moment she looked dazed, as though she was unaware of what was happening around her. Then she sat up and smoothed the creases from her silk gown as though she were ready to step out of her bedchamber to greet a guest. But the horse. It was so close to her!

"Move, move!" I screamed. If only I was closer to her; if only I could push her aside.

She turned toward me, saw the horse, and her face changed. But it was too late—the horse pranced and struck her forehead.

"Noble Lady!" My heart wrenched, and a shower of black splashes blinded my vision.

The horse turned around and raced toward the gate, its tail sweeping my shoulder. Hot tears burning my eyes, I crawled through the crowd to reach her. Someone stepped on my hands. I could hardly feel it. Inch by inch, I crawled to her. When I finally found her, I held her close. I could not bring myself to look at her face, for what was left was not the face I had so loved. But she was still in my heart, no matter what had befallen her, no matter what she had done. She had forgiven me when she could have punished me. She had stood with me when I was alone. She could have been my enemy, but she opted to be my friend. "My lady, my lady. You should have listened to me. You should. Why, why you didn't move?"

She would never reply to me.

"Mei! We need to go." Plum shook me. "We need to get out of here."

"The Noble Lady…"

"My heavens." Plum covered her mouth. "We'll get to her later, but we must leave now."

"I can't… No… Wait…"

In a moment, I was in the corridor. The howling was louder there, and I shivered. The revolt was far from over. I wiped away my tears. I would tell the Noble Lady's son of the last moment of his mother, but first I had to survive. "Where are we going?"

"We can go to our bedchamber," Plum said nervously. Some ladies ran out of the courtyard; some gathered around us.

I shook my head. "How do you know Taizi hasn't invaded there? Besides, we can't get there all by ourselves."

To reach our bedchamber, we had to travel through a dozen halls, gates, and gardens. With Taizi's rebellion, some rebels must have crossed the Tongxun Gate to the Inner Court. We would be captured before we passed one hall.

"Where can we go then?"

"We must get out of the palace," I said. The men's shrieks grew louder, and everywhere, entangled shadows fought each other. I felt naked standing there without protection.

"All right. Let's go now."

A group of men emerged in the dark in the distance and shouted at us. I pulled Plum aside. We stayed behind the wall of a building and listened to the men's footsteps. After a while, the voices faded, and it seemed we had lost them. "Listen to me, Plum. When you pass three halls down this way, you will see the kitchen area for the eunuchs. You know the area, don't you? There are many storage buildings, but if you keep running, you'll see the canal and the west entrance where the eunuchs leave to purchase groceries in the morning. You will be safe there. The rebels will not go there for plunder. You can take the other women with you. Go now."

"Yes, we'll go." She turned around. In the dark, her face was difficult to see, but I could feel she was nervous and frightened. "Come on."

I shook my head.

"You're not coming?"

"I...I have to find someone."

"What on earth are you talking about?"

I did not explain. Plum would not understand.

"Who are you trying to find, Mei?"

"I'm going to look for Pheasant, Plum," I said. I could hear some metal clang from somewhere close. "I have to. I need to know if he is all right."

"You are crazy!" she said. "The rebels are everywhere! What will happen to you if they catch you?"

"I...I..." I swallowed. "I'll be careful."

"Don't be stupid, Mei. You must not think of him now. It's too dangerous to go to the Eastern Palace. You will fall into rebels' hands. How are you going to get there?"

I did not know. Eastern Palace was even farther than my bed-chamber, and it was where the revolt had started.

In the dark, another group of men raced toward us in the distance. I pushed her. "Go, Plum. Don't worry about me. Go before it's too late."

The other ladies urged her too, and finally, Plum ran down the path. Soon my friend and the others receded into the darkness.

Footfalls pounded closer from the other side of the wall. I wished there had been bushes or trees so I could hide, but there was only a terrace and kylin statues. I darted to a statue and couched behind it, my hands around my knees. Men's voices grew louder. Torches sputtered in the air. I was surrounded. My eyes became damp, and I held my breath.

It seemed ages had passed before the men finally left. I dashed from behind the statue and ran. A few times, the voices of the men were so close, I crawled on the ground so they would not notice me. When I found trees, I pressed myself against a trunk, waiting for the men to pass, and ran again. The distance to the Eastern

Palace seemed farther than the earth to the sky, and I wished I could turn into a crane and fly over the halls' roofs.

Finally, I glimpsed the roofs of the Ninth Heaven Hall, a building near the Eastern Palace. Seeing no one around me, I dashed behind the building.

I froze. Smoke. Layers of smoke. Rising from dried leaves on the ground to the elms, birches, and oaks decorated with rows of lanterns celebrating the festival. Still hanging, the lanterns were blazing fireballs.

I coughed. Smoke choked me, or perhaps it was my fear.

Something growled in the smoke. I froze. Animals. Everywhere. Deer darted into the chrysanthemum bushes; monkeys squeaked across the mulberry trees; hunting hounds snarled in the corridors of the Ninth Heaven Hall; a rhinoceros paced in the front yard; a leopard scoured the flower beds; a wolf with glinting eyes perched on a man-made mountain in the center of the yard. And overhead spiraled falcons, vultures, and many owls.

They must have come from the imperial stables and corrals. That meant the rebels had attacked there already.

My legs trembling, I raced down a trail near the trees. Body after body lay still on the ground. The Gold Bird Guards. The Emperor's men.

"Hell is rising," someone screamed.

Eunuchs, servants, palace maids, and ministers poured out of the darkness. A servant who had served in the feast hall earlier fled. He carried a gold statue—loot, most likely—high above the crowd. A eunuch bumped him from behind, and the servant smacked him with the statue. "All is for the taking. Hell is rising!"

I could not turn back. Tongxun Gate was closer. Once I reached the gate, I could run all the way to the Eastern Palace. I pulled up my skirt and rushed down the path along the wall.

I stepped on something marshy. My arms grew rigid. I forced myself to look down. A cluster of coiled ropes. No, too soft. My throat tightened. Snakes?

I faltered.

Angry growls came from behind me. I spun around, my heart

pounding. Two dogs raced past me to the coil. One dug in and pulled out a string of ropes, while the other gnawed the other end. I stepped back, feeling sick. The ropes were not snakes.

Stumbling, I trudged to the back of the hall toward the gate. There, again, clouds of smoke draped in front of me like a vast canopy. I could not breathe, my throat burned, and my legs were weak. Something furry swept by my feet. I did not look down.

Finally, I reached the gate, a formidable building with an arched tunnel. Elated, I ran toward it. The gates were left ajar, and I held on to the bolt and pushed it open.

"Hold!" a voice shouted at me from the other side of the gate, and a torch appeared. The fire almost singed my hair. I had yet to cover my face when a man in a bloody tunic, unlike any outfits the Gold Bird Guards wore, grabbed my arms and locked them tightly behind my back. "Here's another!"

A rebel!

39

I STRUGGLED, KICKING HIM AS HARD AS I COULD. "GET away from me. Let me go!"

"You're not going anywhere." The man dragged me to a vast open area in the Eastern Palace. Everywhere, I saw people. Their faces smeared with blood, their heads drooped as they knelt. I could not see who they were, but I would never forget those black hats, colorful skirts, and tattered clothes. They were ministers, scribes, palace ladies, eunuchs, servants from the kitchen.

My knees weakened.

Prince Yo had won. The Emperor had lost.

But that could not be possible! The Emperor had never lost a war! He always won! He was Li Shimin, the greatest conqueror of all land and seas! He had flattened the mountains in the west; he was feared even by wolves in the prairies. And now...now defeated in his own home?

I shivered. What would happen to me? To us? To everyone in the palace? And Pheasant. What about him? Did he get away? Did he... A figure, limbs splayed in a weird angle, sprawled against the wall. His head cocked to one side, blood gushing from his slit throat, and his robe, his familiar white robe, was soaked in a pool of blood. Pheasant? My heart wrenched, and I wanted to scream. Then I saw his face. He was only a scribe. I breathed out in relief. But where was Pheasant?

"Move!" A hand pushed me forward.

I stumbled. The torches leaped and wavered before me, burning my face. Anguished groans and frantic screams filled my ears, each sound a stake thrust into my heart. When I was stopped again, I raised my head. I faltered.

In front of me was a tree stump. Near it, a masked man heaved, and an ax fell.

A crunch. A ball-like head bounced, gathering dirt, leaves, and horse dung, hit the bare roots of an elm tree, slowed, and came to a stop at my feet, while thick liquid gushed like maple syrup. The masked man came over. He grabbed the head's hair, wiped the dirt on a body lying nearby, and thrust the head onto a spear.

Sourness rushed from my stomach. I staggered back. Again and again, I swallowed, pushing back the bile.

The hand struck my back again. "Move!"

I stumbled sideways. Before me stood a fence of spears that staked severed heads, their eyes round, their mouths contorted, their faces etched in blood and agony.

I bent and vomited.

"Move!"

I could no longer walk.

"Move!"

"Please...no...please..."

"Move now!"

I did not want to die. I did not want to become one of those faces on the stakes. A blow fell on my back, and the ground slammed into my face. I lay there, numb. A strange sensation seized me. I was floating, riding in a roofless carriage that raced in the air. Around me, the sound of horse hooves echoed. *Clop, clop, clop*. It drove and drove, pushing through dark tunnels, diving into the clouds of smoke, flying through the frozen sheets of rain, and reaching stands of cypresses and stone statues that shed drops of red tears. Love and destiny were two wild horses that could not be curbed...the thought came to me. So there I was. Riding on the back of the horse I chose...

A melodious voice came from somewhere, so smooth, like milk, and so pure, like the summer sky. It tempted me to follow it, like the sound from a distant dream.

"Oh, weep, my child, weep,
let the mist of your eyes flow
over the mountains of sorrow.
Oh, weep, my child, weep,
let the wind of your thoughts blow
passing the empty meadow.
For the clouds are gathering, and the storms are coming,
drowning the moon, and tearing the sky of eternity.
Let go the tethers of your heart, knotted, drifting like feathers,
and the light of your memories, fading, fleeing with night's fireflies.
And into the pond, your soul gazes
and shivers,
at fate's reflection, luminous, inevitable,
like a tear on a shallot."

Tears poured out of me. I closed my eyes. "No." I clenched my hands. "No."

A pair of hands pulled me up, and I stared into Daisy's teary eyes.

"Mei..." Her clothing was torn, and her hairpin was askew. Around her were other palace women. Their shawls were missing, and their faces were stained with blood and tears.

I sat up. "Daisy. Poor Daisy, are you all right? Are you hurt?"

"Plum... Plum..." Daisy glanced at the tree stump. "She... She...."

My heart wept.

"Bring the women!" a voice shouted.

A man grabbed my arms. All around me, women wailed, their pitiful cries tightening around me like a noose. Too soon, I was stopped again. Before me were Prince Yo, the Pure Lady, the Emperor's uncle, and Taizi.

"Get off me." I shook off the arms and stood. If I was going to die, I would die standing. "Let me ask my last question, Taizi. Where's Pheasant? Let me see him before I die."

"Pheasant?" He frowned.

"What did you do to him?"

He did not answer at first. "What are you talking about?" His voice was thick, and he looked larger than ever.

I was no longer afraid. "You know what I mean. He went to talk to you. He found out you kept the weapons. He wanted to talk sense into you. He had faith in you!"

He was quiet. "I didn't see him."

"You didn't?" I was confounded. "You didn't see him tonight? He didn't talk to you?"

"That's what I said."

Had the rebels killed Pheasant? I could not understand. "He left me before the insurgence started."

"He's a man. He knows where it would be safe," Taizi said.

"Then where is he?"

Taizi spun, his hands on his hips. "Has anyone seen Pheasant?" he shouted at the crowd.

He still cared about him.

"Pheasant is a traitor, like everyone else," Prince Yo said.

"He's not a traitor!" I turned to Taizi. "You know he's not. He loves you. He cares about you. He will not let anyone harm you. Find him! Find him before these people kill him. Before it's too late."

Taizi folded his arms across his chest. He frowned. He knew what I had said was true.

"Nonsense," Prince Yo said. "We have a lot to do. Don't waste time on Pheasant."

"You don't tell me what to do." Taizi balled his hands.

"You'll listen to a woman?" Prince Yo spat. "Are you crazy?"

I had not thought of what to say when Taizi lunged at Prince Yo. His hands circled Prince Yo's neck. "Send men to find Pheasant. It's my order. Do you hear?"

Prince Yo gurgled, his face red and his feet dangling above the ground. I could hardly breathe. Would Taizi strangle him? I hoped so. If Prince Yo died, the rebellion perhaps would end.

But then without warning, Taizi's hands left the prince's throat, and he stumbled back. Slowly, he turned around.

A dagger had sunk deep into his back.

"I was looking for an opportunity to put you down," the Pure Lady said, wiping her bejeweled hand on her silver gown. "You don't think we went through all this trouble for you, do you?"

To my horror, Taizi swayed and dropped to the ground. They had used him. They had used his grief to break the palace's gates, and then they simply stabbed him and let him die.

"Good riddance." Prince Yo turned around and shouted, "Now bring my father!"

He had caught the Emperor?

I felt chilled, as though the prince had just stabbed me with a dagger, and all around me, the women and ministers screamed and cried.

And he came. The mighty one, the One Above All, and the lord of all the land and the seven seas, was dragged across the blood-soaked earth and, his head lolling to one side, he knelt before his son.

"So what do you say, Father?" Prince Yo laughed. "You never cared about me. You sent me into exile. For what? I did nothing wrong, I told you. You wouldn't listen. You never listened. During the months of my exile, I swore that since I could not make you listen to me while you were on your feet, I must have your ears while you are on your knees."

"You are as foolish as you are devious." The Emperor's voice, slow and slurred, was filled with venom. "I do not have a son like you."

"Are you sure, Father?" Prince Yo leaned over. "Can't you see it? I am your true son. I did precisely what you have done. I am like you, exactly like you, and when I rule, I shall rule like you."

The Emperor's body trembled, as though he were seized and shaken by an invisible hand again. For a moment, I thought he would tumble to the ground, just like he had surprised us

in the Audience Hall. But he did not. He held on, his head
jerking repeatedly.

"You're an old man, Father. You're going to die." Prince Yo
shook his head. "You will die now. Tonight. Face it."

"I—will—not—"

"Then be proud of me! Look at me! Why are you not proud of
me? What do you want that I don't have? I deserve so much more.
I can do so much more. Why? Why?" he screamed.

The Pure Lady put a hand on his arm.

"Very well," Prince Yo said, panting. "I will finish you myself.
But you should have seen this coming, Father."

I wanted to close my eyes. I had never loved the Emperor. He
was not a good man or a good lover, like Jewel had said, but had
I wished him to die?

Perhaps.

But not like that.

Prince Yo raised his sword. I shivered, and without thinking, I
closed my eyes.

"No!" a voice shouted.

My eyes flew open. Pheasant!

His sword paused in the air. Prince Yo turned.

From behind the tree stump, many shadows sprang, carving
the night's black shade like thunderbolts. For a second, I thought
the rebels had all converged from the corners of the kingdom and
tried to cut a slice of the Emperor and us. Then I saw the Captain's
bloodstained face, his men swarming behind him, and among them,
riding on a horse, was Pheasant.

I straightened. Oh, Pheasant! The bonfire blazed near him and
illuminated his face. He looked golden, supreme, and magnificent,
and his motion, steady and determined, glimmered with brightness.
He thrust his arm forward, shouting, and the men around him
roared, invigorated.

Tears rolled down my cheeks. I wanted to run and embrace
him. I could not, because a surge of commotion had engulfed me.
A scream rent the sky, and around me, shadows leaped and fell,

chasing one another. Swords, daggers, spears, and lances flew in the air and entangled. Men groaned. Bones crushed. Knuckles cracked. Skulls collided against one another. I drew back, my gaze still fixed on the lithe figure on the horse.

"Pheasant!" I shouted.

He turned his head in my direction but did not seem to see me. It did not matter. I ran. Every part of my body ached as I limped toward the arched gateway. I found Daisy and helped her rise. Another palace woman groaned at my feet, and I pulled her up too. Together, we trudged across the sticky ground, while the sharp clang of weapons rang in my ears. Finally, we crossed the archway of the Tongxun Gate and arrived at the vast area in the Inner Court. I slid down the wall and stretched out my legs. I was spent.

"I've got the Emperor!" someone cried out on the other side of the gate. "Keep him safe!"

"No one touches my brother!" Pheasant's voice. "Leave Taizi to me!"

"My son!" a woman shrieked. The Pure Lady. "Oh, my son! You murderer—"

Then all of a sudden, her piercing voice ceased.

I wanted to see what was happening to her, but I was too exhausted. Warm liquid splashed my face, and I did not trouble to wipe it away. I was used to blood, the sticky liquid with a thick odor. A man wielding a sword raced through the archway and dove toward us. He was about to reach me when he fell to his knees. A sword—the Captain's—had sunk into his back. More rebels poured through the passage but sagged, and finally, the only people who stood before me were the Captain and his men.

40

LIGHTS—SHINING AND BRILLIANT—PIERCED MY EYES.
Dots of red, green, and orange swirled before me. It was morning.
The sky looked clean, tinted with a shade of indigo the silkworm
workers used to dye the threads. For a moment, I thought that what
had happened the previous night was a nightmare. Then I looked
around me.

A forest of head-pierced stakes sprouted in front of me, while
sharp blades, severed limbs, and headless bodies littered the ground.
A few paces from me, some guards, holding their legs, groaned;
near them the ministers, their hats askew, their beards speckled with
blood, slumped against the wall, like me; and farther along were
the ladies and eunuchs, their arms supporting one another, limping
along the wall.

We had survived, but we would never be the same, or feel the
same, or think the same of the life in the Inner Court again.

"Hey, there," a voice said beside me. His hands held my shoulders.

"Pheasant." I faced him, my heart warm with happiness. "You're
here. You saved us. You came! I was so worried about you."

"It's over." He slid down the wall to sit with me.

"I know. I saw it all."

"I was too late." He drooped his head, his face speckled with
blood.

I touched his sleeve. "What happened to you? Why did Taizi say he did not see you?"

"I was kidnapped by the Pure Lady's men, right after I left you." He grimaced. "I thought they would kill me. But the Captain came out of the feasting hall. The men were frightened. They hid me behind a tree and tied me up. I don't know why the Captain would go to the Eastern Palace—"

"I told the Emperor about Taizi's plot."

"You did?"

"Please don't be angry. I was worried about you."

"I suppose I must thank you. If you hadn't, the Pure Lady's men would have killed me."

"So the Captain saved you?"

He shook his head. "He didn't see us. But the lady's men saw him and were worried something was wrong. Two fled to warn her, and the rest ambushed the Captain. Only one man was left to watch me. I kicked his manhood when he was distracted and escaped. I came across the Captain so I told him about Taizi's plot."

It was then he heard the bell tolling from the watchtower, Pheasant said. He knew the palace was being attacked, but he did not know it was Prince Yo, and while he fought against the rebels with the Captain, the Emperor had ordered the Duke to hold the front gate and had gone himself with his uncle to subdue Taizi. But the Uncle deceived him, leading him directly to the Pure Lady and Prince Yo.

I gazed at the guards who were throwing some bodies into a wheelbarrow. I recognized the Pure Lady's gown. The body of her son, Prince Yo, was next to her.

"Where is Taizi?" I asked carefully. Somehow I pitied him. Unlike Prince Yo, he was not evil. Perhaps he had never even cared about the throne; perhaps he had cared about his lover more than anything. He had made a choice too, and Pheasant was right to love him.

"The imperial physicians are caring for him right now."

So he had survived. I hoped he would recover soon. But he would need to pay, either with his life or something else.

Pheasant stretched out his legs. With the wall against our backs, we stared at the gruesome scene without saying anything. He reached for my hand.

"What a night," he said. "So many lost their lives. Is this worth it?"

His words, tinged with sadness, drifted in the air. His face was serious and weary, marked with lines of determination and sorrow that did not belong to his age. I wished I could say something to make him feel better.

"I don't know," I said.

He squeezed my hand.

"And the Emperor?" I asked finally.

Pheasant nodded at a group of people under a tree. They hoisted up a stretcher upon which the Emperor lay. He had lost his hat, his robe was torn, and his whiskers, curled in a sad shape, stuck to his cheeks. When the porters passed us, I could see he was trembling, his right hand bent awkwardly to his chest, his eyes closed. Then suddenly, he opened his eyes and gazed at me. Instantly, I looked away and shied away from Pheasant, my throat tightening. Would he order my death?

Nothing.

"I have to go." Pheasant rose. "Will I see you...again?"

Of course. I would run through a forest of fire to meet him if necessary. I wished to tell him just that, but then I remembered the people around me. I dipped my head. "Yes, Prince Zhi. Yes."

He walked to follow the stretcher, a waterfall of golden lights covering his back like a cape. Near him, the branches of the elms and oaks swayed gently. A soft whistle rang as a gust raced down the street, sending a wave of fetid air toward me. I covered my nose. When I put down my hand again, the breeze had changed to a breath of fresh morning air.

Greedily, I inhaled. Thinking about Pheasant's question, I asked myself, *Is it worth it going through all this trouble for him?*

I had risked my life and pleaded with the Emperor. I had stumbled across the blood-soaked ground. I had watched people lose their heads and knelt before a tree stump, waiting for my own death. I had almost been beheaded. I had survived, and the Emperor had simply gone away.

It was worth it. I had made my own destiny.

Before me, the sky brightened, the hue of indigo dissolving, replaced by an intense shade of milky white.

✦ ✦

Soon after, the punishment for the rebels was announced. The Emperor's uncle was beheaded, along with all his immediate family, including his wife, his wife's family, his concubines, his concubines' families, their children, their grandchildren, and their families. Their family's estate, their wealth, their titles, and their yearly allowances were confiscated.

The Pure Lady's entire family line was eliminated. All of her blood-related kin—her parents, her grandparents, her siblings, her siblings' families, their children, and their children's families—were beheaded.

On the day of their deaths, I heard, the execution grounds in the Western Market were flooded with rivers of blood.

Because Pheasant begged for Taizi's life, the Emperor banished him to the southern edge of the kingdom, where he would live in oblivion, but at least he was still alive. His household, however, was disbanded, and all his women and servants became slaves. All his associates, tutors, aides, and even the wrestlers invited to his bouts were all beheaded.

I heard Chancellor Wei Zheng had died that night too, but no one seemed to be aware of his involvement in the revolt, and the Emperor decreed a generous funeral and sent condolences to his family. Secretary Fang had a minor injury to his shoulder. It took him a month to recover.

The Duke survived. When the Emperor ordered him to hold the front gate, he had taken some guards with him, but by the time he'd arrived, the gate had already been broken into. He had been forced to pull back and never quite faced the rebels himself. Nonetheless, he was rewarded for his stalwart support. When I saw him days later, he did not have a scratch or a bruise on his face. I suspected there was more to the story as to what really happened that night. Perhaps he had hidden in a latrine.

I told Prince Ke about his mother. The poor prince's delicate face crumpled, and his willowy frame doubled over. When he went to fetch her body, he cried like a child. My eyes growing misty, I recounted to him how brave the lady was at the moment of her death. I did not tell him what she had said about poisoning Jewel. It was better for him not to know.

The wind of the rebellion did not die off easily. A few months later, one of the Emperor's vassals in the northeast, a Koguryo general, encouraged by the rebellion, murdered the obedient boy king the Emperor had groomed and proclaimed his own dynasty. The Emperor, infuriated, decided to start a punitive war and led the army himself. Unable to mount a horse, he put on his breastplates and a cape, hiding his useless right arm, and rode in a cushioned carriage to the eastern border while he ordered the Captain to lead with the cavalry.

The Captain proved to be the most vital force on the battlefield. His cavalry broke through the rebels' front line, leaving many dead and entire villages engulfed in fire. In three months, he took over ten forts, driving the Koguryos all the way back to the heart of their land. It was said that the Captain was so fierce, the mere mention of his name would send the rebels fleeing. But when the army arrived at Anshi Fort, the final stronghold of Koguryo, the army was threatened with food shortages and brutal winter weather and was forced to withdraw. Finally, the Emperor returned home, without touching the rebellious general's flag.

Nonetheless, a song of victory was sung across the kingdom to praise the Emperor's valor and supremacy. Indeed, the Emperor had taught his vassals a lesson, people said, and the ministers cheered.

But the Emperor, haggard, sickened by the weather and rough traveling conditions, would never walk on his own again. Unable to see well or stand on his own feet, he was carried in a stretcher draped with thick curtains when he attended the audiences, and for the next two years, he spent many months in a mountain spa in hopes of regaining his health.

When he was well enough, he took Pheasant with him to the Audience Hall, and he asked Pheasant to sit with him, dine with him, and together they watched polo games and laughed.

Naturally, people whispered. Would the Emperor name Pheasant his heir?

For the disgraced Taizi had died in exile, and with two sons gone, the Emperor had to choose one among his remaining sons. Two were toddlers, and the others were borne by women with low ranks; thus, they were out of consideration for the throne. Only Prince Ke, Prince Wei, and Pheasant were serious contenders. Both princes, Ke and Wei, were senior to Pheasant, and the succession rule favored them, but Pheasant had saved the Emperor's life.

"Of course, Prince Zhi shall be the heir. He saved us, every one of us," I once heard the sweepers saying under the eaves. "What did Prince Wei do?"

Even the Duke made a formal petition to the Emperor. It was time the kingdom chose a new heir, he said, and the heir should be the eighth living prince, Prince Zhi.

And then, on a warm summer night, after the Emperor returned from the mountain spa, for the first time since the rebellion, he ordered all of us to attend a feast. Even though he did not declare it openly, his meaning was clear.

He would announce his heir.

AD 648

the Twenty-Second Year *of*

Emperor Taizong's Reign

of Peaceful Prospect

SUMMER

41

THE MUSIC OF ZITHERS, LUTES, FLUTES, AND CHIME BELLS filled the hall, and Lady Obedience, leading a group of dancers, twirled in the open space between the tables. The feasting hall was crowded with ministers, princes, titled ladies, and servants.

Sitting near the end of the hall with the other surviving Talents, I peered at the Emperor. He slouched at the feasting table in the center of the hall, for he was easily tired and could not sit for long periods these days. He wore a bejeweled mortarboard, the crown reserved for audiences in the Audience Hall, and his face, clouded with grave sullenness, remained crooked. But he looked somber and at ease.

My heart clenched in anticipation. Would the Emperor choose Pheasant? Would he announce it now?

The three princes, Prince Ke, Prince Wei, and Pheasant, sat near the Emperor, but as it had often appeared lately and against the traditional seating arrangement, Pheasant sat closest to the Emperor. And the Duke, who had often been serious and scowling, grinned, his hawkish nose looking less sharp. I wondered if he had succeeded in persuading the Emperor to choose Pheasant as the heir. He certainly wanted that, for he was his uncle, and he would be a powerful man if Pheasant became the Emperor.

Secretary Fang sat with the other ministers. They ate heartily, although they looked expectant, their eyes flicking from the Emperor to Pheasant, Prince Wei, and then Prince Ke. Even the servants, pausing in the midst of serving, cocked their heads, glancing from the Emperor to the princes.

The only person who seemed detached from the crowd was the Captain. Standing a few paces behind the princes, he was not eating, nor was he looking at anyone. His purple birthmark smeared across his face like a pool of dried blood, he stared at a pillar silently. I wondered what was in his mind. During the rebellion, his sword had slashed many rebels' throats, and it had slashed more when he broke into forts in Koguryo. The Emperor had promoted him, praising his might and loyalty. He was now the General, the commander of all armies in the Four Garrisons, ninety-nine legions of Gold Bird Guards, and all the cavalry. He was the sharpest sword the Emperor would ever have.

I looked at the titled ladies gathered around me. None of them were smiling, but they all looked calm, as though they were not concerned about the announcement of the heir. I thought of Pheasant's wife, Lady Wang, whom he had been married to for almost three years, and Rain. Both were living outside the palace and had not been invited to the feast tonight. If they had been here, they would certainly have been excited.

The servants placed some saucers filled with cooked leeks, stewed donkey meat, and slices of marinated tiger meat on the Emperor's table. The leeks would improve his appetite, and the meat would repel evil spirits and lift his mood. But he did not touch them. I was not surprised. He had long lost interest in eating, and these days, he dined only on soft, glutinous rice cakes.

Finally, the Emperor cleared his throat. The hall quieted, the music ceased, and only the scent of food and wine drifted through the air.

"Ministers, I have gathered all of you to witness the crucial moment of our kingdom. I shall announce my heir today and show the kingdom what a capable son I have." The loose skin on his right cheek swayed visibly, and his voice was a slow, slurred drawl.

Those who had not seen him lately would have been surprised at his indistinct voice, but I could tell he had put great effort in enunciating the words, and I could also tell the effort was costing him strength. He was having a hard time catching his breath. "From this moment on, our kingdom shall rejoice, for I declare one of my sons has proved himself, for all his valor and honesty, as a worthy heir of mine. Come up, Pheasant."

Pheasant hesitated. He looked around, pushed away his food, and slowly, but steadily, walked to the Emperor's table.

My heart raced faster. I had mentioned the rumor of him being the heir when we were alone together, and he had shrugged it off. But the moment had come.

"Look at all these people; look at their faces, Pheasant. And remember them. They are your servants, your advisers, your family. Understand them, understand them well, for one day, you will need their help to rule. Everyone"—the Emperor, his hands shaking as usual, held Pheasant's shoulders—"here, I give you my heir, the future Emperor of Great China."

The crowd roared. Waves of praise poured out of their mouths, and joyous shouts filled the hall.

My heart bloomed with happiness. Pheasant. The future Emperor of Great China!

But he looked shocked, and a shadow of panic raced across his face.

"What do you say now? You have made me proud, Pheasant," the Emperor said, his voice less grave, his face softening with what looked like a smile. "Now sit with me and drink."

A servant filled a goblet with some wine, and Pheasant drained it. "Father, ministers." He paused. "I hope I will not disappoint you."

"Praise our prince!" Secretary Fang stood and bowed. "It is our fortune to have a valiant heir!"

The other ministers all bowed, beaming with joy. Pheasant bowed back to each of them, one by one, and when he was done, he straightened, smiling, looking relaxed.

The Duke ordered the musicians to play again, and immediately, the hall was alive with the notes of zithers. Colorful ribbons whirled, and long dancing sleeves twirled. Everyone nodded, praising what a wise choice the Emperor had made.

The Duke laughed. Of course he was pleased. His enemy was dead, and Pheasant, one of his nephews, was the heir. Pheasant would be kind to him, paying him the respect and prestige that was due to an elder. And with the Emperor still unable to hold a calligraphy brush, I suspected the Duke would be indispensable for a while.

My heart swelling with happiness, I sat and watched. I wished the Noble Lady could have been there. She would have been surprised, but she would have been gracious and given Pheasant her blessing. I knew she would.

Rain, and Pheasant's wife, Lady Wang, would rejoice too when they heard the news. I had yet to meet Lady Wang, but I would meet her very soon, whether I liked it or not, because once the announcement of Pheasant as the heir was heard by the whole kingdom the next day, both Lady Wang and Rain would relocate to the Eastern Palace, and Lady Wang, as the wife of the heir, would take over the Eastern Palace.

A few hours into the feast, the Emperor retired. The candles dimmed, the servants yawned, and the ministers fell asleep at their tables. When no one seemed to notice us, Pheasant nodded at me and slipped out. I followed. We went to a corner near a bamboo grove behind the hall.

"Ah, so good it's quiet here," Pheasant said as I sat next to him. The wall felt cold against my back, but I could feel the warmth from Pheasant's arms.

"My emperor." I dipped my head toward him.

He took a flask from his belt and sipped. "This is madness, isn't it?"

He did not look happy. I searched for his eyes. "You will make a righteous ruler, Pheasant."

The Emperor had once said Pheasant could not rule the kingdom because he had too much love. But he was wrong. An emperor with love did not rule a kingdom; he conquered it.

"I don't know... It's a serious business to rule a kingdom, Mei. I did not wish to believe it when they talked... But now..."

"You saved us. You saved everyone."

He shrugged. "Anyone would have done the same, not just me. But Father doesn't think so. He wants me to be the heir. He is adamant. He will announce the news to the whole kingdom tomorrow. He even promised me that he would build a Buddhist pagoda for my mother, as I requested."

"Buddhist pagoda?"

Pheasant nodded. "Yes, I want to pay respect to her. My uncle recommends a Taoist abbey, but I want a Buddhist pagoda. After all, she was a Buddhist, and I think she would like to have an official Buddhist building dedicated to her."

I turned to him, touched by his kindness. Buddhism, after all, was not a popular religion in our kingdom and was looked down upon by the nobles, but if Pheasant wanted to honor his mother and offer his support, perhaps people's view of the religion would change. And many Buddhists, for sure, would benefit from that. I remembered the monastery where Mother stayed and how it was falling apart. "That is a fine idea, Pheasant. I am certain people will like that."

"I hope so. The years have been hard on us. The rebellion, wars…"

"I know." I sighed, leaning back. So much had happened. So many people had died…and I had nearly died too, and now Pheasant was the heir. Who would have expected that? For all the talk, the prophecy was wrong after all…

"Are you all right?"

"Yes. I was thinking about the prophecy." When I had overheard the Uncle talking to the Chancellor, he had mentioned the Wu Man, and he had believed it was Prince Yo…

"Don't believe it; it's just gossip. If it had been true, Prince Yo would have lived."

"You're right. He was not the one." I considered the clue again. The Wu Man, the Uncle had said. Could it be possible I was the person who would end the Emperor's reign and rule the kingdom? Could it be possible that Tripitaka's prediction about my fate, made so long ago, was correct after all? But then why had the prophecy mentioned a man? I did not understand it, but the thought of me being the one in the prophecy was frightening. I shivered.

"You look like you're freezing. Come on, drink. You will warm up." Pheasant handed me the flask. "What do you say we finish this?"

I decided to forget the prophecy. "Is that a challenge?"

He laughed. "Do you wish to have some food? I bet you are hungry. I did not see you touch anything."

"I was too happy." He was right. I was starving. I drank some wine and gave back the flask. "I want to ask you something, Pheasant. Will you tell me the truth?"

"What do you wish to know?"

"What will you do when you become the Emperor?" His father was stable, for now, but the rebellion and his ride to Koguryo had crippled him. It was possible he would never recover…or he could have another mysterious attack, and then he might never wake up. The forbidden thought leaped into my mind, and I hastened to smother it.

Pheasant gulped some wine and wiped his mouth. "I will make your wish come true. Any wish." Then he put up one finger.

"Only one?" I laughed. The sensation of the alcohol, or perhaps the prospect of a beautiful future that I had never imagined before, brewed in my head.

"Yes, make it good."

"I would like to have a copy of *The Art of War*." I wanted to read the master's words again and explore all those direct and indirect methods. Who knew? I might understand them better this time.

"Done. I shall steal it for you."

"I'm counting on you," I said. "But seriously, is this what you're going to do when you're the Emperor? Steal?"

"No, of course not. I will order you to drink the whole flask, get drunk, and lie down with me."

I did not get a chance to speak before he pulled me into his arms. I gazed at him. A surge of euphoria filled me, and my head felt light with sweetness. I raised my head to kiss him. He tasted like wine, but he was stronger and more savory than any spirit.

After a while, we lay together, our arms behind our heads. It was so dark, and I could see only the two red lanterns near the feasting hall. Flute notes lingered and drifted toward us, growing faint, and finally it was lost in the wind.

"Look." I pointed up. "There is the moon. So bright."

In the sky, the stars blossomed like silver flowers floating in a black river, and the clouds flowed slowly, like spilled ink. The full moon, bright and serene, cast a luminous net around us. What a fine night it turned out to be.

"Remember once when we were in the garden?"

"Yes." I nodded. "I told you about the story of Chang E, who wanted immortality rather than her husband. You said she was foolish."

"I said that?"

"You forgot?"

"Well, I still think she is. But never mind that now." He stroked my shoulder. "When I become the emperor of the kingdom, you will be the empress. The empress of bright moon."

I turned to him. What about his wife, Lady Wang? But I knew Pheasant did not care for her, and he looked so serious, and I knew I should trust him. "You mean it?"

He squeezed my hand and nodded.

I smiled. His voice wove around me like a spell of promise. The empress of bright moon. I liked the sound of that. Father would have liked it too. I was twenty-two years of age. It was not too old to be an empress, was it?

Above my head, the stars flickered like shiny seeds. Near them was the moon, inside which the fabled palace radiated. It did not look so lonely or distant; in fact, it looked closer, and it seemed to walk toward me, approaching me, beckoning to me. All I had to do was reach out and touch it.

AUTHOR'S NOTE

The story of Wu Mei is based on a historical figure, the one and only female ruler in China, Wu Zetian, also known as Empress Wu. All the male characters in the novel, except the eunuchs, are actual historical figures; some of the female characters, including the Noble Lady and Mei's mother, are real women who lived and were recorded in history as well. Others, such as Jewel, Plum, Daisy, and the other Ladies, are fictional.

The birth date of Wu Mei was not recorded. It is likely that she was two years older than Pheasant, but in the novel, I chose to portray them as the same age. It is also unknown whether Mei had a romance with Pheasant while she was serving Emperor Taizong.

The formal name of Emperor Taizong's firstborn son, the heir, was Li Chengqian, but I chose to use Taizi, which means "the crown prince" in Chinese. It is unknown whether he was homosexual, but records showed he was rather attached to his Turkic heritage.

The assassination attempt on Emperor Taizong and the rebellion of Li Chenqian and Prince Yo appear in historical records, but the two princes' plots were planned separately and were discovered before they caused damage to the palace.

All the quotes from Sun Tzu's *The Art of War* were translated by Lionel Giles (1875–1958), with one slight change in the line *"ju qiu hao bu wei duo li."* Giles translated it as "To lift an autumn's hair is no sign of great strength." I changed it to "To lift a feather is no sign of great strength," as "*qiu hao*" refers to a very fine down feather in the autumn in archaic Chinese.

I used the modern pinyin system for the majority of the Chinese names, but I used the names of Confucius, Lao Tzu, and Sun Tzu as they are commonly known to English readers.

The city Chang'an is now known as Xi'an. The kingdom Koguryo is now the modern North Korea.

READING GROUP GUIDE

1. How much did you know about the palace women in ancient China before you read this novel? In what ways do you think the palace women in China were similar to those in Europe?

2. Discuss the many facades of love in the novel and how it manifests itself in the following characters: Mei, Pheasant, Jewel, Emperor Taizong, Taizi, and the Noble Lady.

3. Discuss the theme of deception. How does the Emperor deceive the kingdom? How does Jewel deceive the Emperor and the other women?

4. The novel opens with the monk's prediction of Mei's destiny. How would you define the concept of destiny? How does Mei perceive her destiny?

5. Compare the relationship between Mei and Jewel and the relationship between Mei and the Noble Lady.

6. For nearly two thousand years, Confucius's instruction of five virtues—filial piety, tolerance, courtesy, faith, and wisdom—determined the values of ancient China. Describe how filial

piety is demonstrated in Mei and how it motivates and suppresses her.

7. Have you heard of Sun Tzu's *The Art of War*? Do you think the master's insight in strategies set up a tone for this novel? Do you think the master's teaching helps Mei in the Inner Court? How?

8. Silkworm farming was an important industry in ancient China, and silkworms were often revered, but Mei is forced to destroy them in the novel. Do you agree with what she did?

9. Discuss the relationship between Mei and Pheasant. When does their relationship begin to grow? At what point does it begin to deepen and change?

10. How would you describe Jewel's character? Do you consider her to be a sympathetic figure or an evil one?

11. Discuss the intricate relationships within the imperial family. How do these relationships affect the Emperor and his sons?

12. What do you think the title *The Moon in the Palace* means?

13. The descriptions of nature, animals, birds, and sceneries are very rich in this novel. Discuss the symbols of the sun, snow, and rain. Where do you see them? What do you think they symbolize?

14. If you were one of the Emperor's hundreds of concubines confined in the Yeting Court and Inner Court, how would you attempt to rise within the palace hierarchy?

Read on for an excerpt from

the *Empress* of *Bright Moon*

Available April 2016 from Sourcebooks Landmark

WOULD HE DIE TONIGHT?

The thought flickered in my mind as I dabbed at a brown stain on the Emperor's chin. He did not respond, not even to twitch his lips or blink. He lay there, his mouth open, his gaze fixed on the ceiling. The right side of his face was a ruinous pool of skin, and his good left eye was opaque, like a marble that the light of candles failed to penetrate. Now and then, there seemed to be a spark in that eye, as though his old valor was struggling to come to life, to surface, to fight the fate that conquered him, but the light flashed like a fish in a murky pond. It was there, swimming, but it did not come up to the surface, not even for a breath of air.

He did not see me. He was gone, I could tell—a once-powerful whirlwind of wrath and will, now a bag of slackened skin, a shell of vaunting vanity.

I straightened, and an ache shot through my back. How long had I been kneeling at the bedside, watching him? I could not remember. All of us—the Talents, Graces, and Beauties, once the bedmates of the Emperor—had been his caretakers for the past ten months. Every day, we took turns feeding him, cleaning him—for he had long ago lost the ability to control his fluid—and carefully we watched him, listening to his every labored breath and every painful groan.

When the Emperor had announced Pheasant as the heir of the

kingdom last year, he had been frail, and he had collapsed a few days later, shaken by the mysterious hand that had tormented him all these years. Writhing, gushing white foam from his mouth, he fell out of a stretcher on the way to his bedchamber and had not wakened since.

The water dropped in the water clock beside me. Nine. Where were they? They must hurry...

I rose, patting the side of my Cloudy Chignon, the elaborate hairstyle I had finally mastered. A few strands had fallen on my shoulders, and the loose knot that should have sat on top of my head had slumped sadly to my right ear. I wished I could make myself look more presentable, but we were not allowed to leave the chamber. The physicians had ordered me and the other Talents to stay with the Emperor at all times. I had not bathed for two months, or looked at myself in the bronze mirror, or put on my white face cream. My hair, which had once been soft and fragrant, now felt heavy and lumpy on my neck, and the green robe I wore had turned brown, stained with splashes of herbal remedies.

The thought whispered to me again. I peered at him. What if he died tonight? What would happen to me and the other women who served him when he did die? I quickly smothered the thoughts. I should not think of those questions, for it was treason to ponder on the Emperor's mortality...

But all the titled women in the Inner Court must have wondered about their fate these months while he lay there unresponsive. After all, it was the unspoken law that we, as the Emperor's women, should never feel the warmth of another man's arms again after the Emperor's death. There must have been a plan for us. Yet no one openly talked about it, even though the ladies gathered together in the courtyard every morning, whispering, their eyes misty with tears.

I wished I could listen to the Duke and the Secretary, the two highest-ranking ministers, when they came to visit the Emperor. But they had many important matters to discuss and did not seem to pay attention to us. And Pheasant. He was busy too, and I had not yet had an opportunity to ask him about our fate.

But no matter what the plan was for us, I knew one thing was for sure: after the Emperor's death, Pheasant—my Pheasant—would be the ruler of the kingdom. He would look after me and my future.

And he had promised... *The empress of bright moon,* he said...

My heart warm with joy, I glanced at the doors. Pheasant and the Duke should have arrived by now. I wondered what the delay was.

A soft drizzle fell outside, light, persistent, carrying a pleasing rhythm that reminded me of the sound of baby silkworms devouring mulberry leaves. It was the fifth month of the year, a good time to have some rain. I yearned to go outside, feel the raindrops on my face, and smell the fresh air, for the bedchamber was veiled with the thick scent of incense, ginseng, musk, clove, dried python bile, and the unpleasant odor of death. I had been inside for so long, I supposed I smelled just like the chamber. I knew my fellow Talent, Daisy, did, as well as the others who yawned in the corner. Each time one of them passed me, I could name the herb in her hair.

Footsteps rose in the dark corridor, and red light from many lanterns poured through the doors. Finally, Pheasant and the Duke entered the chamber, their wet robes clinging to their chests. The physician, Sun Simiao, followed behind.

I retreated to the corner, giving them space, as they had asked each time they came, although I wished to stand right beside them and listen to what the physician had to report. When he examined the Emperor earlier, he had sighed heavily.

The men whispered in low voices, their eyes on the Emperor. The Duke sighed and sniffed, running a hand over his face. Pheasant, surprisingly, looked somber, although his eyes glittered.

"Crown Prince," the physician said, stepping aside to the screen, and Pheasant and the Duke followed him. "We have done the best we could. But I'm afraid I must tell you the dreadful news. The One Above All will not see the dawn's light."

My heart jerked. I tried to remain motionless.

"I understand." Pheasant's voice was soft and sad, and I stole a look at him. His eyes sparkled in the candlelight near the screen. His face was thinner, his jawline more refined than ever, and he had grown a beard.

I remembered how grief-stricken Pheasant had been when he learned the Emperor had become ill last year. For days, Pheasant had stood by the bedside, with us women scurrying from the physicians' herb chamber to the courtyard, carrying bowls of medicine. When we fed the Emperor, Pheasant, careless of his own life, would taste the liquid first, to ensure it had not been mixed with any pernicious ingredient by a vicious hand. When some of us fell down in fatigue after days without sleep, he would tell us to rest and watch the Emperor himself. He was a dutiful son, and I was not sure the Emperor deserved him.

"If there is anything you need, Crown Prince," the physician said, "we're here to serve you."

"You have my gratitude, Physician Sun." Pheasant nodded solemnly. His gaze swept past me. A swift look, but long enough to warm my heart. We had seen each other more often recently, as he came to visit his father almost every day. Sometimes, when the other Talents were not watching, he would brush my arm or hold my hand, and sometimes, when he went to use the privy chamber, I would follow him. There we would share some precious private moments, and it would be the highlight of my day. "Uncle?"

The Duke bowed slightly. "Nephew."

The old man looked his usual self, his face long and hard and his gaze arrogant. I wondered how the Duke managed to stay in good health. He was the Emperor's brother-in-law, and they were the same age, but while the Emperor was in the throes of death, the Duke still stood strong. For the past three years, he had been the Emperor's close assistant, taking direct orders from him, writing edicts for him when he lost control of his arm. Since the Emperor had become ill the year before, the Duke had acted on the Emperor's behalf, giving orders to the ministers. At the moment, he was the most powerful man in the kingdom.

"I must prepare for the inevitable," Pheasant said. "I would like you to arrange a meeting with the astrologers, Uncle, and report to me the auspicious dates for burial in the coming months. Also, summon the mausoleum's mural painters for me, as well as the craftsmen who will build the four divine animal statues for the burial. I would like to examine their works and make certain all matters regarding the funeral are taken care of."

His voice was loud and steady, full of command and authority. I was proud of Pheasant. During the past months, he had shown a strength that was unknown even to himself. He had learned the rituals of worshipping Heaven and Earth and the judicial and penal processes, and familiarized himself with the governments of the sixteen prefectures of the kingdom. He had gathered ministers together, charmed them, and even won the support of the General, the commander of the ninety-nine legions of the Gold Bird Guards, who safeguarded the palace.

"Of course, Nephew," the Duke said, looking hesitant, "yet I would advise you not to tell the women of this devastating news at the moment."

"Why?" Pheasant looked surprised.

The Duke coughed, and when he spoke again, his voice was so low I had to strain to hear. "For the women are most petty minded and troublesome... If they know their fate..."

"What fate?"

"Naturally, your father's women shall never be seen or touched by any other men, and he has ordered that those who have borne him children must dwell in the safe Yeting Court for the rest of their lives."

Pheasant frowned. "I see. But what about the women who have not borne a child?"

"They will be sent to the Buddhist monasteries around the kingdom, where they will pray for the Emperor's soul. This is for the best and a fine tradition that dynasties follow."

I froze. Buddhist monasteries? He was banishing us. He was demanding we become Buddhist nuns, the ones who severed their secular ties to the world, the ones who forsook joy and desire, the ones with only past and no future. If we were banished there, scattered to the remote corners of the kingdom, we would hear nothing but the sound of misery, feel nothing but sorrow, see nothing but death. Our lives would end.

A chill swept over my body. The Emperor's death would be my noose.

A Conversation with the Author

What inspired you to write this novel?

I first had the idea of writing about women when I studied No Name Woman in Maxine Hong Kingston's *The Woman Warrior: Memoirs of a Girlhood among Ghosts* in graduate school. Because that story was so depressing, I wanted to show my classmates that not all women had that kind of fate in China. I decided to write stories of Chinese women who succeeded in controlling their destinies. And who controlled her destiny better than Empress Wu? But I realized Empress Wu was so misrepresented, to understand her better, we had to start from her earlier years. That's where *The Moon in the Palace* begins.

If you could spend one day with an author, dead or alive, who would it be and why?

Can I mention two authors? I love Arthur Golden's *Memoirs of a Geisha*, and I must have read and reread it five times over the course of ten years. I would love to meet him someday!

I would also love to spend a day with Mary Stewart, who unfortunately passed away. Her Merlin trilogy made such an impact on me at a time when I sought guidance during the early years of my writing. I learned so much from Merlin's smart voice and also the way Stewart plotted her scenes. I used to take each chapter, study the structure of the scenes, and analyze how the story progressed. I also admire the voice of her female characters in her romantic suspense books. I love her strong female characters and how Stewart transmitted their intelligence through dialogue.

What research or preparation did you engage in before writing this book?

Oh my. I did a tremendous amount of research on this book. I read Wang Pu's *Tang Hui Yao* and Liu Xu's *The Old Tang Book* in archaic Chinese script, the earliest historical record about the Tang Dynasty. And then I read *The New Tang Book*, *Book of Odes*, Confucius's *Analects*, Lao Tzu's *Tao Te Ching*, Sun Tzu's *The Art of War*, Ban Zhao's *Lessons for Women*, poems before and after the Tang Dynasty, all in archaic Chinese texts and English translations, if I could find them. I spent three years reading and decoding them before I started to write the novel and then continuously reading and studying them as I wrote.

Because the archaic Chinese script is very condensed and the meanings have altered considerably in modern time, I sometimes spent hours just trying to decipher one word. To understand two couplets would sometimes take days. But thankfully, many British and American scholars were fascinated with ancient China and wrote extensively on many subjects in ancient China, so I was able to refer to them and compare the sources. But sometimes problems arose too. Many misunderstandings happened, words were misinterpreted, or sometimes the translations did not appear as graceful as the original texts. In those cases, I resorted to my own translation.

I also read extensively about the world of Tang Dynasty so I could furnish my characters with a truthfully historical setting. I also studied the world history at that period so readers could place China in a global scope and understand the country better.

But my ability to understand the archaic Chinese was not always enough. Once, I came across a Japanese author who wrote five books about Empress Wu, but I was unable to read Japanese. So I dug out a Chinese translation of the books and borrowed those books from a remote library in the United States with the help of my local library. They turned out to be very useful.

Not all of my research findings were pleasant. I found it hard to digest the derogative and disparaging opinions about Empress Wu, and women in general. Sometimes I grew upset, and I simply wanted to throw my findings out the window.

Which character do you feel most closely connected to?

I feel most affinity with the young Mei, which was the main reason I decided to write a young Empress Wu, who was still at an age when romantic love mattered most for her, before she was embroiled in political games.

I can identify with the thrill, the innocence, and the sweetness essential to young love since I was a teenager once. I also have some understanding of forbidden love. When I grew up in China, I was told any expressions of affection to boys were ruinous. Education was the only path that would help me find a better future, so it was most important for me. My parents forbade me to date, and teachers thought it detrimental to cast amorous glances in the classroom. I never dated anyone in school, but I saw how my rebellious friends stole away and met their lovers in secret. So I suppose I can say that I had a taste of love blossoming on discouraging soil.

I can also identify with Mei's love for her parents, as filial piety is ingrained in the Chinese culture and I was taught so at an early age. As a little girl, I knew the importance of obeying my parents' will and pleasing them. I think this sentiment was manifested in Mei as she tried to become the Empress to please her father.

Are any of your characters inspired by the people around you?

I hope not! Especially Jewel. I love her as a character—devious, ambitious, but tragic—but I never personally knew anyone like her in my real life.

Acknowledgments

A Chinese adage says, "It takes ten years to sharpen a sword." Well, this book took ten years to write. Ten years is a long time, and I have many people to thank over this long journey.

My first and foremost gratitude goes to my husband, Mark, who encourages me to pursue my dream and supports me during the writing process. You always have the magic to inspire me and make me laugh, and this will not change no matter how many years pass. And to my two adorable children, Annabelle and Joshua, my passion in real life: I love you through and through.

Thank you to my gentle and brave editorial director, Shana Drehs. I cannot believe you took a chance with a first-time author like me and agreed on a two-book deal before you even glimpsed a word of the second book. I am so grateful for your faith in me. It must have been my destiny to meet you years ago.

Thank you to my gifted editor, Anna Michels. You have put in many hours perfecting this manuscript, and your suggestions were invaluable. I am fortunate to be in your good hands.

Thank you to my amazing agent, Shannon Hassan, who burst into my life and helped my dream come true. I love your decisiveness and efficiency.

Thank you to Deb Werksman, from the bottom of my heart,

for your email that brought me to this beautiful outcome. The wait would have been much longer without you!

Thank you to the most generous Jeannie Lin, for passionately helping me with the query letter and offering me publication insights.

Thank you to Diana Gabaldon, for providing me with confidence when I was enveloped in the dust of doubt and disappointment.

Thank you to Christy English, for reading my manuscript and offering me excellent feedback and encouragement.

Thank you too to Dianna Rostad, Karen Walters, Cindy Vallar, and Laura Vogel, for critiquing my pages. To Dianna, especially, for leaving feedback in my mailbox whenever I asked, and to Karen, for inspiring me to rewrite the first chapter.

Thank you to Renae Bruce, who would search tirelessly for a word that I needed, and Lei Zhang and Elaine Cho. You are my friends for life.

Thank you to Katrina Kuroda, for picking up my boy at pre-school so I could attend critique groups.

Thank you to Sheila Randel and Ray Randel, for welcoming me to your family with open arms and reading my pages whenever I asked. I am so grateful for your love and acceptance.

Thank you too to all the people who offered generous help when I was in desperate need: A. Lee Martinez, Deborah DeFrank, Stephany Evans, Katie Grimm, Natalie Lakosil, Dawn Frederick, Rachel Udin, Deborah Needleman Armintor, Carolyn Woolston, Jeanne Ledwell, and Lisa Stone-Hardt.

Last, but not least, thanks to my family and friends in China, whom I have not seen for ten years. This was never meant to be a bet, but now that the book is published, I can go home.

About the Author

Weina Dai Randel was born and raised in China. She has worked as a journalist, a magazine editor, and an adjunct professor. Her passion for history tells her to share classical Chinese literature, tales of Chinese dynasties, and stories of Chinese historical figures with American readers. She is a member of the Historical Novel Society and currently lives in Texas. *The Moon in the Palace* is her first novel.